THAT
CARE
FORGOT

A gripping serial killer thriller

JAMES WARREN

THE
BOOK
FOLKS

Published by The Book Folks

London, 2024

ISBN 978-1-80462-261-2

www.thebookfolks.com

Prologue

March 1994
St. Charles Parish, Louisiana

The Broussard family's Southern plantation home sat in the middle of a twenty-acre lawn, with mature live oak trees surrounding the property. Greek columns supported the two-story mansion, and a wrought-iron balcony wrapped around the second floor. Shutters matched the wrought iron's color. Dormer windows protruded from the roof, and two chimneys completed the exterior's notable features.

An interior designer had converted the back parlor into a children's playroom, complete with little red and blue handprints on the walls. Terrance Broussard, a slender man in his early forties with thinning brown hair, stood in the doorway. While cleaning his wire-rimmed glasses, he focused his attention on Abigail, his nine-year-old daughter. She reclined on a red beanbag chair and watched a cartoon on television, while absentmindedly fiddling with one of her light-brown, shoulder-length pigtails.

Terrence donned his glasses and stepped into the playroom. "Abby, please turn off the TV."

"Okay, Daddy."

As Terrance sat down on a tan leather couch, Abby stood next to him by the armrest.

"How are you feeling today?" he asked.

"Tryin' not to think about it," she said with a straight face.

Terrence saw no tears. Abby was an emotional child, but also displayed resilience and strength. He suspected his mother had a heart-to-heart talk with Abby in the days leading up to her death. If so, it would have been one of their secret conversations, which Abby would never reveal.

He sighed. "I know what you mean. I'm sad too. Grand-mère's passing is tough on all of us, but we can try to be positive."

"We can?"

"Oh, sure." Terrance forced a grin. "We can remember the good things. Wasn't it wonderful Grand-mère lived with us for the past three years? She spent so much time with you. Didn't you love that?"

Abby smiled and nodded.

"Let's not forget Grand-mère was a mighty fine lady. That's why we named you after her."

"I know."

Terrence gave a light chuckle. "Of course you do. You know, the whole family's getting together to say goodbye to Grand-mère, and we're having her funeral on Saturday. After that, there'll be a private ceremony at the mausoleum. Since you're getting pretty big, you can be there with the adults."

"Wha'bout Timmy?"

"Your brother's too young. He might find it too scary."

Her face lit up. "Oh yeah! It's kinda dark. There's kinda scary statues, and a..." She squinted and twisted her mouth. "A sar–? Sarco sumthin."

"A sarcophagus, a big stone coffin. How'd you know about all that?"

"Mommy told me."

"I guess she did. Two of our ancestors are inside the sarcophagus, and the rest are interned along the back wall."

"Mommy told me that too."

"Right." Terrence placed his hands on his lap. "You know what? I was about to go inside the mausoleum to see if everything's all right. I'll check for cracks and make sure there are no icky bugs, like spiders. Want to come along?"

"Sure!" Abby said with a wide smile. "If I see spiders, can I kill them?"

"You bet."

Terrance stood and took Abby's left hand as they walked outside and across the lawn toward the family resting place at the right rear of the estate. The structure was comprised of light-gray stone, and its foundation formed a square, twelve feet on each side. To match the family residence, Greek columns rose ten feet to support the roof, and the family crest appeared on the mausoleum's double doors. A wrought-iron fence and gate encompassed it.

As he walked, Terrance heard two sparrows chirping in the distance. He also noticed the smell of freshly cut grass and observed wheel tracks from a riding lawn mower.

"It certainly is a nice day," he said. "The lawn looks mighty nice too. Our new groundskeeper, Mr. Brett, must've been here this morning when I was out. Have you met him?"

"Uh-huh. I like him more than Mr. Chase."

"How come?"

"He's nicer and talks more. Mommy told me Mr. Chase died from drugs. I promise I won't do drugs, Daddy."

Terrence grinned. "Good girl. How'd you get to be so smart?"

She shrugged. "I don't know."

After they stopped at the wrought-iron gate, Terrence pulled a key from his right pocket and opened the lock. The gate creaked as he swung it open.

"We'll need to get that fixed," he said.

They crossed six feet of grass to reach the mausoleum's entrance. Terrence then used the same key on the doors. As he opened the right one, the stench of death overwhelmed them. Abby let out a blood-curdling scream, which magnified inside the chamber. Terrence looked down and saw the naked body of a dead woman, bloated with blue and black patches of skin. She stared at him through eyes glazed over in white, her mouth agape in eternal horror.

Chapter 1

Early April 2019
Downtown Los Angeles, California

Twenty-five years later, Rebecca Holt, a first-year associate with Nelson, Estes & Cosentino, examined her reflection in the elevator's shiny doors as it ascended to the fifteenth floor. Her red hair, big brown eyes, fair skin, and freckles made her appear too young. Even her shoulder-length hair in a French twist did not give her a more mature look.

As soon as the elevator doors opened, Rebecca dashed past the reception desk. Once she arrived at her office, she noticed the blinking voicemail message light, which was unusual. Her parents and friends called her cell phone, and other attorneys communicated through email. None of the law firm's clients knew her office number because she had no direct contact with them.

Rebecca put her purse on one of two guest chairs and hung her jacket on a hook behind the door. She kept her workspace free of clutter, and everything was in its place. Her office did not feature any expensive furniture, such as leather chairs or an antique desk. Once she made partner, perhaps the law firm would provide them.

Rebecca sat at her desk and punched in the code for her voicemail. An automated voice said, "Message from 3627," the extension belonging to Carter Patterson, a senior partner, both in rank and in age. She then heard, "Hello, Rebecca. As soon as you get in, please stop by my office. I'd like to speak with you about the pro bono program."

Rebecca was elated. The pro bono team represented two environmental groups suing the federal government, and she was eager to get involved. Patterson's message also surprised her. All the pro bono attorneys had at least five years' experience, and the firm had hired her only six months ago. Her work product had been superior, but only Patterson had given her any praise. She glanced at a framed photograph of her and three friends standing on top of a massive boulder at Joshua Tree National Park. She could not wait to tell them the good news.

Rebecca hustled to Patterson's corner office, which was in its usual disheveled state. Paperwork covered his solid ash desk, except for the portions underneath his keyboard and computer screen. Two other computer screens and keyboards sat on a side table. To the left of the table stood three filing cabinets filled with folders, and several drawers were partially open. Patterson had scattered more paperwork on a windowsill, while various plaques and awards covered the walls.

Even in his mid-sixties, Patterson's slender build towered over Rebecca's five-foot-five frame. The office lights bounced off his wrinkled and milky dome, and his remaining curly gray hair was past due for a haircut. He sat in his black leather chair and rummaged through the debris on his desk. His red-and-blue striped tie hung across two hooks on a freestanding wooden coat rack, and his jacket was missing in action.

Patterson shook his head. He scurried to the filing cabinet closest to the computer table and opened the second drawer. "No." He pushed the drawer back and opened the fourth one. "There it is," he said with a quick smile. He removed a file, and when he returned to his chair, Rebecca knocked on the doorframe.

"Oh, there you are!" he said. "A little late this morning?"

"Sorry, I thought I told you about it. I had to take my parents to the airport."

"Yes, yes, of course." He smiled again and waved his right arm dismissively. "Please sit down."

Rebecca examined a black leather chair to check for more stray paperwork and then took a seat. "You wanted to talk to me about the pro bono program?"

"Correct." He leaned forward and dropped his hands onto a stack of papers. "We're adding another person, and any hours count the same as billable hours towards the monthly quota. Interested?"

"That'd be great! Thank you!"

"You're welcome. You've performed well and deserve to be added. So, have you heard about the team representing female inmates during parole hearings? They're incarcerated in Chino, which is about, oh, forty miles or so east of here."

Rebecca's enthusiasm disappeared, and her heart sank. Instead of working in the field of law she loved the most, she would instead toil in her least favorite. She found everything about criminal law distasteful and depressing. In fact, she did not watch the evening news due to its constant reporting of one violent incident after another, and now she faced interacting with a convicted criminal. Despite her aversion, she would not turn down the assignment. She needed to make an excellent impression during the next few years to improve her chances of making partner at one of the largest and most prestigious law firms in the Greater Los Angeles area.

"I suppose you're not familiar with that portion of the team's work," Patterson said cheerfully. "Doesn't matter, I suppose. This time, we're assisting a male inmate housed in Eastvale, which is a little further away. His name is Nicholas Malone, and he's sixty-two. Sister Catherine Sullivan told me about him. I've known her for decades, and I trust her insights. Sister Catherine met Malone at the county hospital, where he had prostate surgery. She said he's rough around the edges, but still a suitable candidate for parole. Would you believe while incarcerated, Malone obtained bachelor's and master's degrees in psychology?" He chuckled. "How about that! So, any interest in taking his case?"

"Uh, sure… Why not?" Rebecca realized her assignment was even less palatable, as her new client would be a male prisoner, not a female one.

"Marvelous!" Patterson said, as he slapped the paperwork on his desk. "Earlier this morning, Sister Catherine gave me a case file she created." He scanned his desk. "Huh. Where is it?" He studied the filing cabinets and then turned his attention to the documents on the windowsill. "Ah!" He rolled in his chair and grabbed a one-inch-thick brown file. He rolled back to his desk and handed it to Rebecca.

"Please review it and get a copy of the parole packet from the librarian. Go see Malone as soon as you can and then report back to me."

"Fine. I'll get right on it," she said flatly.

Rebecca returned to her office and closed the door. She dropped Malone's file on the desk and slumped into her chair. Yesterday, another partner had assigned her the dreary task of reviewing several thousand pages of documents, which the firm had received through discovery concerning a massive civil suit. Now she had this additional, awful assignment. She needed a brief distraction and turned on her computer. She reviewed emails, one of which contained a lengthy summary of the firm's recent litigation. In other words, the partners were bragging about themselves again.

Rebecca spun in her chair and through her north-facing window, she gazed at the nearby mountains, a place where she loved to hike. Over the coming Fourth of July weekend, she planned to spend three nights with friends in Humphreys Basin, high in the eastern Sierras. She would, if paperwork and onerous deadlines did not overwhelm her around the same time.

Rebecca sighed. "Might as well get started," she said to no one.

She opened Malone's file, and the cover page stated in bold letters, "California Department of Corrections and Rehabilitation." Rebecca flipped to the next page, a court record entitled "Abstract of Judgment." Near the top, she spotted two alarming words:

VOLUNTARY MANSLAUGHTER

She had difficulty believing Patterson wanted her to represent a criminal who had killed someone. For a moment, she wondered if he had read the file and then realized it was a ridiculous notion. Patterson was a legal genius who had won several cases before the Supreme Courts of California and the United States. He knew every tiny detail of his cases and probably committed Malone's file to memory before giving her the assignment.

Rebecca grimaced at the idea of sitting face to face with a convicted killer. She also wondered if Sister Catherine was too naive and saw the good in everyone, regardless of whether it existed.

Rebecca reflected on her criminal law professor's explanation as to the difference between manslaughter and murder. He had said, "Manslaughter involves the intentional killing of the victim in the heat of passion." He had also supplied the classic example. A married man came home to find his wife in bed with his best friend. He became enraged and shot one or the other. The married man's emotional state was a mitigating factor, which meant he committed manslaughter, a less egregious yet still horrific offense.

The criminal record stated the judge had sentenced Malone to eleven years of imprisonment, the maximum term allowed under the law. The next few pages discussed the homicide's circumstances. Malone had owned a bar in Central California, and one evening, he had a heated argument with a customer. He forced the victim outside and shot him in the parking lot. Given her lack of experience in criminal law, Rebecca did not understand how this crime was more serious than other manslaughter offenses, thus warranting the maximum sentence.

Rebecca took some solace in that Malone hadn't committed a hate crime or engaged in gang violence. There also hadn't been sexual assault, harm to a child, or an assault on an elderly person. But did any of that make a difference? She concluded it did not. Malone had still ended someone's life, and once released from prison, he could kill again.

Rebecca flipped to another page and read that Malone had been convicted of battery of a police officer, which appalled her. The same judge had given him a concurrent two-year prison term. The next few pages contained a police report, which stated officers arrived at the bar after Malone shot the customer and that instead of surrendering, Malone slugged an officer in the stomach, causing him to drop to his knees.

Rebecca dug deeper into the file and found a third conviction record. "What a surprise," she said sarcastically.

Two years into his incarceration, Malone had been convicted of battery on a prison guard, which had added another year in prison. The file did not have any documents discussing the attack's details.

Rebecca surmised that even if Malone had decent qualities, as Sister Catherine had supposedly asserted to Patterson, a mountain of them would not overcome his criminal history. Rebecca had heard parole concerned rehabilitation. She also assumed the parole board members were compassionate people, but they also likely feared violent convicts, and a severe criminal record could weigh on the scales of justice as heavily as a pile of bricks, resulting in the denial of an early release.

The bottom portion of Malone's file contained part of his prison record. During his last six years of incarceration, the authorities had not cited him for any violations. It was something in his favor, but it only really reflected his ability to control himself under close supervision. He could return to his old ways once on the outside. Rebecca wondered how he felt about lawyers, given their poor reputation. Regardless of his opinion, she did not want to meet him on the street or anywhere else.

Chapter 2

Given her reluctance to work on Nicholas Malone's case, Rebecca had been tempted to leave the office for a few hours and spend time at a local mall. Once she returned, she would inform Patterson she went to the prison, and Malone told her to buzz off. However, she was a poor liar and did not want to deceive him. Besides, Patterson could send another attorney to meet Malone, which would reveal the truth. She would not risk this scenario, as she was not foolish enough to put her career in jeopardy.

Rebecca resolved to do her best, but if Malone rejected her for being too young, a woman, or any other reason, she would report it to Patterson with a clear conscience and move on with her life. If she had to represent Malone, there was a silver lining. According to the law firm's parole packet, preparing for and attending a parole hearing did not take an inordinate amount of time. On top of that, every minute counted towards an attorney's monthly quota of billable hours, even the time driving to and from the prison.

Before leaving her apartment in North Hollywood, Rebecca made certain she understood the rules for the men's state prison in Eastvale, otherwise known as the Inland Empire Institution for Men. Among other things, the prison's website listed many restrictions on a visitor's appearance. A visitor could not wear clothing resembling a prisoner's attire, including blue denim pants and a blue chambray shirt. Clothing mimicking prison staff uniforms, consisting of forest-green pants and tan shirts, was also prohibited. The prison also banned camouflage and any provocative or outlandish outfits.

On one level, Rebecca did not have an issue with the restrictions because none of her professional attire fell into a banned category. She also intended to dress conservatively while at the prison so she would not bring unnecessary attention to herself. On another level, the clothing rules made her feel intimidated, as they reflected the authorities' ability to control her while she was in their custody.

Before Rebecca pulled her white Honda Civic into the visitor parking lot, she knew the prison in Eastvale did not have stone walls typical of older penitentiaries. Nevertheless, the prison still made an imposing presence, with its double fence topped with razor wire and guard towers placed in strategic locations. In other words, it screamed, "Go away!"

Rebecca had a knot in her stomach as she passed through the visitor entrance, and tightly clutched her black satchel. She eased her grip once she realized her fingernails were digging into the leather.

She waited in line for the security check, staffed by dour guards almost as intimidating as the prison itself. She was surprised the checks were no more intrusive than the procedures at an airport. Individuals simply placed their belongings on a conveyor belt and passed through a metal detector. Nevertheless, she could think of many things she would rather be doing, such as a root canal or suffering through an IRS tax audit.

Once Rebecca stepped into the visitor center, a sea of humanity overwhelmed her. Most individuals were young women and their children, ranging in ages from a few months to twelve years. They sat in rows of rigid plastic chairs bolted to low metal rails, which were affixed to the concrete floor. The constant noise from various conversations and crying babies made the experience even more unpleasant. Rebecca found a seat next to a teenage mother holding a sleeping toddler in her lap. On her other side sat a young woman with acne, bleached hair, and a scowl.

As Rebecca waited for her name to be called, she scanned the individuals in the crowded room. She wondered how their loved ones' incarcerations had affected their lives. She imagined they suffered emotional and financial hardships, but also realized she had no genuine point of reference. She had never lived in a high-crime area, and the police had never arrested a family member, not even for a minor offense.

After waiting about ten minutes, a tall and muscular Latino guard called out Rebecca's name. Without saying a word, he escorted her toward a metal door with thick glass in the center. She again became apprehensive as she realized that once she passed through this door and an identical one about ten feet down the hallway, she would be trapped.

The guard opened the first door. Upon closing it behind them, Rebecca jumped at the sound of metal slamming on metal. Even though she expected the same sound a second time, it still was unnerving. She noted a third metal door further down the hall, which was probably for the prisoners.

The Latino guard took Rebecca down the stark corridor. The hallway was eerily quiet except for their steps on the concrete floor. In a control room above them, an African American guard with a thick mustache stared at her.

The Latino guard stopped in front of an open door to a cramped room with off-white walls covered in scratches, scuffs, and dents. Scuff marks also marred the baseboards, and florescent lighting glared overhead. The room was bare except for a small plastic table with a stand bolted to the floor and two freestanding plastic chairs.

"Your client will arrive in about twenty minutes," the guard said in a deep voice. "If you're still waiting after thirty, please let us know."

"Why the long wait?"

"Just standard procedure." He then departed.

Rebecca was enveloped in silence except for a faint buzz from overhead. She tried to remain calm despite her unnerving situation. She chose to sit in the chair between the table and the far wall. As she pulled it away from the table, she grimaced upon seeing a thick metal ring bolted to the floor. The guards probably chained prisoners to it so they could not rise and attack their lawyers.

After taking her place, Rebecca retrieved a pad of paper and a pen from her satchel and placed them on the table. She intended to pass the time by surfing the internet on her phone, but to her disappointment, she had no reception, which forced her to be alone with her thoughts. She shuddered as she created mental images of Malone, each more intimidating than the last. She tried to imagine more pleasant matters yet kept returning to the same horror show.

After twenty-five minutes in the tiny room, Rebecca heard approaching footsteps. Others had walked through the corridor, but she believed this time Nicholas Malone the killer was coming. Her body became tense, and she developed another knot in her stomach. The same guard returned with an older inmate in tow, with handcuffs on his wrists and shackles around his ankles.

Rebecca felt relieved when she saw Malone. As opposed to her imaginary inmate with a burly frame, menacing tattoos, and a vicious snarl, she observed a pale, stooped-over man with bags under his eyes, deep forehead wrinkles, and a gray crew cut. His small, misshapen nose indicated at least one break. He also had flabby arms and some excess weight around the waist. Even without handcuffs and shackles, she concluded she could handle a physical confrontation if he stepped out of line.

With a groan, Malone lowered himself into the other chair in the room. The guard did not use a chain to attach Malone's handcuffs or shackles to the ring on the floor, which signified he was less dangerous. The guard instead closed the door and left them alone.

Rebecca forced a smile. "You must be Nicholas Malone. Can I call you Nick? I'm Rebecca Holt. Pleased to meet you."

She held out her hand, but Malone did not reciprocate.

"Rebecca who?" he asked hoarsely while staring at her. "You're not on my visitor list. What the hell are you doing here?"

"I'm Rebecca Holt, your new attorney."

"My what? I didn't hire anyone."

Despite Malone's hostile tone, Rebecca remained calm. In the past few months, she had gained considerable experience dealing with egotistical attorneys and their hot tempers, so Malone's attitude did not faze her.

"I know you didn't ask for any help," she said, "but I'm here to provide it. I'm representing you for your upcoming parole hearing pro bono, which means free of charge."

Malone scoffed. "Yeah, right. A kid like you can help me. Who sent you?"

"My boss and Sister Catherine."

He threw back his head. "That passive-aggressive bitch!"

Rebecca was shocked and did not hide it. "What did you just say?"

"Passive-aggressive bitch! She wouldn't leave me alone when I was lying in bed at the hospital, and now she's sent someone to bug the crap out of me some more."

"I'm not here to bother you. I'm here to help."

"Oh really?" Malone said as he raised his eyebrows. "You're too young to be a lawyer. With that red hair and freckles, who are you, the Wendy's girl?"

She smirked as a defense mechanism. "Nice one. It's not as if I haven't heard that before. Believe it or not, I'm an adult and a licensed attorney in the state of California."

"They give licenses to twelve-year-olds?"

"Wrong again. I'm actually twenty-five."

Malone glared at her. "Big deal. You're still a kid to me. Where'd you go to law school, Pretty Girl U?"

"Hardly. I attended Pepperdine, which is an excellent school, and I graduated second in my class." She did not want to mention the other reasons she appreciated her law school, including Dean Edwards and his spouse providing her moral support during a family crisis. She doubted whether she would have received such support at a secular institution.

Malone feigned surprise. "What? I'm only worthy of number two, not number one?"

"Afraid not. Jeffrey Blake was first in my class, and he's a tax attorney in Washington, DC, so, he's out. Getting back to me and my firm. We have an excellent parole program, and we've assisted many female prisoners in securing their releases."

"So what! The board is soft on women, but they'll screw me over. You're just wasting your time and my time, Wendy."

"It's Rebecca, and you're wrong."

"Bullshit! You're just doing this because you're a liberal do-gooder who wants to make points with her law firm. Bucking to make partner, right?"

To an extent, the answer was yes, but Rebecca did not want to share her thoughts, including taking delight in his hostility. If he continued to resist, at some point she could give up guilt-free.

"My reasons for coming here are irrelevant, and we should discuss your life, not mine. With that in mind, please tell me why you committed manslaughter?"

"Because he deserved it," Malone said. He continued to stare at her.

"Did the police officer and the prison guard deserve to be attacked?"

"Pretty much, yeah!"

"Is that what you'll tell the parole board?"

He scoffed. "Why the hell not? They won't release me, no matter what I say."

"I doubt that's true. Besides, there must be some good things to say about you," she said, even though she did not believe her own words.

"Aren't you afraid I'll beat the crap out of you?"

Rebecca paused and gave a wry smile. "No, not really. I'm a third-degree black belt, and you're older and slower than me. You make one move, and I'll block it. Then I'll drop you to the floor and crack a rib or two for good measure. It won't be so hard."

That should be it, she concluded. He'll curse me out and leave.

Malone instead gave a faint smile and leaned back in his chair. He turned his attention to a wall and appeared deep in thought.

Rebecca noticed he became less hostile when she showed some backbone. In the continued silence, she considered her options. She could walk out and risk offending Patterson, the only supportive partner at the law firm, or she could press Malone a little more. Maybe dealing with him would not be so awful for a brief period if he could not push her around. It could be better than plowing through endless stacks of documents.

"What do you say, Mr. Malone? Can I be your attorney?"

"Don't think so," he said, while continuing to look away.

"Okay," she said nonchalantly. "But consider this. You'll deal with me, or Sister Catherine will be your next visitor. Your choice."

He furrowed his eyebrows and exhaled through his nose. "Damn. Those are my choices? I'll take the one who needs a sippy cup." He turned his head to face her and leaned forward. "But you can only be my lawyer if you listen to a story."

"What story?"

"The one about the Crescent City Killer, who was on the loose in New Orleans about twenty years ago."

Rebecca was taken aback as the mere thought of a serial killer sent a chill down her spine.

"I'm sorry, but I'd rather not hear that story. I don't see how it has anything to do with you."

Malone smirked and rose from his chair. He then twice pounded the door with his handcuffed fists. "Guard!" he yelled. He turned back and said, "No story, no attorney. Think about it."

Chapter 3

Rebecca returned to her car in the prison parking lot and sat in the driver's seat. She retrieved her phone from her satchel and searched the internet for articles on the serial killer. She found at least thirty websites discussing him. The first one stated he had slaughtered twelve women. Another site said fourteen women had been murdered, and many more had never been found. A third site claimed the serial killer had taken the lives of thirteen women and two men.

Rebecca was uncertain which version was the most accurate. At least all three gave the same account regarding what happened to the serial killer, which was not ending up in a California state prison. So, Malone would not offer a confession, at least not a genuine one.

The internet articles were consistent regarding two other disturbing matters. This gave Rebecca more reasons for not wanting to hear Malone's horrific story.

* * *

Once she returned to the law firm, Rebecca reported to Patterson, who was typing on a keyboard sitting on top of clutter. He stopped working upon noticing her.

"How'd it go?" he asked with a smile.

Rebecca scoffed. "'Interesting' would be the diplomatic word to sum up our meeting. Malone's a difficult person and has a bad attitude. He's certain he'll get denied parole, and he won't let me represent him unless I listen to his story about a serial killer in New Orleans. Do you remember the Crescent City Killer?"

"Perhaps. Was he active in the nineties?"

"Yeah, that's him."

Patterson nodded. "Yes, yes. I remember vaguely… Very curious… Did he say why he wants to talk about it?"

"I'm afraid not. Sorry."

"Hmm… Let him tell the story, and his reasons should become clear soon enough. You can still count all the time with him towards your hours."

"Okay, thanks."

Rebecca walked away disappointed. She had hoped Patterson would have concluded Malone was a lost cause and told her to forget about him. Instead, it seemed she was stuck with him for a while.

* * *

Two days later, Malone stepped into the same visiting room with a swagger, despite once again being restrained at the wrists and ankles.

"Look what the cat dragged in," he said as he eased into a chair. "You really want to do this, huh? Can I call you Becky?"

"Only if I can call you Little Nicky," she deadpanned.

"I prefer Nick."

"Fine. How are you feeling today? You still sound hoarse."

"It's nothing. I have nodules on my vocal cords, and I always sound this way."

"Can't a doctor remove them?"

He rolled his eyes. "What for? I don't like going under the knife, and it doesn't bother me."

"But you had prostate surgery," Rebecca said.

"No shit. I had cancer, no choice."

"Are you going to provide me with any details of your medical history?"

He gave a light chuckle. "Why? I have some aches and pains, which is normal for someone my age. I won't get sympathy from anybody."

Rebecca grabbed her pen and was ready to take notes. "You might if a board member has the same thing. Let's start with your life prior to your incarceration. Where'd you grow up?"

"Uh-uh. The serial killer story comes first."

The pushback annoyed Rebecca, but she remained calm. "We need to get ready for your parole hearing."

"There's plenty of time for that. Serial killer first."

She sighed. "Fine. Go ahead."

Nick leaned back in his chair and tilted his head towards the ceiling as if he were looking back in time. "Our story begins twenty years ago."

Chapter 4

Early March 1999
New Orleans, Louisiana

Assistant District Attorney Cassandra Morgan and several others stood in a hallway inside the criminal courthouse moments before a press conference would begin.

"Are we all here?" Detective Pamela Swanberg asked.

Cassandra glanced at the thin woman with her dark-blonde hair in a bun. "Not quite. Dennis went to the restroom."

Pamela sauntered a few steps toward the front entrance and peered outside for a moment then returned to the group. "The vultures are ready for us."

Cassandra heard chuckles. While she did not care for the media, she did not have an equally low opinion of them. Some reporters were too pushy or too sensationalist, but overall, she thought they were simply doing their jobs, so the occasional press conference was nothing more than a necessary nuisance.

Cassandra spotted the curly brown hair and husky physique of Dennis Kowalski as he shuffled out of the bathroom and down the hallway. She also noticed his dress shirt was partially untucked and made a corresponding gesture to him. He nodded and made himself more presentable. While Dennis was an excellent prosecutor, he always had a sloppy appearance.

"Would you like to make any comments after my prepared statement?" Cassandra asked as Dennis reached the group.

He held up his hands. "No way. You can have all the fun."

"Anyone else?" she asked, while scanning the rest. She saw nothing but shaking heads. "Fine. Let's just do this."

There were six microphones standing on the courthouse steps, a gaggle of reporters and photographers, and television cameras behind them. A gentle breeze blew strands of Cassandra's shoulder-length auburn hair across her face, and she tucked them behind her left ear to preempt any complaints from the photographers. After she heard several cameras click, she put on sunglasses to shield her green eyes from the late-morning sun, even though the local television stations would not appreciate it.

Cassandra stepped in front of the microphones. "Thank you for coming. I'd like to make a few remarks before answering questions. The district attorney's office and the New Orleans Police Department thank the jury for their careful consideration over the past four weeks. We appreciate their patience during the trial and their thoughtfulness during deliberations. While we're pleased with the verdict, no one associated with this case is ecstatic. The death of Dr. Horace Bellflower was truly horrific and tragic. I sincerely hope the verdict gives some closure and peace of mind to his family, even though nothing can replace the loss of a father and a husband."

Cassandra heard more clicking of cameras and noticed two reporters jockeying for position, which she found childish and annoying.

"It took a great deal of time and effort to reach this moment. I'd first like to thank my co-counsel, Dennis Kowalski." She gestured to her right as he nodded and kept a serious demeanor.

"Dennis worked far too many hours, both before and during the trial. I'd also like to thank the detectives and officers of the New Orleans Police Department for their tremendous amount of work over the past year. In fact, without the tireless efforts of Detective Pamela Swanberg," she said and gestured to her left, "Dr. Bellflower's killer would have never been brought to justice. Besides the individuals before you today, others in law enforcement made significant contributions, and I'm very proud to be associated with all of them. I'll now take questions."

The reporters spoke at once, creating an unintelligible noise. Cassandra spotted a reporter from *The Times-Picayune* and casually pointed to her. "Go ahead, Melanie."

Cassandra strained to hear the question as a bus passed on the street below.

"I'm sorry. Did you ask about sentencing?" she asked.

Melanie nodded. "Yes. What will the prosecution ask for?"

"After careful consideration and consulting with Dr. Bellflower's family, the district attorney's office has decided not to seek the death penalty. Given the truly heinous nature of Samuel Johnston's crime, we'll request life imprisonment without the possibility of parole, which is the only reasonable option."

Cassandra did not inform the media she had an intense disagreement with District Attorney Philip LeMay concerning sentencing. She had argued for the death penalty, but he had refused and had never supplied an explanation. His Highness had spoken. End of discussion.

Cassandra noticed an African American reporter from a local television station. Since he had been kind and respectful to her, she called upon him next. "Lee, I believe you have a question?"

He nodded. "Yes, thank you. Ms. Morgan, now that the trial's over, what are your plans?"

"Starting tomorrow, I plan to be on vacation."

The reporters laughed.

"Sorry, I wasn't trying to be funny," she said lightheartedly. "I really need a vacation. I haven't taken a day off in the last seven or eight months."

"That's not what I meant," Lee said. "What are your plans for your career? We've heard rumors you'll run for district attorney. Can you confirm them?"

Cassandra paused and then gave a thin smile. "Oh... I don't know. Who knows what the future holds?" Out of the corner of her left eye, she noticed Dennis step backwards toward the courthouse entrance.

The reporters again asked questions simultaneously, which frustrated her. She spotted an older woman in the front row and gestured toward her.

"Are you running for political office?" the reporter asked.

Cassandra sighed inwardly as she had already given an answer. "I'm sorry. We're not here to talk about me. Are there any other questions about the case?"

"When will the sentencing hearing take place?" another male reporter asked.

"In thirty days, unless defense counsel requests a continuance."

Cassandra had seen the same reporter in the courtroom when the judge stated the sentencing date and wondered if he had paid attention.

"Why aren't you seeking the death penalty?" another journalist asked.

"I'm sorry I can't go into the reasons at this time. Please review the earlier press release on the subject."

Cassandra heard Dennis blurt out, "Another body! Where'd they find it?"

She also noticed Detective Swanberg swivel her head but saw no reaction from the reporters. Murders occurred far too often in New Orleans, so his outburst over one more surprised her.

Cassandra would allow the press conference to last only a few more minutes. The reporters would inevitably repeat their questions again, and when they did, she would leave with a polite "thank you for coming" and a wave.

Chapter 5

Ten days later, Cassandra Morgan was working in her office. Three volumes of Louisiana case law lay open on her desk, as she researched an unusual issue concerning Samuel Johnston's upcoming sentencing hearing. Gustav Holst's *The Planets* played on her portable stereo, and the recording was in the third movement for Mercury. The violins were reaching a crescendo when she heard a knock.

She peered through the window in the office door and saw Andre Armstead, the district attorney's chief of staff, a slender, six-foot-tall African American in his early thirties. He had a shaved head and wore a black three-piece suit, a dark-gray shirt, and a solid-black tie. She had never seen him with any hair or different attire. With his chin thrust in the air, his body language projected arrogance, which was also nothing new.

Cassandra motioned for Armstead to enter and used the remote to turn off the music. While doing so, she glanced at her most prized possession, a framed and autographed photo of Itzhak Perlman, the world-famous violinist.

"Welcome back," Armstead said as he entered. "How was your vacation?"

Cassandra knew he did not care. "It was a nice break. Thanks for asking."

"Have you heard about our local serial killer?"

"A little bit. Someone has been murdering prostitutes and dumping their bodies in other parishes. Last I heard, the count was up to eight or nine women. So far, homicide has no leads and no suspects, which means they have a hopeless investigation."

"Your information is out of date," Armstead smugly said. "It's now eleven dead hookers. The sheriff's deputies in St. Bernard Parish pulled the last victim out of a bayou on the same day the jury convicted Johnston."

"Okay, I stand corrected. It's eleven. What's your point?"

"Well..." Armstead clasped his hands together. "The media has finally got wind of the murders, and they've been asking many questions. Both the chief of police and the district attorney have been taking a lot of heat."

Something was amiss. Her boss should not be feeling any pressure because his prosecutors rarely got involved before the police had any suspects. She stared at Armstead and recognized his body language which indicated he was pleased with himself as he was about to deliver unpleasant news.

"So," he said with a snicker. "Mr. LeMay decided his office will head a new task force."

"Are you serious? We don't lead criminal investigations."

"Perhaps, but it's different this time, and congratulations... Mr. LeMay put you in charge."

Cassandra's eyes bugged out. "What! I don't have time for that. I already have plenty on my plate."

Armstead gave a lopsided grin while again raising his chin. "Not anymore. Your caseload will be reassigned, including sentencing for Johnston. Peterson will handle it."

"This is ridiculous! Someone else can lead the dog and pony show! I'm going to talk to LeMay about it right now."

Cassandra rose from her chair and stepped around her desk. She could move no further, as Armstead slid over and stood in her way.

"Speaking with Mr. LeMay won't make a difference," he said. "A press release has already gone out with your name on it, and he has no time to discuss the matter. He's preparing for a press conference, which will begin in fifteen minutes, and–" he chuckled "–your presence is required."

Cassandra was so shocked she could not respond.

Armstead continued. "By the time it's over, copies of the personnel folders for your new team members will be on your desk. Others will be added if any positive developments arise… which seems unlikely. In addition, Mr. LeMay will provide a toll-free number for the public to call with any relevant information."

"Terrific! All kinds of kooks and nuts will flood us with calls!"

"Perhaps," Armstead said with a faint smile, "but we might learn something useful. You and your team won't handle the calls alone. Chief Baxter has ordered the Explorer Scouts to assist."

"Kids, just what I need. Any more good news?"

"Oh, yes. Are you aware of the trailer behind police headquarters? It's the war room for the investigation. Tomorrow morning at nine, you'll meet with the outgoing lead detective at the trailer. He'll give a briefing and pass the torch to you. Oh… One last thing." He inched forward and in a quieter voice said, "I suggest you look at yourself in the mirror because you might be wearing too much blush."

Armstead left Cassandra's office with a wide smile, while her blushless face burned with fury. She flopped in her chair and tried to calm herself. She had to attend the press conference and couldn't afford to make a terrible impression. For whatever reason, she was already in enough trouble with the district attorney, and she didn't want to dig a deeper hole.

Cassandra racked her brain to determine why LeMay had sidelined her career. Her most recent trial victory reflected well on him and the office. She reviewed her performance over the past few years, consisting of one trial victory after another, while only losing an inconsequential motion or two during the same period. No other prosecutor in New Orleans could match her record of success.

Cassandra speculated LeMay was upset over the Johnston case, yet their only disagreement had concerned the death penalty. She had lobbied for it in private, and after he had decided otherwise, she never opposed his position in public or within the office. She did not appreciate LeMay's personality as he was too aloof toward his attorneys and support staff. However, she did not express her opinion to anyone because she didn't know who would relay any comments to him.

With only ten minutes until the press conference, Cassandra focused on controlling her anger, or at least the appearance of it. Early in her legal career, she had learned to keep a serious and composed look no matter what occurred in court. She could not appear bored if a judge rambled too long lest she offend the judge or make an unfavorable impression on the jury. She could not appear flabbergasted when a witness gave an unexpected answer or amused when a potential juror gave an ignorant response to a question during *voir dire*. Once again, she would have to rely on her ability to suppress her emotions to endure the painful media event.

* * *

At the scheduled time, reporters assembled in the main conference room. The police chief and the captain in charge of the Field Operations Bureau stood to the left of the podium. Cassandra and Armstead stood to the right. She was seething yet presented a serious, professional appearance.

Phillip LeMay entered the room with his chest puffed out, too confident for his own good. His tan size-forty-four suit and belt struggled to hold in his frame, especially around the abdomen. His smile and pinkish hue on his cheeks created the illusion of innocence and boyish charm, while his bald head and wrinkles reflected his fifty-six years.

"Good morning. Thank you all for coming," LeMay said. He grabbed the podium with both hands.

Before he uttered another word, Cassandra tuned him out. There was no need to listen as everything he said about the investigation and the serial killer would be predictable. She suspected LeMay had a few canned speeches, picked one, and filled in the blanks. She also didn't want to listen to LeMay talk about himself, which would definitely occur. Cassandra also knew no one else would speak. When His Highness was in the room, he did not allow anyone else near the microphones.

At one point, a reporter asked a question and used the term "Crescent City Killer."

That's just wonderful, Cassandra said to herself. *The serial killer has a nickname, which will help drive up the number of phone calls from the wacky and delusional.*

After a few more questions, the press conference came to a merciful end. LeMay rushed from the podium to a side door, and Cassandra followed him.

"Mr. LeMay," she said.

He ignored her and kept moving.

She quickened her pace and touched his left shoulder. "Mr. LeMay, do you have a few moments? I need to speak with you about my reassignment."

LeMay spun around, revealing his scowl. "Not now. I'm overdue for a meeting with the mayor. Besides, I'm not putting anyone else in charge of the task force. I picked you because you're the best candidate for the job. Now, if you'll excuse me." He then made a quick exit.

Cassandra sulked and returned to her office, where three manila folders sat on her desk. She was surprised LeMay had assigned so few individuals. Then again, three team members or thirty would not make a difference. The serial killer had been too smart and too careful to get caught. And besides, given her team's size, she wondered if LeMay or any other city leader cared whether they apprehended him or not. After all, the victims were prostitutes, not tourists or captains of industry.

Cassandra closed her office door and sat down. She rubbed her forehead. Her body craved alcohol, something more substantial than beer or wine, but unfortunately, LeMay had banned all such substances from his domain.

Since Cassandra no longer had anything better to do, she opened the top folder, which revealed the face of Detective Tyler Winfield, a pale twenty-six-year-old. His buzz cut was the color of straw gathered in the fields, and his skin had a yellow tinge. Tyler's beady dark-brown eyes stared at her, and his face had a blank expression. He also had a small nose and thin lips. In fact, Tyler resembled Winnie the Pooh, and after searching her memory, she recalled others had called him the same thing. His voice even sounded like the bear of very little brain.

According to his file, Tyler had become a detective nine months ago and had been assigned to the vice squad. Given everything Cassandra had heard about him, the promotion seemed undeserving. He had not performed well as a uniformed officer, and no one in the district attorney's office had much confidence in his abilities. The file said Tyler recently spent four months on sick leave, followed by one month of personal leave, and the corresponding reasons were absent. He returned to active duty only a week ago. Since he had never worked a homicide case or distinguished himself, he was clearly a poor choice for the so-called task force.

Cassandra flipped open the next file and saw the image of an overweight Caucasian male with mild acne scars and greasy brown hair. She recognized Mike Beaumont, another vice squad detective. He had the physique of a bowling ball and almost always gripped a can of Diet Coke in his left hand. His file confirmed what she had suspected. Mike had been passed over for a promotion three times, and his request for a transfer to the homicide unit had been denied. Cassandra had not worked with him for a few years. However, through the rumor mill, she heard his career and work ethic were in cruise control until he reached the mandatory retirement age of fifty-five for detectives near the year's end.

Just when Cassandra thought her day couldn't get any worse, she opened the third file. Her last team member was Donald "Donnie" Green, a sixty-four-year-old African American who walked with a limp. He had a toothy grin and a full head of gray hair about half an inch long. Donnie was nothing more than a part-time personal assistant for the district attorney, running errands and driving him to various events. When he was present in the office, he rarely remained in his cubicle. Donnie instead chatted with others, especially the young women. Some affectionately called him "Grandpa Gabby," but Cassandra had a much lower opinion of him, and when he made his rounds in the office, she kept her door closed to discourage him from bothering her.

Cassandra threw the files at a wall. She loathed the sight of LeMay and concluded he had set her up to fail. She looked to her left at the diplomas from the University of Washington and the Tulane University School of Law, which were hanging on the wall. Next to them was a photograph of her shaking hands with the governor, who had congratulated her when she had been named the Louisiana Prosecutor of the Year. Despite all her success, LeMay had thrown her in the garbage.

Chapter 6

After fuming in her office for several minutes, Cassandra marched out of the building and climbed into her fully restored, dark-blue 1969 Ford Mustang Fastback. She drove to the nearest convenience store and bought a six-pack of Michelob and a bottle of Jack Daniel's. She intended to have a couple of beers and a couple of shots during the evening or even earlier.

Cassandra headed for the Garden District and parked on Washington Avenue, across the street from a charming creole cottage painted light blue with dark-blue shutters and white trim. Professor Lillian Adams, a wiry, elderly woman, was on her hands and knees, working in her garden filled with red, pink, white, and pale-lavender rosebushes. Even though it was a warm day, Adams wore a long sleeve shirt, long pants, and a wide-brim straw hat, protecting her fair skin from the sun's rays.

Upon Cassandra closing the driver's side door, Adams turned her head and gave a brief wave with a gloved hand.

"Good morning!" Adams said while rising to stand. "Most of the roses have amazing blooms, especially the pink ones. Don't you agree?"

"Oh yes," Cassandra said as she approached, even though she had little interest in gardening.

"The pale-lavender ones have a lovely color, but no matter what I do, they won't bloom as large as the others." She chuckled. "Oh well. Would you care for some sweet tea?"

"No, thank you." Cassandra never enjoyed the taste of any tea, sweet or otherwise.

"Suit yourself. I'm still getting some. Please sit down over there." Professor Adams gestured toward a small, white, round metal table and two purple rattan chairs.

Adams brushed off her pants and stepped onto the large porch. She removed her gardening gloves and deposited them on the metal table. Her hat remained on her head as she ambled into the house.

Cassandra sat in the chair further from the door and examined the well-maintained neighborhood filled with colorful homes and mature trees. While the area could be described as picturesque, Cassandra paid little attention to such things. She instead briefly thought of a cold beer and wondered why Adams was taking so long.

When Adams returned, she lowered herself into the other chair and placed a glass of sweet tea on the table. She smiled, which made the wrinkles around her mouth and eyes more visible.

"It's so nice to see one of my favorite students, but it's too bad you missed Ted. He's in Baton Rouge for a couple of days. Would you believe he and his brother are building a playhouse for some of the grandchildren... at their ages?" She chuckled again and gave a dismissive wave.

"What about you, Professor? Are you enjoying retirement?"

"I certainly miss teaching, but I knew it was time to leave. Fortunately, I still have a productive and fulfilling life."

"How so?"

"Besides gardening and visiting with family, Ted and I have taken a few trips. Next month, we're going to Hawaii. Also, a movie production company hired me as a consultant, and they'll be shooting some scenes here in the city. The working title of the film is *Big Easy Blues*." She shook her head. "My first piece of advice was to change the name, because the movie is about lawyers, not musicians. By the look on your face, I take it you don't approve?"

Cassandra shrugged, while Adams took a sip of tea.

"Not really. It's just, uh... How can I put it? You were a distinguished law professor, held in high esteem. Now you're getting involved with Hollywood. It seems beneath you."

Adams grinned. "Oh please. I'm not allowed to have a little fun?"

"Sorry. It's just my opinion."

"No need to apologize. I asked for an honest opinion, and you gave it. Perhaps you should loosen up every now and then. Don't you ever do anything for fun?"

"I recently read a book," Cassandra said.

"Oh, that's nice. What was it about?"

"High-tech surveillance and the Fourth Amendment."

"My, my, you haven't changed a bit, serious all the time." Adams took another sip of tea. "Correct me if I'm wrong, but you didn't come here to talk about my life or what you do for fun. Care to tell me what's on your mind?"

"Okay," Cassandra said with resignation. "Did you see the press conference?"

Professor Adams put down her glass. "Do you mean the one after the guilty verdict in the Johnston case?"

"No, the one this morning."

"I'm afraid not. I suppose it'll be on the evening news. I take it something unusual happened."

"You could say that," Cassandra said and then sighed. "The one this morning concerned a serial killer who's been murdering prostitutes. Once the media found out, the police and my boss have been taking some heat, or so I was told. It doesn't make sense for anyone to be after LeMay at this point. Anyway, to show he takes the case seriously, LeMay announced a new task force. He put me in charge and assigned three losers to assist me. He wants to torpedo my career, and I have no idea why. I don't think I've done anything to offend him."

Adams leaned back in her chair. "Are you sure about that?"

"Yes, of course."

"I hate to break it to you, but you got on the district attorney's bad side. You're not aware because there's a difference between you and him. He thinks like a politician, and you think like a lawyer."

Cassandra frowned. "I'm sorry, I don't follow."

"After the Johnston verdict, a reporter asked if you were going to run for district attorney. You replied you weren't sure and didn't know what the future held, correct?"

"Yes, and I never wanted to run. I only said it to be polite."

Adams nodded. "That's all fine and good. Unfortunately, that's not the way LeMay would've taken it. He strongly suspects you might run for his office, which makes you a political threat. And why not? You're the rising star, and you've received better media coverage than him. So, he put the brakes on your career and forces you out of the limelight."

"Terrific," Cassandra said sarcastically. "I never thought about it that way."

"That's because you're not a political animal. Ordinarily, there's nothing wrong with it, but you need to know how the game is played. For those holding public office, you always need to consider their backgrounds and the political angle."

Cassandra sighed. "Yeah, I guess so."

"Also keep in mind LeMay's political backers probably don't want him to leave office."

"Huh? Are you talking about donors or corruption?"

Professor Adams took a sip of tea and then held her glass in her lap. "Could be both. There's been plenty of corruption in this city over the years. It wouldn't surprise me a bit."

"Suppose so," Cassandra said. She had heard rumors about LeMay's ethical lapses but paid little attention to them. She vowed to pay more attention to potential signs of it. "Getting back to my situation. Do you think LeMay assigned his assistant to my team as a way of keeping tabs on me?"

"Possibly," Adams said as she placed her glass on the round table. "Please don't take your current situation too hard. Tracking down a serial killer is next to impossible, but sometimes they're apprehended. Besides, sooner or later, you'll return to LeMay's good graces, and your life will return to normal."

Cassandra frowned again and hung her head. "I'm not so sure of that."

"If you don't want to ride it out, you have other options. You could quit and work in the private sector or teach. There's one other possibility. You could get lucky, solve the case, and apprehend the serial killer. If you do, you'll become the most famous prosecutor in the country and make a fortune from book deals, movie deals, and public appearances."

Cassandra scoffed. "Let's face it. Solving the case isn't a realistic possibility. Besides, being a celebrity isn't for me."

Adams chuckled. "Oh please. I've seen you in front of the cameras. You're comfortable in the spotlight, and you enjoy it whether you're willing to admit it or not. Just give it some thought before you do anything rash, because it's always best not to act in the heat of the moment. Regardless of what you decide to do, make your best effort, and the rest will resolve itself."

Chapter 7

Cassandra stared at the double-wide trailer sitting in the parking lot behind police headquarters, a miserable location. A fence topped with barbed wire separated it from the grounds of the Orleans Parish Prison. She also noticed a large dumpster to the trailer's right, which seemed appropriate given her present situation. At least she couldn't smell any rotting materials. Based upon the puddle of water underneath the bin, she surmised sanitation workers had emptied it and hosed it out earlier in the morning. She thought she would not be so fortunate on other days.

While staring at the trailer, Cassandra considered her options. She wanted to remain a prosecutor but not under these circumstances. She could apply to the US Attorney's Offices in New Orleans and Baton Rouge, although at present, attempting to make a move was not the best idea. If she did, someone from either office could contact LeMay and inquire why she was leaving. LeMay could then devise another way to make her life more miserable by giving a scathing review.

Perhaps Professor Adams correctly assumed LeMay saw her as a political threat. Given his nature, he would probably run for reelection or some other office. Cassandra didn't know when the next election would be held, but she reasoned LeMay needed to announce his candidacy for any position by a much sooner date. She made a mental note to determine the deadline, and once it passed, perhaps she would return to his good graces. Unfortunately, that point in time was probably too far away. She decided she would give this rotten assignment six months and no more. If her situation had not changed by then, she would seek other employment.

Cassandra entered the trailer and scanned the room. Four filing cabinets were in a row alongside the left wall. Someone had posted a map of southeast Louisiana on the left-hand side of the back wall. In the middle of the room sat four rectangular white tables made of rigid plastic and metal legs, the same as those used in school cafeterias. They were bunched together to form a larger rectangle. Eight equally cheap-in-quality chairs were scattered around the tables.

In the back stood two whiteboards with eleven columns, six on one board and five on the other, one column for each murdered prostitute. On the right, the trailer held four small offices. The bottom of the walls and the doors consisted of pine or another cheap wood. The door's top halves were glass, except for the frames. Cassandra had no doubt the parish spent as little as possible to create this working space.

She inspected the map in the far-left corner. Someone had placed numbered red dots on it, which formed an uneven semi-circle to the west, south, and east of New Orleans. No dots were north of the city and Lake Pontchartrain. She deduced the numbers stood for the order in which the victims were murdered.

Cassandra made a closer examination of the whiteboards, which the police also called murder boards. A deceased's name and photograph topped eight columns. The remaining three had no picture and listed the victims as Jane Does 1, 6, and 11. The bottom of the first column, the one for Jane Doe 1, had the name "Chase Unger," and his photo appeared below it.

Every column listed the female corpse's date of discovery, the corresponding location, and relevant biographical information. Except for all the women being Caucasian and in their twenties, they had little in common. Their heights ranged between five one and five ten. Some women had been slender, and some had been curvy, but none had been obese. The killer also did not discriminate as to hair color or eye color. For seven women, the murder boards listed out-of-state arrests for prostitution, and the columns for the eight identified women stated the local hotels where they stayed before their deaths.

Cassandra heard the front door open and turned around. She saw Detective Ken Blankenship, a man in his late thirties with average height, short blond hair, and an athletic build. She also noticed a black eye.

"Long time no see," she said with a smile.

"Morning. Same to you."

"What happened?" She pointed to her eye.

He smirked. "A jackass did it and got payback."

Ken's comment amused her. "Details, please."

"Okay. Prior to joining the homicide unit, I arrested this jerk a couple of times for minor offenses. I guess we got along since I gave him some respect. Anyway, he moved up to bigger and better things, meaning he was using his place as a stash house for coke. Narcotics got a search warrant, and they wanted me to be there to make things easier." He shrugged. "I said sure, why not?"

"And things didn't go as planned?"

Ken pointed at her. "Right. Early yesterday morning, I go to the door with another detective. We knock, and he answers. The jackass sees us and a couple of uniformed officers. He gets this panicked look and takes a swing at me." He pointed to his black eye. "The idiot takes off and tries to escape through the backyard, but four officers are waiting for him. He takes another swing at one and misses, which starts a fight. One officer got banged up a little, and the jackass had to be taken to the hospital. He'll live."

Cassandra made a half-frown and shook her head. "What an idiot! He was lucky he didn't get himself killed."

"Yeah."

"Are you glad you're saying goodbye to this case?"

Ken dismissively waved his right hand. "Uh, I don't know. I wish I could've seen it through until we caught the bastard, but I'm tired of spinning my wheels. Hey, even though homicide's no longer on the case, if you need our help, we'll be ready, willing, and able."

"Thanks." She heard the front door open again, looked past Ken, and saw Donnie Green hobble his way inside.

"Greetings, Cassandra, Ken," he said with a toothy smile.

"Good morning," Cassandra replied in a matter-of-fact way, while Ken nodded.

A moment later, Mike Beaumont waddled through the door with a can of Diet Coke in his left hand. Cassandra had a tough time believing anyone so overweight and out of shape could remain on a police force.

"Morning, everyone," Mike boomed. "I see two of my fellow inmates. Where's the third one?"

"Right behind you," Tyler Winfield said as he entered the trailer. He approached Cassandra and put out his hand. "Pleasure to meet you, Ms. Morgan."

She shook it. "Same to you, and please call me Cassandra. We're going to be stuck with each other for some time. So, there's no need to be formal. How about we all take a seat? I'm sure Ken wants to get this over as soon as possible."

Ken smirked. "I'm not in a big rush." He moved closer to the whiteboards and waited until the others sat down. "Okay, here's what we know so far, which isn't much. There's been twelve murders in the past five years, eleven women and one man. All the women were found naked and were listed as Jane Does until identified."

Cassandra glanced at her teammates and noticed six eyes watching Ken, which meant they were paying attention. At least that was something. On the other hand, Tyler had a blank stare, not a good sign.

"I'll start with the first two victims," Ken said. "Our best guess is Chase Unger was the first one to die." He pointed to his picture in the first murder board's lower left-hand corner.

"Unger was the groundskeeper and handyman for the Broussard and Robinette families in St. Charles Parish. The local sheriff's department initially believed Unger died of an accidental drug overdose, but they later concluded he was murdered, once they made the connection to the first female victim.

"Terrence Broussard and his nine-year-old daughter later discovered Jane Doe 1 in the family mausoleum. The coroner said she'd been dead for about two weeks, which corresponded to Unger's time of death. If you haven't seen a two-week-old corpse, you'd better get prepared. It's a truly awful sight."

"You got that right," Donnie said grimly.

Ken nodded. "Even though it's been five years, I imagine the daughter might still be in therapy. Fortunately, the mausoleum was completely sealed, which meant no insects had started on the corpse."

Mike stood and appeared nauseated. "Give me a sec," he said as he stumbled toward a small office and then placed his right hand on the door. He hung his head for a few moments and then returned to his seat. "Sorry about that. Please continue."

"Welcome to homicide," Cassandra said sarcastically.

Mike returned the comment with an icy stare. Cassandra didn't care. He couldn't be an asset if he couldn't handle the subject matter. She also noticed Tyler remained silent and still. His apparent lack of curiosity was not an outstanding quality for a detective.

Ken continued. "We believe the killer murdered Unger first so he could get access to the mausoleum and dump Jane Doe 1. Unger had a key to the gate for when he would mow the fenced-in part of the grass around the mausoleum, which the local sheriff found at his place. The same key opened the mausoleum doors. The killer must've met Unger somewhere and took it from there. He injected Unger with a lethal dose of heroin or somehow convinced the poor sap to do it. The killer then stole the key. After that, he brutalized and murdered Jane Doe 1, then he put her in the mausoleum and returned the key to where he'd found it."

"What were the extent of Jane Doe 1's injuries prior to her death?" Cassandra asked.

"Given her state of decomposition and discoloration, it was difficult to notice any bruising, but the coroner found several during the autopsy. They were all over her body, except for her face. The killer also dislocated her right shoulder and fractured three ribs. Even with all that, the cause of death was strangulation. A red thread, possibly from a scarf, was embedded in her neck. Despite her decomposition, ligature marks were still visible around her neck, wrists, and ankles. Given these injuries, the coroner concluded Jane Doe 1 was tied down and physically assaulted for quite some time prior to her death."

"Were the other women abused and murdered in the same manner?" Donnie asked.

"Yeah," Ken said with a grimace. "Same ligature marks and strangulation, plus many bruises, broken bones, and internal injuries. Some victims had cigarette burns, but none had injuries consistent with sexual assault."

Mike held his stomach and shook his head.

Ken sighed. "Can you handle it?"

"Eventually I will," Mike said. "This is like the first time I saw a stabbing victim but worse. I can handle it, honest."

Ken glanced at Cassandra with a look she interpreted as a sarcastic, "Really?" She held the same opinion.

"Moving on," Ken said. "Our serial killer left all the other women in remote locations about one hour away from New Orleans. Some were found in wooded areas, others in marshes, bayous, and lakes. The killer never returned to the same location twice. Except for Jane Doe 1, all the female victims had been dead three to eight days by the time they were discovered. We identified seven women by matching their prints to ones entered into the FBI database following their prostitution arrests in various states. Evelyn Moore's prints were recognizable, but she had no prior criminal history. However, she had breast implants, and using their serial numbers, we tracked their journey from manufacturer, to doctor, to patient."

"And you have no solid leads as to the identities of the three Jane Does," Cassandra said.

Ken nodded. "That's right. I doubt we'll ever identify Jane Doe 1. While Jane Doe 6 was nude, like the others, her high school class ring was on a chain around her neck. It has the initials 'LHS' and a dragon, which isn't helpful. Do you have any idea how many high schools start with the letter *L*? Jane Doe 11 was only in the water for about three days, which means she still had visible fingerprints. We ran them and found no criminal history. No clue who she is."

"Where were the women abused and killed?" Mike asked.

"We never figured it out. Maybe the serial killer planned to leave no physical evidence. The bastard didn't shoot anyone, which would've made too much noise. He could've used a silencer, but he'd still have to clean up the blood. Same goes if he stabbed them. Maybe he simply enjoyed murdering his victims up close and personal."

Mike let out a groan.

"The killer probably gagged the women so no one would hear any screaming," Ken said. "However, some bodies showed no marks consistent with gagging. The killer could've tortured and murdered them in a remote cabin, where a gag would've been unnecessary."

"He could've stuffed socks or something else into their mouths," Donnie said.

Ken nodded. "That's true. We also don't know where he disposed of their clothes and shoes. Chase Unger and Jane Doe 1 had no post-mortem injuries. Other bodies sustained minor ones after death, such as bite marks from small animals. I'm surprised a gator didn't take a bite out of at least one of the bodies dumped in the water."

Ken coughed twice into his left arm. "Excuse me. Evelyn Moore had deep lacerations on her back. After she was murdered, the killer tied a couple of barbells around her and threw her off a private dock. She was found when a swamp tour boat full of tourists cruised over the corpse. Its propeller severed the rope and sliced up her back. A moment or two later, a 'lucky' tourist saw the body rise to the surface."

Even though Cassandra had viewed many crime scene photos, mental images of Moore's body made her sick to her stomach. Tyler grimaced and looked away, while Donnie frowned and shook his head.

Ken continued. "Moving on to our next topic, which is—"

Mike again appeared queasy and jumped up from his chair. "Excuse me." He headed towards the front door, opened it and slipped out of view.

Cassandra then heard gagging and coughing. Mike vomited and coughed about five more times, which was followed by several moments of silence. He then waddled back inside.

"I'm okay now," he said as he sat down.

"Are you sure?" Ken asked.

Mike nodded.

"Any evidence indicating the killer's identity?" Donnie asked.

"That was my next topic, and there is none. If he left anything of himself on his victims, it had washed away or degraded by the time the bodies were found." Ken shrugged. "Well, that's about it. Anything else I can do for you?"

Mike Beaumont and Donnie Green took turns peppering Ken with questions, while Tyler Winfield did not utter a peep. Cassandra paid little attention and instead focused on the whiteboards. Eleven women had been murdered, and their predator would never stop because he would never lose the desire to kill. He had been too good and too careful with his grisly craft. Only two things would halt his killing spree: his own death or an arrest. She feared neither would occur before the next victim was found. She also wondered if other victims were out there somewhere, waiting to be discovered. By the time she refocused her attention, the question-and-answer session had concluded.

"Okay," Ken said. "All the reports are in the filing cabinets. The physical evidence, what little we have, is locked away in the property room, except for the bodies, of course. I really wish you good luck. Sadly, you're going to need a miracle."

"Thanks," Cassandra said. "We'll see you around."

Donnie, Mike, and Tyler echoed her sentiments.

After Ken left the trailer, Cassandra addressed her new colleagues. "I usually listen to classical music while I'm working. Does anyone mind? If not, I'll start with a compilation of Mozart's chamber music."

Tyler shook his head.

"Fine by me, so long as we mix in some jazz and the blues," Donnie said.

Cassandra smiled. "Sounds like an incredibly reasonable request. What about you, Mike?"

"Sure, but, uh… what's that song they play all the time at weddings?"

"John Pachelbel's *Canon in D Major*?"

"If you say so. I heard it during both of my weddings, and I don't need to relive them."

Chapter 8

Over the next few days, Cassandra and her team reviewed all the reports and photographs associated with the Crescent City Killer. Meanwhile, police cadets and Explorer Scouts answered calls to the toll-free number. Every day, Mike Beaumont arrived with a can of Diet Coke and was the loudest and most verbose person in the room. Tyler Winfield was the quietest, and Donnie Green was the most engaging.

At one point, Cassandra read the autopsy report for Jane Doe 1 while a Miles Davis tune played on her portable stereo. The coroner had found no illegal drugs in her system and no evidence of prior drug use. Perhaps the coroner's findings were not conclusive due to the extent of decomposition. Even so, his conclusions piqued her interest.

Cassandra plowed through the files on the plastic tables and found an autopsy report for Evelyn Moore. Once again, the coroner had found no drugs in her bloodstream. He also found no needle marks or damage to the nose's mucous membrane linings consistent with snorting cocaine. In fact, the victim's internal organs showed no evidence of a drug habit or recent drug use. Cassandra thought it was quite odd because many prostitutes engaged in their trade to support their drug habits, but not these two.

Cassandra grabbed an autopsy report for a third victim. She had tested positive for marijuana, but there was no evidence of long-term drug use. The toxicology report for a fourth victim had come back clean. She grabbed two more coroner reports out of the pile and retrieved the rest from the filing cabinets. One more victim had used marijuana before her death, but her corpse had no evidence of habitual drug use. All the other victims had been drug-free.

Cassandra then had a revelation – Ken Blankenship and the other homicide detectives had been looking at the wrong group of women! They had deduced the victims were streetwalkers, but the lack of drugs pointed to a higher level of prostitutes, who also held day jobs, such as office workers and dental assistants. They came to New Orleans on the weekends when the conventions were in town and trolled for horny businessmen with money to burn. She also realized prostitutes from out of town made ideal victims because probably no one noticed their disappearances. Even if a potential john suspected an absent woman was no longer around, he would have assumed that perhaps she'd made enough money and went home. By the time a friend or family member had reported her missing, the killer would have been long gone.

Cassandra used the remote to turn off her stereo. "Hey, Mike, how long were you assigned to vice?"

"Too long. Why?"

Cassandra explained what she had just discovered. "Does that seem consistent with street-level hookers?"

"No way! They were higher-end prostitutes. Right, Tyler?"

Tyler shrugged. "Don't ask me. I wasn't with vice too long, but it sounds right."

"Do you know where these sex workers congregate and meet their johns?" she asked.

Mike gave a wide smile. "Oh sure. They frequent several upscale bars and clubs in the city. We never arrested them because we were told to only go after the streetwalkers. Even so, some detectives harassed them for fun."

"Did you ever bother them?" Tyler asked.

He scoffed. "No way. It would've ticked off my ex-wife."

"Which one?"

"Both," Mike said with a chuckle.

"It looks like some potential witnesses were missed," Cassandra said. "Mike and Donnie, this weekend please go to the bars and clubs where the higher-end prostitutes hang out. Show them pictures of the victims. Wait... I mean show them the DMV photos, not photos of the corpses. While I highly doubt it, someone might remember seeing a victim with her last client."

"This weekend?" Donnie asked.

"Yes, this weekend. It's only for a few hours on Friday and Saturday night. Do you have anything better to do?"

Donnie held up his hands to shoulder level. "All right, all right."

"On another note," Cassandra said. "Has anyone read the FBI profile report?"

"I did. It's right here," Mike said. He grabbed the corresponding file and opened it. He skimmed to one section. "It says the serial killer's a single, white male between the ages of twenty-five and thirty-five. Now that's *really* helpful."

He handed the report to Cassandra, who scanned through it.

"You got that right," Donnie said. "Everyone knows all serial killers are single white males."

Mike raised his eyebrows. "That's not true. What about Richard Ramirez, the Night Stalker, in California, and Aileen Wuornos in Florida?"

"And Wayne Williams in Georgia," Tyler said.

Donnie waved his right arm at Tyler. "He wasn't a serial killer. No brother would do that!"

"That's enough," Cassandra barked. "A discussion on the history of serial killers is pointless," she said more calmly. "Bottom line, the profile isn't particularly helpful, although it's not completely worthless. It says the serial killer is a sociopath, very charming, and very confident. That's most likely true. He didn't break into homes and attack his victims. Instead, he used his personality and money to lure his victims away from wherever he met them. We can also assume he's physically strong. He needed it to kill the women and carry off their corpses."

"Sounds about right, but it could be more than one person," Mike said. "Remember the Hillside Stranglers?"

She rolled her eyes. "Again, not helpful. Let's not speculate and get back to reviewing what's in front of us, okay?"

About forty minutes later, a skinny, pale Explorer Scout with pimples and braces walked into the trailer. "Miss Morgan?"

"Yes, Jeremy. What is it?"

"There's a woman in the other building." He pointed behind his back. "Her name's Cynthia Stevenson, and she said she drove down from Fort Worth. She says her daughter, Denise, could be one of the victims."

Cassandra groaned. "She's the third one this week. Did she give a description of her daughter?"

"Yeah," Jeremy said. "Just a minute. I wrote it down." He pulled a paper out of his shirt pocket and unfolded it. "I asked her the questions you told me to ask." He looked at the paper. "She said her daughter is five feet, five inches with an average build. Her hair's brown, and she sometimes dyed it red. She has two little moles next to each other on her right thigh, and her wisdom teeth were removed."

"What about any healed fractures?"

Jeremy examined his notes again. "A long time ago, Denise broke her left wrist when she fell out of a tree. Another time she broke her right ankle while playing soccer."

The news hit Cassandra like a ton of bricks. She glanced over at Mike, Tyler, and Donnie. Their dejected facial expressions showed they came to the same conclusion: Denise Stevenson was Jane Doe 11.

Donnie got out of his chair. "I'll talk to her mother."

"Thanks," Cassandra solemnly said.

Chapter 9

Early April 2019
Eastvale, California

Rebecca had bought a book about the Crescent City Killer, which according to the author, was the definitive work on the subject. So far, Nicholas Malone's narrative had been consistent with the book and the contents of several websites. He'd also provided details not found elsewhere. She wondered how Nick had obtained the information and whether it was accurate. She wanted to interrogate him about it, but currently cared more about something else.

"So far, your story is interesting," she said, "but we need to talk about you."

"But I'm not finished," he said in his usual hoarse voice.

"Is it a long story? I suspect it is. We can take a break from it."

"But I want to continue."

Rebecca inched forward with a serious expression. "And I say no. Would you like to have a little talk with Sister Catherine?"

Nick scoffed. "Are you going to throw her in my face every time we have a disagreement?"

"Probably."

He paused and then gave a half-smile. "You're a bit of a hard-ass, aren't you? Where were you twenty years ago?"

"In kindergarten and far too young for you."

"Good one. Do you have a boyfriend?"

Rebecca did not appreciate Nick prying into her personal life. She also suspected he was trying to deflect the conversation away from himself.

"We're not here to talk about me," she said.

"Do you have one?" he asked as he leaned forward.

"Sorry, none of your business."

He chuckled quietly. "You don't. I can tell by the look in your eyes."

"Fine. I'll put a nice deerstalker cap on your head and call you Sherlock Holmes, okay? In the meantime, we need to focus on you. I've reviewed some of your criminal records, and I'm trying to get some more. I also need more details about your life. So, were you born in California?"

Nick rolled his eyes. "We're starting there? Ah, what the hell. I was born in Chicago, and there was nothing special about my childhood." He bounced his head to the left. "Daddy wasn't an alcoholic who beat me." He bounced it to the right. "Mommy wasn't a nutcase who popped pills." He returned his head to its original position. "And I wasn't a juvenile delinquent who dropped out of high school."

"How'd you do in school?"

He shrugged. "Average student, nothing special."

"Did you have any learning disabilities?"

"Does apathy count? To answer your next question, I was never arrested in Illinois or in any other state besides California. That means my first arrest was for murder. Nice way to start a life of crime, huh?"

"Not really," Rebecca said. She was tired of Nick's sarcasm. "My next question concerns your work history. What have you done?"

"Hell, lots of things. My first job was in a warehouse, and I worked in a few of those. I was a bartender at a couple of places before drifting out west. I worked in construction in Denver and Vegas, but those jobs didn't last too long." He paused for a moment. "I was a blackjack dealer at the Tropicana for a few months. I quit after I'd had enough of Vegas. I moved to California and worked as a longshoreman in Long Beach. Since the pay was really good, I did that for a while and then bought a bar."

"Okay. How'd you find out about the bar?"

Nick smiled and tried to cross his arms before realizing his hands were still cuffed. "Back then, I rode my Harley up and down the coast. One day, I noticed a bar in Santa Maria was for sale. I'd been there before and liked the place. So, I said to myself, 'Why not?'"

"Uh-huh. How'd you purchase it?"

Nick smirked. "With money, how else?"

Rebecca groaned in her mind. "Hilarious. Where'd the money come from?"

"I had savings, and an uncle died and left me a few bucks. I had to negotiate with the prior owner to get the price down. He wouldn't budge until I threatened to break his legs."

Rebecca's mouth dropped open in shock.

He chuckled. "Gotcha. I didn't threaten him."

"That wasn't funny."

"Oh yeah? The look on your face was."

"Great. Glad to be of service. How was life as a bar owner?"

Nick leaned back in his chair. "Good, pretty good. It was a nice place. At night, we were always busy, but not too busy. It was a decent crowd."

"Decent? It was a biker bar."

Nick's eyebrows narrowed as he leaned forward and dropped his forearms on the table. "Yeah, so what? It wasn't a biker gang bar. Not everyone who rides a Harley and wears leather is a hard-core criminal. Most bikers are regular people with regular jobs. You need to grow up and experience the real world."

Rebecca did not flinch and pointed to the scars on his right knuckles. "Is that how you got them, handling a decent crowd of bikers?"

Nick smiled, leaned back, and admired the scars. "Oh, that. There was this idiot causing problems at the bar. His friend grabbed him and told him they should leave. The idiot gave his friend a wild look and hit him." He scoffed. "Some people, right? I told him to leave, and he shoved me. Big mistake. I responded by connecting my fist to his face, and I caught him right in the teeth. That's how my hand got sliced up and later got infected. No big deal."

Rebecca raised her eyebrows. "It's a big deal to me, and it'll be for the parole board. They'll see it as another violent act." She hesitated before asking her next question. "Was that the only time you hit someone while you owned the bar?"

Nick paused and stared at the wall for about thirty seconds. When he returned his focus to her, he said, "Yeah. There were some tense moments, but nothing got out of hand."

Rebecca reasoned killing someone must have followed a tense moment. "Why were you convicted of manslaughter?"

"I thought you had my criminal records."

"I have some, not everything. What happened?"

Nick exhaled. "Cheryl was one of my bartenders, and her ex, Denny, was an asshole. He used to smack her around when they were together, then Denny kept bothering her after they broke up, even after she got a restraining order."

"Did you have a relationship with Cheryl?"

"No, I was banging another bartender. Man, Brenda was one hot piece of ass." He smiled and rubbed his chin. "Wonder what happened to her?"

Rebecca frowned.

He smirked. "What? Not being sensitive enough?"

"Not really." In fact, she found his view of women disgusting. "How long were you and Brenda together?"

Nick leaned further back, and his chair's front legs lifted off the ground. He looked at the ceiling. "Uh, about a year and a half, give or take."

"Why'd you break up?"

Nick stared at her.

She felt embarrassed. "Oh, sorry about that. The answer is obvious."

"Yeah. Getting locked away in the county jail and then in prison has a certain effect on relationships. But now that I'm thinking about her, it's too bad I couldn't have seen her one last time for a conjugal visit."

Rebecca's embarrassment turned to revulsion. "So, you thought Brenda was only a piece of meat?"

Nick's face turned red. "Hey, I never laid a hand on her, and I never treated her like dirt. No one was allowed to disrespect women in my bar."

Rebecca was uncertain as to his meaning of "disrespect." "Fine. Let's get back to Cheryl and Denny."

"Yeah, okay," Nick said calmly. "Like I said, he wouldn't leave Cheryl alone. I warned him to stay away, but he wouldn't listen. One evening, Dumbass came to the bar again. I had two or three shots of tequila in me, but I wasn't drunk, and I was sick and tired of seeing that clown. I got my gun in the office, and I put it in my back pocket. I tried talking to him again, and he wouldn't leave. So, I got more physical and forced him outside. I waved the gun in front of him and told him to leave and never come back. Instead of wetting his pants, Dumbass cursed me out. This really ticked me off, so I shot him right there in the parking lot."

Nick didn't need to summarize the aftermath as Rebecca knew it too well. The district attorney's office had charged him with first-degree murder. Nick's defense counsel had never claimed he was innocent because too many witnesses had seen what had occurred. Several people in the bar watched him force Denny outside, and two others saw the shooting. Since Denny was unarmed, claiming self-defense was not an option. Nick's lawyer did the best he could by arguing for manslaughter instead of murder, and the jury agreed. During the sentencing hearing, both Nick and his lawyer asserted they would not appeal the conviction.

"Why did you get eleven years, the maximum sentence?" Rebecca asked.

Nick held up his cuffed hands. "How the hell am I supposed to know? The judge said he was throwing the book at me, and then he gave a concurrent sentence, no extra time, for hitting the cop."

"Why'd you hit the police officer?"

He shook his head and frowned. "I was in a really bad mood and didn't give a shit. When the cops came to arrest me, one of them gave me attitude. I reacted by punching him in the gut, and he fell to the floor. I was in a lot better shape back then."

Nick looked at the table, and about fifteen seconds of silence followed. "That's enough about me," he said eventually. "Let's get back to the story."

Chapter 10

Late March 1999
New Orleans, Louisiana

The following Monday, Cassandra arrived early at the trailer behind police headquarters. She was anxious to hear about Mike and Donnie's interviews at the bars and clubs, even though they probably had little to report. She suspected that if they had found a prostitute or customer who had remembered something significant, they would have called her.

Once Cassandra stepped into the trailer, she noticed some changes. The four filing cabinets on the left sat closer to the front door, and someone had moved the map of southeast Louisiana next to them. Six partially folded maps of the parishes surrounding New Orleans to the west, south, and east were taped to the back wall's left-hand side. As with the original map, they featured numbered red dots, indicating each victim's location and the order in which they were murdered.

A third whiteboard stood to the right of the other two and had a timeline in three colors. Five black horizontal lines signified the years 1994 through the spring of 1999. Cassandra also noticed breaks in the first four lines, showing the timeline skipped the summer months. This made sense because no murder occurred during that time of the year. Short vertical lines marked the beginning and end of every month listed, and even shorter vertical lines divided each week.

There were twelve red Xs on the timeline. The first two were next to each other, which represented the murders of Chase Unger and Jane Doe 1. Cassandra examined a handwritten legend at the bottom, which explained that an X stood for each victim's estimated date of death. The timeline also contained four short blue horizontal lines and two small blue circles. According to the legend, the blue lines stood for the dates of the annual New Orleans Jazz and Heritage Festival, which took place in late April and early May. The blue circles signified the dates of other large-scale jazz concerts.

Cassandra felt a chill as she understood the timeline's significance. Seven of the twelve murders occurred within days of the jazz festival's start or finish, and three women died within seventy-two hours of the jazz concerts marked with blue circles.

Cassandra surmised the serial killer did not live in New Orleans because no murders had occurred from late May through October – perhaps he detested hot and humid weather. She also concluded the killer did not appreciate Carnival, otherwise known as Mardi Gras, as no murders had occurred between its start and its conclusion on Fat Tuesday. He did not strike around the holidays at the end of the year, which possibly meant he was home with family during Thanksgiving, Christmas, and New Year's Day.

Cassandra then had a horrifying thought. The serial killer murdered at least one prostitute around the same time as the last four jazz festivals, and the next one was not too far away. Narrowing the potential suspects to jazz lovers who lived elsewhere was a nice theory yet made little difference. She guessed there were tens of thousands of men who loved jazz, lived elsewhere, and came for the festival. She hoped she could narrow the potential list of suspects with the information in front of her.

Cassandra stared at the third whiteboard with her hands on her hips. There had to be something else, something she could deduce. She closed her eyes and rapidly reviewed the evidence in her mind. There was nothing. She performed the exercise a second time and still had no revelations. She took a step away from the whiteboards and then it came to her.

The Crescent City Killer was not a local and had to stay somewhere while in town. A hotel was not an option. He had beaten and tortured the prostitutes for hours before their deaths. If the killer had taken a victim to a hotel room and had gagged her, others could have still heard noises and would have become suspicious. Hotel walls were too thin after all. On top of that, the killer would not risk being seen while carrying a corpse down a hotel hallway. He was too smart and too thorough to take unnecessary chances.

Cassandra asked herself where the killer had stayed. She immediately ruled out apartments or condominiums because most had common walls. She grimaced at the possibility he could be rich and an absentee homeowner. If so, it would be next to impossible to determine which residence belonged to him.

She came up with one other option: short-term rentals of vacation homes with garages or secluded carports. Such places would provide the killer some privacy and enable him to put a body in a car's trunk without anyone noticing. Unfortunately, she didn't know how many vacation homes existed in the city and only had a decent working theory with no supporting evidence. Nevertheless, she continued with her train of thought.

Cassandra considered how the killer got around town. If he lived within a two-hundred-mile radius, he could drive to New Orleans and use his own vehicle. She then dismissed the notion. If the killer could not stand the heat and humidity in the Big Easy, he did not live somewhere close to the Gulf Coast. Thus, the killer must have flown in and rented a car, most likely one with a large trunk for obvious reasons – like a sedan. The trunks for sports cars were too small, and placing a body in the bed of a pickup truck would be too conspicuous, even with a tarp or another cover on top of it.

Cassandra then addressed another issue. The killer was not a local and deposited the bodies in remote locations. He wouldn't have driven around the countryside with a corpse until he found a suitable spot. Instead, he had searched for a location in the daytime during a prior trip and had taken good mental notes. Someone living in a rural area could have noticed a strange car but thought little of it and forgot about it. Weeks or months later, the killer returned to the same area with a different rental car late at night, when most everyone was sound asleep. Even if another local spotted the vehicle, it would not have raised an alarm.

Dropping a corpse in the woods would not make enough noise to awaken the neighbors, especially if the nearest one was over one hundred yards away. Sliding a body into the water was also a quiet matter. If the killer left any footprints on solid ground, he could brush them away. If he left shoe prints in a marsh, they would be likely to have disappeared before someone discovered a body.

Cassandra reasoned the third whiteboard's creator could have come to the same conclusions. Since the work impressed her, she did not believe any member of her team would have made the effort over the weekend. Tyler Winfield – aka Winnie the Pooh – had displayed no drive or initiative, and Mike Beaumont – Burnout Mike – and Donnie Green – Grandpa Gabby – were supposed to conduct interviews, and she doubted they would work any extra hours at the trailer. Cassandra didn't worry about the mystery person's identity as someone would take credit soon enough.

Cassandra was still staring at the third whiteboard when she heard the trailer's door open and a cheerful, "Good morning."

She turned her head and saw Tyler wearing a wide smile. "Did you do all this?"

"Yup."

She was amazed he was more than a bear of very little brain. "Nice work!"

"Thanks," he said as he approached.

"Why'd you get the extra maps?"

Tyler walked toward them, and Cassandra moved to her left to join him.

"I got them to pinpoint where the women were found," he said as he casually pointed. "You probably figured that out. I used them to determine who were the closest neighbors to the bodies. Then I read the police reports to see if those people were interviewed. They were." He shrugged. "So much for that."

"Anything else?"

"Yeah. The last victim was found in St. Bernard Parish, right here." Tyler pointed to the map on the lower right and the red dot with the number twelve. "She had been in the water for about three days. I've got a friend who's a deputy sheriff in those parts, and he's really familiar with the local bayous. Yesterday afternoon, we interviewed homeowners close to where the last victim could've been dropped into the water. No one saw anything unusual, which was not surprising. The killer probably arrived late at night."

"It was at least worth a try. Where'd you get the third whiteboard?"

Tyler gave a weak smile. "Don't ask."

Cassandra did not inquire any further and concluded Tyler "borrowed" it from a room inside police headquarters. "I bet you also concluded the serial killer loves jazz and doesn't live in New Orleans."

"And he uses short-term rental homes."

Cassandra gave a thin smile. "What's the old saying, great minds think alike? Any idea how many of those homes are in the city?"

"Not really, but we can figure it out. Have you heard of Vacation Rentals by Owner? It started up around '94 or '95. We can check their listings, and there might be other companies with listings on the internet. The classifieds section for newspapers in other major cities probably have ads for short-term rentals in New Orleans. We could ask other police departments to send them to us."

Cassandra nodded. "Yeah. You've really put in a lot into this. Nice work, Winnie." She grimaced and then said, "I mean Winfield. Sorry."

Tyler's smile disappeared, and his shoulders slumped. He shuffled towards the large plastic tables and parked himself in the closest chair. "Yeah... I know people call me Winnie the Pooh. There's not much I can do about it."

While Cassandra had difficulty empathizing with others, she still felt terrible and eased into the chair next to him. "Maybe, but sometimes appearances matter. You could grow out your hair."

He shook his head slightly. "I'd end up looking worse, because I've got a bad cowlick in the back. It's either this or shave my head." He looked down. "I'm aware people underestimate me due to the way I look and the way I talk. That's why I was put on this team." He looked at her. "We're not expected to succeed, right?"

Cassandra did not answer, but she knew it was true.

"That's why Mike's here too," Tyler continued. "He's been passed over for promotion, which made him bitter, and he also doesn't respect the chain of command." He perked up. "But he's excited about this case. He knows it's a long shot, but he wants to do everything he can to catch the serial killer."

Cassandra was taken aback. "No kidding?"

"Nope. Believe it or not, Mike's got a good head on his shoulders. He's given me great advice over the years and really helped me out when I was a rookie. He also told me he wants to get back into shape."

"Really?" Cassandra said. She sincerely doubted Mike would have the desire or drive for the many months or even years needed to lose all his excess weight.

"I hope so… We'll see." Tyler paused for a moment. "There's one thing I can't figure out. Why is The Legend working with us?"

"The what?"

Tyler popped back his head with a quizzical expression. "Come on, you don't know Donnie Green is The Legend? How long have you lived in New Orleans?"

"No, I didn't. I've been here about twelve years, the first three at Tulane and the past nine with the DA's Office."

He smirked. "Oh, that sort of explains it. We don't mention it because Donnie doesn't like people calling him that. Too modest, I guess. He picked up the nickname about fifteen years ago, but you should've heard it at some point."

"Why do people call him that?"

Tyler leaned back in his chair. "Donnie was probably the best detective in the city, great instincts, an organized mind. Even the smallest clue didn't get past him. He even had a way of charming suspects into making confessions. Donnie was really amazing, but that's not how he got the nickname…"

"Geez! Don't leave me hanging!"

"Sorry about that." Tyler swatted his hand dismissively. "Ah, you wouldn't believe me. Besides, Donnie might show up any minute, and he wouldn't be thrilled with me telling the story. Just look up what happened in February 1984."

Cassandra was about to access the internet using the computer in her office when she suspected Tyler wanted to continue their conversation.

He inched forward. "Do you mind if I ask you about something else?"

"Sure. What is it?"

His eyes shifted toward the front door and back to her. "It's about the DA, Philip LeMay. Some people say local business leaders have him in their back pocket. Do you know anything about it?"

Cassandra considered whether she should mention her opinion. "You won't repeat anything?"

"Won't tell a soul."

"Okay. Before, I could barely put up with him, and then he banished me to this crummy trailer. So, I'm definitely not his friend. Yeah, I've heard the rumors too. If he's dirty, I'd love to take him down, but rumors are just that, rumors. It's possible his political opponents started them."

Despite her own comments, Cassandra wondered whether LeMay was corrupt. He drove an expensive car, and his suits looked too high-end for a person on a public servant's salary.

"As long as we're sharing, do you mind if I ask you a personal question?" Cassandra asked.

"No. Go ahead," Tyler said. He relaxed in his chair with his arms open.

"Why were you out on leave for five months?"

"Oh, that," he said as his cheeks turned red. "My partner and I were talking to a couple of hookers on the sidewalk. We're trained to always pay attention to our surroundings, but I didn't notice the drunk driver coming right at us. He jumped the curb and clipped me in the left leg. I went flying in the air and came down hard. I broke both lower bones in my left leg and tore some tendons. I had three surgeries and some physical therapy, and I'm okay now."

Cassandra was stunned. "That's just awful. I'm sorry you had to go through all of that."

"Thanks." He shrugged. "It happens."

"Was anyone else injured?"

"I got the worst of it. My partner and one of the hookers had scrapes and bruises, nothing serious. The other hooker got a mild concussion."

"The accident explains the four months of sick leave, but why'd you take one month of personal leave?"

"My mother was very ill for a while, but she's better now."

"What was wrong with her?"

Tyler gave another weak smile. "She barely confides in me about her health. Out of respect, I'd rather not share any details. I hope you don't mind."

"No, not at all. Thanks for the info."

Cassandra stood and took two steps to her office, intending to access the internet on her desktop computer. She then stopped and again sat in front of the plastic tables.

"Anything else?" Tyler asked.

"What happened to Donnie?"

"He'll be coming in any moment, and like I said, he doesn't want others to bring it up."

Cassandra leaned toward him. "Oh, come on. He's not here. What happened?"

Tyler sighed. "Okay, but if Donnie or Mike open the door, I'm stopping, even if it's in mid-sentence."

Chapter 11

February 8, 1984
New Orleans, Louisiana

On a cool and overcast day, Donnie Green parked his car in front of the Seventh Street Elementary School, an impressive two-story brick building. He arrived to pick up his youngest child, his seven-year-old daughter, Hannah, for a medical appointment. As he exited his car, he adjusted his windbreaker to make certain no one could see his service weapon.

It was lunchtime, and the first- and second-grade children were playing and talking in the yard to the left of the front entrance. The kindergarteners were to the right, and Donnie took particular note of three little tykes playing hopscotch on the blacktop close to the fence. They wore light jackets in bright colors. One was red, the second purple, and the third yellow. Happy, young children always brought a smile to Donnie's face.

Four teachers stood next to the front entrance, including Hannah's teacher, Miss Ellington, a young and slender African American, who motioned for Donnie to join them.

"Good morning, Detective," she said pleasantly.

Donnie smirked. "I'm not on duty. So, around here, I'm just another dad."

"Oh, I'm sorry. You told me that before. Please stand to the side so we can see all the children."

Donnie nodded and stepped onto the walkway in front of the entrance.

Hannah appeared out of nowhere. "Hi, Daddy!" She turned toward her teacher. "I need to go to the bathroom."

"That's fine," said Miss Ellington. "After you're done, please report to the office so your dad can check you out."

"Okay," she said with a wide smile, and then headed inside.

"Her tonsils?" Miss Ellington asked, while keeping her focus on the children.

"Yep," Donnie said. "This is a follow-up to her last infection. The pediatrician wants to take another look and discuss possible surgery with my wife and me."

"Sorry to hear that."

"Thanks."

Miss Ellington returned to her conversation with the other teachers, while Donnie scanned the school grounds to pass the time. Moments later, he saw an older, dark-blue pickup truck park across the street. A scruffy, pale man with intense eyes exited the driver's side door. He wore a tan trench coat, which was not unusual given the cool temperature and the possibility of rain. However, Donnie noticed the coat's left side hung lower than the right, indicating he was carrying a concealed firearm.

Donnie continued to look at the scruffy man without making it obvious. "Miss Ellington," he said in a low voice, "the students need to leave right now."

"Why? The bell will ring any moment."

"They need to leave now! Don't stare, but see that man across the street? He could be packing."

"Oh," she said nervously.

Miss Ellington stepped in front of the other teachers, and at that moment, the bell rang. Donnie noticed the scruffy man walking toward the school. Meanwhile, Miss Ellington and two other teachers quickly rounded up the first- and second-graders, and the fourth teacher hurried toward the kindergarteners. The scruffy man reached the edge of the school grounds, and with his right hand, he reached into the left side of his trench coat.

"Gun!" Donnie yelled as loud as he could. "Run!"

The children to his right screamed and ran past the brick building. The scruffy man removed an Uzi submachine gun and fired wildly, hitting the building's corner and a window as the kindergartners ran away in terror around the other side.

Donnie was horrified when he noticed the little girl with the yellow jacket was still on the blacktop, apparently frozen in place from fear. He ran toward her, and with his right hand, he reached for his semi-automatic pistol tucked into his waistband. With his left, he pushed the girl down, while he fell to shield her. The gunman pivoted the Uzi in his direction. Donnie said the quickest prayer of his life and aimed his weapon.

Donnie and the scruffy man simultaneously opened fire. Donnie got off two shots and saw the other's muzzle flash at least three times. He was about to pull the trigger again when he felt an incredible pain in his left hip. In a split second, he regained his focus and re-aimed his weapon at the scruffy man, who was face down on the ground with a pool of blood forming underneath his chest.

The man didn't reach for the Uzi, which was about three feet from his hand. Instead, he stared at Donnie and took one labored breath. He took another as Donnie continued to aim his weapon. The scruffy man took one more breath and then stopped moving. Donnie was certain he was dead, and the pain in his hip once again became overwhelming.

Donnie heard a blood-curdling scream from behind and realized it was coming from the little girl in the yellow jacket, who must have been wailing the whole time. He tried to turn to check on her, but the pain was excruciating. He saw blood at his waist and on his pant legs. Donnie tried one more time to turn toward the little girl. He forced himself onto his back and then passed out from the pain.

* * *

When Donnie awoke, he realized he was in a hospital bed with an IV attached to his left arm. Even though he was groggy, he tried to push himself up to a sitting position.

An attractive nurse with red hair rushed to his bed. "Not now," she said while touching his chest. "The doctors said you need your rest."

Donnie nodded and returned his head to a pillow. "What about the children?"

She looked at him with a sense of awe. "You saved them, you saved them all."

"I guess so," Donnie said as he tried to focus. "How bad am I?"

"You need to speak with your doctors about that. One of them is making rounds on this floor right now. Please lie still, and I'll be right back."

Doctors? How many of them worked on me? he thought. He noticed a dull ache in his left hip and left knee and concluded the IV contained morphine.

The nurse returned with a middle-aged man in a white coat who had unruly hair and a handlebar mustache. Donnie had a hard time believing this man could be a doctor.

"Hello," he said in a deep voice. "I'm Dr. Cromwell, one of your surgeons."

"So, how am I doing?" Donnie asked.

"The good news is you'll live."

"Tell me the details, all of them... please."

"You're really not up to it right now."

"Please tell me now. I can handle it."

Dr. Cromwell sighed. "Very well. According to the police investigation, that maniac fired five times before you ended his life. One bullet hit your left pelvic bone and did significant damage to it and the surrounding tissues. You've already been through two surgeries, and your hip is being held together with rods, pins, and wires."

"What about the rest of me?"

"The other bullets were fired too low and broke apart upon impacting the asphalt. Shrapnel struck you in the lower right abdomen and both femurs. It also struck your left patella, which turned into another jigsaw puzzle that we had to put back together. I'm afraid to say, given the extent of your injuries, you may never walk again."

"Oh yeah, we'll see about that," Donnie said with a grin. "Can I see my family now?"

"Only for a little bit. You need to rest and recover."

"They'll be here when visiting hours start in ten minutes," the nurse said. "They've been here every day."

Chapter 12

Late March 1999
New Orleans, Louisiana

Even though Cassandra was a hard-boiled prosecutor and was too familiar with violent crime, Tyler's story about the shooting shocked her. After he finished, she sat in a daze and tried to imagine the horrific scene at the school. She now regretted she had not treated Donnie with respect. He couldn't return to the field, but he deserved to remain on the payroll for the rest of his life.

"Yeah. I, uh, don't know what to say," Cassandra uttered. "Is Donnie in much pain these days?"

Tyler's eyes darted to the front door and back. "I heard he's on heavy-duty pain meds and needs another surgery. I'm not sure how many he's had so far. I won't ask him about it because he'll brush it off. He really doesn't like to talk about it."

"Uh… Yeah… What happened to the little girl with the yellow jacket?"

"She only had a few scrapes and bruises from being pushed onto the asphalt. After she finishes college, she wants to join NOPD."

"No kidding? That's nice," Cassandra said with a thin smile. "What happened to Donnie's daughter?"

"Nothing too bad. She was inside the office and wasn't injured. The school didn't let her go outside and see her dad lying on the ground, covered in blood. Obviously, she eventually found out what happened."

"Yeah… of course. Thanks for the info."

Cassandra retreated into her office and considered everything she had learned. To her surprise, Tyler Winfield turned out to be more than Winnie the Pooh. He was a valuable part of the team, given he was intelligent and took the initiative. She reasoned she needed to listen more to the meaning of his words as opposed to the sound of his voice.

However, despite what Tyler had told her, Cassandra was not convinced Mike Beaumont was an asset. Mike had told Tyler about his motivation to work on the case, but she questioned whether his enthusiasm would last. After all, he had been burned out for too long. He could get frustrated again, give up, and simply wait for retirement.

Cassandra again kicked herself for her previous low opinion of Donnie Green. Upon searching her memory, she recalled one or two others had called him The Legend. At the time, she had assumed they were only being sarcastic and had not inquired about the nickname. She made a point to be more respectful toward him, yet was uncertain he could knock the rust off and revive his detective skills. Perhaps too much time had passed.

Cassandra then considered her team as a whole. Even if they turned into the best detectives in the world, it probably wouldn't matter. They needed clues and suspects to solve a case but all they had were dead bodies and educated guesses. She feared the only way they would catch the serial killer was after he made a mistake, which meant leaving behind evidence after he brutalized and murdered another woman.

Chapter 13

That same morning, Donnie arrived at the trailer in his usual good mood. He greeted Cassandra and Tyler with a wave and a loud, "Good morning!"

"Are you sure? It's Monday morning," Cassandra said as she hid her newfound respect for him.

Donnie smiled. "Mornings are always good for me."

Immediately thereafter, Mike made a more dramatic entrance by strutting through the door while his right arm and head moved back and forth to an imaginary beat. He sang off-key and with intensity, "They whisper promises in the… dark!" He then thrashed an invisible guitar and made noises corresponding to the final chords of Pat Benatar's song.

Tyler and Donnie tried to hold back their laughter, while Cassandra asked, "Fond of the rocker chicks, aren't we?"

"Yeah!" Mike said. "That song was on the radio on the way over here. How can you not love Benatar?"

"I'll find a way," she said with a half-smile. "Let's get down to business." Once Donnie and Mike had taken their seats around the plastic tables, she said, "Tyler believes the serial killer is a jazz lover and lives in another city. Sounds like a good theory, and we'll go over it later. Donnie, as of now listening to jazz would be too creepy. Can you stick to the blues?"

Donnie nodded. "How about the blues and R&B?"

"Deal. Now, I'd like to hear about your fun weekend."

Donnie scoffed. "I wouldn't call it fun, especially around my family. They don't want to hear about me talking to a bunch of hookers."

"It wasn't all bad," Mike said. "Some of them were attractive."

Cassandra gave a scornful look.

"What?" Mike uttered with his hands held out. "They were."

Donnie smirked. "As you asked, on Friday and Saturday night, Mike and I went to the bars and clubs where the prostitutes hang out. A few of them told us to get lost, but some others talked to us after we said we weren't vice."

Mike chuckled. "That and mentioning the serial killer made them a little more cooperative. Too bad they didn't have any useful information. A couple of them remembered a victim or two, and they couldn't recall who were their last customers. Not a big surprise. We handed out our business cards and told them to be careful. Maybe some of them took our advice seriously."

"Yeah, but there's a problem," Donnie said. "It's not the same group of prostitutes all the time. Do we have to interview them every weekend?"

"Good point," Cassandra said. "Probably not. Maybe one weekend, Tyler and I'll make the rounds."

"Huh?" Tyler said.

Cassandra glanced at him. "Hey, they can't have all the fun. I'll bring extra business cards and see if I can get the owners and bartenders to hand them out. We might twist their arms and coax them to help us. If not, I'll advise them law enforcement might constantly show up."

"Which would be bad for business," Mike said with a devilish grin. "Me thinks they'll fall in line."

* * *

Over the next several days, Cassandra and her team determined New Orleans had fifteen single-family residences with garages or carports that were rented for periods of two days to one month. Nearly all the homes were in the Lakeview and Gentilly neighborhoods. Donnie, Tyler, and Mike spoke with the property owners of fourteen of the fifteen homes, and the owners supplied lists of renters for the past five years. They also asked the owners if anything unusual had occurred during the same period. Some owners were oblivious because they were never on site. They had property managers who also had no useful information. Unfortunately, no one could reach the fifteenth owner, Millicent Thornwell.

Tyler generated a massive spreadsheet containing fifteen columns, one for each vacation home, and rows for the weeks around the time of the murders. He also entered the renters' names into the database. After he finished inputting the information for the first fourteen columns, Cassandra reviewed the spreadsheet and found all the names and dates overwhelming, and unfortunately, no single name appeared eleven times. While several names appeared more than once, the spreadsheet had too many to narrow down the potential suspects. She speculated the killer could have used multiple aliases or even a new name each time he came to the city.

* * *

Cassandra decided to make in-person contact with Millicent Thornwell, who rented a bungalow in Gentilly. Since she lived in Algiers Point, Cassandra and Donnie took the short drive in her Mustang across the Mississippi River. They parked on a tree-lined street in front of Thornwell's home, a two-story Victorian painted pale yellow with white trim. The front porch and second-story balcony welcomed visitors, and the well-maintained front yard contained grass and a few bushes. Thornwell's house was, in fact, the nicest one on the street.

Cassandra noticed Donnie wince when he exited her vehicle. She felt awful for him and surmised his pain medication was insufficient.

"Are you all right?" she asked.

His grimace turned into a smile. "I'm okay. No complaints, no worries." He motioned with his left arm for her to proceed to the front door.

Cassandra did not want to push the issue and make him feel emotionally uncomfortable on top of his physical pain. She strolled to the front entrance with Donnie limping beside her and then rang the doorbell.

A tiny, elderly woman wearing thick glasses answered the door. Her wrinkles and gray hair in a bun contrasted with the gleam in her eyes and her endearing smile. Cassandra thought if Thornwell removed her glasses, she would look like Jessica Tandy in the movie *Fried Green Tomatoes*.

"Mrs. Thornwell?" Donnie asked.

"Yes, that's me. Just call me Millie. May I help you?"

"I'm Donald Green, and this is my associate, Cassandra Morgan." Both produced their identification. "We're from the district attorney's office. Could we speak to you for a few minutes?"

Millie released a little laugh. "The District Attorney? Why would he have any interest in Old Millie? Oh, never mind. Please come inside." She held the door with one hand and motioned for them to enter with the other.

Cassandra and Donnie followed her as she shuffled into the living room, which was clean and free of clutter. A flower pattern covered a large couch and two chairs, and an elegant oak coffee table sat between them. Many family photos and artwork depicting rural Louisiana graced the walls. A portrait of a younger Millie and a man of the same age hung above the couch.

Millie held out her left arm. "Please have a seat on the couch. Would either of you like some tea?"

Cassandra didn't like tea and was about to politely decline, but before she could, Donnie touched her arm.

"That'd be nice," he said, "but we wouldn't want to put you through any trouble."

Millie let out another little laugh. "It's no trouble at all. I just made a new kettle, and there's plenty for all of us."

Cassandra was upset at first, but then concluded Donnie's approach with a potential witness was the better option.

While Millie shuffled to the kitchen, Cassandra glimpsed its light-gray marble countertop, white cabinets, and plenty of natural light.

"I've never been in trouble with the law," Millie called out. "My daddy was a bootlegger during Prohibition, not me. I was too young for such nonsense... Here we go."

She reentered the living room carrying a silver tray and a tea set. "I hope you don't mind Earl Grey. Oh, I know full well it's not very Southern. My dear departed husband was stationed in England during the war, and he brought some home. I still need a taste of it every now and then. Of course, I added a bit of milk."

"Earl Grey's just fine, thank you," Donnie said.

Cassandra would have preferred an excessive amount of milk to mask the taste.

Millie placed the tea set on the coffee table and almost fell into a chair. "I may be eighty-four, but I can still get around."

"Yes, ma'am," Donnie said. "We came to talk to you about your bungalow in Gentilly. It's a short-term rental, I believe. People stay there for a few days, a week, or two weeks at a time."

"That's right."

"If it's not too much trouble, we need a list of the renters for the past five years."

Cassandra took a sip of tea. As expected, she found its taste too harsh for her palate. She hid her displeasure and glanced at Donnie, who took a sip from his cup and appeared to enjoy it. She couldn't understand how anyone could enjoy such a foul beverage. Perhaps Donnie was an excellent actor.

"You need a list of renters?" Millie said. "You'll need to talk to my second oldest son, Jimmy. He takes care of business matters for me." She held up her bony left index finger. "Don't call my oldest. He lives in Baton Rouge. Now, Jimmy lives across the river. I have his number written down next to the phone on the end table." She gestured to her right.

Donnie retrieved a small notepad and pen from his shirt pocket and scribbled Jimmy's name and number.

Millie chuckled and waved her left hand. "I declare, my memory isn't what it used to be. I tend to forget numbers, even the ones I call over and over again. I seem to remember everything else, especially the important things."

Donnie smiled. "That's great, ma'am, because we need to search your memory. Do you remember any time when something unusual happened at your rental home? The neighbors complained about a noise, or they saw something suspicious?"

Millie's face went blank for a moment, and then she appeared to regain her focus. "Oh, not that I recall. We've always had such nice tenants. Jimmy might remember something unusual, but I don't think so. He would've told me about it. He's such a good boy, but he worries about me too much."

"Do you remember anything being broken or damaged at the bungalow?" Donnie asked.

He took another took a sip of tea, and Cassandra did the same to be polite. Her second sip was as awful as the first, a truly foul beverage.

"Oh, yes," Millie said as she patted her left hand on her lap. "One time a child dropped a glass, and it broke. Before his parents caught him, he tried to pick up the pieces with his hands, and he cut one of his fingers. You wouldn't be talking about that, are you?"

Donnie grinned. "No, ma'am. Anything else?"

Millie closed her eyes. "Anything else… Oh, I remember now!" She opened them and gazed at Donnie. "A gentleman broke a lamp. He called Jimmy and was so apologetic." She let out another little laugh. "Such a fuss over nothing."

"What happened?" Cassandra asked.

"Jimmy and I went over to take a look. He said he accidentally knocked over an old lamp, and he offered to pay for a replacement. It wasn't necessary, but he insisted." Millie smiled and shook her head. "Bless his heart. Jimmy and I weren't sure how much the lamp was worth. I asked for two hundred dollars, just to make him happy, and he gave me five hundred. He wanted to give extra for my trouble, as if there were any." She struggled to push herself forward in the chair. Then in a quieter voice, she added, "He *said* he accidentally knocked it over. However, I strongly suspect something else was going on."

"Which was?" Donnie asked and took another sip of tea.

Cassandra did not touch her cup and anxiously waited for the answer.

"I suspect he had a lady friend over," Millie whispered. "They got a little, shall we say, rambunctious, and they broke the lamp." She leaned back and in her normal voice said, "However, one's romantic affairs are none of my business, which is why I didn't inquire any further."

Donnie placed his teacup on the coffee table. "What did the gentleman look like?"

"Oh, he was tall and rather handsome. He had a cleft chin, just like my late husband." Millie glanced at the portrait above the couch then returned her attention to Cassandra and Donnie. "Even though he was a Yankee, he had Southern manners, *quite* charming actually. The next time he rented the bungalow, Jimmy and I invited him over here for tea. I certainly thought he'd decline. Such a nice young man would have better things to do, but he came over," she said with a wide smile. "That was a very pleasant afternoon."

"That's nice," Donnie said. "Do you remember what he looked like, besides the cleft chin?"

"Oh, I'm not so sure."

"If we came back another time with a sketch artist, do you think you could describe the gentleman?" he asked.

Millie sighed. "I'm sorry, but I sincerely doubt it. My eyes aren't what they used to be. I just remember he was handsome, and he had a cleft chin. So did my late husband."

Cassandra noticed Millie had repeated herself, indicating her mental faculties could be failing.

"What about your son? Could he describe the gentleman to a sketch artist?" she asked.

"No, I don't think so. Jimmy was never very good at remembering faces, and he's been so busy these days. His mind is filled up with everything else, the poor boy."

Donnie nodded. "I understand. What was the gentleman's name?"

"His name was…" She placed her left hand on her chin. "His last name was common… Smith, Jones, Johnson? One of those." She returned her hand to her lap. "Jimmy keeps the books, and he should know. I hope you don't think my visitor caused any trouble."

"I'm sorry, but we can't discuss the matter," Cassandra said. "We'd appreciate it if you didn't mention this little talk to any future tenants, including the polite Yankee."

Millie chuckled. "No trouble at all. Besides, what's there to tell? Is there anything else?"

"No, ma'am," Donnie said. "We've taken enough of your time."

Cassandra smiled and nodded. "We appreciate your cooperation and your hospitality."

Millie beamed. "Oh, my pleasure. Please stop by anytime for another cup of tea. Nice visitors are always welcome here."

"That'd be nice, very nice," Donnie said as he stood. "We'll see ourselves out."

As they walked outside, Cassandra noticed Donnie limping again. He also grimaced when he descended the four steps from the porch to the front yard.

"Good job with Millie," she said once they were in her Mustang.

Donnie grinned. "It wasn't much. Just talk nice to people, and they'll open up. I'm pretty sure she would've responded the same way if you'd taken the lead."

"Maybe, and maybe Millie had tea with a serial killer. I'd rather not inform her if it turns out to be true."

Donnie shook his head. "I'm not volunteering for that conversation," he said with a straight face. "Breaking a lamp isn't much, but it's consistent with a struggle. At least we know the same man rented her bungalow twice. It shouldn't be too hard to determine how many of her tenants rented the place more than once around the time of the murders."

"Right. We just need to get the list from her son."

Chapter 14

The next day, Cassandra arrived at the trailer with a six-pack of Michelob bottles and stowed them in the small refrigerator she had wedged into her cramped office. Tyler and Mike were sitting at the plastic tables with a coffee mug in front of Tyler and a can of Diet Coke in Mike's left hand. Cassandra sat down to join them.

"Drinking on the job. Isn't that against the rules?" Mike asked.

"So what? No one ever comes back here, and frankly, no one cares about us. It's not for now. We could have a beer or two during lunch. You should've seen Ken Blankenship and me when we were waiting for the verdict in the Reynolds case. The jury was out for days, and we passed the time by going through an entire bottle of Jack Daniel's."

Tyler gave a weak smile, and Cassandra was uncertain what was happening underneath his straw-colored buzz cut.

Mike frowned. "Is Donnie joining us?"

"No," Cassandra said while ignoring Mike's disapproval. "He has another doctor's appointment. Afterwards, he's going to contact the St. Charles Parish Sheriff to set up a meeting. I'd like to talk to him about Chase Unger and Jane Doe 1."

"What do you hope to accomplish?"

She shrugged. "Not sure. I'm looking for anything at this point. Have you been going through the lists of renters?"

"Yeah," Tyler said. "We've started with the names that appear multiple times, running their addresses, credit checks, and criminal histories. So far, nothing significant pops out."

"Yeah, it figures," Cassandra said as she brushed her auburn hair away from her face.

She was disappointed, even though she didn't expect any positive results. Since most serial killers worked alone, she had considered eliminating any couple or family who rented a vacation home. On the other hand, she suspected the killer could have pretended to be traveling with a wife and children. The owners and property managers would have met him, not the rest of his imaginary family, and would not have cared if they met anyone else.

* * *

About two hours later, Andre Armstead arrived with his shaved head, same black-and-gray attire, and the same arrogant attitude. "Good afternoon… people. The district attorney requested that I check on your progress."

Cassandra was suspicious of Armstead's motives. She assumed Donnie gave periodic briefings to Philip LeMay, as Donnie saw him from time to time. Perhaps the DA had sent his chief of staff to find fault in her investigation and justification to fire her. Armstead could also be checking whether Donnie had been withholding information. Cassandra wanted to interrogate Armstead but surmised it would be pointless; he was too cold and calculating to satisfy her curiosity. She instead provided the team's working theory and their recent efforts.

Armstead cast his eyes down upon her. "Which means you have no suspects."

"Not yet."

"Hmph." Armstead pointed to the left and middle whiteboards. "Those are summaries of the victims?"

"Correct," she said. "And the board on the right provides a timeline, and the maps in the far corner show where the victims were found."

Armstead approached the whiteboard with the timeline. He examined it for a few seconds and then stepped in front of the maps. He stared at them and kept his back ramrod straight for about fifteen more seconds.

"There's a problem with your theory of the case," he said while still facing the maps. "The bodies were discarded in remote locations. Someone from out of town would be unfamiliar with the back roads. However, someone who drives for a living, making deliveries all over southeast Louisiana, would be familiar with them. I should know. I used to work for UPS."

Armstead walked to the middle whiteboard and stood with his chin in the air and his hands behind his back. "So much fuss over a bunch of dead hookers. Given their... clientele, what should they have expected?"

Cassandra was enraged but did not express it. Any expletive-filled tirade would get back to her boss.

"Enough of this." Armstead gave a dismissive wave. "I have more important matters on my plate." He turned around, nodded once in Cassandra's direction, and departed.

After Armstead closed the door, Mike exclaimed, "What an arrogant prick!"

"Tell me about it," Cassandra said. "Is this your first impression of him? It won't get any better." She became lost in thought and approached the whiteboard on the right.

"I'm double-checking the date of death for the tenth female victim, Misty Thorgenson." She turned around and stared into the distance. "Maybe, just maybe, Armstead's a viable suspect."

"Wait a minute," Tyler said. "Let's not get carried away. We can't stand him, but there's nothing to indicate he's violent."

Cassandra's temper was about to flare when her ability for rational thought took over.

"I know. I get it," she said. "I'd love nothing better than to throw him in the dumpster outside and have it hauled away. But please hear me out. Armstead's never seemed fond of women in general, and you just heard his comments about prostitutes. He also knows the back roads." She tapped the plastic table closest to her. "I could be wrong, but I remember his hand was wrapped in gauze around the same time as Misty's murder. Armstead said his girlfriend's cat scratched him. I didn't buy it back then, and I certainly don't buy it now."

Tyler scoffed. "Armstead has a girlfriend? No way. Trust me on this one, no way."

"Why do you say that?" Mike asked.

"Simple, he's gay."

That last piece of information caught Cassandra's attention. She suspected if Armstead were hiding his sexuality, he could also hide other aspects of his life.

"Are you sure?" she asked.

Tyler smirked. "Yeah. I saw him at the King Philip."

Mike nearly jumped out of his chair. "That's a gay nightclub! What were you doing there?"

Tyler crossed his arms and smiled.

"You're gay?" Cassandra asked.

Tyler shook his head and continued to smile.

"Bisexual?"

Tyler smiled wider and touched his nose with his right index finger.

"How about that!" Mike said. "Hey, are you attracted to me?"

Tyler smirked again. "No, not really."

Mike chuckled. "Hey, why not? I'm a good catch."

Cassandra rolled her eyes. "Are you sure it was Armstead at the nightclub?"

"Yeah. The first time I saw him there, he was hanging all over a guy. The second time, another guy was hanging all over him."

Mike groaned. "I didn't need to hear that part."

Tyler's brow furrowed, and he made a slight frown. "Wait a minute. You're joking about it, but you really can't handle two men showing affection for another?"

"Hold on," Mike said as he held up his hands with the palms out. "I can so long as one of them isn't that prick who was just here."

Tyler gave a weak smile. "Got it."

"Was Armstead dressed in black and gray?" Mike asked.

"Yeah. Dark-gray shirt and black pants, both times."

"Oh man! Even I have better fashion sense," Mike said. "Cassandra, do you really think Armstead could've done it? I've never heard of a black and gay serial killer."

She sighed. "Let's not get into another discussion about who can be a serial killer. All I have right now is speculation and conjecture, but it's worth taking a good, hard look at him. Besides, do you have anything else to do? Very quietly, could you please check him out?"

Tyler nodded.

"Sure," Mike said. "Don't worry. We know the drill."

Cassandra knew what he meant. Mike and Tyler would pull Armstead's credit card statements. When Armstead's arm got scratched, he could have used a credit card to make a co-payment to a doctor or a clinic, which could have occurred around the same time as Misty Thorgenson's murder. Other credit card purchases could place him close to where the authorities discovered another body or two. Credit card activity could also show Armstead was away from New Orleans when some murders occurred, which would eliminate him as a suspect. She also knew Mike and Tyler would subpoena his home phone records. A lack of calls for a few days would show he was not in New Orleans. The detectives would also check Armstead's bank records to determine where and when he made cash withdrawals from ATMs.

Cassandra sat down. "I need a small favor."

"What is it?" Tyler asked.

"My father's a history professor at the University of Washington. Right now, he's attending a seminar in Atlanta, and he'll be coming to town this weekend. I need an excuse to ditch him sometime Saturday afternoon."

"Okay," Mike said. "What's the big deal? You don't like the guy?"

"No, it's nothing like that." She inched forward. "I love my dad, and most of the time, he's a really great guy. Every time I go back home, I enjoy his company. Two years ago, he was in Denver for a couple of days, and I flew out and met him for dinner. It was a really fun night."

"So, what's the problem?" Tyler asked.

"Things are so different when he comes to New Orleans. He's absolutely obsessed with the city and its history. Every single time, he tells me the exact same stories, over and over. He wants to go to the same places and do the same things. I can handle dinner this Friday evening because we're going to Commander's Palace." She smiled briefly. "However, his stories will be so tiresome by Saturday afternoon when we're having beignets at Café Du Monde *again*."

"Why don't you go to that place on St. Charles Avenue?" Mike asked. "Their beignets are just as good, and it'll be less crowded."

"I know, I know. I've told him, and he doesn't care. Dad apparently needs to eat a beignet in the French Quarter, or his brain will melt down."

"Okay, I get it now," Mike said. "What do you need?"

"Please get me out of there. On Saturday, call me at two. Make up some excuse... Say there's been a break in the case. Tell me I need to come to the office right away, and when you call, make certain your voice is loud enough so Dad can hear you."

"Sure. Whatever you want."

Chapter 15

On Saturday afternoon, Cassandra spotted her father, Gary Morgan, standing in front of Café Du Monde's outdoor seating which consisted of metal tables and chairs. It was easy to locate him amongst the crowd due to his distinctive appearance, which included thick and dark hair, deep brown eyes, thick eyebrows, and a vertical inch-long scar on his chin. He waved at her with the enthusiasm of a young boy on his first trip to Disneyland.

Her father's actions embarrassed Cassandra, but she did her best not to show it. She did not understand how he could get so excited. Earlier in the day, they had brunch at the Court of Two Sisters and had only separated for a couple of hours while he had taken a nap in his hotel room.

Even though the café was busy, Cassandra secured a table close to the railing, which allowed her to feel less crowded. Her father told another story about New Orleans while savoring a powdered-sugar-covered beignet and drinking coffee and chicory. Her coffee sat on the table despite its enticing aroma. She tuned out her father's ramblings while watching others pass through Jackson Square. Between bites, her father continued to talk, apparently unaware she wasn't listening.

About thirty feet behind Cassandra's father, a young woman with dishwater-blonde hair wore a red scarf, which was like a violent gash on her pale skin. She stood silently as if she was waiting for someone and provided Cassandra a startling reminder of Jane Doe 1. Cassandra returned her attention to her father because she feared if the woman looked at her, she would become more unnerved.

Her father was still oblivious to her mood and continued to enjoy himself. Cassandra shifted her eyes to spot the young woman again, but she didn't find her. She scanned the surrounding area and still did not spot her. A moment later, Cassandra saw her at a distance, walking away with a man. She quietly breathed a sigh of relief and returned to her boredom.

As the time approached two o'clock, Cassandra kept glancing at her watch in anticipation of Mike's phone call. She then saw Tyler and Mike walking toward her and felt relieved. Mike waved at her, and she reciprocated. Mike's clothes were looser due to recent weight loss, but he needed to lose much more, and she wished he would do something about his greasy hair.

When Tyler and Mike reached the railing, Mike said, "What a nice surprise! We just finished lunch and happened to see you. Is this your father?"

"Yes, it is," Cassandra said. She noticed Tyler had a mischievous grin, which she found suspicious. "Detectives Mike Beaumont and Tyler Winfield, this is my father, Professor Morgan."

"Please call me Gary," he cheerfully said. He rose and shook the detectives' hands. "Are you my daughter's colleagues?"

"Yes, we are," Mike replied. "We heard you attended a seminar in Atlanta."

"You did? Oh wow! Cassie, you're going to make me a celebrity in the Big Easy!"

Mike mouthed, "Cassie?" and appeared to hold back his laughter.

Cassandra hated the nickname because to her it sounded too juvenile. "Dad, let's not get carried away. Is there a reason you guys needed to talk to me? Does anything need my immediate attention?"

"No, no," Mike said nonchalantly as he flicked his right hand. "Nothing like that. We just saw your father and thought it'd be nice to meet him." He flashed a wide smile.

In her mind, Cassandra swore at Mike and Tyler.

"And it's nice to meet you too!" her father said. "This is great! Would you like to join us?"

"I'm terribly sorry, but we can't," Mike said. "We have plans. Tyler's on his way to see his mother, and I… well, you don't need to hear about it. It was great to meet you, Gary. Enjoy the rest of your afternoon."

Tyler nodded. "It was nice to meet you."

Gary smiled back at them. "You too, both of you!"

Mike and Tyler walked away with big smiles on their faces, while Cassandra's father returned to his seat.

"Boy, that was great! What an awesome couple of guys. Right, Cassie?"

"Yes, Dad," she answered calmly even though she was seething.

"Hey, doesn't Tyler look like Winnie the Pooh?"

"You shouldn't say that!" Cassandra said.

"What?" her father said as he raised his eyebrows. "It's a good thing. Winnie the Pooh was one of my favorite Disney characters from childhood. Now if Mike looked like Tigger or Eeyore?" His eyes nearly popped out of their sockets.

"I know, Dad. I get it."

"Okay. How long have you known Mike and Tyler?"

Too long, she thought. "Mike… about five years, and I met Tyler rather recently."

"That's great! Really great! Are they working with you on the serial killer case?"

Cassandra crossed her arms. "Sorry, but I'm not allowed to talk about an ongoing investigation."

Her father chuckled and pointed at her. "And the look on your face means yes! If they're working with you, they must be the cream of the crop." He leaned forward. "How are things going? Are you developing any leads, any good clues?"

"Like I said before, I can't talk about it."

He leaned back and chuckled again. "Not even with your dear, old dad? Come on. We've never kept secrets from each other."

"About our lives, that's true, but this is different. For an investigation, there are rules that must be followed."

"Sometimes rules are meant to be broken, right?"

"I don't think so." Cassandra tired of her father's good-natured badgering.

"Do you have any good suspects?"

"Come on, Dad. I—"

"Oh, look!" He pointed again. "There's another tell. You can never play poker with me and win because I can read your face. You don't have any suspects."

She groaned. "You're too happy about a mass murderer on the loose."

Her father's smile disappeared. "I'm sorry, Cassie. I didn't mean it that way. It's just so exciting that my daughter is involved with such a huge case." His smile returned. "I have a great idea. Why don't you let me look at the evidence? I could review it with a fresh set of eyes."

Cassandra rolled hers. "That's not allowed. Besides, the photos of the victims are really gruesome."

"I can handle it," he said with a straight face. "Remember, I'm a professor of modern American history. I've seen photos of the Dachau concentration camp and the war in Vietnam. I don't have a weak stomach. Honest, I can handle it."

"It's not just that—"

"Don't consider me a member of the public or your dad. Think of me as an expert or a consultant."

Cassandra threw up her hands in frustration. "Why not? It's Saturday, which means no one will be in the office to catch us."

"Great!"

* * *

Twenty minutes later, Cassandra and her father stood in front of the whiteboards. She supplied a running commentary and showed him photos of the victims and the crime scenes. At the same time, he closely examined the materials, asking questions.

"Wow!" her father said with his hands on his hips. "It might be morbid to say out loud, but I now better understand why you became a prosecutor. This is fascinating and a lot to take in. I imagine you're frustrated because you don't know who's been committing the murders."

"'Frustrated' is an understatement."

"Uh-huh. I bet. Why are the two unidentified women called Jane Doe 1 and Jane Doe 6? Shouldn't they be Jane Does 1 and 2?"

"Each victim was called Jane Doe until they were identified. Six stands for the sixth female victim."

Her father nodded. "Oh sure. I get it. And you really don't know who they are?"

Cassandra exhaled through her nose. "Unfortunately, no. Jane Doe 1 was found naked in a family mausoleum. She wasn't wearing any jewelry, and she didn't have any implants or any other medical devices with serial numbers, like another victim. Plus, her fingers were too decomposed to get prints. We can't compare her teeth to any dental records, and the same goes for her DNA. It's sad to say, but we may never know who she was."

Her father nodded again. "I see what you mean. It's terrible. Someone must miss her. She must have family somewhere. What about Jane Doe 6?"

"As you saw in the photos, she was found in the woods. She hadn't been dead too long, which meant the patterns on her fingers were still identifiable, but there was no match to prints in any criminal database. While the others had been stripped of jewelry, Jane Doe 6 still wore her high school class ring on a chain around her neck. She must've really loved her school because the ring is rather ugly. It's too bad we have no idea where it came from."

"Can I see it?" her father asked.

"It's locked up in the property room, and members of the public can't get in. No way I can sweet-talk the clerk into allowing you access to the room. We have photos of the ring. Is that good enough?"

"Might be. Doesn't hurt to look."

Cassandra walked to the filing cabinet furthest to the left and opened the third drawer. She removed a thin manila folder, brought it to the large plastic tables, and flipped it open.

"There it is," she said. "It's from some high school with the initials 'LHS.' The year 1992 and a dragon also appear on the ring."

Her father sat and studied the first photo with a laser focus. He then turned the page and examined three more images of the same ring.

"Cassie, do you have a magnifying glass somewhere around here?"

"Sure, one moment." She strolled to her crummy office, opened a desk drawer, and grabbed it. She returned and gave it to her father.

"Thanks," he said with a grin.

He spent another minute examining the first photo through the magnifying glass and another minute staring at the second one. He then raised his head, and his face lit up.

"See, I knew I could help! I know where the ring came from!"

Cassandra's mouth dropped open. "You're kidding?"

"Would I kid you? Do you remember my colleague professor, Douglas Stottlemeyer? He has a ring just like this one. It's encased in Lucite and sits on the desk in his office. Some of us have given him a hard time about it. He's a tenured professor, and he cares about a high school class ring. And yes, it's ugly. Would you like me to call Doug to confirm?"

She was stunned. "Yes, of course," she said. "Call him right now, but don't tell him about the investigation." She took a seat and felt a rush of adrenaline.

Her father removed his cell phone from a pant pocket and punched in a phone number. "Hey Doug," he said a moment later. "It's me, Gary … Uh-huh … Yes, it was a good conference. I'm now in New Orleans with my daughter … Of course, I'm having a good time!" He laughed. "She's well … Uh-huh … Uh-huh … That's great news! Congratulations! … Uh-huh … Two weeks early … Very healthy, awesome! … What's the height and weight?"

He put his hand over the mouthpiece and glanced at Cassandra. "It's his second granddaughter."

He redirected his focus, "Great! … Sure … We'll do it when I get back into town … Uh-huh …"

Cassandra grew impatient and touched her father's left arm. "Ask him about the ring," she whispered.

He nodded. "Doug, guess what? I just saw a class ring that looks like yours … Yeah, that's right … That's what we were thinking. Someone went to the same high school … No, I couldn't talk to her."

Cassandra was impressed her father could hide the truth without being dishonest.

"Doug, where'd you go to school? … Uh-huh. Could you look at your ring so we can compare the two? … Oh yeah, not in your office. Do you remember what it looks like? … Terrific! What are the letters on the ring? … LHS."

Cassandra felt a wave of goose bumps while she hung on her father's every word.

"What font was used? … Uh-huh. What about the year, same font?"

He gave her a thumbs-up sign.

"There's also a dragon, right? … How many talons are visible? … Does the dragon grab any letters or numbers?

… Uh-huh … What does the dragon's eye and mouth look like? … Uh-huh … Do you remember if the class rings were ordered from one of those companies that makes them for all the schools? … They don't, huh … Yeah … Okay, sounds good … Thanks, goodbye."

Gary hung up and smiled.

"Just don't leave me hanging!" Cassandra said.

"Sorry about that. I was enjoying the moment. This is awesome."

"Well?"

"Both Professor Stottlemeyer and Jane Doe 6 attended Lodgepole High School. Lodgepole is a small town west of Minneapolis."

"Are you sure? They went to high school many years apart."

"Doug said they've been making the same class ring for decades."

Cassandra was ecstatic. "This is great news, in more ways than one."

"Terrific! I'm glad I could help."

"And thank you, but you can't tell anyone because this is an ongoing investigation. If you'll excuse me, I need to make a short call."

"No problem. I need to call your mother and check in with her."

Cassandra clasped her hands together. "Please don't tell Mom about what we've been doing?"

Her father chuckled. "What? I can't keep something like this from her. Don't worry, your mother isn't a blabbermouth."

"I can't win," she said under her breath. She hurried into her office, closed the door, and called Mike on her cell phone. "Hey, that was a cute little prank."

Mike chuckled. "I knew you'd enjoy it."

"Oh, I did, and not in the way you intended. Dad was driving me nuts, asking me one question after another about the case. To placate him, I let him review the evidence, and guess what? He just identified Jane Doe 6's class ring."

"Holy crap! Are you serious, or are you trying to get back at me in some way?"

"Yes, to both questions, and congratulations, you've won yourself a trip to Minnesota. I hope you own a parka."

Chapter 16

Mid-April 2019
Eastvale, California

Rebecca once again arrived at the visitor parking lot for the Inland Empire Institution for Men. While she still found the facility intimidating, it did not bother her as much as during her first visit. Since she arrived early in the day, the waiting room was only one-quarter full. Instead of a room full of noise, two women sat in one corner and engaged in a hushed conversation. In another corner, a baby fussed while other young children remained quiet. Rebecca barely had time to place her satchel on the floor and check her cell phone when a tall African American guard arrived. He escorted her to an attorney visit room, which had a similar pattern of scuff marks, nicks, and dents as the room she had previously visited.

About ten minutes later, the same guard arrived with Nicholas Malone.

"Oh my!" Nick said, upon entering the tiny room. "You're here on a Saturday! I'm so honored." He eased into his chair.

Rebecca ignored the comment and addressed the guard. "You can take off the handcuffs and shackles."

He responded with a blank stare.

"I'll be fine. Please remove them."

The guard made a half-frown, grabbed a key from his pocket, and uncuffed Nick's wrists. While still bent over, he turned his head toward Rebecca. "That's the best I can do. The shackles on his ankles stay on." He left the room and closed the door.

"Thanks," Nick said as he rubbed his wrists.

Rebecca gave a genuine smile. "How are you feeling today?"

"About the same as always."

"We need to talk some more about you."

He exhaled through his nose, and the lines in his forehead became deeper. She thought he would protest, but instead he said, "Fair enough. What do you want to know?"

"We already talked about your manslaughter conviction and the one for hitting the police officer. No need to go over those again. I received a complete copy of your prison record, and I have a few questions. Let's talk about the first few years of your incarceration. You had some write-ups, and you were convicted of assaulting a guard. Please tell me first about the write-ups."

Nick shrugged. "There wasn't much to them. After the judge sentenced me, I was transferred from the county jail to one prison and then to another, just routine stuff." He scratched his forearm. "I got written up for having contraband in my cell. Someone got ahold of a *Playboy*, and it ended up with me. Not a big deal. Another write-up was for disobeying an order, which was a bunch of bull. I also got into a fight, and it wasn't my fault."

"What was the fight about?"

Nick chuckled. "A gang member challenged me, the new guy, and he should've known better. Back then, I worked out every day, and I was ripped." He clenched his fists and expanded his chest. "The dumbass tried to attack me, and I responded by knocking him out. He got sent to the infirmary, and word got around fast. After that, no one tried to take me on solo."

Rebecca concluded if Nick's story were accurate, he had acted in self-defense, but the authorities had cited him for a rule violation. Something didn't seem right to her. She would again read the relevant section of his prison record and then determine if she would further question him about the incident.

"Why'd you assault the prison guard?" she asked.

"I wouldn't call it an assault, because I was defending another inmate."

"How so?"

Nick looked to the right, and his eyes flashed. "Mitchell Colfax was a guard in our cell block and a real sick bastard. He was also a big guy, around six four and a lot of muscle. Colfax tried to intimidate everyone around him, and he targeted this skinny kid, Carson Williamson, who was about twenty or twenty-one."

Rebecca saw fire in his eyes and the muscles in his lower jaw tighten. Even though Nick's demeanor made her nervous, she didn't fear for her safety. Nevertheless, she was somewhat relieved he was staring at the wall and not at her.

"Shortly after the kid arrived, he starts acting all weird and jumpy," Nick said. "I knew it wasn't drugs. It was weird in a different way. After a couple of weeks, I confronted him, and he admitted Colfax had been molesting him."

"Did you report it to anyone?"

He scoffed while continuing to look away. "Hell no. It would've done no good. If a report had gotten to the warden, he wouldn't have cared."

"Why do you say that?"

"Colfax would've denied it," Nick retorted. He turned his head to glare at her. "Who would the warden have believed, Colfax or me?"

"Did you try reporting it to someone on the outside?"

Nick slammed his right palm on the table. "Man, you really don't know much about the real world, do you? So, I'll have to spoon-feed it to you. Suppose we'd contacted the ACLU or other liberal do-gooders. So what? They couldn't swoop into the prison and rescue the kid. Months would've passed before someone did something about Colfax, if they did anything at all. By then, the kid might've committed suicide."

"So, what'd you do?"

"I decided to remove the sick bastard from the prison, but I couldn't force a transfer. Also, I didn't want him to victimize a weakling at another prison. He needed to take early retirement involuntarily. Colfax was bigger and stronger than me, but I had the element of surprise."

Nick rose to his feet with his face red from anger and hate. Rebecca was unnerved as his right hand formed into a tight fist. Despite being a black belt in karate, she felt intimidated.

"I snuck up on him from behind and coldcocked him in the back of the head," he growled while he swung his fist toward the wall. "Colfax stumbled and was barely on his feet." He held out both hands with the palms facing each other. "I grabbed his head and slammed it into the wall. Wham!" he said as he mimed the action. "I heard Colfax's skull fracture, and he was knocked unconscious." Nick's face became less tense and turned a lighter shade of red as he sat. "Other guards rushed to the scene and beat the crap out of me. I spent a week in the infirmary, but it was worth it. Colfax lived and was gone for good."

Nick's presentation and the revelation of his darker side horrified Rebecca to the extent that she couldn't speak or move.

He turned his head toward her and grimaced. "Oh, I'm sorry. I got a little carried away, I just really hated that guy. Are you all right?"

"Not really," she said nervously.

He exhaled. "Ah, crap. Hey, I'm usually not like that. I hadn't thought about Colfax in years and got carried away." He held up his hands. "Don't freak out. I swear I've never hit a woman, not even one who's an attorney." He gave a quick half-smile. "I'm fine now, okay?"

"Fine," Rebecca said, her pulse racing. She did her best to collect herself and focus on the task at hand. "If you nearly killed Colfax, why were you only sentenced to one more year in prison?"

Nick chuckled. "Politics might be the correct answer. At first, I was charged with attempted murder. I told the public defender what happened, and he contacted his liberal do-gooder friends, who were part of a civil rights group. Can't remember the name. It wasn't the ACLU. The do-gooders got on their high horse and raised a big stink. The prison authorities wanted to keep things quiet, and the DA got on board. My PD wanted the case dismissed, but the DA wouldn't go that far. He said if I pled guilty to aggravated assault, he'd recommend a one-year sentence. If I refused, we'd go to trial on attempted murder, and I could get a lot more time. An extra year didn't sound too bad. So, I took the deal."

Rebecca thought his explanation made sense. "Did the civil rights group make demands for prison reform?"

He smirked. "Those idiots wanted a show trial, and they were really ticked off when I took the deal. Screw them! I was the one facing more time, not them. They only knew about Colfax and had nothing serious on the other guards. Other minor stuff happened, and no one wanted to talk about it. Life inside is never fun, but we're not a bunch of whiners, at least most of us."

Nick grimaced and rubbed his forehead.

"Something bothering you?"

"It's nothing." He continued to rub his head. "It's just a headache. I've been dealing with them for a few days. Let's keep going."

"Are you sure?"

"Yeah." He put his hand down. "I'm not dying. Besides, you'll bug me some more sooner or later."

Rebecca could handle Nick's attitude as long as he didn't act out any more violent scenes from his past.

"After the conviction for assaulting Colfax, you weren't cited for any more violations."

"Yeah, that's right. I was transferred to another prison and then to here. The guards didn't hassle me as much as I got older. The other inmates knew about me and gave me a certain level of respect. Now I'm some kind of elder statesman or whatever, and everyone treats me pretty good, or at least good for in here."

"Why'd you get bachelor's and master's degrees in psychology?"

"Something to do."

"That's not much of an answer."

"Too bad."

"Are you going to have the same attitude with the parole board?"

"Maybe. It won't make a difference if I'm polite to them or not."

Rebecca sighed. "You don't know that. Let's try again. Why did you pursue the degrees?"

Nick shrugged. "Something to do. You can only work out in the yard for so much time each day, and after a few years, reading books and watching TV became boring."

"Why psychology as opposed to anything else?"

"It interested me. Do you need a more complex and sophisticated reason?"

"Not really, I guess."

In Nick's prison file, Rebecca had seen a letter from a chaplain, thanking him for starting anger management and drug addiction support groups.

"Why'd you start an anger management group?"

"I was bored."

She gave him a hard stare.

He exhaled and looked away. "Whatever. I wanted to help some guys deal with their anger and hostility. Acting up with the guards or other inmates would hurt their chances at parole. They also needed to learn how to better interact with others once they got on the outside."

"What about the drug counseling?"

Nick opened his mouth and then gave a wry smile. "You wouldn't like the snarky answer."

No kidding, she said to herself.

"Again, I was just trying to help. For some idiots, their problems stemmed from illegal drugs. If you get them off the stuff, they wouldn't do stupid things on the outside and end up back here."

"You can get drugs in prison?"

Nick groaned and rubbed his forehead again while placing his elbow on the table. "You really need to wake up. You can get anything – drugs, alcohol, cell phones, other contraband."

"How do drugs and alcohol get into the prison?"

He put down his hand. "Through family members, the delivery guys, guards looking to make a few extra bucks. If you want something and have the money, you can get practically anything."

"Have you been using drugs and alcohol?"

"Not for a very long time." He grimaced.

"I think we should stop for today. Shouldn't you go to the infirmary and get yourself checked out?"

"Thanks, Mom, but I'm fine."

"Then perhaps you'd like to discuss something else, something like your favorite subject."

His eyes flicked toward Rebecca, and he perked up.

Chapter 17

The day after Professor Gary Morgan flew back to Seattle, Cassandra and Donnie headed out to meet with Sheriff Jefferson "Red" Burkett, who had led his department for twenty-three years. Cassandra wanted to talk to him about one of the Crescent City Killer's first victims, Chase Unger. She rode in the front passenger's seat of Donnie's government-issued sedan, which had a dent in the front bumper, door dings, a cracked windshield, and a worn interior. She imagined Donnie had been driving this car far too long.

On the way, Donnie raised an issue. "Please don't take this the wrong way, okay? Sheriff Red has a… prickly personality. If you go after him… well, our meeting will go downhill very quickly."

"What the hell?" Cassandra said, offended. "I don't go after people."

Donnie kept his left hand on the steering wheel and used his right to press down twice on an imaginary flat object, indicating "calm down."

"I'm afraid you do, but it doesn't happen very often. I've only seen it twice, and both times it was well deserved. Remember the detective who called you 'babe' and 'honey' in the same conversation?"

"Oh yeah." She recalled he was a sexist jerk and a loudmouth.

"No doubt he had it coming. Then there was Lieutenant Garson, who was about to retire. He touched your shoulders, like he was going to give you a massage, and he made an offensive comment. From the look on your face, I thought you were about to tear his arm off."

Cassandra scoffed. "You still remember that? It happened years ago."

Donnie nodded. "I know. My point is you can get hot under the collar. Ordinarily, that's not a problem, but you need to keep your temper in check today. You can't go after Sheriff Red even if he deserves it, okay?"

She exhaled through her nose in frustration. "I'll be a good little girl. Is that what you want to hear?"

"Not exactly, but the correct sentiment is in there somewhere."

Cassandra now had another reason not to look forward to meeting Sheriff Burkett. She had heard bits and pieces of gossip about him. Based upon this information, she concluded he was "old-fashioned," meaning he did not want women working in law enforcement, which most likely included female prosecutors. Women worked for the sheriff in various roles, including as deputies, but if he had his way, female employees would perform clerical work and nothing else.

While Cassandra did not appreciate the sheriff's sexist attitude, there was nothing she could do about it. On the other hand, she was unaware of him having any issues with African Americans, so even though she wanted to show she headed the investigation, she would let Donnie take the lead.

After about two minutes of silence, Cassandra said, "There's been rumors about our DA being corrupt. I don't know if they're true, but some things look suspicious, such as the fact that he and his wife both drive top-of-the-line Mercedes, and she doesn't work."

Donnie kept his eyes fixed on the road. "I've heard those rumors too. LeMay told me his aunt died, and she had no children. She left him three houses, including two rentals, and LeMay sold all three." He scoffed. "Dumb move if you ask me. I would've rented out all three houses for the income and sold them after I retired."

Donnie and Cassandra crossed the Mississippi River on the Hale Boggs Memorial Bridge and headed northwest to Hahnville. They traveled on a narrow two-lane road with a grass-covered levee on their right. Small businesses, homes of various shapes and sizes, and a scattering of trees dotted the landscape on their left. About three miles past the bridge, they came to the parking lot for the local courthouse, which was much larger than the other buildings in the immediate area. A smaller building next door contained the sheriff's office.

Donnie parked his vehicle and winced as he exited it. Cassandra noticed but said nothing this time. She could not imagine the constant pain he endured. They entered the sheriff's office and approached a middle-aged receptionist with a crooked smile and a medium-brown bouffant hairstyle.

"How may I help you?" she asked.

"Afternoon," Donnie said in a soothing voice. "We're with the Orleans Parish District Attorney's Office, and we have an appointment with the sheriff. Could you tell him we're here?"

"Sure will, sugar. Be back in a jiff."

As the receptionist rose from her chair, Cassandra smelled the half-can of hairspray she must have used earlier that day.

The receptionist performed a balancing act on three-inch heels toward the door with the sheriff's name and logo behind her desk. She knocked and poked her head inside. About thirty seconds later, she left the door open and returned to her station.

"He'll see you now. Y'all have a blessed day."

"You too, ma'am," Donnie said.

Before Cassandra and Donnie reached his office door, Sheriff Burkett stood in front of it. Cassandra surmised the sheriff had obtained the nickname "Red" because he previously had red hair, which was now thin, gray, and slicked back. She also noted his wiry frame and his face made of cracked leather.

"Afternoon, Sheriff," Donnie said as he held at his hand. Since Burkett did not reciprocate, he put it down. "It's been a while since I last saw you, maybe at a conference in Baton Rouge."

"I reckon," Burkett uttered through yellow teeth.

Donnie nodded. "We're working on the Crescent City Killer case, and we wanted to talk to you about Chase Unger."

"Uh-huh." He smacked his lips, which deepened the cracks around his mouth. "Got more evidence?"

"Well, no," Donnie said sheepishly. "We just wanted to go over a few things, and uh–"

"Waste of time." He turned toward his office.

"Wait a minute," Cassandra said, which caused Burkett to pause. "So far, the serial killer has murdered twelve people, and three of them were found in your parish. You might not care about the two hookers, but what about Chase?"

Burkett turned around to face her with narrowed eyes and a scowl.

"Sheriff, I'll be honest with you," Cassandra continued. "We're grasping at straws, but we've got to keep trying. Hopefully, we'll discover some little piece of evidence, which will lead to something else, then something else, which will lead us to the killer. Let me ask you this. If he's caught, what should happen to him?"

"Bring him to justice."

"Okay, that's you answer on the record. How about off the record?"

Burkett stared at her, sizing her up. He pursed his lips. "Shoot him in the head."

Cassandra slightly shook her head and frowned. "That's it? He brutalized and tortured the women before killing them. A quick death isn't good enough. I say burn him with a blowtorch, take a baseball bat to his hands and feet, and shoot him in the stomach. After that, tie him down in the hot sun and leave him there until he dies."

Burkett gave no visible reaction. He instead stared at Cassandra until the silence became uncomfortable. Without taking his eyes off her, he yelled, "Boone!"

From the back of the room came a voice. "Yeah, boss?"

"Git out here!"

A large man in a deputy's uniform strode towards them. Boone was six feet tall with a broad chest, big arms, and thick thighs. He also had short, light-brown hair and a baby face. Cassandra concluded he was a thirty-year-old country bumpkin.

"Yeah, boss?" he asked again.

Burkett's eyes shifted to his deputy. "Help them." He stepped into his office and closed the door.

"Afternoon," Boone said with a smile. "I'm Travis Boone, and you are?"

"I'm Cassandra Morgan, and this is Donnie Green. We're from the Orleans Parish DA's Office. We'd like to talk to you about Chase Unger for a few minutes."

"Pleased to meet both of you," Boone said as he shook their hands. "Want to talk about Chase, alrighty. Uh, we can use the interrogation room." He then grimaced and snapped his fingers. "No, someone's usin' it for an interview with a job applicant. Where else… Oh yeah, we can sit in the breakroom. Follow me, please."

Deputy Boone guided them past several occupied cubicles and desks. Some individuals wore uniforms, while others were in civilian clothes. They came to a dated kitchen with a four-burner stove, a microwave, an old refrigerator, and a sink. Various notices had been affixed to a large bulletin board, and a hodgepodge of chairs surrounded two round patio tables.

"What do you want to know about Chase?" Boone asked once all three had taken their seats.

"Did you know him?" Cassandra asked.

Boone leaned back. "Oh yeah. We went to high school together, in the same graduatin' class. Took a few subjects together and that was it. We weren't buddies or anythin' like that. Not sure if he had any. He was the quiet type, a loner."

"Did he ever get in trouble with the law?" Donnie asked.

Boone nodded. "Oh yeah. After high school, he had a serious drug problem: cocaine, meth, prescription meds. Back when I was a rookie, I arrested him, which was his last one." He released a chuckle. "Get this. I brought him into the station, and I looked him square in the eyes." He pointed with his index and middle fingers spread apart. "I told him to stop with the drugs cuz they were takin' him down the wrong path. He just looked at me for a spell, just contemplatin' things. Then he said, 'You're right.' That was it! He quit drugs right then and there."

"No fooling?" Donnie asked.

"Nope. Chase had been clean and sober for about three years before he was killed. By that time, he seemed to have his life in order. He was workin' as a groundskeeper for the Broussard and Robinette families and sometimes picked up work as a handyman. Chase never smiled, but he appeared content. He must've enjoyed workin' outside."

"Where'd he live?" Cassandra asked.

"He had a trailer just outside of town, tucked away behind a bend in the road. Chase liked the location cuz it gave him privacy."

"If a visitor parked his car out front, would anyone see it from the road?"

Boone shook his head. "Nope. No one saw him come and go." He sighed. "You know, we all thought Chase was doin' fine, and then he died from a heroin overdose."

"It's a shame," Donnie said. "How'd you find out?"

"His mom was worried cuz she couldn't get ahold of him. She called the station, and I drove out there. I knocked and rang the bell. No answer. I peeked inside and saw him lyin' on the couch, been dead for a couple of days. Poor bastard," Boone said as he shook his head. "No sign of foul play, and we figured it was an accidental overdose. Far as we knew, Chase never tried heroin, and for his first time, he shot up too much."

"Right," Cassandra said. "Was there any evidence Chase had a visitor before he overdosed?"

"No."

"Uh-huh," Donnie said. "And the connection between Chase and Jane Doe 1 was the key to the Broussard's mausoleum."

"Yeah. Kinda creepy to have one at your own place, even for these parts. Chase needed the key to open the gate and mow the grass between the fence and the mausoleum. The same key opened the mausoleum's doors. After we found the body inside, we figured someone killed Chase to get his key."

"Makes sense," Cassandra said. "After you found Jane Doe, did you go back to Chase's trailer to look for evidence of a visitor?"

"Yep. Chase's mom was gettin' ready to clean the place before she put it up for sale. Didn't matter – we got there before she started. The only prints we found belonged to Chase and his mom. His killer must've been really careful."

"There's something else I can't figure out," Cassandra said. "The Broussards own a large piece of property. From the road to the mausoleum, it's a long way to carry a corpse, even for a strong man. If the killer parked in front of the garage and passed by the house without anyone noticing, it's still a long haul."

"That's right, and I reckon the killer got to the mausoleum another way. There's an access road behind the Broussards' place. From there, it's a short walk through the oak trees to the gate, 'bout a hundred feet."

"Huh," Cassandra said. "I didn't see any access road on the local map."

"Oh, it's there," Boone insisted as he pressed his right index finger into the table. "I can show you, no trouble at all."

"That won't be necessary. We suspect Chase met the killer in New Orleans. Do you know why he'd go there?"

Boone stared into space and then shook his head. "Sorry, can't come up with a reason. I didn't know him too good."

"Did he have any hobbies?" Donnie asked.

"Uh, maybe, but I doubt it."

"Did he like jazz?" Donnie asked.

Boone's eyes lit up, and he pointed his index finger at Donnie. "Oh yeah! It was the one thing you could get him fired up about. He told me the one thin' missin' from his life was musical talent. If he had it, he would've formed a jazz band." He held up his hands. "Whoa, hold the phone! I get it. Chase might've met the killer at a jazz club in the city."

"Possibly," Cassandra said. "Anything else that's important? Anything we haven't covered?"

Boone gazed into space again for a couple of moments. "No, not really." He then focused on Cassandra. "I really hope you catch the guy and identify Jane Doe 1."

She gave a half-smile. "So do we. That's it for now, and we really appreciate your time. If you think of anything else or something comes up, please give us a call right away."

"Will do, ma'am."

As Cassandra and Donnie left the building, she considered pulling Chase Unger's credit card statements to determine which jazz clubs he had frequented, but immediately dismissed the idea. No club employee or musician would remember a time five years ago when someone – the serial killer – met a quiet man – Chase Unger – who didn't socialize with others. She had met nobody with total recall and doubted such an ability existed. Once they reached Donnie's sedan, she stood by the passenger door and gave him a wry smile.

"What is it?" he asked.

"Oh…" She held out her hands. "I don't know. Don't go after the sheriff. Oh really? And who got some cooperation?"

Donnie chuckled. "Yeah, you got me. The torture-and-kill angle didn't pop into my head."

"Hey, whatever works, my friend. Whatever works."

Donnie chuckled again, and then the levity reflected in his face disappeared. "You weren't serious about what you said, about beating him and shooting him, were you?"

"Does it matter?" she said with a straight face. It didn't to her.

Chapter 18

The morning after speaking with Sheriff Burkett and Deputy Boone, Cassandra arrived at the trailer shortly before nine. Tyler, Mike, and Donnie were already present and seated around the large plastic tables. As always, Mike had a can of Diet Coke in close proximity, and Cassandra still could not get over his greasy hair.

"Man, the Green Wave really got screwed over," Mike said while acknowledging Cassandra's presence with a nod. "Right before halftime, Billingsley lunged for the ball before it went out of bounds. He flipped it back to Mouton…" Mike motioned as if he were taking the shot. "Swish! Three points, but no! The ref made a late call and said Billingsley had stepped out-of-bounds. Give me a break!"

"No doubt about it," Tyler said. "They were robbed."

"What the hell?" Cassandra interjected. "You're talking about a basketball game from months ago. Get over it. That game didn't make or break Tulane's season. Even if they had won that game, they still would've finished with a losing record."

"It was still a bad call," Mike said.

"I hate to inform you, but he was out," she said. She sat down. "I had a better view than either of you. It happened right in front of me, four rows up from the floor."

"You're kidding?" Mike said with a grin.

"Nope. I was there with my boyfriend, and he's a big Tulane sports fan."

"What does he do?" Donnie asked with a smile.

"Chemical engineer."

"You never told us anything about your personal life before," Mike said. "Did you accidentally let it slip out?"

"No. There was no reason to mention him before."

"Hey, want to hear about my marriages and divorces?" Mike asked. "It's highly entertaining."

"No thanks," Cassandra said with a grin.

Mike turned to Tyler. "Hey, what about you? Care to share?"

"Pass."

"What about you?" Mike asked Donnie.

Donnie paused for a moment and then said, "I was married for thirty-nine wonderful years, and last August, my beloved passed. After her diagnosis, she slipped away pretty fast, and I'm thankful she didn't suffer much."

Cassandra was flabbergasted, and Tyler stared at the plastic table in front of him.

"I'm really sorry to hear that," Mike said sullenly. "I swear I didn't know."

Donnie gave a weak smile. "I know. I told the boss not to say anything because I didn't want people to constantly remind me of her passing. Since she's been gone, it's not been all bad. I'm surrounded by my family, and one day, I'll see her again."

The room fell silent for a few moments.

"What's your secret to a long and happy relationship?" Tyler asked.

Donnie smirked. "Oh, that's simple. Don't marry Mike."

All present laughed, including Mike, who appeared to enjoy the joke the most.

"How'd things go yesterday?" Mike asked once the laughter had died down.

Cassandra rolled her eyes. "Meeting Sheriff Red was… an experience, and let's just leave it at that. We talked with his deputy, who knew Chase Unger. Based upon what he told us, there's a little more support for our theory that the serial killer is a jazz lover… Wait a minute. Aren't you and Tyler supposed to be freezing your butts off in Minnesota?"

"Nope," Mike said with a devilish grin. "We didn't need to go."

"Why not?" she asked.

Mike lifted his chin. "Drum roll, please."

Tyler beat the tabletop with both hands in quick succession, then pretended to strike a cymbal with a drumstick and made the corresponding sound effect. Donnie chuckled, but Cassandra was not amused.

"Our work is done!" Mike said. "Yesterday, we called the Lodgepole Police Department and explained we needed help tracking down a 1992 class ring. They were more than willing to assist. You gotta love small-town cops, right? The local high school told them the '92 class president was Melanie Stockwood."

"Stockwell," Tyler said.

"Stockwell." Mike pointed at him. "Thanks. Two officers went to her home, and she was there because she's a stay-at-home mom. The next thing you know, we're on the phone with her. Man, she loved to talk about high school a little too much. Stockwell keeps in touch with most of the 'old gang.' Her words, not mine. She said Lodgepole High's class of '92 had 112 students, and fifty-eight were women, which the school confirmed. About two months after Jane Doe 6's murder, there was a class reunion, and fifty-four women showed up."

Tyler held up four fingers.

"That means four did not," Mike said. "Stockwell knew good old Sheila couldn't come, since she was sick and living in Chicago. They've gotten together since the reunion."

Tyler pulled down one finger, which left three.

"Stockwell lost track of the others. Two of them had credit card activity after the murder of Jane Doe 6, which leaves…"

Tyler showed one finger.

"…one," Mike said. "Marissa Olson. The same patrol officer spoke with her parents yesterday. They told him, sometime after high school, she had a falling-out with them. So, she and her boyfriend moved to Houston. After they broke up, he moved back to Minnesota, and she stayed behind. A couple of months later, Olson disappeared. We're mailing out DNA kits today. Lodgepole PD will collect samples from her parents and send the kits back to us. That means we… are… done!"

Tyler and Mike high-fived each other while Donnie shook his head.

"Mike, you're infecting Tyler and not in a good way," Cassandra said. "You're also congratulating yourselves, but you didn't have to do much, including notifying Olson's family about her death. You stuck the local cops with that awful task. Let's not forget we have no clue who murdered Olson and the others, and we still don't know Jane Doe 1's identity."

* * *

The following Saturday morning, Cassandra sat alone in the trailer, while staring at the whiteboards containing the victim summaries and the timeline Tyler had created. Her hands were on top of her head, and her fingers pulled back her auburn hair behind her ears. Even though it was a futile exercise, she studied the whiteboards and mulled over the evidence in her mind, hoping to find even the tiniest of latent clues that could start her on a trail to the killer. A symphony played on her portable stereo at a soft volume. The horn section marched forward, carrying the orchestra, and reaching a crescendo.

The case was eating at her. An inability to solve any case would have bothered her, but this one affected her on a deeper emotional and psychological level. She knew she was not an empathetic person and could never relate to a murder victim's family. It was not in her nature to offer a shoulder to cry on. She had instead told the victims' families she would get justice for their loved ones. As for their emotional struggles, she had told them to speak with a religious leader, attend a support group, or call a psychiatrist. She had also hoped a trial victory would give some closure.

This time was different as she had nothing to offer. As a result, for the first time in her legal career, she felt ineffective and useless, even though she doubted whether the most brilliant detective in the world could solve the case. She also feared the killer would torture and murder another woman during the upcoming jazz festival, which would devastate another family she could not assist.

Another woman. She no longer viewed the victims as merely prostitutes and low-level criminals. They were human beings, just like her, and this realization had hit her harder the previous day. Betty Moore, Evelyn Moore's mother, had called her. Betty had spoken for a long, painful hour about her daughter. There had been so much more to Evelyn's life than being a part-time prostitute. Cassandra promised Betty she would catch the serial killer, the most foolish pledge she ever made. Her thoughts about Evelyn and Betty caused her to lose sleep last night. She imagined she would lose more sleep after the serial killer slaughtered more women and more families wanted to speak with her. She was uncertain whether she could handle it if the killer remained at large much longer.

Cassandra heard the front door open. She looked over her shoulder and noticed a familiar African American with short gray hair and a limp approaching her.

"Sorry to interrupt," Donnie said. "I accidentally left my cell phone in my office yesterday."

She spun around in her chair while the symphony continued to play. The violins took their turn, rising to the occasion to match the majesty of the horns.

"Hey," he said. "That's a really nice piece of music."

She smiled. "Yes, it is. It's the fourth movement of the *New World Symphony* by Antonín Dvořák." She turned it off with her remote. "Do you have a few minutes?"

"Sure, I've got the time," he said as he pulled up a chair.

Cassandra summoned the courage to talk about a personal matter, something she was reluctant to do with anyone, including her significant other and her parents. She leaned toward him. "This is just between us, okay?"

"Sure. I'll keep it confidential."

"Okay… Has this case been getting to you? Getting you…"

"Frustrated?" Donnie asked.

She nodded and hung her head.

"And it's weighing heavily on you?" he said.

With her head still down, she said, "Yeah. Doesn't it get to you?"

"I try my best not to let it beat me up."

"How do you do it?" she asked. She lifted her head and brushed several strands of hair away from her face.

"Oh, lots of ways… I spend time with my family and my church. Your parents live in Seattle, right? So, I guess getting together with them isn't so easy. Don't you spend time with your boyfriend? Are you doing anything with him this weekend?"

Cassandra gave a weak smile. "Yeah. He's a gourmet cook, and tonight, he's making a mole."

"Mexican food, right?"

"Right. I'm not a chocolate lover, but I'm willing to try it."

Donnie nodded and grinned. "Okay, okay. That's a good distraction. Do you cook?"

She shrugged. "I can boil pasta and heat a can of soup. How about you?"

His face brightened. "Oh yeah. I'm the cook for all the family reunions. Nobody, I mean, nobody makes a better crawfish étouffée than me. I also make a mighty fine fried alligator. You should try both sometime."

"Just say the word, and I'll be there."

Donnie pointed at her. "I'll let you know."

"It's a deal, but… I hope you don't mind me asking… Doesn't anything ever get to you?"

"What do you mean?"

"Aren't you still in pain because of…"

"My knee? It's nothing I can't manage, and there's not much I can do about it. I just live my life as best as I can from day to day, and the Lord willing, there'll be more good days than bad. So far that's been the case."

"Yeah, but sometimes it's hard to have a positive outlook."

"It's all a matter of what centers you, grounds you. Give it some thought, okay?" Donnie rose out of his chair. "If you need to talk again, I'll be there for you. Anytime, anywhere, all right?" He lumbered into his office and grabbed his cell phone. As he stepped out, he said, "Don't stay too long and let this case continue to chew you up. You need a mental break. Once we catch him, you'll be too busy for months or even years. Please take some time to enjoy life while you can."

"Thanks. I'll keep that in mind."

Donnie lumbered out the front door. Once he closed it, Cassandra spun back around in her chair and stared at the whiteboards again. She could not take a mental break because she was too obsessed with the case. They had to stop the monster no matter what it took. She didn't care if he were arrested and put on trial because a bullet in the head would be an acceptable way to end his murder spree. Unfortunately, she didn't own a firearm, but she ultimately didn't care who ended his life or by what manner.

Cassandra longed for a stiff drink, but as there was no hard liquor in the trailer, she walked to her office, opened the small refrigerator, and settled for a bottle of Michelob. The cool liquid soothed her throat yet did nothing to ease her mind. She turned on her computer and opened the spreadsheet for the list of short-term renters. She studied it intensely, desperate to discover something, anything.

Chapter 19

Mid-April 2019
Eastvale, California

Three days after her last visit, Rebecca returned to the state prison. Given Nick's recent outburst, she would let him talk about Cassandra Morgan and her team instead of himself. Whenever he had spoken about them, he had seemed totally engrossed in the story and never shifted into a hostile mood.

Nick had, so far, been consistent with the general consensus of what had happened, except when he had provided details about Cassandra, Donnie, Mike, and Tyler, which Rebecca found nowhere else. Despite her thorough search on the internet, she found few personal details about them. She located the most materials on Cassandra, but it still wasn't much. Various sources provided the usual reporting about a prominent prosecutor, and some discussed the rumors of what had happened. Rebecca had also found old news articles praising Donnie for saving the children at the elementary school. She read a few webpages that mentioned Mike but found nothing, absolutely nothing about Tyler.

Rebecca wondered if Nick had inside information, or if he had created certain details out of thin air. She speculated he could have first-hand knowledge, but when he provided his personal history, he never mentioned living in Louisiana. She'd eventually have to confront Nick as to the veracity of his story as diplomatically as possible.

Once again, Rebecca stood in line for the security check at the prison. She brought a paperback novel to read while sitting in the waiting room, but ended up having no free time. As soon as she passed through security, she saw a heavyset female officer with black hair pulled into a tight bun approaching her. The flap on her breast pocket said her name was Zuver.

"Are you Rebecca Holt?" the officer asked bluntly.

She forced a smile. "Yes, I am."

"I need to see your ID." Zuver held out her hand.

Rebecca had produced her identification for another officer during the security check. She could have objected but believed it was better to not argue. She provided her driver's license.

Zuver stared at the card. Without a hint of emotion, she returned it and said, "Follow me." She then marched through the middle of the visiting room.

The officer's actions confused Rebecca, as her other visits had occurred in one of the tiny rooms in another direction. Zuver headed in the wrong direction by ninety degrees. Rebecca suspected there were similar rooms in another part of the building and so she followed.

Officer Zuver used a key to unlock a thick metal door, which she held open for Rebecca as she passed into the adjoining hallway. As Rebecca followed her to the end of the hallway, she looked through thick windows into various offices but didn't notice any spaces designated for attorney visits and she started to become concerned.

Officer Zuver led Rebecca past another metal door and then a third. Once the last door opened, Rebecca found herself at the prison yard's edge. At least one hundred inmates were exercising or talking to each other. She became alarmed and clutched her satchel tightly. Her martial arts training would be useless if several men attacked her at once.

Rebecca trailed Zuver across the yard while doing her best not to reveal her terror. She kept her focus on the officer, and in her peripheral vision, noticed inmates staring at her, some less than ten feet away. Most of them possessed harsh facial features and apparent gang tattoos. She expected to hear wolf whistles or sexual propositions, but none were forthcoming.

About two-thirds of the way across the yard, Rebecca looked past Officer Zuver and spotted an older man with a gray crew cut, Nicholas Malone, sitting on one side of a picnic table behind a double fence topped with razor wire. This time, nothing restrained his wrists and ankles. A portable structure about the size of a two-bedroom trailer was to the left of him and the picnic table, and another double fence and razor wire was behind him. Rebecca quickened her pace to exit the yard into the smaller fenced area. Getting to it a second or two sooner would make an enormous difference to how she felt.

Officer Zuver unlocked the first gate, and once Rebecca was inside, she closed it and unlocked the second one. She gave Nick a quick wave, and he smiled and waved back. Rebecca entered the smaller area and watched the officer close and lock the second gate. Zuver did the same with the first and then stomped toward the building across the yard.

Rebecca examined the picnic table and the area to its left. Given it was early afternoon, the trailer cast a shadow toward the table but did not yet reach it.

She turned her attention to Nick. "Good afternoon."

He responded with a half-smile. "Same to you."

"Anyway, we could move this bench over a little bit?"

"Huh?" he uttered.

Rebecca cocked her head and held out her hands. "Hello? I'm a fair-skinned redhead and would rather not be in the sun."

"Oh, right. I can't move it because it's bolted down. We can't go inside," he said as he pointed at the trailer, "since the guards need to always see me. Sorry about that."

"Okay," she said with a tinge of disappointment. "At least we'll be in the shade fairly soon." She sat on the other side of the picnic table from Nick. "What is this place?"

"It's for conjugal visits."

Rebecca's mouth dropped open, and her eyes became wide as saucers.

Nick laughed hard and slapped the table twice.

"It's not funny!" she said.

Nick continued to laugh. "Yes, it is." He laughed again. "You got it wrong, it's…" He chuckled. "It's a place for conjugal visits and visits with family, but…" He chuckled again. "For us, it's an attorney visit."

"It's still not funny."

"Oh yes, it was. The look on your face was hilarious! Thanks. I haven't had a good laugh in a long time."

"Terrific," Rebecca said while feeling annoyed and embarrassed. "Now, can we end the entertainment portion of the afternoon?"

He released one more chuckle. "Yeah, sure. Sorry you were taken across the yard. Not sure why that happened. When other people from the outside come into this area, they go through a back gate."

Rebecca looked to her right, towards the other inmates. "I thought some of them would've given me a hard time, but it didn't happen."

"For good reason. They know if they screw with the visitors, someone will beat the crap out of them."

Rebecca was caught off guard and looked at him. "Who'd do that?"

"Take your pick."

"Who?"

He held his hands up. "I'd rather not say."

"All right," Rebecca said out of reflex. She was uncertain how to interpret Nick's last bit of information. Perhaps he or a larger prisoner with respect for women was ready to "discipline" an unruly inmate. Perhaps the guards would commit an assault. One part of her wanted the answer, but another did not.

"So, why are we meeting here?" she asked.

"I thought you needed a nicer setting after my outburst the last time. I sort of called in a favor so we could meet here. Don't get used to it because we can't do this all the time."

"That's fine. How are you feeling?"

"The headaches come and go. Right now, I'm fine."

"Did you go to the infirmary?"

Nick groaned. "What is this? No, I didn't go. It's nothing serious."

"You really should go."

"If the headaches come back, I'll have a doctor examine me, okay? Can we move onto something else?"

"Sure. Do you want to get back to New Orleans in 1999?"

Nick grinned. "You read my mind."

Chapter 20

End of April 1999
New Orleans, Louisiana

With the annual jazz festival fast approaching, Cassandra's anxiety level increased with each passing day. It seemed inevitable the Crescent City Killer would strike again, even though Mike and Donnie had reminded the higher-end prostitutes of the imminent threat and implored them to either stop turning tricks or stick to clients who lived in the city. However, she feared their advice had fallen on mostly deaf ears.

Cassandra and her team again touched base with the owners of all fifteen vacation homes, including Millie Thornwell and her son Jimmy. The owners gave the names and contact information of those who would occupy their homes before, during, and after the jazz festival. One owner was too trusting of others. Before his tenants arrived, he mailed the keys to his colonial cottage in Lakeview and asked them to leave the keys behind when they exited the premises.

The owners reported most tenants during the jazz festival were couples and families, but Donnie, Mike, and Tyler interviewed them as they came to town to confirm it. Cassandra's team also came up with a ruse. They told the visitors someone had committed burglaries in the area and asked them if they had seen anything suspicious. In doing so, they confirmed couples and families truly rented most of the homes.

Single males rented three vacation homes, and for these individuals, the team assessed whether they had personalities consistent with the typical serial killer. They ruled out one man who was a senior citizen and a trumpet player for a jazz band scheduled to perform. The second man was much younger but was also five foot two and rail-thin and appeared too shy and meek to be a murderer.

Cassandra received a phone call regarding the third single occupant.

"Hey, are you in the office right now?" Mike asked hurriedly.

"No, but I can be there in ten. What's up?"

"Something big. Tyler and I caught the last tenant on his way out. He told me his name is Patrick Walsh, and he fits the profile of our serial killer."

Cassandra's heart skipped a beat, and goose bumps formed on her arms. "Why do you say that?"

"He's good-looking, intelligent, and looks physically strong. He's also too willing to appease law enforcement. Yeah, it's not much, but he's agreed to follow us to the station. I'm in the car, and Tyler's waiting for him outside. We ran the plates on his sedan, and it's a rental. We haven't mentioned the phony burglar story yet. Better to wait until we question him over there."

"Yeah, good thinking. Please bring him to interrogation room one, if it's available."

"Right. We'll try to get his fingerprints or DNA. Are we searching his car?"

Cassandra considered the question for a few moments. "We don't have probable cause to search the interior. We can have someone dust the driver's side door for prints and attach a tracker to the car."

Shortly thereafter, Cassandra waited inside the police station, on the other side of a two-way mirror for a stark interrogation room consisting of bare cinder block walls, a rectangular table, and four metal chairs with white plastic seats and backs. Her mind raced with speculation that Patrick Walsh could be the monster, but she also knew this could be an enormous ball of nothing.

Tyler popped into the room where Cassandra stood and closed the door.

"We won't have any luck getting prints off his rental car," he said.

"Why not?"

"Take a look."

Tyler pointed as Mike and Walsh entered the interrogation room. Mike sat with his back to the two-way mirror, which forced Walsh to sit on the other side.

Cassandra noticed Walsh wore black leather driving gloves and wondered who in the world still wore them. Perhaps someone who did not want his real identity exposed. She also noticed Walsh was about thirty and six foot two with an athletic build. His thick chestnut brown hair was parted at the side, and not one strand was out of place. He wore expensive, business casual clothes, including a sport coat and a gold watch. As Walsh sat down, he revealed a pleasant smile and perfect teeth. Cassandra also noticed his cleft chin and remembered Millie Thornwell's short-term renter had one. She found Walsh attractive, but that didn't mean anything. After all, Ted Bundy had also made a decent appearance.

Mike pulled out a small pad and a pen. "All right," he said. "This shouldn't take too long, but you might as well take off your gloves."

Walsh slowly removed them and placed them on the table. He then put his hands on top of them. Cassandra groaned as her person of interest was careful not to leave any fingerprints on the table.

"I'm sorry. What was your name again?" Mike asked.

"Patrick Walsh."

Tyler left Cassandra alone, entered the interrogation room, and sat next to Mike. Meanwhile, Cassandra watched intensely from the other room.

"Do you have any identification?" Mike asked.

"Of course," Walsh said with a brief half-smile. He reached into his sport coat and removed his wallet. He flipped it open to his driver's license, which was too far away for Cassandra to make out the details.

"Do you mind taking it out?" Mike asked.

Walsh smirked. "As a matter of fact, yes. It's a real pain to get in and out."

"Damn," Cassandra said to no one. Walsh dashed another opportunity to lift a fingerprint.

"That's fine," Mike said while writing something in his notepad. "Brookline?" he asked.

"Yes. It's a Boston suburb."

Once Mike finished writing, he tore off the small sheet of paper and handed it to Tyler.

Tyler stood and asked, "Would you like some coffee or water?"

Walsh smiled politely. "No, thanks."

Tyler left the room while Cassandra shook her head. So much for obtaining DNA or prints from a cup. Walsh had not asked why the police were questioning him, which she found odd. She surmised he was creating the appearance of being cooperative when he was not. Everything about him, including his mannerisms and his choice of words, seemed deliberate, and thus, she concluded he was hiding something.

"What do you do for a living?" Mike asked.

"I'm an investment banker."

"Sounds like it's a pretty high-stress job."

"Yes, at times," he said with a thin smile.

Tyler reentered the room on the other side of the two-way mirror. "Someone's running a check with the Massachusetts DMV." He raised a small camera.

"Did you place the tracker on his car?" Cassandra asked.

"Yeah. Right under his rear bumper."

In the other room, Mike nodded. "So, when did you move to New Orleans?"

"I haven't. I'm just here for the jazz festival."

Cassandra heard two clicks from Tyler's camera.

"I see," Mike said. "Have you seen anything suspicious recently?"

Walsh did not flinch. "No, why do you ask?"

"There's been a few burglaries in the area."

"That's disturbing."

Cassandra noted Walsh's face reflected no alarm to the news, as if he knew Mike was lying to him. She heard two more clicks from Tyler's camera. Walsh's eyes darted to the right and above Mike, directly at her. She suspected somehow he knew she was watching him. He then turned his attention back to Mike.

"Why did I have to come down here? You could have asked me these questions at the house."

Cassandra knew Mike was stalling for time, waiting for the DMV check.

"Uh… I'm not sure how to put this," Mike said while shifting in his chair. "Well… you sort of fit the burglar's description."

"Oh really?" Walsh held up his right hand to the side of his face. "Do I look like a common criminal?" He then dropped his hand onto the driving gloves.

Mike chuckled. "Not really." He inched forward and leaned in. "Look, I'm going to level with you. My lieutenant is—"

Cassandra disregarded the conversation in the other room when she heard the door next to her open. A slender white male handed a piece of paper to Tyler and departed.

Tyler skimmed the paper. "The information on his license matches what's on file, but we don't have immediate access to the Massachusetts DMV photo. Since it's after hours on the East Coast, we'll request it first thing in the morning."

Cassandra stared at Walsh while Mike continued to engage in idle conversation with him. Walsh appeared too smart and too confident. Coming to a police station probably annoyed him, but he refused to show it. He was also too smug and acted as if he was fooling the police. Cassandra's gut told her Walsh was the serial killer, but they had no evidence connecting him to the crimes, and this reality ate at her.

Since there was no legal basis to hold Walsh any longer, Cassandra told Tyler, "Cut him loose."

He rapped on the mirror and moved toward the interrogation room.

"That's about it," Mike said. "Thanks for your time."

Tyler opened the door to the interrogation room just as Mike snapped his fingers and said, "I almost forgot something. Could I have one of your business cards?"

Walsh offered a smile that didn't appear genuine. "Sorry. I don't carry any when I'm on vacation." He then donned his driving gloves without once touching the table, and another chance to lift a fingerprint disappeared. Cassandra wanted to hit something.

"Okay," Mike said. "Detective Winfield will show you the way out."

Walsh glared at Mike before leaving the room.

Seconds later, Mike entered the room on the other side of the mirror. "He was a little too slick."

Cassandra scoffed. "Yeah, I know. How long before we hear something from the DMV in Massachusetts?"

"A couple or three days."

"Please contact Brookline PD and Boston PD to see if they have anything on him."

"Sure thing. It was already on my list."

* * *

The following morning around eleven, Tyler, Mike, and Cassandra gathered around the plastic tables in the trailer behind police headquarters, while Donnie had another medical appointment. Cassandra wondered if he was consulting with an orthopedic surgeon because his limp had become more pronounced.

She looked toward Mike. "What do we have on Patrick Walsh?"

"We're waiting for a copy of the DMV photo, obviously. Boston PD never heard of the guy, and Brookline PD promised to interview the Patrick Walsh who lives at the address listed on the driver's license I saw."

Cassandra groaned. "As of right now, we can't even arrest him for providing a phony ID. Tyler, what about the motion tracker?"

"According to it, Walsh drove from the police station directly to his rental house, and after that, the car didn't move the entire night. He probably got around town another way, or he found the tracker and removed it."

"What do we have on Armstead?"

"Not much," Mike said. "You were right about when Armstead went to a clinic. According to his visa card, it was the day after the estimated date of death for Misty Thorgenson. Due to privacy laws, I can't get his medical records on a hunch, and the timing could be coincidental. We found nothing placing him close to the bodies, and nothing to show he was out of town when any of the murders happened. It'd be great if we could arrest him for something, anything at all. Is being a total prick against the law?"

"I'm afraid not," she said with a frown, "and it doesn't matter. I have a strong feeling Patrick Walsh is the serial killer." She grimaced and smacked the table. "Maybe we should've followed him last night and not just stuck the tracker on his car."

Mike exhaled. "Yeah, I know, but he's too slick. If someone had tailed him, he probably would've noticed and behaved himself."

Chapter 21

Sunday, May 2, 1999, marked the end of the jazz festival, and Cassandra remained on edge. Nobody reported a new victim of the Crescent City Killer, but then again, on some previous occasions, no body had been discovered until several days after the festival had ended. Soon enough, her worst fear became a reality.

Early Tuesday morning, Cassandra was asleep in bed when her cell phone rang. She reached for it while avoiding a two-thirds full bottle of Southern Comfort resting on her nightstand. She glanced at the clock on her dresser: 6:23.

"Ms. Morgan, this is Deputy Travis Boone."

She coughed away from the mouthpiece. "Uh, hello. Why are you calling?"

"Do you remember when you told me to give you a holler if somethin' else came up? Somethin' came up. We found another dead body. The injuries and manner of death are 'bout near consistent with your serial killer's MO. I thought you'd like to see the corpse and the crime scene."

Cassandra rose to a sitting position and became fully alert. "Yes, of course. Where's the body?"

"Do you know Des Allemands? It's in the southern portion of my parish."

"Maybe. Down Highway 90, right?"

"Right. Just before you get there, look for Wenger Road on the right and make the turn. There's a cemetery ahead on the left, and that's where we are."

"All right. I'm on my way."

Cassandra's mind raced. While she had not wished torture and murder on anyone, she hoped this time there would be a silver lining. The killer – probably Patrick Walsh – could have left evidence of himself behind, something starting the trail leading to his arrest and conviction. On the other hand, she remained pessimistic, as the killer had been too smart to make a mistake. She conceived of no reason he would have deviated from his normal pattern of behavior. If the killer were indeed Walsh, he would have been even more careful after his recent encounter with law enforcement.

Before leaving her apartment, Cassandra placed a call to Tyler.

"We have another dead body, and it's in St. Charles Parish. We need to find Walsh ASAP. Please start with the data from the motion tracker on his car. Check for his current location and where the car was for the last twenty-four hours."

"Got it," he said.

* * *

Forty-five minutes later, Cassandra found Wenger Road, a residential street providing access to an eclectic mix of quaint cottages, larger custom-made homes, and double-wide trailers. Pine trees of varying sizes dotted the landscape. She parked her Mustang behind the last of four squad cars.

Cassandra made the short hike toward the cemetery. On the way, she first heard and then spotted a red-headed woodpecker tapping on a pine tree close to the road. As expected, up ahead and to the left, she observed about 300 white and light-gray above-ground slabs in a rectangular pattern with the longer side running perpendicular to the road. An enormous live oak with Spanish moss hanging from its limbs provided shade for the cemetery's far-right corner, while the rest of the well-maintained property was exposed to the sun.

Three deputies in uniform stood to the left of the cemetery's entrance engaging in idle gossip. Two more deputies were at the far end. On the narrow street's other side, Cassandra spotted Deputy Boone's burly frame and walked towards him. Boone was speaking with an older man seated in a battered dark-green pickup truck with rust spots on the hood and roof, then Boone slapped the truck's side and the older man gave a quick wave and drove off.

"Mornin', Ms. Morgan."

"Who were you talking to? He could pass for the sheriff's brother."

Boone chuckled. "Funny you should say that. That's who he is."

"No kidding. What was he doing here?"

"Identifyin' tire marks. I'll show you."

As they headed toward the cemetery, Cassandra put on her sunglasses. "Where's Sheriff Burkett?" she asked.

"He'll be back tomorrow."

"Won't he get mad because he isn't here?"

Boone stopped and turned to face her. "Yeah, and there's nothin' I can do 'bout it. He doesn't own a cell phone. Can't go get him cuz he never tells us where he goes on his fishin' trips." He turned to face the cemetery and pointed. "Okay, see this path down the middle? Please stay to the right of it."

Cassandra walked behind Boone until he stopped in the middle of the graveyard, where a shorter path intersected the longer one they had followed.

"Ms. Morgan, check out these tire marks. A car stopped here and turned around. Sheriff Red's brother said Goodyear tires made these marks, their most pop'lar model for sedans."

"How does he know that?"

"He owns the local Goodyear store and has been in the tire business forever."

The answer satisfied her. She made a mental note to have her team call rental car companies to determine if they equipped their cars with the same tires, especially the four-door sedan Patrick Walsh drove.

"Can your forensic team make a cast of the tire marks?" she asked.

"Of course. Now, look over here." Boone pointed to two footprints next to the tire marks. "The killer probably wears a size 12. Must be a pretty big guy, right? We'll get a cast of them too. We've got to walk around some gravesites to get to the body."

"Who found it?"

"Nosy neighbor who lives over there." He pointed across the street. "See the three white cottages?"

"Yeah."

"He lives in the middle one." Boone put his arm down. "The neighbor saw a dark-colored sedan pull into the cemetery right before dawn. The car parked, but the lights stayed on, and a minute later, it drove away. The neighbor suspected somethin' was fishy. So, he put on his bathrobe and grabbed his shotgun, then he hustled over here and found the corpse."

"Did he get the license number of the sedan?"

"Nope."

It didn't surprise Cassandra as fate would not give her many breaks, if any. The weather was also not cooperating. It was already warm and humid, and the sun beat down on her. She wished she hadn't left her water bottle in the Mustang.

Cassandra's cell phone rang. "Hang on a sec," she told Deputy Boone while stepping away from him. "Hey, Tyler. What'd you find?"

"According to the motion tracker, Walsh's rental car remained in the garage at the vacation home all night. He drove it to the airport and arrived about ninety minutes ago. He's probably gone by now."

She groaned. "Not good."

"No argument here. I'll bet he found the tracker and removed it before leaving the house with the body inside, then he came back and returned the tracker to where he found it."

"Yeah, but good luck proving it. Have someone check the passenger manifests for the outbound flights earlier this morning."

"We already did," Tyler said. "No Patrick Walsh on any flight. He must've used an alias."

"Terrific. Please call the rental car agency at the airport. Hopefully they won't have cleaned Walsh's car yet. We need the crime lab to go through it thoroughly. Tell the rental agency why we need it without giving away too much, and you might scare them into giving us the car without a warrant."

"Will do."

"Also, you, Mike, and Donnie should go to the airport with some uniformed officers. Interview the ground personnel and see if anyone remembers Walsh. We might get lucky and figure out which flight he took. We can then ask the local police to interview him once he lands. They can also search his luggage before it's returned to him."

"Got it," Tyler said.

"One other thing. Call Ken Blankenship and get some homicide detectives to assist. Have them contact the owner of Walsh's rental home, and let's see if they can get a consent to search. If not, have Ken and company sit on the house until we get a warrant."

"Got that too."

"Thanks, bye." Cassandra swore to herself and walked back to Deputy Boone.

"What was that?" he asked.

"Probably nothing but bad news. Tell you later."

"Okay," he said as more of a question than an acknowledgment. "Let's head on over to the body."

Boone led Cassandra past a handful of slabs and corresponding markers. She then saw the nude corpse of a young Asian woman, lying on her stomach with her head facing sideways and her eyes open. Cassandra guessed the victim was in her late teens or early twenties, about five foot one, 105 pounds, and either Chinese or Vietnamese. She had black wavy hair reaching to the middle of her back, most of which lay on the grass.

Ligature marks were present around the young woman's ankles, wrists, and neck, and many bruises covered her back, buttocks, and legs. On the back of her right leg, Cassandra noticed three marks, each about two inches long, containing charring and blistering consistent with third-degree burns. They were worse, deeper and more extensive than the cigarette burns on other victims. She guessed the killer heated the metal part of a flathead screwdriver or another long metal object before burning the young woman.

Given the victim's left arm was bent at an odd angle, Cassandra concluded the killer had dislocated her shoulder. The left hand rested almost flat, revealing manicured fingernails with French tips, while the right arm lay by the victim's side. Based upon everything she saw, Cassandra did not need an autopsy report to tell her the victim had been tied down, abused for hours, and strangled to death. While the killer had brutalized his other victims, he took it to another level with his latest one.

Boone squatted next to the body, and Cassandra did the same. He put a light-blue glove on his right hand, and with the same hand, he raised the corpse's left arm an inch, which appeared stiff.

"When the first two deputies arrived, the body was still fresh," he said. "Now, rigor has set in but no lividity. Best guess, she passed three, four hours ago."

"Sounds about right."

Cassandra also noted the serial killer, probably Patrick Walsh, neglected to deposit the corpse in a remote location. Instead of being more cautious after his encounter with the police, he had become overconfident. The killer wanted the victim to be discovered quickly to show off his latest conquest. He mocked law enforcement and was certain he would never be caught.

"Other than her race and where she was found, everythin' else fits the other murders," Boone said. "We have a real sicko on the loose, don't we?" He pointed to the corpse's mouth. "There's somethin' sticky on her lips and around it."

Cassandra stared at the dead woman's mouth and eventually spotted it. "This is something new. Looks like it came from duct tape."

"Right." Boone pointed toward the corpse's back at waist level. "There's a strand of chestnut-brown hair. Must've fallen off the killer when he set her down. No root, which means no regular DNA. However, the shaft has… Shoot, I just read about it."

"Mitochondrial DNA," Cassandra said. She knew it couldn't provide an exact match to anyone, but it could narrow down the list of possible individuals significantly. It was better than nothing by a slim margin. Cassandra also remembered Walsh's hair had the same color and texture, which was not much of a coincidence.

Boone took a duckwalk step towards the corpse's left hand and pointed to the fingers. "No doubt she got a piece of him."

Cassandra rose, took a step, and then squatted next to the hand. The French tip for the middle finger had a tiny chip. She also observed what could be blood and skin underneath the nails for the index and middle fingers.

"Our forensics team and coroner should be here any minute," Boone said. "I didn't bag the hands so you could take a look."

"Yeah… Good work, Deputy. Really good work." Cassandra rose as her knees became sore. "I imagine you don't have too many homicides in your jurisdiction. Have you been moonlighting as a crime scene investigator in New Orleans or Baton Rouge?"

Boone grinned as he stood. "No, ma'am. I attend seminars from time to time and read a lot. Paid off cuz we get more homicides than I'd like."

"More than I'd like as well," she said, rage burning inside her. "This makes thirteen victims. We really need to stop the serial killer by any means necessary."

"Amen to that."

Chapter 22

Late April 2019
Downtown Los Angeles, California

Rebecca was in her office, reviewing a mountain of discovery related to a products liability lawsuit. She wondered if her superiors stuck her with the arduous task of summarizing medical records because she had majored in biology in college. She also grumbled over some partners characterizing the term "summarize" as a complete understanding of all the documents. A partner could ask, "What's this on page 1,246?" and "I don't know, it's not legible" would not be an acceptable answer. Such demands were ridiculous. Typewritten reports within the discovery documented the same thing and more clearly.

Rebecca was about to take a break due to eye strain when Carter Patterson popped into her office and sat in a guest chair. She noticed his remaining gray hair was a quarter-inch long.

"Are you busy?" he asked pleasantly.

"Always, but it's okay," she said. While other partners were too demanding and rude, he was the exception, so she always set aside time for him. "When do you have another oral argument before an appellate court?"

Patterson gave a wide smile. "How'd you know?"

"Your haircut."

"Ah! Am I that predictable? I'll be arguing before the Ninth Circuit. Have you ever seen the courthouse in Pasadena?"

"No, not yet."

"Oh, it's extraordinary," Patterson said as his eyes lit up. "There's a rose garden in front, and it's nicely decorated inside, and not too opulent. It's a very relaxing atmosphere. Perhaps you should tag along if you have the time." He crossed his legs and leaned back. "Anyway, enough of that. I'm interested in Nicholas Malone. How are things coming along?"

Rebecca sighed. "He's still a difficult person, and he consistently uses blunt and crude language. He mostly wants to talk about the Crescent City Killer, which means we've made little progress."

"You'll need to speak with him about his manner of speech. A person's tone and the proper use of words can make a significant difference."

Rebecca glanced at the ceiling. "I know, but I don't want to push him too hard. I'm still trying to build a good rapport with him."

Patterson pursed his lips. "Good, good, I suppose. You must take a different approach with him as opposed to that of a company's CEO. I'm a bit concerned about Malone's reluctance to talk about himself, however. Can you nudge him along and be ready for the parole hearing?"

Rebecca paused. She was uncertain he would cooperate given his fatalistic opinion about the parole board. "I'll give it my best shot," she said.

Patterson nodded. "Aren't you learning anything about Malone when he discusses the serial killer and the corresponding investigation?"

"What do you mean?"

"Aren't you picking up on some of his personality traits? Reading others can be an important skill for an attorney."

"Huh. I never thought about that. Are you good at reading others?"

He gave a wry smile. "Not really, but it's not so critical for appellate work. I only have to know the minds of the judges, which are reflected in their past decisions."

"Mr. Patterson, Malone has been chewing up more of my time than expected, and I need an extension on the discovery deadline for the Kessler case."

Patterson crossed his arms. "Why are you telling me? I'm not the partner overseeing it. Have you spoken with Vandemere?"

"Uh, no. I wanted to run it by you first."

"What will Vandemere say?"

"He'll say no. Would you mind speaking to him?" she asked awkwardly.

He frowned and exhaled through his nose. "Rebecca, you need to manage your own schedule and fight your own battles." His jaw muscles became tense, but he did not raise his voice. "Vandemere won't be sympathetic, and neither will the client. When you joined the firm, you knew this was not a nine-to-five work environment. You'll need to juggle assignments and figure it out. Sometimes we must work nights and weekends. It's simply the nature of the beast."

Patterson's response disappointed Rebecca yet it didn't surprise her. "Yeah, okay," she said. She suspected she wouldn't be able to make the day hike with her friends on Saturday. Perhaps she could work late Thursday and Friday, but then she'd be too tired on Saturday morning. She could put in a few hours on Sunday and wouldn't be the only one in the office. She didn't favor either option and questioned whether this was the best way she should live her life.

* * *

An hour later, the receptionist called Rebecca.
"Yes, Ms. Willingham?"
"Nicholas Malone's on line 4387."
"Did he call collect?"
"Yes, he did, and I accepted the charges."
"Thank you. Please put him through."
Seconds later, Nick's hoarse voice came on the line. "Hey, got a pen and paper ready?"
"Huh?"
"You said you couldn't visit, and you told me to call you at 3:30."
Rebecca felt embarrassed. "Oh, that's right. Sorry, I forgot. Let me grab your file. There are a few more things we need to discuss about your life."
"Nope. We're going back to Louisiana, and we're getting to a good part."
"The last part was very good, and we can take a break from the story. We need to get ready for the parole hearing."
"Nah. There's still plenty of time. The next part is even better, and it's my favorite."

Rebecca remembered Patterson's advice. The way Nick told the story could reveal something about himself. Thus, she did not object any further.

"Fine," she said, "but the next time I see you, we'll talk about you. Okay?"

"Yeah, whatever."

Chapter 23

Early May 1999
New Orleans, Louisiana

Late afternoon, Cassandra was in the trailer behind police headquarters when Jeremy the Explorer Scout arrived. He no longer wore braces but still had pimples. He handed Cassandra a report from the New Orleans crime lab.

The first part said Walsh's rental vehicle had the same tires as those that left tread marks at the cemetery in Des Allemands. It also said Walsh had left no fingerprints or DNA inside the car. She took the news in stride, given his performance in the interrogation room and his use of driving gloves.

Cassandra read the next section, which gave her a punch to her stomach. There was no evidence of the Asian woman's presence in the car's interior or trunk, not a speck of blood, a strand of hair, or one skin cell. She tossed the report aside in disbelief and wondered how Walsh could have pulled it off. Perhaps he had wrapped her in plastic before placing her in the trunk. If so, she wondered where he disposed of the plastic and the victim's clothes.

About fifteen minutes later, Ken Blankenship called. "Bad news," he said.

"Don't tell me. Besides coming up with nothing on the initial search of Walsh's rental home, the more intensive one turned up no fingerprints, no hair follicles, and nothing else containing his DNA."

"Yeah," he said with a groan. "He really cleaned up after himself. He even made certain there was no hair in the shower drain, and the entire bathroom was wiped down with bleach. We found traces of it everywhere."

"Damn it."

"I bet he didn't use the kitchen because there was no bleach in the sink or on the countertops."

"Yeah, maybe. How'd he pay for the rental?"

"Up front and in cash," Ken said. "The owner deposited the money the next day. So, it's long gone and back in circulation."

"Did the owner take a credit card number for any possible damages?"

"Yes, and the number was phony."

"Terrific… Sorry it was all a waste of time, and thanks for the assist."

"You're welcome. Any time you need us again, just call."

By the time Cassandra had calmed down, Mike Beaumont came barreling through the front door and sat next to her.

"Hey, I need to talk to you about a few things," he said. "We spoke with some employees at the airport who work the evening shift just in case anyone knew something about our so-called Patrick Walsh."

"And?"

"Same as the morning crew. A couple of people thought he looked familiar, but no one could remember where he was from. Sorry about that."

Cassandra sighed. "I figured it was a long shot."

"We're going with another one. Donnie is getting the passenger manifests for all the flights that departed within two hours of the phony Walsh dropping off the rental car. It'll be a lot of names, but maybe something will pop out."

"Uh-huh. Anything else?"

"Remember when Walsh showed me a driver's license with an address in Brookline, Massachusetts?"

"Of course."

Mike nodded. "Well, Brookline PD got back to me. They sent officers to the address on the license. They found an individual by that name with the same address, same date of birth, and same driver's license number as what the other guy provided to us. Brookline sent me the real guy's photo, and… surprise! He's not the guy we met, not even close. On top of that, the real Walsh said he's never been to New Orleans."

"Shocking," Cassandra said sarcastically.

"No kidding. Did you see how many times the name Patrick Walsh appeared on our list of short-term tenants?"

"Yeah. Three times for the same house, all around the same time as three murders. I'll bet the killer used other aliases with other property owners. Why don't you, Tyler, and Donnie send our photos of the fake Walsh to police departments in other major cities and see if he looks familiar to anyone? It might be a big waste of time, but you never know."

"And like you've said before, do we have anything better to do?" Mike said with a wink.

Cassandra rolled her eyes. "You're a little too happy about the whole situation. You know another woman was just brutalized and murdered."

"Hey, I'm not happy about that. It's that we finally have something. We now know what the Crescent City Killer looks like. We'll figure out who he is, and time is on our side, since he doesn't come to New Orleans during the summer. We'll get him."

* * *

Even though Cassandra knew it was futile, she checked a database to determine if anyone had recently reported a petite and young Asian woman missing. None had been made to the New Orleans Police Department or to any other law enforcement agency in the state.

Cassandra considered releasing the bogus Patrick Walsh's photo to the media. Besides the nutty and delusional making outrageous claims, perhaps someone with actual knowledge of his whereabouts would make a call. However, a national press release would alert the killer and then he could leave the country. In any case, neither the district attorney nor the chief of police would approve a press release because no hard evidence tied the fake Walsh to the murders. She also could not run amok and talk to the media on her own. She further knew at present she could only charge him with presenting false identification, not a severe enough crime to get him extradited back to Louisiana.

About an hour later, Cassandra received a report from the St. Charles Parish crime lab via email, which concerned an examination of the Asian woman. As expected, the lab reported the single hair found on her body did not have its follicle, which meant the lab could only extract mitochondrial DNA. They also found no fibers or other hairs. However, there was enough skin and blood underneath two fingernails to run a DNA test, which would take three to four weeks. But Cassandra feared both DNA samples meant very little because they had nothing for comparison.

Chapter 24

Around ten the next morning, Jeremy again returned to the trailer. "Excuse me, Miss Morgan?"

"Yes?"

"There's someone out front." He pointed behind him, towards police headquarters. "The watch commander says you should talk to her."

"Why is that?"

"She said her friend's missing."

A light bulb went off inside Cassandra's head, and she felt a rush of adrenaline. "An Asian friend, college age?"

"I think so," he said sheepishly. "I'm not sure."

"Have someone bring her to an interrogation room. I'll be there shortly."

"Yes, ma'am."

Five minutes later, Cassandra and Donnie arrived at the same stark interrogation room where Mike had questioned the phony Patrick Walsh. From behind the two-way mirror, Cassandra noticed a young woman pacing behind the table and chewing on a fingernail. She stood about five foot six and had an hourglass figure. Despite her apparent anxiety, she made a striking appearance due to her flawless skin, light-brown hair in a chin-length bob, and piercing blue eyes.

As Cassandra and Donnie entered the interrogation room, Donnie placed a manila folder on the table.

"I'm Assistant District Attorney Cassandra Morgan, and this is my assistant, Donnie Green. Please have a seat."

The young woman sat in a chair in front of her, while Donnie and Cassandra took chairs on the table's other side.

"I'm Lynne, Lynne Covington."

"I believe you're here to report a missing friend, right?" Donnie asked.

Lynne nervously nodded. "Uh, yeah. Her name's Amy Nguyen, and we're students at LSU. I'm a junior, and she's a sophomore. We came to New Orleans last weekend to have some fun, and... I haven't seen her since. I've called her a bunch of times, and I– I can't reach her." Tears welled up in her eyes. "I checked around, and... no one else has seen her. I talked to one of her professors, and he said Amy didn't attend his class yesterday morning."

"Did you make a report with the police in Baton Rouge?" Cassandra asked.

"Do I need to? I last saw Amy here, not back at school."

"Did you talk to any of her family members?" Donnie asked.

"I don't have her parents' number. They live somewhere around here... maybe in Metairie."

"Okay," he said. "When was the last time you saw Amy?"

"Last Saturday night when we were barhopping." Lynne held up her palms. "Okay, we're both underage, and we had fake IDs. It's no big deal. I mean, we never get wasted."

Donnie gave no indication that he was being judgmental. Cassandra suspected his present body language and manner of speech were intentional, to entice Lynne to be honest and open.

"Where'd you last see your friend?" Donnie asked.

"Uh, I'm not sure." Lynne fidgeted in her chair. "We... we were with a group of guys. Two of them wanted to go to another bar, and Amy joined them. I stayed behind with some other people." She looked away.

Donnie leaned to the right so he could again make eye contact. "Are you sure that's what happened? I think you're leaving something out."

Lynne folded her arms and leaned back. "Of course I'm sure. What else could've happened?"

Donnie stared at her as if he were trying to make her more nervous. "How about you and Amy were turning tricks?"

Lynne opened her mouth as if she were shocked, but Cassandra believed it was an act.

"What? No way!" Lynne said. "We'd never do that!"

"Are you sure about that?" Donnie asked. "We have reason to believe you and Amy have worked as prostitutes. Do you want to tell us what really happened?"

"Who told you we were hookers? It's not true!"

Cassandra sighed. "Okay, it's my turn. Do you see that?" She pointed toward the manila folder. "It contains photographs taken two days ago. Want to take a guess what they're of?"

"Uh, no," Lynne said. Her lower lip quivered.

Cassandra opened the folder, revealing a full-length view of the young Asian woman's battered and naked body lying on the grass in the graveyard. Lynne screamed in horror and burst into tears. Cassandra closed the folder, and Donnie gave her a harsh look. She didn't care. Donnie could have continued with a softer approach, and it would have taken too much time. Cassandra thought Lynne needed shock treatment to get her cooperation.

Lynne cried for a couple of minutes while the others remained silent. Once crying turned into sniffles, Cassandra asked, "Can we continue?"

There was no response.

"Let's try again," Cassandra said. "What happened?"

Lynne gazed at the table. "Uh, we were… um…"

Cassandra leaned toward her. "Look. We don't care about underage drinking, smoking pot, turning tricks, or anything like that. This is a homicide investigation, and your friend was murdered. We just want to know what happened to Amy. That's her in the photo, isn't it?"

Lynne nodded nervously and then sat quietly for a few seconds. She sniffled once more and lifted her head. "Yeah, okay. Sometimes I worked as a hooker on the weekends in New Orleans. My parents don't have a lot of money, and it's an easy way to pay for tuition and other expenses."

"What about Amy Nguyen? Was she a hooker too?"

"She was sexually active, but last weekend was her first time doing it for money. Amy was about to lose her scholarship because her grades stunk. I guess she spent too much time partying. She didn't want her parents to find out, and she needed some cash quick. So, I told her what I did, and I didn't think it was a big deal. I only met guys in nice places, and I made certain they weren't creeps."

"Didn't you hear about the serial killer preying on prostitutes on the news?"

Lynne shook her head.

Terrific, Cassandra said to herself. "Where was the last place you saw Amy?"

"At Rousseau's. It's an upscale bar in the French Quarter."

"Uh-huh," Cassandra said. "The hookers pay the bartender to look the other way, right?"

Lynne nodded.

"Did Amy hook up with anyone while at Rousseau's?"

"Yeah."

"What did he look like?"

"Uh, let's see…" Lynne looked at the table. "He was a white guy, around thirty, brown hair… maybe six feet or six two. He was sitting down, so hard to tell. He wore a dress shirt, might've been silk." She lifted her head.

"Did you see his face?" Donnie asked.

"Not really. I was busy talking to another guy."

"If we showed you some photos, could you identify him?" he asked.

Lynne paused for a moment and then shook her head.

"Did you see Amy leave the bar with this man?" Cassandra asked.

"No. I left first, and she was still talking to the guy in the corner." A tear fell from her left eye, which she wiped away with her hand.

"Who was working at Rousseau's that night?" Cassandra asked.

Lynne looked at the table again. "Let me think… There was one or two women. I don't know their names." She lifted her head. "Brody, Brody was there. He's the bartender."

"Please describe Brody," Donnie said.

"He's a white guy... thin, about five nine, short black hair, and he always wears a white dress shirt and a vest."

"What's Brody's last name?"

"I don't know."

Donnie flashed a half-smile. "Well, we can figure it out."

"Did I say anything that'll help you guys?"

"I certainly hope so," Donnie said. "Until the serial killer's apprehended, I strongly suggest you refrain from turning any more tricks. Got it?"

"Yeah, okay."

Chapter 25

Late afternoon, Cassandra and Donnie arrived at Rousseau's, and once again, Donnie carried a manila folder. The establishment had the feeling of a high-class but informal French restaurant, with its massive antique mirror behind the mahogany bar and covered armchairs around small and elegant round tables. A plethora of expensive wine and spirits lined a shelf in front of the mirror, and soft jazz wafted in the air through camouflaged speakers.

Cassandra spotted a man wiping down a table, who matched Lynne's description of the bartender. "Brody Robertson?" she asked.

He turned around. "That's me. Sorry to disappoint you, but we don't open for another twenty minutes."

"It doesn't matter. I'm Cassandra Morgan, and this is Donnie Green. We're from the district attorney's office."

Robertson smiled at her. "Oh yeah. I recognize you from the news. I'm sorry, but I can't open the bar early, not even for a local celebrity."

"We're not here to drink," she said. "We're conducting a homicide investigation."

Robertson laughed nervously. "Homicide? Why do you need to talk to me? I didn't kill anyone."

"I never said you did," Cassandra said. "We just need to ask you a few questions. Were you working here last Saturday night?"

"Yes, of course."

"Did you notice Amy Nguyen, a young Asian woman, in the bar that night?"

Robertson flinched. "I don't know. She could've been here. We were really busy, and I can't keep track of everyone."

"I'm sure that's true, but you probably don't have many Asian women as customers."

"Oh, we get our fair share."

"Perhaps a photo of her would jog your memory."

Donnie removed Nguyen's Louisiana DMV photo from the folder and showed it to Robertson.

He flinched. "No, I don't recognize her. Is she dead?"

"That's right," Cassandra said. "Are you sure you didn't see her?"

"No, I didn't," Robertson said. He broke eye contact and looked at the nearest table.

Cassandra took a step closer to him. "We have a witness who saw this woman in the bar with an attractive man, about six feet or a little taller. Ring any bells?"

"No, sorry," Robertson said with his head still down.

Donnie removed a photo of the phony Patrick Walsh from the folder and showed it to Robertson. "Was this man in the bar last Saturday? Perhaps he met the Asian woman?"

Robertson glanced at the photo and nervously shook his head. "Haven't seen either one."

"All right," Cassandra said. "Thank you for your time."

Robertson returned to wiping down a table, while Cassandra and Donnie left the bar and walked about half a block.

Once they stopped, Donnie said, "He's lying."

Cassandra donned her sunglasses. "Yeah, it was pretty obvious. Tomorrow morning, please run the phone numbers for the bar, his personal cell, and his home number. Let's see who he calls."

"You got it, but aren't you concerned Robertson will tip off the fake Patrick Walsh?"

"Or whoever else is scaring him? To an extent, yes, but it's worth the risk. We might get a better idea as to the serial killer's identity."

Chapter 26

"Hey, boss," Donnie said with a serious look. "I got the LUDs for Rousseau's and Brody Robertson. Since yesterday afternoon, Rousseau's phone activity has only been local calls, both incoming and outgoing. Nothing special about any of the numbers, but we can investigate further."

Cassandra groaned. "Is there any reason we should bother?"

Donnie sighed. "Yeah, I get it. It's probably another dead end, but we need to be thorough. Like you told Sheriff Red, one little thing might make a big difference in the long run."

She gave a weak smile. "You're right. I'll help out with that. What about Robertson's phones?"

Donnie scoffed and waved his right hand. "It's not much better. He received a few calls on his cell. He made a couple of local ones and another to someone in Baton

Rouge. Two people called his home number last night. Both calls were brief, which probably means they only left messages. No outgoing calls from his home number. Ran all the numbers for both the incoming and outgoing. Nothing raises an alarm. We'll look further into those calls too."

"Okay. Thanks for checking."

"Should we take another run at him?"

Cassandra arched her back and grimaced. "I need to get in better shape. Let Robertson stew, and we'll get back to him in a little while."

* * *

Several hours later, Cassandra once again arrived at Rousseau's, and this time, she entered alone and noticed the absence of music. Since it was early, no customers were present. Robertson was behind the bar, wiping the shelf for the bottles with his back facing her.

"I'm back!" Cassandra announced with a smile.

He glanced at her and frowned. "Yeah, so what?" He returned to wiping the shelf.

She closed the distance between them until she stood halfway between Robertson and the front door. "Perhaps after our little chat yesterday, you remembered something important."

"Like I told you before, I don't know anything!" he barked without looking at her.

"Are you sure?" She took two steps forward.

He turned around, and his face was red. "You heard what I said. Back off, bitch!"

Cassandra continued to smile as she strolled to the nearest table. She then ran her right index finger over the tabletop.

"My, my... Such a nasty attitude for someone who works at a classy place. Does your employer know about your potty mouth?"

"Fuck off!"

Cassandra turned her arms outward at the elbow. "Okay. Looks like we'll do it the hard way."

"What the hell is that supposed to mean?"

She put down her hands and strode towards the front door. Before crossing the doorway, she turned her head toward Robertson and flashed a devilish grin. Then she left the premises.

Seconds later, Elroy Dupree, a massive Cajun in overalls, barreled through the front door. His shaved head and sneer made him appear even more menacing and intimidating.

Cassandra reentered the bar behind him and locked the door. "Let's try again."

Dupree growled and raised his massive arms. He bounded towards Robertson, whose whole body shook. Robertson ran toward the back door and was one step away when Dupree grabbed him with both hands and tossed him like a rag doll. Robertson landed back first on top of a table. With his legs in the air, he slid off the table and onto the floor, bringing the table down with him.

Robertson panicked and tried to stand. Before he could, Dupree seized him on the sides of his torso and slammed his back against the wall. Robertson's head crashed against it, but he somehow remained conscious. Dupree raised him to where his legs flailed two feet above the floor. Dupree then used his left hand to press him against the wall, and his right to choke him. Cassandra moved closer, within a few feet of Dupree. She saw the fear in Robertson's eyes and heard him gasp for air.

She glared at him. "Care to say something now?"

Robertson tried to speak but he could only make rough sounds. With a sneer, Dupree looked at Cassandra, who nodded. Dupree eased his grip around Robertson's neck and kept him pinned against the wall. He inhaled a large gulp of air, and his eyes darted back and forth between Cassandra and Dupree.

"Well?" she asked.

"No! I can't!" Robertson said in a panic. "I swear, I swear I can't. He'll, he'll kill me if he finds out."

"Who'll kill you?"

"I can't say. I can't."

Cassandra raised her right index finger to her chin. "Huh… That's interesting. Your boogeyman might kill you later, but my friend's upset and can kill you right now." She nodded.

Dupree growled and increased his grip on Robertson's neck, who then gasped, "O–kay."

She came within two feet of him. "So, you'll talk?"

He nodded nervously.

"Put him down," she said.

Dupree complied yet still held Robertson against the wall. Cassandra reached into a suit jacket pocket and retrieved a folded photo of the fake Patrick Walsh. She unfolded it and showed it to Robertson.

"Was this man with Amy Nguyen last Saturday night?"

Roberson's terrified eyes darted to the picture. "Yeah, yeah."

"Who is he?" she asked as she returned the photo to her pocket.

"The nephew of The Saint."

"What? He's a nephew of a New Orleans Saint?"

"No, not the football team. The Saint of New York."

"Who's that?" Cassandra asked.

Robertson's eyes bugged out. "Are you that stupid?"

Dupree used his right hand to slam Robertson against the wall, which resulted in a moan escaping from him.

"Better watch what you say around him," Cassandra said. "What's the nephew's name?"

"I– I don't know. Ryan, Bryan, something like that."

"What's his last name?"

"I don't know."

Dupree turned his head toward Cassandra, who nodded.

"I swear, I swear," Robertson said in a higher and louder voice before Dupree could make his next move. "I don't know his last name! I never saw him before!"

"Hang on," Cassandra told Dupree.

"All I know is what the owner told me," Robertson said in a less panicked voice. "The Saint's nephew was coming to town, and I needed to treat him very well. It wasn't a suggestion. It was an order. The owner also told me to let him drink for free. I swear that's all I know."

"How do we get a hold of the owner?"

Robertson shuddered. "You– you can't. If– if you talk to him, he'll figure out I talked to you. He'll then tell The Saint, who'll make certain I'm dead. I– I swear I told you everything."

Cassandra leaned toward Robertson until her face was inches from his. "Fine, but if you're not telling me the truth, we'll be back. You can count on it." She stepped back and addressed Dupree. "Let's go."

Dupree shoved Robertson against the wall one more time and then stomped toward the front door. Cassandra unlocked it and closed it behind her.

Once outside, Dupree's face lit up. "That was really fun, Miss Morgan! Thanks for gettin' me out of jail two weeks early. Momma's gonna be so surprised!"

She gave a thin smile. "You're welcome and be sure to tell your mom I said hello."

"Yeah, I will."

"And please stay out of trouble. I don't want to find you in jail again."

Dupree nodded with a grin. "Yeah, okay. See ya!"

Chapter 27

Late April 2019
Downtown Los Angeles, California

Cassandra's actions against Brody Robertson horrified Rebecca. Overly aggressive tactics played well in movies and television, but real life was another matter. Even though she didn't know the ethics rules in Louisiana, she was certain Cassandra had violated them because she had also broken the law. She concluded Cassandra had committed multiple criminal acts, including aggravated assault, criminal threats, and false imprisonment.

Nick had a much different opinion and laughed as hard as his hoarse voice would allow.

"Oh man, I wish I would've been there to see the bartender's face when that big gorilla went after him!" He laughed again.

"It wasn't funny. It was awful!" Rebecca said into the phone.

He scoffed. "Give me a break! It's not like anyone got stabbed or died."

"Oh, that makes a huge difference," she said sarcastically.

"It does to me. I guess you can't see the humor, since you live in a different world. Ignore the PR put out by the prison system, okay. Inside it's dangerous, and you build up a tolerance to the violence."

Rebecca did not want to argue the matter anymore. She was about to mention preparing for the parole hearing when she had another thought.

"Are you sure everything happened at Rousseau's the way you said it did? You weren't there, right?"

He scoffed and after a long pause said, "No, I wasn't, and yes, I'm sure. I had a very reliable source. I wouldn't screw with you."

"Okay," she said slowly. She was uncertain whether Nick had told the truth. She suspected he could have exaggerated what happened at the bar or had just made it up. Either way, pressing the matter further would probably get her nowhere, and her primary interest was the upcoming hearing.

"Let's talk a little bit about you. Previously, you claimed you committed manslaughter because Denny deserved it. Did you really mean it?"

After a moment, Nick said, "I guess I was a little pissed when we first met. Hell, I was surprised you showed up. Around here, surprises aren't good things, you know what I mean?"

"Not really."

"A surprise can be getting shanked in the back."

Rebecca grimaced. "Sorry about that. So, how do you really feel about killing someone?"

He exhaled. "It wasn't the smartest thing I ever did. I was trying to help an employee deal with her ex, and I got carried away. I should've just stuck the damn gun in his mouth and watched him wet his pants."

She shook her head. "That's still assault with a deadly weapon."

"So? He would've been alive, at least for a while longer. Denny was a complete moron, and he would've gotten himself killed sooner or later. He was out of control, and something needed to be done since the restraining order against him was worthless."

"You could've called the police. They could've arrested Denny for violating the protective order and stalking."

Nick scoffed again. "Hey, what the hell do you want from me? I was never an expert in criminal law."

Not for the first time, Rebecca asked herself if representing irritable convicts was why she became a lawyer.

"You need to really consider what you're going to tell the parole board," she said firmly. "They won't brush off your manslaughter conviction. What you say must be from the heart and honest."

He chuckled. "From the heart. Yeah right. I'm not a touchy-feely kind of guy."

"Okay, think of it another way. You and I need to make the best possible presentation. I mean, you want to get out of prison, right?"

"Yeah, sure."

"We also need to address your swearing and your attitude."

"What the hell?" he said loudly.

Rebecca shook her head. "My point exactly. When you speak to the board, you need to be more professional. That means no cursing and no crude comments about anyone, especially women. You should practice using better language when you talk to me. If you get used to talking that way, it's less likely you'll slip up during the hearing. Got it?"

"Yeah, yeah. I guess you don't have to tell your other clients to watch their language."

"I don't meet with other clients."

"What the hell? I mean, what the heck — better? What do you do all day long?"

"I've been processing discovery," Rebecca said, "which means going through documents by the thousands."

"What are you going to do after you're finished?"

"Probably the same thing for another case."

There was silence. "That's all you do? I thought attorneys went to court all the time."

"I never do."

"Oh man!" he said. "Your job is crap! No wonder you're willing to talk to me so often."

"My job isn't that exciting right now, but in three or four years, I'll be going to court. Plus, eventually I'll make partner, and my salary will dramatically increase."

He sighed. "Money isn't everything. It's better to go to work because you want to instead of because you have to. Do you know the difference? You sound as if you're trying to convince yourself you're in a good situation."

"No, I'm okay," Rebecca said, although she conceded Nick could be correct. She worked too many hours for too little satisfaction. She had assumed her situation would improve, yet now realized she could be mistaken.

"Whatever. After dealing with lovable old me, don't you want to become a criminal defense attorney?"

She smirked. "No thanks. I'm not interested in criminal law. So, promise me one thing. After you get released, please don't commit any more crimes, and if you do, don't ask me to represent you again."

Chapter 28

This time, Rebecca waited five minutes in the visiting room before Nicholas Malone arrived. Without being asked, his accompanying guard removed Nick's handcuffs and shackles. Nick took a seat with a wide smile.

"Hello, Ms. Holt. Aren't you tired of coming here?"

Rebecca was taken aback. "Ms. Holt? Why so formal?"

"I don't know. At least I caught your attention."

She gave a half-smile. "You caught my attention a long time ago. How are you feeling?"

He shrugged. "No recent headaches. Yesterday, I had to see the doc, a follow-up to my prostate surgery, and he said I'm doing fine."

"Sounds good. Did you tell him about your headaches?"

"No, that's not his specialty, and they're gone," he said. "Stop pretending to be my mother."

"Sorry about that. Let's get back to preparing for the parole hearing."

Nick folded his arms and frowned. "What for? They won't order my early release."

She leaned forward and put her right hand on the table between them. "You don't want to even try? That's not a positive attitude."

He waved a dismissive hand. "Oh really?" he said. "You try being positive if you're in my situation. I'm not getting out early. Let's get back to New Orleans twenty years ago."

"No way. Last time, we agreed during my next visit, we'd talk about you. I'm here, so..." She held out her hands.

He exhaled while still crossing his arms.

Rebecca pulled a notepad and pen from her satchel and placed them on the table.

As she cast her eyes on her notes, she said, "We already discussed your manslaughter conviction and the two assault convictions. You have bachelor's and master's degrees in psychology. We also discussed the anger management and drug counseling programs you started."

"They weren't programs."

She looked up. "Then what would you call them?"

"Don't know."

"You need to come up with an appropriate term sooner or later." She tapped her pen on the next line in her notes. "There's something else bothering me. Why didn't you tell me about all of your activities in prison?"

Nick pulled his head back. "What? I haven't left out anything."

"Yes, you have. I found out you started a literacy program."

He rolled his eyes. "Ah geez. I didn't tell you because I didn't start much of anything."

"Then what happened?"

Nick opened his arms and put them on the table. "Just after I was transferred to Eastvale, I met this guy who couldn't read, and I offered to help him out. At first, he refused, since he thought it was some kind of trick. Moron." He shook his head. "He must've been dropped on his head a few times when he was a kid, and that's why he ended up here."

"Just stick to what happened without the derogatory comments."

"Whatever. Eventually, the kid realized I was on the level, and I helped him. It didn't take too long before he was reading at the fourth-grade level. That's not great, but it's better than nothing, and he's getting better. Later, I taught five others, no big deal. Then the liberal do-gooders found out." He flashed a scowl and threw back his right arm, then returned it to the table. "Those idiots. They took it over and screwed it up, almost put an end to the whole thing."

"You still did something else positive while incarcerated." She inched forward and touched his left hand. "You need to stop downplaying your accomplishments. We should mention them during your parole hearing. Presenting every little bit of positive information will make a difference."

Nick pulled his hand back. "Forever the optimist, aren't you?"

"Guess so... Moving onto another topic. You can get illegal drugs in prison, right?"

He glared at her. "Yes, of course. I already told you about it."

"Did you ever use drugs?"

"We already went over this."

"Not exactly," Cassandra said in a non-confrontational manner. "You told me you hadn't used drugs or drank alcohol in a long time. I'm asking you about *any* drug use."

"Whatever," he said as he crossed his arms. "I smoked a joint or two in high school, and that was it. No other illegal drugs. I'm taking pills for high blood pressure, and I might need another pill for high cholesterol. It's part of the joy of growing older."

Rebecca sighed. "If you get asked about drug use, please give the same answer – the first part, I mean, and without the sarcasm. Using marijuana in high school isn't a big deal and admitting it isn't a bad thing. Then when you deny other drug use, they'll be more likely to believe you. Anyway, onto another topic. Can you get any letters of recommendation?"

He chuckled and relaxed his arms. "Are you nuts? The only people I know are cons and guards. There's no one on the outside."

"Are you sure there isn't anyone who could vouch for you? Who has personal knowledge about what you've been doing? What about the chaplain? He previously wrote a nice letter, and it's in your file."

"Don't think so."

"Wouldn't the chaplain know about what you've been doing?"

"Maybe."

"That's good enough for me. I'll contact him and a staff psychologist."

Nick looked away.

"Have you been attending church services?" Rebecca asked.

"Yeah. Every Sunday for the last few years. Don't remember the exact date when I started."

She nodded and gave a thin smile. "That's okay. The chaplain can mention your attendance in a letter. Can you talk about your faith?"

Nick turned his head and stared into her eyes. "Are you religious?"

"Uh, sure. I was raised in the Lutheran Church."

"Do you still attend church?"

"Sometimes."

"Are you willing to talk about your faith and what it means to you?"

She was uncomfortable discussing it and didn't want to admit it. She instead replied, "I see your point."

"Besides, so many clowns talk about 'Jesus this' and 'Jesus that' before the parole board, and they're completely full of it. Even if I talk sincerely about my faith, they won't listen."

Rebecca was uncertain whether Nick's last comments were correct. Nevertheless, she deferred to him because he probably knew more about parole hearings than she did.

"Okay," she said. "At least we can mention your church attendance. Moving on. Do you have any family ties?"

He crossed his arms again. "Not anymore. My parents are dead. I have a brother, but I lost contact with him years ago, before I was sent to prison. Don't know if he's dead or alive."

"Anyone else, such as children, aunts, uncles, cousins?"

"No kids, and my aunts and uncles are probably dead. I have cousins, but I haven't talked to any of them in a very long time. I don't even know where they live. Are we done?"

"For now, yes. We might need to prepare some more closer to the hearing."

"Yeah, whatever. Why don't we talk about something else?"

"Like what?" Rebecca asked with a smile. "I'll take a wild guess and say the serial killer story."

Nick chuckled. "No, not that. Something else. Don't take this the wrong way... you're sort of... attractive. You look too young for your age, but you look good."

Rebecca was uncomfortable with the comment. "Thanks, I guess. What's your point?"

"Why don't you have a boyfriend?"

She smiled out of reflex. "Sorry, that's none of your business."

He chuckled again. "Now that's not fair. You know so much about me. Why can't I learn a little about you?"

"I'm not the one up for parole."

"Oh, come on," he said with a devilish grin.

Rebecca reasoned it wouldn't hurt to provide him a few details to humor him. "Fine. I go on dates once in a while, but I'm not seriously interested in anyone right now."

"What's once in a while?"

"Uh... four dates in the past six months."

"That's it!" Nick eyes popped as he held his hands in the air. "I sometimes had four dates in two weeks. Don't you want to have fun and meet people?"

"Yes, of course, but it's not so easy. I don't like the bar scene, and work keeps me very busy."

"Work can't keep you that busy."

"Mine does. I work sixty hours per week and sometimes even more."

His eyes bugged out again. "That's nuts! Did you know about this before you took the job?"

"Of course," she said as she leaned back and crossed her arms. "It's typical for a first-year attorney in a big law firm."

Nick smirked. "Yeah. The partners use their underlings to milk their clients for as much money as possible. What's next?" he asked incredulously. "After you make partner, you take your turn and grind the new attorneys into the ground."

"That's a crude way of putting it."

"And accurate, isn't it? Do you enjoy your life right now?"

She kept her arms folded and said nothing.

"Uh-huh. And down the road, you want to inflict the same life on others? That's really messed up."

"When you put it like that, it sounds bad. It's not really like that though."

"Oh yeah? Do you like the people at your firm?"

"I like Carter Patterson," Rebecca said. "He's my supervisor for your case."

"That's one. What about the other partners? Are they a great bunch of guys?"

She remained silent.

"Yeah, that's what I thought."

"Look, we're not here to talk about me."

"Whatever. I've heard enough."

When the law firm had offered Rebecca a position during her third year of law school, she had jumped at the chance to join them due to its excellent reputation, and her starting salary had been higher than expected. During law school, she had paid little attention to the rumors about the firm overworking its associates. She lived by the Golden Rule, treat others as you wished to be treated, and others did the same.

Rebecca then had a rude awakening. The work had been duller than expected, and the hours had been much longer. Most partners did not treat their subordinates well and were only interested in expanding their bank accounts. Many associates would not assist their colleagues out of fear someone else would make partner first. Rebecca also did not appreciate the impact her job had on her social life and began to question whether accepting the position in the first place had been a mistake. On the other hand, she had heard the first two years at the firm were the worst and then life got better. She considered discussing her situation further with someone, but her client was not the proper candidate for that conversation.

"Why don't we talk about something else? Have any ideas?"

Nick gave a wide smile. "Yeah, I do."

Chapter 29

In the morning, Cassandra's team would once again assemble at the trailer. She knew the assault on Brody Robertson at Rousseau's was wrong and didn't care. Only the result mattered, which was a lead on the Crescent City Killer. She surmised Robertson was too scared to tell anyone what had happened and was confident Elroy Dupree, the massive Cajun, would keep quiet.

Mike and Cassandra arrived at the trailer early, before the others. She noticed his jeans and new hairstyle, which was shorter and drier, a vast improvement.

"New pants?" she asked. "Aren't they a little tight?"

"Yeah. I bought them that way on purpose. It encourages me to lose more weight. I threw out my fatter clothes. So, there's no going back now," he said with a wide smile.

"How much have you lost so far?"

"Thirty-seven pounds." He grabbed his beer belly with both hands. "Still too much here. The doc said I should lose another forty, but I'm shooting for sixty because I want to get back to what I weighed in college."

"Good for you. Keep it up."

"Thanks."

Several minutes later, Donnie and Tyler arrived.

"Thanks for everyone being on time," Cassandra said. "I have some good news. It looks like we got a break in the case."

Both Mike and Tyler leaned in while Donnie dropped his elbow on a table and put his hand to his chin.

"On a whim, I went back to Rousseau's late yesterday afternoon, and I convinced Robertson to cooperate."

Mike jumped back in his chair. "How'd you do that?"

"Oh… I was just a little more direct and persuasive. It really didn't take much. Robertson said Amy Nguyen was at the bar with someone named Ryan or Brian. He didn't know the last name. He said the guy is the nephew of The Saint, some notorious criminal. Anyone heard of him?"

Tyler and Mike shook their heads.

"I think I've heard of him," Donnie said. "White guy, right? From New York City?"

"That's what Robertson said, and he couldn't tell me anything else. I'm sure Ryan or Brian was the phony Patrick Walsh. Donnie, please contact NYPD and ask about The Saint and his nephew."

"Will do." He stood and went to his office.

Cassandra directed her attention to Tyler and Mike. "Where do we stand on the killer's possible aliases?"

Mike held up his hand. "I got this one. As you know, he used 'Patrick Walsh' three times, and he came here around the same time as three of the murders. That helped us narrow down the names of short-term renters who were here when the other murders happened. We also eliminated anyone who was not Caucasian and anyone over fifty."

"All right," Cassandra said. "Did you come up with anything?"

"Oh yeah," Mike said. "Someone using the name Jonathan Smith stayed at Millie Thornwell's bungalow around the same time as when the eighth and ninth women were killed. He provided Thornwell an address in Chicago, which was probably bogus, and we're checking on it. A Kevin O'Malley from Philly was in town at the time of four other murders. The DMV photo for the real O'Malley looks nothing like the suspect we interrogated."

"I guess we're making progress," she said. "That's three aliases associated with nine murders, which means we don't have a name connected to four other women."

"Right," Tyler said. "We're still looking into renters in town when the first couple of victims were killed. Maybe the killer used his real name back then. We can narrow down the list to English, Irish, and Scottish names. Given the pattern, I doubt he used names that originated from any other country. Even if the info on The Saint pans out, we still need to associate names with the other murders."

"Sounds good. Here's what I'm thinking," Cassandra said. "We should—" She paused when she heard the door open.

Andre Armstead entered the trailer with his shaved head and typical black-and-gray attire. Once again, his chin was in the air, and his hands were placed behind his back.

"Good morning... people," he said. "The district attorney wants an update because the media has been flooding his office with inquiries since the last murder."

The sight of this arrogant piece of work did not thrill Cassandra. At least he had rarely bothered her since Philip LeMay had banished her to the trailer. She also still didn't trust Armstead, and there was no need for an update because Donnie was in contact with LeMay from time to time. Perhaps LeMay sent Armstead to determine whether she would give an inconsistent summary of the investigation, which he could use to further punish her. Donnie would have provided LeMay with truthful and accurate information. She would do the same for Armstead and then get rid of him.

"Mike and Tyler, you can take off," she said. "I can handle it."

Neither detective needed to be told twice. They bolted out the door without being too obvious.

Cassandra spent the next thirty minutes informing Armstead of the recent developments while leaving out the massive Cajun's role. She was pleased he had few questions, and after he had departed, Donnie came out of his little office.

"I purposefully waited until after Andre left. I try to see the good in everyone, but I'm not too fond of him."

"No argument here."

"Anyway, I just got off the phone with NYPD. I was put through to their organized crime task force or something like that. The Saint's real name is Conor McCarthy, and NYPD has plenty on him. One of their detectives will fly down to meet with us, and he'll bring copies of a few files."

Cassandra perked up. "Very nice. You must've worked your charms on them. Why don't they mail off the documents?"

"Apparently, they're too sensitive to be entrusted to the Post Office."

"Okay. When's the detective coming?"

"The day after tomorrow. He'll meet with us at two."

Cassandra couldn't wait that long for more information. She went into her office and ran an internet search for The Saint. The result was many links to websites about the New Orleans Saints, the British television show *The Saint*, and Catholic saints. She ran another search for the name "Conor McCarthy." More links popped up, and none referenced an arch criminal.

Cassandra was undeterred. She drove to the New Orleans Public Library and made a beeline to the non-fiction section. The library had books discussing the Italian Mafia but no publications addressing other criminal organizations. She assumed the library's collection reflected America's almost singular fixation on Italian organized crime due to movies such as *The Godfather* and *Goodfellas*.

Cassandra next proceeded to one of the libraries at Tulane University, and this time, she was in luck. She found a book called *Irish Mobsters*, and the back cover said the author was a *Boston Globe* reporter. The index stated several pages mentioned Conor McCarthy. She found the nearest empty chair and started reading.

According to *Irish Mobsters*, The Saint was a legendary hit man. He had never been a member of any organized crime group and had accepted assignments from the Italian crime families in New York City and the Russian mob. The authorities also suspected him of working for mobsters in other cities. Some also believed he carried out several assassinations overseas, possibly on behalf of the CIA.

The book claimed McCarthy had killed people in many ways. He was an expert with a sniper rifle and was not afraid to shoot the target at point-blank range. Other times, he employed a knife or poison. He also staged accidents. Nobody knew how many murders he had committed.

Cassandra was somewhat relieved *Irish Mobsters* did not mention the murder of law enforcement officers. Perhaps McCarthy lived by the same code as the Italian Mafia, which included, "Don't whack the FBI," which she interpreted as covering anyone associated with law enforcement, including assistant district attorneys.

The *Boston Globe* author explained McCarthy got his nickname because of his lifestyle. He apparently never smoked, drank, or used illegal drugs. He never swore and didn't allow it in his presence. A member of his crew once cursed in front of him and McCarthy had him beaten to a pulp. The author also claimed McCarthy never cheated on his wife. In his later years, he made generous donations to various charities, and civic leaders treated him like a pillar of the community. He attended Mass every Sunday and gave generously to the Catholic Church. The man evidently had some kind of deranged moral compass.

Chapter 30

Two days later, a tall, slender man in his mid-fifties wearing a dark-gray business suit and carrying a black leather briefcase arrived. He had wavy gray hair, a large, distinguished nose, and a gray mustache. He appeared unfazed by the trailer's shabby interior or the files scattered everywhere.

"Good afternoon," he said cheerfully. "I'm Detective Scott Langford with the NYPD, and you must be Cassandra Morgan."

"That's right." Cassandra shook his hand and gestured toward her colleagues. "These are my associates, Tyler Winfield, Mike Beaumont, and Donnie Green."

"Pleasure to meet all of you."

Langford also shook their hands, and Donnie was the last one.

"Donnie?" Langford said. "You must be the one who called."

Donnie gave a toothy smile. "You got it."

"Very good. Shall we get started?" Langford asked.

He took a seat at the head of the plastic tables and in front of the whiteboards. Cassandra and Tyler took their places to his left, while Donnie and Mike sat to the right. Langford opened his briefcase and removed four brown folders, the largest almost two inches thick.

"I was told you have an interest in Conor McCarthy, aka The Saint, and one of his nephews. Whoever spoke with Donnie didn't pass along the nephew's name, so I brought the files for all three, plus the one for McCarthy." He lined up the folders side by side and opened each one, revealing a large photograph of each family member.

Mike pointed to the photo on the right, depicting a handsome man with dark hair and a cleft chin. "That's the one who called himself Patrick Walsh."

"I see," Langford said. "His real name is Ryan Parkhurst, and you believe he might be a serial killer?"

"He's our best suspect," Cassandra asserted. "In fact, he's currently our only one."

"If you're going after Parkhurst, you need to know what you'll be facing," Langford said with a stern expression. "It won't be just him. You'll have to deal with his uncle and his uncle's right-hand man. I'll explain in detail. Just give me a moment, please."

Langford returned the files for the two other nephews to his briefcase and then pushed the one for Parkhurst toward the middle of the plastic tables. He opened the thickest file, which contained a photograph of an elderly Caucasian couple and two younger men seated at a round table. All four were wearing formal attire. The older man had thick white hair, an oval face with wrinkles etched in stone, and yellow-tinted glasses. The woman also had white hair, diamond earrings, and a diamond necklace.

Langford pointed at the elderly man in the photograph. "This is Conor McCarthy, and he's now seventy-six years old. This was taken at a charity event sixteen months ago. To his left is his wife. They've been married for fifty-one years."

In the photo, the two younger men sat to the right of McCarthy. The shorter one had a scowl, a buzz cut, and a broad chest. To Cassandra, he looked like a cross between a bulldog and a Sherman tank. The taller man had dark hair in a ponytail. His rugged face and cold, dead eyes made him appear even more out of place than the other younger man.

"The one with the ponytail is Lazlo Janka, nothing but a thug in a suit," Langford said. "Don't worry about him for now. The man next to him is another matter. That's

Tommy Hanson, McCarthy's bodyguard, driver, confidant, and whatever else McCarthy wants him to be."

Langford coughed away from the others. "Excuse me. My allergies are acting up again. Getting back to McCarthy. He was born and raised in Queens. The day after the Japanese attacked Pearl Harbor, he joined the army and became a sniper, one of their best. After the war ended, McCarthy remained in the army, but from '45 to '48, there's no mention of a duty station in his DoD file."

"Why is that?" Tyler asked.

"He was assigned to classified missions." Langford coughed again. "Excuse me. After McCarthy was discharged in '49, he became a hired assassin. He—"

Cassandra lost focus as Langford discussed portions of McCarthy's life she already knew and had told her teammates. Nevertheless, they remained polite and quiet while Langford gave his oral presentation. While he spoke, Cassandra fixated on the images of Tommy Hanson and Lazlo Janka. Despite her years as a prosecutor, there were few, if any, occasions in which she had come across individuals who appeared as fierce and intimidating. She imagined that with a nod or a snap of McCarthy's fingers, they would kill anyone without hesitation.

Langford coughed again and cleared his throat. "Over the years, McCarthy's reputation and his bank account grew. He invested in legitimate businesses and became very wealthy. He now owns about fifteen apartment buildings in New York City, mostly Manhattan, and a couple more in Connecticut. McCarthy also owns three security companies and a limousine service. His only child, Conor Junior, runs the day-to-day operations, but The Saint is still in charge. McCarthy has business interests in other cities, including New Orleans. One of his companies provides security for the riverboat casinos here and in Biloxi, Mississippi. Obviously, he has an enormously large bankroll at his disposal and can hire an army of lawyers to defend his nephew."

"Does McCarthy have a criminal record?" Donnie asked.

Langford shook his head. "He's highly intelligent, and when he was an active assassin, he kept his mouth shut and covered his tracks. No one around him cooperated with us or the FBI out of respect or fear. We came close one time tough, and that's where Tommy Hanson comes into the picture." He pointed to Hanson in the photograph.

"Conor Junior was sixteen when he had an appendectomy. He had a semi-private room at the hospital, and twelve-year-old Tommy was in the other bed. Tommy was a wimpy, skinny kid who had several bruises and internal injuries. Conor Junior asked him what had happened, and at first, Tommy didn't give him a straight answer. Eventually, he admitted his stepfather, Jack Kressel, had been abusing him since marrying his mother three years beforehand. At least it wasn't sexual abuse."

All eyes in the room were fixed on Langford.

"Just before Conor Junior was discharged from the hospital, he invited Tommy to join his family for dinner. Tommy knew nothing about Conor Senior's occupation, but Conor Junior had an inkling. Once they had finished dinner, Conor Junior pushed Tommy to tell his father about Kressel. Conor Senior said he'd take care of it." Langford raised his eyebrows. "Any guesses what happened?"

Mike smirked. "The Saint paid the stepfather a visit."

"Close. Three days later, two members of The Saint's crew snatched Kressel off the street. They drove him to a warehouse, where they threatened his life. They took a hammer to his left hand and a power drill to his right knee. Once they were done, they threw him out of a moving car in front of his home."

"Holy crap!" Mike said. "The Saint's men were that brazen?"

Langford held out his hands. "What can I say? By the way, you can't say 'holy crap' in front of The Saint." He gave a half-smile. "Just food for thought…

"Tommy's mother wanted to press charges. At the time, the police started a vigorous investigation, but they had no idea who had attacked Kressel. About a week later, McCarthy's goons arrived at the family home, where they spoke with Tommy, his mother, and especially his stepfather. They said they worked for McCarthy. They also explained who McCarthy was and what he did for a living. Apparently, they didn't hold anything back.

"Then the goons gave an ultimatum. They said Tommy goes to live with McCarthy, and his mother and stepfather leave the city for good. If they disagreed, the goons threatened to kill them in a way that would've made their prior attack on Kressel seem like gentle kisses. Of course, they left in a big hurry. I can only imagine what was running through Tommy's mind at the time."

Cassandra was stunned and speechless. While she had heard plenty of horrific stories over the past several years, this one was different and more shocking. Unfortunately, it also made a lot of sense.

"I take it The Saint didn't make them disappear after they moved," Donnie said.

"Oh no. There was no need for any further bloodshed. They simply moved to Boston and refused to cooperate with us."

"What happened to Tommy?" Mike asked.

"Conor Senior took him under his wing and obviously became a father figure. His men taught him how to fight and defend himself. He started a weightlifting program and must've never given it up. Tommy enlisted in the army and joined the Rangers. After being discharged, he's been at McCarthy's side ever since. Thanks to him, Tommy's a very disciplined person and can also be very violent. Do you remember an incident about two years ago at a New

York nightclub, the one involving Blake Wilkins, a backup linebacker for the Jets?"

Donnie, Mike, and Tyler nodded in the affirmative.

"Sorry, not really," Cassandra said.

"Let's just say Wilkins got into a… scuffle with Tommy and lost," Langford said. "Tommy and Wilkins were sitting at different tables. Wilkins had been giving a woman a hard time, and Tommy told him to leave her alone. Wilkins was offended and started a fight, which Tommy ended by breaking the linebacker's jaw and ending his football career. We didn't arrest Tommy because witnesses confirmed he had acted in self-defense.

"That was him? Damn!" Mike exclaimed.

Langford chuckled. "That's another word you can't say in The Saint's presence. Anyway, moving on to his nephew, Ryan Parkhurst. He's twenty-nine, single, and about six two. He's had a couple of arrests for assault but no convictions. Before Donnie called us, we only considered him a rich playboy. He receives a generous allowance from his uncle's family trust, and he owns two jazz clubs and an upscale bar."

Cassandra looked at Tyler. "Looks like we were right."

"What do you mean?" Langford asked.

"We have a theory the serial killer is a jazz lover and lives out of town."

Langford nodded. "Unfortunately, there's a serious problem. Parkhurst was never on our radar, and he has no driver's license, ID card, passport, or known address. He doesn't own any credit cards or have any utility bills in his name. To an extent, he's a ghost. Parkhurst could be living in one of his uncle's apartment buildings rent-free and off the books. His allowance and his businesses allow him access to plenty of cash. If he's traveling to New Orleans, he's probably using credit cards in another name. Bottom line, there's no easy way of tracking him down."

"That's some wonderful news," Cassandra said sarcastically.

"What can I say? I'll leave the files for McCarthy and Parkhurst for your review. If you have more questions or need further assistance, please call me anytime, day or night."

"Detective, we really appreciate you coming down here," Cassandra said. "It was a long trip for a short meeting."

Langford gave a wide smile. "It's my pleasure in more ways than one. I brought my wife along, and we're having dinner tonight at the Gumbo Shop, one of our favorites. Tomorrow morning, it's brunch at the Court of Two Sisters before catching our return flight. For the food alone, I'm more than willing to come to your fair city." He rose from his chair. "Pleasure to meet all of you." He left and closed the door on his way out.

Cassandra then addressed her team. "Parkhurst might never return to New Orleans, but his attraction to the city remains."

"The jazz scene," Tyler said.

"Correct. I know he hasn't come here during the summer, but maybe they'll be some special event or concert that'll lure him here. I think he's arrogant enough to believe he can slip in and out the city undetected. After all, he left Amy Nguyen's body where it would be readily found, probably to us. Donnie, you're the resident jazz lover, can you keep track of all things jazz?"

"You got it," he said with a smile.

"We need to make a flyer with Parkhurst's name, aliases, and photo," Cassandra said. "We'll distribute it to the property owners of the short-term rentals and show it to whoever we can find at the clubs and bars where the prostitutes congregate. It might not be a bad idea to gives copies to the managers of Preservation Hall and other music venues."

"Should we tell them Parkhurst is a suspected serial killer?" Tyler asked.

"Hmm…" Cassandra leaned back in her chair and mulled it over. "Probably not. We'll just tell them he's wanted for questioning about a homicide. That should be enough to get everybody's attention. We'll also provide the same information to the rental car companies at the airport."

"We could also give the flyers to the airlines," Mike said.

"The ground personnel here only deal with him when he's leaving," Donnie said. "What we need is advance notice when he's coming though, so it's probably better for NYPD to reach out to the airlines out there."

Cassandra pointed at Donnie. "Good idea. I'll talk to Langford about it, although Parkhurst could avoid the airlines and take a private jet. Even so, he'd still need a rental car. He won't use a limo service once he gets here."

Mike chuckled. "Yeah, I can just see it. Excuse me, sir. Please ignore the corpse in my hands and drive me to the nearest swamp."

Both Tyler and Donnie laughed, but Cassandra didn't enjoy the gallows humor.

"Let's not forget Parkhurst has used phony IDs with addresses in Chicago, Boston, and Philly," Donnie said. "He might travel to those cities. We should alert their police departments about our latest info."

"Right," Cassandra said.

"What about the media?" Tyler asked. "Should we tell them anything?"

"It might be a good idea," Mike said.

"Hold on a sec," Donnie interjected. "Parkhurst is loaded, and if the media broadcasts his name and face, he'll run away. The next thing you know, he'll be drinking a rum and Coke in the Caribbean while laughing at us."

"Good point," Cassandra said. "He could have a passport under a fake name, and even if he doesn't have one, he can drive to Mexico and figure it out from there. Let's table informing the media for now."

After their conversation ended, Cassandra thought sipping a rum and Coke was an excellent idea but had neither ingredient in the trailer. Instead, she slipped into her office and settled for a bottle of beer from the small refrigerator.

Chapter 31

The next day, Cassandra and Donnie traveled again to Algiers Point and parked in front of Millie Thornwell's charming Victorian home.

Once Cassandra parked her vehicle and opened the driver's side door, she saw a little blonde girl, about four years old, riding her red tricycle further down the street.

"Tessa, please come back!" her mother called out. "You've been riding long enough!"

Cassandra couldn't take her eyes off the red tricycle. The color seemed to pulse and distort her vision. She suddenly saw Jane Doe 1 being strangled, her eyes bulging. Panic filled Cassandra's body, and she closed her eyes. She grimaced as she tried to shake the image. She then felt someone grabbing her left arm and shaking her. While still in a panic, she opened her eyes and realized it was Donnie.

He looked at her with worry lines evident on his forehead. "Are you all right?"

"Yeah, I'm fine," she lied. She felt her accelerated heart rate and tried to calm down.

"I don't think so," he said. "Do you remember our little talk? You can tell me anything in confidence."

Cassandra stared at Donnie, deciding whether to say anything. "Don't tell anyone else, okay?"

"Of course."

"Did you see the little blonde girl with the red bike?"

"Sure, I did and…?"

"Blonde hair, red bike, red scarf…"

"Jane Doe 1. Yeah, I get it. This case is getting to you too much. I'm not your daddy, but please take my advice, go see someone about it."

Cassandra didn't respond. She feared if she sought professional help, LeMay would take her off the case or even bench her permanently.

"You at least need to come to my place for dinner," Donnie said. "You can bring your boyfriend and meet some of my family. We won't mention the case at all, and we'll have a lot of fun. Remember when I told you I was a great cook? That's reason enough to come over."

Cassandra gave a sad, little smile. "Okay, I'll think about it."

"No way. That's not good enough, and we'll talk about it later." He smirked. "By the time we're finished, you'll have no choice but agree to come for dinner."

Cassandra gave a light chuckle.

"That's a little better," Donnie said. "Are you now okay to talk to the Thornwells?"

"Yeah, sure. Given what Millie said the last time we were here, do you really think either of them can identify Parkhurst?"

"You asked me before, and I'll give you the same answer. We're about to find out."

Moments later, a man in his late fifties answered the door with a smile as warm as Millie's. Faint wrinkles surrounded his blue eyes, and his hairline had receded to the crown. His remaining hair was light brown with gray peppering his short beard.

"Good morning, I'm James Thornwell," he said. He put his right hand on his chest. "Yes, I know Mama still calls me Jimmy, and I suppose there's nothing I can do about it." He put his hand down. "You're Cassandra Morgan and Donnie Green?"

"Yes, sir," Donnie said.

Jimmy gave a surprisingly weak handshake to both. "Pleasure to meet you. Since Mama's been expecting you, she made tea and croissants, and they're already on the coffee table. I respectfully request you indulge her before we get started with the business at hand."

"Not a problem," Cassandra said with a fake smile, while on the inside, she cringed at the word "tea."

Jimmy escorted Cassandra and Donnie into the warm and cozy living room. A familiar, tiny woman with gray hair in a bun and a gleam in her eyes peeking through her glasses sat on the couch. Millie rose to greet them.

"It's so nice to see you folks again. Please have a seat." She gestured to the two chairs on the other side of the coffee table. "I made Earl Grey tea and croissants with butter and blackberry jam. I grew the blackberries myself."

"Thank you," Cassandra said genuinely as she sat in one chair. She loved blackberries and hoped their taste would overcome the vile liquid's harshness.

Donnie took the other chair and slid the manila envelope he was carrying underneath it. Jimmy joined his mother on the couch.

"How's your health, Miss Millie?" Donnie asked as he buttered his croissant.

Millie chuckled. "As about as well as one can expect at my age. I take good care of myself, but my fussy son over here thinks I eat too many sweets."

Jimmy patted her thigh. "Now, Mama. We don't need to discuss it in front of company."

Cassandra sipped the tea to be polite, which tasted as horrible as the last time. She then tore an end off a croissant and found it light, flaky, and delicious. She slathered a layer of the jam on the rest and savored every bite. Donnie addressed a more serious matter as she started on another delectable roll.

"Miss Millie, we need to talk to you a little more about the polite Yankee who stayed in your bungalow," he said in a soothing voice. "Do you remember who I'm talking about?"

Millie beamed. "Oh, yes. He was such a nice man."

Donnie nodded. "Yes, ma'am. We brought some photos. I'd like you and Jimmy to look at them and tell us if you recognize anyone. We'll ask you first and have him step into another room. Then we'll ask him. Does that sound okay to you?"

"I guess that's fine."

Jimmy rose. "I'll step out onto the porch," he said.

When he was out of sight, Donnie retrieved the envelope from below the chair and removed a photo array of six men with similar appearances. All of them had cleft chins, the same hair color, and the same complexions. Numbers one through six appeared below their images.

Donnie placed the array on the coffee table. "Please take your time and tell me if you recognize anyone."

Millie's smile disappeared as she adjusted her glasses and strained to view the photos. She grabbed the photos so she could study them closer. "Oh my. These gentlemen all look quite similar. You certainly aren't making it easy for Old Millie."

She examined the array for several more moments. She then pointed a bony finger at the fifth photo, which depicted Ryan Parkhurst. "I believe he was number five, although I'm afraid I can't say with certainty. Number three also looks a lot like the polite Yankee. I'm sorry."

"That's quite all right," Donnie said as he gently retrieved the array and set it face down on the coffee table. "You did your best." He went to the front porch to retrieve Jimmy.

Cassandra gave a thin smile. "Please don't help your son with an identification. He has to rely on his own memory."

Millie didn't respond and instead watched Jimmy reenter the room and sit on the couch.

Donnie returned to his chair. "Please take your time looking at the photos and tell us if you recognize anyone."

Jimmy nodded and looked anxious. Once Donnie turned over the array, Jimmy's eyes widened. Without hesitation, he pointed to the middle photo in the bottom row. "That's him," he said, "number five."

The quick response surprised Cassandra. "Are you sure? I imagine it's been some time since you saw him."

Jimmy put his hand to his chest again. "I swear I'm certain. I should remember him because he was the only renter who had tea with Mama and me. Something like that sticks out in one's mind." He put his hand down. "One other thing I should've mentioned previously. Before you got here, I looked over our guest list, and number five is Jonathan Smith."

"Thank you for confirming it," Cassandra said. "That name is an alias, and his real name is Ryan Parkhurst."

Jimmy grimaced. "That's disturbing."

Millie glanced at her son and then focused on Donnie. "Would you mind telling us why you're so interested in him?" she asked.

"I'm sorry, ma'am," Donnie said. "It's still an ongoing investigation, which means we can't provide you the details."

Jimmy turned his gaze to Cassandra, and his face went blank and turned pale.

"Are you okay?" Donnie asked him.

Jimmy appeared to regain his focus. "Uh, yes. I'm fine. What do we have to do?"

"Not much," Cassandra said. "If Parkhurst gets in touch with you again, please let us know and give us his contact information. It's urgent that we speak with him."

"I guess we can do that," Millie said.

"Please don't create any alarm about Parkhurst and don't tell anyone about this conversation," Cassandra said politely but forcefully. "Just keep renting out the bungalow as you always have, including to Parkhurst. In addition to that, we'd greatly appreciate it if you would keep giving us the names of your renters."

"Is there anything else?" Jimmy asked.

"That's it," Donnie said. "We really appreciate your time."

"Yes, it's been a pleasure," Cassandra said.

"I'm sorry, I wish I could say the same," Millie said and then sighed. "I thought he was such a nice young man, but the police want to speak to him."

Jimmy turned to his mother. "Yes, Mama, I know. It'll all be fine. I'm going to escort these nice people to their vehicle. You just sit here, and I'll clean up in a bit."

Millie waved her left hand. "There you go again, babying me. I can manage one tray."

"Very well, Mama."

Millie addressed her guests with a wide smile. "Feel free to come again any time. But next time, we must discuss something more pleasant."

"Yes, ma'am," Donnie said.

"Yes, ma'am," Cassandra echoed. "Thank you for your time and hospitality. I hope you enjoy the rest of the day."

Jimmy escorted Cassandra and Donnie outside. Once they reached the front yard, Jimmy said in a low voice, "I didn't want to say something that would alarm Mama. I follow the news, and eventually I recognized you, Ms. Morgan. You're the one going after the Crescent City Killer."

"That's right."

"And Smith, Parkhurst, or whoever he is, is your man?"

"Correct," she said.

Jimmy's eyes rolled to the back of his head. "Oh, this is all too much for me right now. I can't believe Mama and me had tea with a serial killer." He groaned. "And he might've murdered someone in our bungalow." He swallowed and refocused on Cassandra. "That's what you believe, isn't it?"

"Unfortunately, yes."

Jimmy closed his eyes. "Oh, how am I supposed to maintain my composure if he calls again to rent the bungalow?"

"You must do your best," Donnie said. "Can you handle it?"

Jimmy opened his eyes and stared into the distance. "I– I don't know."

"I'm going to be honest with you," Donnie said. "Please look at me."

Jimmy complied with Donnie's request.

"As of right now, we don't know where Parkhurst is, and we really need your assistance to apprehend him."

"Are you serious?" Jimmy asked. He put his hand to his mouth.

"Yes, I am," Donnie said. "If Parkhurst calls you, act like you know nothing, and get him to the city, okay? Has he met your wife?"

"I don't think so. Wait…" Jimmy stared at the ground. "No, no. They haven't met."

"Good," Donnie said. "A female undercover officer can pose as your wife and meet Parkhurst under the pretense of giving him the keys to the bungalow. When she does, other officers will be nearby, ready to take him into custody. In fact, unless Parkhurst specifically asks for you, you don't need to be there."

"I– I don't know," Jimmy said as he raised his head.

Donnie looked into his eyes. "You can do it. You only need to talk to him on the phone. That's it."

"I'll try, but promise me one thing. Please don't tell Mama the whole truth. She's a fragile woman, and her heart can't take it."

"We won't tell her," Cassandra said, even though she thought Millie would eventually find out.

"Thank you." Jimmy grabbed his stomach. "We have to part ways now. If I think about this whole affair any longer, I'm going to be sick." He gave a quick wave and hurried into his mother's home.

Cassandra and Donnie climbed into her Mustang. She gave him a wry smile.

"What is it this time?" he asked.

"Have a female officer pose as his wife. Very nice. I wish I would've thought of it."

Donnie chuckled. "Thanks. Sometimes something clever pops into my head. It looks like we're making progress, but I'm not sure Jimmy could handle it if Parkhurst returns."

"Yeah, his mother's heart could probably take it more than his."

Chapter 32

Late April 2019
Santa Maria, California

Rebecca drove to Santa Maria, a town minutes away from California's Central Coast. She pulled her Honda Civic into the parking lot for the Eight Ball Billiard Lounge, where she would meet Brenda Watson, Nick's ex-girlfriend. The building had a generic exterior for California, stucco walls and a Spanish tile roof, which matched the architecture for other businesses and apartments in the immediate area. Without its sign, the pool hall could pass for an office building.

As she stepped out of her car, Rebecca saw a petite woman in her mid-thirties approaching. She had slicked back her mahogany-brown hair in a short ponytail and wore a black T-shirt, black jeans, and black boots. Tattoos covered her right arm, and except for her soft, big brown eyes, everything about her reflected a dark personality. Rebecca had a difficult time believing this woman could be Brenda Watson. She then remembered Watson had worked at Nick's bar. If she had the same appearance years ago, she would have blended in with the atmosphere.

"Are you Rebecca Holt?" Watson asked.

"Uh, yes." She forced a smile. "How'd you guess?"

"No one else around here looks like a lawyer."

"Oh, right." Rebecca felt self-conscious about wearing a business suit. At least Watson didn't make a comment about her appearing too young to be an attorney.

Watson turned around and walked toward the building's front door, and Rebecca followed her inside. The interior smelled like a brewery and featured pool tables, dartboards, and a large banner proclaiming "Raider Nation." Not Rebecca's kind of place, not even close.

Watson approached a gruff-looking bartender with a handlebar mustache and wavy black hair covering his ears. "Give me the usual," she said.

The bartender grabbed a glass mug and poured beer from a tap. He handed it to Watson and then stared at Rebecca.

"Do you have any white wine?" she asked sheepishly.

The bartender scoffed, and Watson shook her head.

"Sorry about that," Rebecca said. "I'll take a bottled water."

With a frown, the bartender grabbed a bottle from a refrigerator with a glass front and handed it to her.

Rebecca made a note to herself. In the future, she needed to be less conspicuous in similar situations. When at a blue-collar bar or a pool hall, wear casual clothes and order a beer or hard liquor.

With the mug in her hand, Watson strode toward a small, square table and sat with her back to the rest of the room. Rebecca sat on the other side. They were far enough away from the bartender and the few other patrons that they could talk in private, if Watson chose to do so.

Watson took a large sip of beer, causing Rebecca to notice her black fingernail polish. Despite her petite frame, she gave off an intimidating presence. Rebecca suspected this quality could have attracted Nick. When Rebecca had stood up to him, he had respected it.

Watson's hostile demeanor did not make it easier to start a conversation.

"So," began Rebecca awkwardly, "as I said on the phone, I'm Nick's attorney. He has a parole hearing coming up, and I wanted to... to talk to you about some things."

Watson placed the beer mug on the table and stared at her.

"Can I ask you a few questions?"

Watson gave no acknowledgment, not even a slight gesture.

"How'd you meet Nick?"

Watson pursed her lips. "I was a customer, and I needed a job. He hired me. That was it."

"How long did you work there?"

"A little over two years. I lost my job after Nick was arrested and the bar closed." She crossed her arms. "I know what you're thinking. How could I be with a man old enough to be my father, right?"

"Well, it crossed my mind. Sorry."

"Yeah... whatever. I never had a problem with it."

"How'd he treat you?"

"Good, really good." Watson unfolded her arms. "He always looked after me and cared about what was going on in my life. He had a temper, like most men, but he only yelled at me once or twice. Never laid a hand on me. When it came to women, sometimes he acted like a pig." She gave a half-frown. "Probably some macho, tough-guy act or other bullshit, but he never let anyone mess with a woman in his bar."

"That's nice," Rebecca said with a nervous smile. "How much did you know about him?"

"That's a hell of a question." Watson grabbed her beer and took another large sip.

"What do you mean?"

She scoffed. "He never talked about himself, like he didn't have a life before owning the bar."

"Did you ever ask?"

"Couple of times, and he blew me off."

"Why was he like that?"

Watson shrugged. "Who knows? Ghosts... demons from his past."

"Were you at the bar when Nick…"

"Killed that guy? Yeah, I was there, but I didn't see it. I only heard yelling and the gunshot. Nick came back as if nothing had happened, which was really freaky."

"Were you scared?"

Watson's eyes became wider. "Hell yeah! My boyfriend had just lost it!" Her face returned to its serious norm. "I also watched Nick slug the cop. It wasn't a fun night." She tilted her head back and drank from her mug until it was three-quarters empty.

"Was your husband, Anthony, at the bar that night?"

Watson gave a hard glare. "It's Tony, and how do you know about him?"

Rebecca was flustered and tried to keep her emotions under control. "My law firm hired a private detective, and it wasn't that hard for him to find information on your husband and your daughter."

Watson folded her arms, and her eyebrows drew together.

"Was Tony at the bar that night?"

"Yeah. He only saw what I saw."

Rebecca needed a moment to collect herself before continuing with the interview. She stalled by unscrewing the cap on her water bottle and drinking about a quarter of its contents.

"Nick's not on Kyra's birth certificate, but he's the biological father, right?"

There was no reaction except for Watson pressing her lips together.

"Nick told me he didn't have any children," Rebecca said, "but the report submitted to the judge before sentencing said you were pregnant."

Watson looked away. "Yeah, Nick's the father."

"Why did he say otherwise?"

She returned her gaze to Rebecca. "How the hell should I know? I haven't spoken to him in years." She finished the rest of her beer.

Rebecca leaned forward. "Yes, you do."

"Fine. After Nick got arrested, we had this talk, and back then, he was looking at a very long time in the can, maybe until he died. He wanted our kid to have a normal life and not to be ashamed of him. He said he didn't want to have a relationship through letters, phone calls, and visits. Nick said forget about him and find someone else."

The news overwhelmed Rebecca. "I'm– I'm sorry. I don't know what to say. It must've been tough."

"Yeah," Watson said stoically.

"Is that why you started a relationship with Tony?"

"Wasn't like that. At first, Tony and I were friends. He knew what was going on and offered to help out. He said I could move in with him and give Kyra a stable home."

"Does he know he's not Kyra's biological father?"

Watson scoffed. "Of course. We're not a couple of fucking idiots."

"What if Nick gets out and wants joint custody of Kyra?"

"Good luck. Tony's listed as the father on the birth certificate."

"Nick could demand a DNA test."

Watson's eyebrows narrowed, and she gave another hard stare. "Is that why he sent you up here?"

Rebecca leaned back and held up her hands. "Wait a minute. Nick doesn't know I contacted you, okay? I haven't even asked him if he wants to meet Kyra. I'm just raising the issue."

Watson folded her arms and gazed to the left.

"I'm not Nick's attack dog, honest. I'm just looking for something to help him get released on parole."

Watson exhaled and continued to look away. "What do you want?"

"Would you be willing to attend the parole hearing?"

"Too far away."

"What about writing a letter or an email and sending it to me? I'll give it to the parole board."

Watson remained silent for too long. Rebecca grew impatient and fought off the urge to check the time on her cell phone.

"Maybe I'll write a letter... maybe on one condition."

"What is it?"

"Kyra doesn't know Nick's her real father," Watson said in a low voice. "If Nick wants to see her, he's gotta be Uncle Nick or a family friend. She's still a little girl, only nine. Tony's her dad and telling her different will hit her too hard." In her normal volume, she added, "Kyra's not tough like me. She can't leave the house unless she's wearing something pink or yellow. I don't know where she gets it from."

Rebecca nodded. "I'll pass the information to Nick. It won't be a fun conversation."

"Right... Your problem, not mine." Watson grabbed her empty mug and strode to the bartender. She paid him and then walked out the front door.

Chapter 33

The following morning, Rebecca had another meeting with Nick. While waiting in a cramped attorney visit room, she noticed an inmate had carved "fuck you" into the table. She wondered if prison officials had punished the culprit.

Upon entry, the guard removed Nick's handcuffs and shackles.

"So, what gives?" he asked as he sat down. "We've got time before the parole hearing, and there's nothing else to talk about."

Rebecca forced a smile. "Actually, there are a couple of things we need to discuss. The first one is your future. Have you thought about what you'll do if you're granted parole?"

He smirked. "You're kidding, right? This is why you drove out here? I won't be granted parole, which means there's no need to make any plans."

She sighed. "You shouldn't be so fatalistic. Besides, you're not serving a life sentence. One day, you'll get released, and you need a plan. It'd be better if you could give one to the parole board."

"Whatever. I'll think about it. What's the other thing?"

Rebecca asked herself whether she should broach the topic. If she did, she feared the next few minutes would not go well. She took a deep breath. "I was looking for something... or someone who could talk about your life before prison, and I..."

"And what?" Nick's eyes bored into her.

"I met with Brenda Watson yesterday."

He flashed a quizzical expression. "What'd you do that for?"

"I– I wanted her to tell the parole board about your relationship with her."

"That's it?" he said as he threw up his arms. "We were together years ago. They won't care about it."

"There was something else... I talked to Brenda about your daughter."

Nick's face became tense and red, and he pounded the table with his fist. "What the hell were you thinking? I don't need that thrown in my face!"

Rebecca pulled back. "But– but I thought it wouldn't hurt to ask about her."

"Yeah right!" he said with fire in his eyes. "I've *never* seen my kid, and do you know why? Do you? Brenda said she didn't want our child to have a criminal for a father! I was pissed when she suggested it, but..." He pounded the table again. "I went along with it." He bent forward to where his head almost contacted the table between them. His face was twisted in pain.

Rebecca felt awful. She reasoned if she brought up Watson's version of events – that it was Nick that insisted he should have no contact with their daughter – the conversation would become even uglier and would hurt him even more. She could say nothing else, afraid of making a terrible situation even worse. She also could not leave and abandon him.

"Why the hell did you bring this up?" Nick demanded, with his face still red.

Rebecca held up her hands. "I'm– I'm sorry. I wanted to tell the parole board some good things about you and– and what you'd do after prison, like meeting your daughter."

Rebecca put down her hands, and tears welled up. She grabbed the strap of her purse to bring it up from the floor. She reached inside to grab a tissue and wiped her eyes. She then peeked at Nick, who still appeared in pain. She looked away.

After several moments, she sneaked another look at him, and noticed the color in his face had returned to normal, although she could tell he was still upset.

"Do you want to contact Kyra?"

He turned his head to the wall. "Don't know... Maybe... I haven't thought about her in a long time."

"There's just... one other thing," Rebecca said and then swallowed. "Kyra doesn't know you're her biological father. She thinks Tony, Brenda's husband, is."

The redness in Nick's face returned, which made her nervous.

"Brenda said she would write a letter for the parole board, but there's a catch. You… you have to pretend you're an uncle or a family friend when you're around her." As soon as the words came out of her mouth, she regretted it. She realized she should have sprung that additional piece of information another time.

Nick was enraged and again slammed his fist on the table. "What the hell! I can't be her dad!" He gave a frosty glare. "What are you trying to do to me? My life is crap, and you just made it worse!"

Rebecca pushed away from the table. "I'm– I'm sorry. I– I was only trying to help."

"Yeah! You did a great job, just great!"

He stood and twice slammed his hand on the door, indicating he wanted the guard to return.

Rebecca was inconsolable and on the verge of tears again. "Wait. Can't we talk about this a little more?"

"Hell no!"

The door opened.

"Let's go," Nick barked at the guard.

* * *

Once Rebecca returned to her office, she dropped her purse on the floor and slumped into her chair. She still felt terrible about what she had done. Perhaps she should have spoken with Nick before contacting Brenda Watson. Maybe she shouldn't have contacted Watson at all. After a period of punishing herself, she placed a call to Carter Patterson.

"Mr. Patterson, can I stop by your office? I need to talk to you about Nicholas Malone."

"Fine, fine, but don't bother coming here," he said cheerfully. "I need to stretch my legs. I'll come to you."

Two minutes later, Patterson plopped himself down in her office. "What's new?"

Rebecca groaned. "Nothing good. Malone told me he didn't have any children, which wasn't the truth. He and Brenda Watson, his ex-girlfriend, had a daughter."

Patterson's eyebrows raised. "Oh, I see. I take it you confronted him about it."

"Yeah," she said sullenly. "But there's more to it. I met with Brenda yesterday. She said Malone wanted no contact with his daughter, since he was going to prison, but when I spoke to Malone, he said not having a relationship with Kyra was Watson's idea."

"Oh dear!"

"On top of that, Watson said Kyra doesn't know Malone's her father. If Malone wants to see her, he must introduce himself as Uncle Nick or a family friend. When I told him, he got really upset. I didn't mean to, but I really hurt him."

Patterson exhaled and ran his right hand through his remaining gray hair. "Oh dear. That must've been an unpleasant experience."

"I should be getting used to them, but this one was really terrible."

They sat in silence for about a minute.

"It's not just Malone's attitude," Rebecca said. "I have to deal with a certain two partners at this law firm." She then regretted opening her big mouth again.

Patterson reached out for the office door and closed it. "You mean Vandemere and Bradford?"

She raised her eyebrows and her hands.

"I know, I know," Patterson said. "I'm not offering excuses, but Bradford's going through a nasty divorce. I'm not sure why Vandemere has such a rotten temper." He shook his head. "He's a very unhappy man. I'll speak with them and not mention your name. Acceptable?"

Rebecca gave a faint smile. "Thanks."

"Perhaps we should get back to Malone and why he doesn't have a relationship with his daughter. Did you confront him about the inconsistency between his story and Brenda's?"

"Oh no. I didn't want to get him more upset."

"Yes, yes. I see your point. Who do you believe?"

"Uh… Not sure," Rebecca said. "Maybe Malone."

"Or maybe you *want* to believe his version. How well do you know him?"

"That's a good question because he doesn't like to talk about himself. Watson said something similar. She said he never talked about his past."

Patterson nodded. "Interesting… interesting. He could be hiding something." He raised an eyebrow. "Or he simply doesn't enjoy talking about himself. Some people are like that." He smiled. "Although I can't imagine one attorney who falls into that category. The next time you speak with Malone, are you going to bring up who was to blame for cutting him out of his daughter's life?"

Rebecca shook her head. "What's the point? Regardless of who's at fault, he doesn't have a relationship with Kyra. He didn't say anything specifically, but I think he has very mixed emotions about her. I got the impression he had put his daughter out of his mind, and he's now having a hard time dealing with thoughts about her."

Patterson cocked his head. "Could be. Could be, but I've never met the man, and I'm certainly not a psychiatrist. Did you ask him about his plans upon release?"

"I did, and he has no clue."

He gave a half-frown. "That's not good, not good at all. He needs to come up with something to impress the parole board. If they ask and he still has nothing, the board might conclude he's more inclined to commit crimes. Please work on that issue."

"I'll try, but it won't be easy. He's still fatalistic."

"I understand, but if Malone attends the hearing convinced that he won't get parole, that's exactly what will happen. I assume he wants to be released. After all, no one wants to remain behind bars."

"Makes sense to me."

* * *

Late in the afternoon, Rebecca's phone rang for the sixth or seventh time in the last two hours. She wondered if others had conspired to prevent her from getting any work done. This time, it was the receptionist. Rebecca was tempted to let the call go to her voicemail yet answered it anyway.

"Yes, Ms. Willingham."

"You have a collect call from Nicholas Malone, and I already accepted the charges. Would you like me to put him through?"

Nick was perhaps the last person with whom she wanted a conversation. She would have preferred to avoid him for a few days.

"Ms. Holt, are you still there?"

"Yes, sorry. Please put him through."

Seconds later, he came on the line. "Hey, I'm surprised you're willing to talk to me."

"So am I."

"Look, I had some time to think things over. I'm still pissed at what you did, but I get what you were trying to do."

Rebecca felt somewhat relieved. "Thanks, I guess."

"Just don't bring up Brenda and my daughter for a while, a very long while."

"Uh, okay."

"Do you have some free time? I still need to finish my story."

Rebecca glanced at the large stack of paperwork on the corner of her desk. She wished she could wave a magic wand and make it go away. "I'm really busy right now, but I'd like to hear what happened next."

"Huh. Now you're interested? You weren't when we first started."

"How'd you know that? Oh wait, master's in psychology."

Nick chuckled. "I could read people even before I started taking college courses."

"Yeah, some people are like that."

"Okay. Now, where were we?"

"Detective Scott Langford from the NYPD came to New Orleans, and he said Patrick Walsh was really Ryan Parkhurst, the nephew of Conor McCarthy, also known as The Saint. Parkhurst once had tea with Millie and James Thornwell, and Cassandra is convinced he's the serial killer."

Chapter 34

Late July 1999
New Orleans, Louisiana

Mid-May rolled into June. By July, there was still no sign of Ryan Parkhurst, despite the New Orleans Police Department and other law enforcement agencies on the alert, which frustrated Cassandra to no end. He must have known he was a wanted man and was probably being extra careful to avoid an arrest. Cassandra also worried Parkhurst would torture and kill in some other city, maybe somewhere on the East Coast, and would never return to New Orleans. He could even be in another country, where local law enforcement was unaware of the prior murders.

The district attorney had not assigned her to any other significant cases, and she suspected Philip LeMay wanted to keep her on the sidelines for as long as possible. At least Mike Beaumont continued to lose weight.

* * *

On a Tuesday morning, Donnie called Cassandra on her cell phone.

"Hey, boss, are you coming in today?"

"Probably not," Cassandra said lethargically. "There isn't much for us to do at this point."

"Maybe not today, but something could be up this Sunday. I just got two tickets to a special event, invite only. Three local jazz greats will be getting together one last time. Since Parkhurst owns two jazz clubs, he might've have scored an invite."

"I appreciate your enthusiasm, but I doubt it. I guess we can make the usual contacts with the property owners. Some of them are probably tired of hearing from us."

"It's still worth going to the concert, and maybe we'll get lucky," Donnie said. "Do you want to go with me? I can't bring Tyler or Mike because Parkhurst knows what they look like."

"No, I have plans," Cassandra lied. "Do you know any detectives or uninformed officers who like jazz?"

"Yeah, sure."

"Great. Invite one of them and enjoy the concert."

* * *

The following Friday evening, Cassandra planned to have dinner with her boyfriend, Brian. They had reservations at Landry's Seafood House on Lake Pontchartrain, one of her favorite restaurants. However, given her depressed mood, Landry's had become nothing more than another place to eat, and dinner was something to do to kill time. She was about to leave her one-bedroom apartment when her cell phone rang.

"Is this Cassandra Morgan?" asked a male voice with a Southern drawl.

"Yes, that's me. Who's this?"

"Grady Jones, manager at Wilco, one of the rental car agencies at the airport."

"Uh-huh. Why are you calling?"

"Well… I reckon some time ago, somebody said to give you a holler if we spotted a guy who resembled… now where's that paper?"

Cassandra felt a chill run up her spine. "Ryan Parkhurst," she said excitedly. "Did you see him?"

"Ah, no. A customer just called and wanted our best sedan, but the computer says it was gone. I didn't know cuz I was out yesterday. Rick said last night a flight from JFK got in really late, and this guy, Shawn Murphy, from hang on…"

Cassandra heard keyboard clicks while her mind raced. "It doesn't matter where he's from."

"Murphy said he was from Middletown Township, New Jersey. Rick gave him the sedan. Dunno why he didn't recollect yer flyer. Is this guy really a big deal?"

"Yes, dammit! He's a serial killer!"

"What?" Jones said in an elevated voice. "Are you sure?"

"Absolutely! Did you show Rick the flyer?"

"Yeah, yeah," Jones said hastily. "Diff'rent name, same fella."

Cassandra's heart pounded harder. "Do you have the info on the sedan?"

"Yeah! I'll shoot it to the email on your business card!"

"And send me his local address."

"Right! Go get the bastard!"

"Bye."

Cassandra's hands shook, and she had difficulty thinking coherently. Nevertheless, she managed to call Tyler.

"He's here!"

"Who? You mean Parkhurst?"

"Yeah! Yesterday, he rented a car at the airport under the name Shawn Murphy, and I just found out. Call Mike and Donnie and get down to the trailer ASAP."

"On it."

She made another call to the New Orleans chief of police. "Chief Baxter, it's Cassandra Morgan. He's here in the city!"

"How the hell did you get my home number and what are you talking about?"

"Ryan Parkhurst, the serial killer. He's here."

The line went silent for a couple of seconds. "Are you sure?"

"Positive. He was spotted at the airport last night."

"And you're just getting around to telling me now? Is this a sick practical joke?"

"No, Chief, it isn't. I swear I just found out. Parkhurst rented a car, and the info on it is being sent to me right now. I'll forward it to you. He gave the rental car company a local address, which I'm about to get, and I bet it's bogus. Please issue an APB and have all available personnel check the higher-end bars and jazz clubs. Also, Parkhurst has stayed at short-term rental houses in the area. My team will contact the owners of each home, and if we can't reach one, please send a patrol unit to check the corresponding rental."

"We'll do our best, but we can't be in a thousand places at once. For good measure, I'll alert the Orleans Parish sheriff and the sheriffs in the surrounding communities. If you need anything further, I'll be in my office in twenty."

* * *

As expected, the address Parkhurst provided to the rental car agency was bogus. Cassandra and her team assembled in the trailer and contacted the property owners, asking them who currently occupied their rentals. With each passing moment, she agonized another woman could already be dead.

After too much time had passed, Mike exclaimed, "Found him!"

Cassandra experienced another chill up her spine. "Where?"

"Do you remember the idiot who mails keys to his tenants? He owns the cottage on Marshal Foch Street in Lakeview. He just told me 'Shawn Murphy' is renting the place. That's got to be Parkhurst!"

Cassandra's hands shook again. "Yeah! Mike and Tyler, I'll head out with you. Donnie, get ahold of the watch commander, and have any officers in the area meet us at the address. Sirens off when they get close. How– how many property owners haven't been contacted yet? Call them just in case."

"Okay," Donnie said hurriedly, "and please get going."

Chapter 35

Tyler drove an unmarked sedan like Mario Andretti at the Indy 500, speeding and weaving in and out of traffic. Mike sat in the front passenger's seat and turned around to speak to Cassandra.

"Having you come along isn't SOP for good reason. Parkhurst could be armed and might not go quietly."

"Yeah, I know it's not standard operating procedure," she said as she held up her hands. "I'll stay away from the house and out of the line of fire."

Mike glanced at the road in front and turned back again. "I really mean it. Stay away. The last time an ADA came along, the suspect stabbed him in the shoulder. So, whatever you do, don't get near the home until we give the all-clear. Understood?"

"Yes," she replied.

Tyler slowed to a reasonable speed. He parked the car two houses down and on the other side of the street from the target residence. As quiet as mice, Cassandra, Mike, and Tyler stepped onto the street and waited for backup. The porch light for the house in question was out, and it was too dark to make out the details. Cassandra could only determine it was a light-colored, single-story colonial cottage with an awning over the front door. No fence separated the small front yard from the back.

About fifteen seconds later, a blue-and-white patrol car arrived, and two uniformed officers exited the vehicle. Cassandra recognized the African American officer, Ernest Washington, a seasoned veteran. The other one was a Caucasian rookie, and his nameplate stated, "H. Conners."

"Another patrol car is two minutes out," Washington said. "We were told we're going after a homicide suspect. Is that right?"

"That's the understatement of the year," Mike said with a smirk. "We're pretty certain the Crescent City Killer is renting out the house over there for a few days," he said, pointing to it. "We're not sure if he's inside right now. Detective Winfield and I'll approach it to see if anything's amiss. If so, the four of us will bust in."

"The Crescent City Killer. Is that the one with all the dead hookers?" Connors asked.

Cassandra glared at him. "Look, moron. The victims were all young women, and the dead should be treated with respect."

Conners lurched back. "What the hell?"

"You can't talk to him like that!" Washington said a little too loudly.

"Hey, keep it down and focus," Mike said. He pointed again at the house. "There's a garage in the back. You two go around the corner and see if you can figure out if the suspect's car is parked inside. It's a silver sedan, license num—"

A woman's scream came from the cottage.

The uniformed officers looked at Mike, who barked, "Go to the back. When you hear Tyler and I bust through the front door, do the same. Go!"

The officers, Mike, and Tyler ran toward the residence. Cassandra stepped behind the unmarked car, her heart pounding. The world around her disappeared as her sole focus was on the colonial cottage. Tyler beat Mike to the front porch and burst up the small set of stairs. He kicked in the door, and Mike ran inside while pointing his pistol in front of him with both hands. Tyler was right behind him and held out his gun in the same manner. Cassandra heard another loud bang, signifying the officers blasting through the back door.

"Police!" she heard Mike yell. "Freeze or you're dead!" A second later, "Keep your hands up! Knees on the floor! Now! Now!"

Then there was silence, and Cassandra's heart continued to pound. Seconds seemed like hours until she saw Mike step onto the front porch with a big grin. He pumped his fist in the air.

"We got him! You can come in."

As she strode towards him, she could barely contain herself.

Another blue-and-white patrol unit parked behind the first one. As two more officers exited the squad car, Mike yelled, "Over here!"

Cassandra wanted to say something, anything, but she was too overwhelmed with emotion. Instead, she listened to Mike, who appeared unfazed.

"When we made it to the master bedroom, she was on the bed, lying face up with Parkhurst on top of her. He looked surprised." Mike chuckled. "Wonder why? I guess we're not as dumb as we look. You won't believe what he said. 'What's the big deal? It's only a little rough sex.' Oh sure. That's why she looked terrified."

The two other uniformed officers arrived at the front porch, and the taller one said, "Who's in charge?"

"I am, Detective Mike Beaumont. We just arrested the Crescent City Killer. Please call it in and wait outside for forensics to show up."

"You really got him!" said the taller officer.

"You bet your sweet ass we did. Now please call it in."

The taller officer gave a quick nod, and then he and his partner returned to their vehicle.

Mike turned to Cassandra. "Follow me, and please don't touch anything."

As they entered the front room, Cassandra noticed Parkhurst standing in the hallway with his hands cuffed behind his back, while Officers Washington and Conners held onto his arms.

Parkhurst laughed. "Lookie here. They brought another little honey to the party!"

Under normal circumstances, such a sexist remark would have bothered Cassandra, but not this time. He could make all the comments he wanted. His reign of terror had ended, and now it was her turn. She knew the wheels of justice were now in motion and would not stop turning until a prison official strapped down Parkhurst and gave him a lethal injection. If it were the last thing she did on this earth, she would attend his execution.

Cassandra glared at Parkhurst and stepped to the side as Officers Washington and Conners jostled him out the door. She then noticed in the room to the left of the front door, a young, fair-skinned woman with a triangular face and chin-length black hair sitting in a rocking chair with her head down. Her blouse was torn at the left shoulder, exposing a bra strap.

Tyler was next to her, down on one knee. He looked at Mike. "Give us a minute."

Cassandra followed Mike through the hallway and into the master bedroom, which had a queen-sized bed with a flower-print sheet covering the mattress. Parkhurst had attached handcuffs to all four bedposts and had wedged pieces of cloth between the cuffs and the posts to prevent scratch marks. There was a switchblade on the nightstand next to the bed. With the closet door ajar, Cassandra observed a crowbar resting on one end in a back corner, no doubt one of Parkhurst's instruments of torture. She returned to the front room, where the black-haired woman still sat with Tyler next to her.

"Can you answer a few questions?" Tyler asked.

The woman picked up her head. "Uh, sure."

"What's your name?"

"Diane, Diane Nickerson."

"Did he hurt you anywhere?"

"No, I'm okay." She straightened her back as if to emphasize she had no injuries.

"We can have you checked out at the ER."

She shook her head. "I'm fine."

Tyler gently touched her left hand. "We'll need to take your statement. We can do it now, or we can talk to you tomorrow morning. Either way is fine with me."

"Now."

"Are you sure?"

"Yeah." Diane pushed her hair away from her face.

Mike retrieved a little notebook and a pen from his pocket.

"Where did you and Ryan meet?" Tyler asked.

Diane looked puzzled. "Ryan? He told me his name is Shawn."

"His real name is Ryan Parkhurst. Where'd you meet him, at a local bar?"

"No, he called my service. I usually meet someone in a public place so I can check him out. You know, make certain the client's not a weirdo or a creep. My service said he'd pay double the normal fee if I met him at his place. I thought, 'Why not?' Stupid me, right?"

"Then what happened?"

"He welcomed me inside, and he was kind of charming. We had some wine, and everything seemed okay." Diane brushed aside her hair again. "Then we went back to the bedroom. I saw the handcuffs, and I told him I'm not into kinky stuff. He got mad and pulled out a knife. That's when I screamed. He told me to shut up and put the knife to my throat. He forced me onto the bed, and that's when you guys showed up." Her eyes got wide. "Hey, wait a minute. How come you got here so quickly?"

"We've been investigating–" Cassandra began.

"It's a long story," Mike interrupted. "Let's just say we were in the right place at the right time."

"Yeah, okay," Diane said. "I didn't deserve this. I hope you nail him to the wall."

"We will," Cassandra asserted. "You can count on it."

Chapter 36

Early afternoon the next day, Cassandra and her team gathered to celebrate Parkhurst's arrest at Willie Mae's Scotch House in the Tremé District. They sat at a plain, square table, nothing fancy for this establishment. While the décor was lacking, the smell of fried chicken whetted Cassandra's appetite.

"Great idea," Mike said. "I haven't been here in a long time."

Donnie smiled. "Thanks. This place has the best chicken in the whole state. The best! No doubt about it."

"Yeah, I can't argue with you, but there's a problem," Cassandra said. "The name includes the word 'Scotch,' and I can't get any alcohol, not even a beer."

Donnie smirked. "Hey, you can't have it all. Besides, isn't it a little early for drinking?"

"Not really."

"Care to make a complaint?" Mike asked. "See the little old lady over there by the front door?" He pointed with the nod of his head. "That's Willie Mae Seaton, the owner. You can tell her all about it."

Both Mike and Donnie chuckled, and Tyler gave a weak smile.

Cassandra turned to Tyler. "Want to get in on this? Care to take a shot at me?"

Tyler waved his right hand back and forth, indicating he declined.

Cassandra grinned. "Guys, I have to tell you something. I really had my doubts we'd pull this off. When it's all over, there'll be a press conference, and I'm going to make certain all three of you get the recognition you truly deserve."

"Thanks," Donnie said. "That means a lot."

"Oh yeah?" Mike said. "You need to give most of the credit to Tyler."

"Why?" she asked.

"We need to tell the serial killer that he was caught by Winnie the Pooh!"

Everyone at the table laughed, including Cassandra.

"Hey, it's nice to see you loosen up," Donnie said to her. "For an occasion like this, I expected to see your significant other. Where is he?"

"He's out of town, visiting family," Cassandra lied. She didn't want to discuss her personal life and avoid embarrassment. Last night, she ran off without informing Brian. When she got home around one in the morning, she realized she had forgotten about their date and called to apologize. Brian said he understood, but the serial killer's capture meant more endless hours in the office for her. He no longer wanted to play second fiddle to her career, and so he had ended their relationship.

Cassandra moved to another topic. "Tyler, did the crime lab get back to you?"

"Yeah, about thirty minutes ago. Besides Parkhurst's cell phone and the crowbar, there was nothing else noteworthy in his suitcase or the master bedroom closet. Nothing special in the rest of the house."

"Who's the judge for Parkhurst's first appearance?" Mike asked.

"Judge Gradisher," Cassandra said. "I've had a couple of trials in his courtroom, and he's somewhat on the conservative side. For bail, Gradisher might focus only on the events of last night, but he'll still order Parkhurst held without bail. Anyone want to sit with me during the hearing? Tyler?"

He shrugged.

"Donnie?"

"Sorry, no can do. I've got a doctor's appointment. Besides, I don't even like looking at the criminal courts building. It gives me the creeps."

Mike was drinking from his glass of Diet Coke. He put it down and sighed. "Fine, I'll go."

"Thanks. Did we get a swab from Parkhurst?"

"Yup." Mike chuckled. "We got him now!"

"Yeah," Cassandra said. "I'm sure his DNA will be a match to what we found underneath Amy Nguyen's fingernails, and then I can charge him with murder. I might also up the ante for last night's festivities by adding an attempted murder charge."

"Will the bartender from Rousseau's testify if the case goes to trial?" Tyler asked.

"What for?" she said. "He lied to us the first time we spoke to him, which will make his credibility suspect. Besides, we don't need him to prove Nguyen and Parkhurst were together. His DNA under her fingernails will be enough, and maybe Nguyen's friend will pick him out of a line-up. If not, she can at least provide a general description of who was at the bar."

Cassandra knew she couldn't call Brody Robertson as a witness because he could reveal the unorthodox way in which she forced him to talk. She also knew her tactics were very illegal but supposed it did not matter anymore.

"What about the other murders?" Tyler asked.

She exhaled. "That's a tougher call. There's no direct evidence, at least not yet. We'll also need to deal with jurisdiction, since we can't tie the other bodies to Orleans

Parish. Don't worry, we'll figure it out, but ultimately, the DA will make the call on any murder charges."

Mike scoffed. "Philip LeMay, *Mister* District Attorney… what a piece of work! Did you see him on TV last week? He was wearing another expensive suit and a gold watch. No way he can afford them on his salary. I've heard rumors that he's corrupt. They've got to be true."

"You can't trust rumors," Donnie said.

"Yeah, I know," Mike said. "But this is the Big Easy, where for some politicians, anything goes. Hey, are you going to stick around for the rest of the fun and games with Parkhurst?"

Donnie smirked. "By next summer, I'll be retired. Doesn't matter what happens between now and then. I'll be retired. The grandkids want to visit some national parks, and I'm more than willing to be their chauffeur. I'll go to any of them except the one in New Mexico… what's it called?"

"Carlsbad Caverns?" Tyler asked.

"That's it. No one's getting me into a hole in the ground, even after I'm dead."

Cassandra smiled. "Mike, you're hitting mandatory retirement by the end of the year. Any plans?"

"Yeah," he said. "I plan to sleep in bed for a month. Then I'll get up, walk over to my couch, and sleep for another month. After that, I'll look for something. I have a cousin who's a manager at a golf course in Biloxi. Maybe I could be his assistant, and it might be fun. What about you, Tyler, sticking with NOPD forever?"

Tyler gave a weak smile and shrugged.

"He's too busy thinking about Leslie," Mike said. "Yeah, I heard you on the phone. Is Leslie a guy or a girl?"

Tyler's face became red.

"Leave him alone," Donnie said. "He doesn't have to tell us about his personal life, even though we desperately need some entertainment."

"Yeah, entertain us, tell us!" Mike said with a wide smile.

"Geez," Tyler said and folded his arms. "There's not much to tell. Leslie's a woman, and I met her about three weeks ago."

Mike chuckled. "Ooh, a girl! Does she know you're bisexual?"

"No offense, but you need to get a life. Yeah, she knows, and she's probably attracted to the 'novelty' of it," Tyler said while making air quotes. "I don't think it'll last because her personality's a little too much for me."

"You mean she's too much like Mike?" Donnie asked. "You need to end it now."

Mike chuckled again. "I can't argue with that. Bail out, bail out now!"

Everyone laughed, including Tyler.

Chapter 37

Early May 2019
Eastvale, California

Nicholas Malone entered the attorney visit room with a swagger, which Rebecca interpreted as an act for her benefit.

"How are you feeling?" she asked as he sat down.

"Same as always. Did you do anything fun last weekend?"

"Yeah, thanks for asking. I took a day trip with three friends to the Pisgah lava tubes. They're out in the desert near Barstow."

Nick raised his eyebrows. "What's so special about lava tubes?"

"They're fun to explore."

"If you say so. Did you go coed?"

"No, just with my female friends."

"You're not interested in any men?"

Rebecca scoffed. "Of course."

Nick put his elbows on the table and leaned forward. "Well?"

"Well, what?"

"Tell me about it."

Rebecca didn't respond.

He rolled his eyes. "Ah, come on!"

After a moment, she relented. "Fine. There's a new paralegal at work. He's cute, but it doesn't matter. I can't ask him out because the firm doesn't allow dating within the office."

He threw up his hands. "What the hell? It's a stupid rule. Break it."

"I don't want to get in trouble, and the rule isn't all bad. It prevents some problems. If a relationship doesn't work out, it'd be awkward for two people to work around each other."

Nick shook his head and frowned. "You've been brainwashed. They work you to death, and you have little time for your social life. You can't meet men at work. Quit and get another job."

"Enough of that," she said. "Let's get to why I'm here. This is the last time I can come out before your parole hearing. We need to discuss a few things one more time."

"Whatever," he said with a dismissive wave.

"First, speak to the parole board in your own words. You're an intelligent guy and should be able to connect with the panel. Please avoid using swear words and crude language."

Nick scoffed. "Do you really have to pound it into me over and over again?"

"Yeah, I do. You have a habit of using harsh language, and your hoarse voice makes it sound even worse."

"Yeah, I get it. You want me to talk like I'm on a job interview, right?"

Rebecca paused and gave a wry smile. "Maybe not all job interviews. When you applied to be a dock worker, crude language might've been expected."

Nick smirked. "Yeah. Some of them were ex-cons. The job wasn't so bad, but having my own place was better." He grimaced. "At least it was until I shot Denny. Do you think any of his family will attend the hearing?"

"Probably. Don't engage with them and please be respectful."

"Should I apologize to them?"

"What do you think?"

Nick sighed. "Yeah."

"Next question. If released on parole, what are you going to do?"

"I've got to support myself somehow. There won't be a rich babe waiting at the gate to take me home."

Is he ever going to get it? she said to herself. "Please try to be more respectful of women. What will you do?"

"I can still be a bartender. I used to drive a forklift at a warehouse and sitting down for a living isn't too bad. There are probably other things I can do, but I'll bet no one wants to hire an old geezer."

"You never know. Where would you live?" Rebecca asked.

"An ex-cellmate's out on parole, and he lives in Canoga Park. Hell, I'll live anywhere after I first get out."

She nodded. "Sounds good and try not to use the word 'hell' during the hearing. We'll also tell the parole board about all your good works in prison. Don't be humble or shy about it."

Nick smirked. "You think I'm humble or shy?"

"Well, not really. What about your daughter?"

Nick exhaled through his nose and looked away. After a couple of moments of awkward silence, he said, "Don't know. I still can't think about it too much."

Rebecca did not want to press the issue any further and get him upset again. I "I'm sure the parole board will ask if you're going to get into any more trouble," she said instead.

Nick chuckled and turned his head toward her. "I'm sixty-two and slowing down. What can I do?"

"What are you going to say about your manslaughter conviction and your other crimes?"

Nick rubbed the back of his neck. "Yeah… Shooting Denny and hitting the cop were pretty dumb moves. I let my emotions get the best of me. Now I have a much longer fuse."

"What about attacking the guard?"

He leaned back in his chair and held out his hands. "Look, I won't lie to you. To this day, I don't regret cracking his skull. He was a sadistic SOB, and I needed to help the kid right away. He received counseling, but he was still messed up. I'm not sure what happened to him after he got released. I wouldn't be surprised if he self-medicated with drugs and alcohol."

"Would you do something like that on the outside?"

"Hell, no! It's different out there. There are other options and…" Nick furrowed his brow and scrunched his nose. "What the…" With his left hand, he reached down and pulled up his left pant leg. He scratched his lower leg and then put his hand on the table between them.

Rebecca saw blood underneath a fingernail. "Are you okay?"

"Yeah, it's nothing."

"Maybe not." She pointed at his fingers.

Nick turned his hand to examine it. "Huh." With both hands, he pulled up his pant leg again and looked down.

Rebecca noticed a small stream of blood inching toward his sock, and just above it, she saw the bottom of a thick, vertical scar.

"Ah crap! Last week, I scraped my leg and reopened the wound. I'll see if a guard can get me a Band-Aid. Hang out here for a bit."

"Yeah, sure."

Nick pounded on the door. "Hey, look at this," he said when the guard opened it. He then raised his pant leg again.

"Let's go," the guard said, and they departed.

Rebecca's thoughts suddenly overwhelmed her. Upon seeing his surgical scar, she wondered if the name Nicholas Malone was an alias, and his real name was Tyler Winfield.

Nick had said that after Tyler was struck by a car, he had surgery on his leg, and the thick line on Nick's leg was consistent with a surgical scar. Both Tyler and Nick had buzz cuts. Nick's hair was gray, and Rebecca could not determine his original hair color. Tyler had a bad cowlick, which was why he kept his hair short. Perhaps Nick's hair swirled to an extent at or near the crown, but she had never taken a good look.

Nick had said Tyler resembled Winnie the Pooh in part because he had a small nose. Nick also had a small nose, though it had been broken at least once. Nick had said Tyler sounded like Winnie the Pooh. Rebecca had no idea what Nick sounded like without the nodules on his vocal cords making his voice sound hoarse.

Rebecca tried to determine why Tyler would change his name and could not imagine a plausible explanation. She had repeatedly searched the internet for any information on him and had found nothing. If he had been part of a significant arrest or a scandal while he was a detective, at least one news article would have mentioned it.

Rebecca had no doubt Nick was a heterosexual and had a fairly crude view of women. On the other hand, according to Nick, Tyler was bisexual and more sensitive. Perhaps Tyler/Nick changed over time, but that seemed unlikely. She also acknowledged Nick could have withheld or altered information about Tyler, and it was even possible Tyler Winfield never existed.

Rebecca didn't want to confront Nick about his identity for the time being as she wanted him to focus on the parole hearing. She feared if she did otherwise, he could get upset, fire her as counsel, and make a terrible impression before the parole board. She had invested too much time and effort to let that happen.

Rebecca then had a horrible idea, which made her shudder. Nick could be the serial killer! If so, it would explain why he had provided so many details. He had committed violent acts and had the capacity to kill. She didn't think serial killers committed murder due to emotional outbursts, however. During her psychology class in college, she had learned serial killers were sociopaths: cold and methodical. Nick had some morals and was highly emotional.

Rebecca laughed to herself at the possibility of Nicholas Malone and Ryan Parkhurst being the same person. Her book and many websites discussed what happened to the serial killer, and the story did not end with him incarcerated in a California prison.

Nick was gone long enough for Rebecca to shelve her thoughts concerning his identity, and she was able to compose herself and create the impression she was bored.

He eventually returned to the room and sat down. "Sorry it took a while. I had to go to the infirmary just to get a stupid Band-Aid. More idiotic prison rules. Is there anything else we need to cover?"

"A couple of things. The chaplain wrote a nice letter for you, and he mentioned your attendance at the Sunday services. I know I'm beating a dead horse, but you need to carefully choose your words during the hearing. Talk like someone with a master's degree and not like a rude and crude, uneducated convict."

He flashed a grin. "Hey, watch it. You're knocking some of my best friends."

"And keep the sarcasm to a minimum."

"Yeah, yeah," he said dismissively.

Rebecca patted the table. "I believe we're done for now. We'll get together an hour or so before the parole hearing for some last-minute prep. I have some free time, sort of. So, we can talk about something else." She grinned. "Do I have to give you another hint?"

Chapter 38

Early August 1999
New Orleans, Louisiana

Brightly painted homes and businesses filled the Big Easy. Their colors ranged from white and yellow to shades of blue, green, and purple. Wrought-iron balconies, charming architecture, and tree-lined streets were also present throughout the city, but the Orleans Criminal District Courthouse bore a stark contrast. The large rectangular building's light-gray walls had turned much darker shades as a result of pollution and the passage of time. The courthouse appeared as if it had risen from the depths to impose its ominous presence and dark powers on anyone who dared to approach it. With the addition of gargoyles and a stormy night, it would make a perfect setting for a horror movie.

Early Monday morning, Cassandra and Mike sat inside a courtroom, waiting for Ryan Parkhurst's initial hearing. Due to his weight loss, Mike wore what he called his "smaller-size" business suit, which was still too large. His dress shirt's collar was at least an inch too big in circumference, and he had cinched up his tie as much as possible to make the collar less noticeable.

Two ceiling fans did little to dissipate the oppressive heat and humidity. Cassandra suspected someone had turned off the air conditioner over the weekend and hoped it would run at full force at any moment. If not, the room would soon become more insufferable as the outside temperature rose. For Mike, the conditions were already unbearable, and Cassandra noticed sweat on his forehead and neck.

Parkhurst reclined on the other side. He displayed a devilish grin and appeared as if he enjoyed the moment. His body language reflected contempt and arrogance, and Cassandra looked forward to wiping the smile off his face in short order.

To Parkhurst's right was Beauregard "Bo" Davenport, New Orleans' most prominent defense attorney, who sported a dark-brown toupee and a goatee streaked with gray. Suspenders held his pants up to his bulging stomach, and his bow tie struggled to retain his double chin. Davenport also wore a bright-blue suit, a flashy watch, a gold ring on his left hand, and a large diamond ring on his right. Cassandra rolled her eyes over such flamboyance.

To the left of Parkhurst sat Morrison Hayworth, whom Cassandra recognized from news broadcasts. He was a New York attorney who had represented notable crime figures. His black suit, grayish complexion, and coal-black eyes gave him a grim appearance. Both he and Davenport used handkerchiefs to wipe sweat from their foreheads.

Conor McCarthy, also known as The Saint, sat in the first row behind the defense counsel's table. Tommy Hanson, the walking tank, and Lazlo Janka, the thug with a dark ponytail, had parked themselves on each side of him. McCarthy's face appeared etched in stone, and fissures broke the surface in numerous places. He wore yellow-tinted glasses and a three-piece, charcoal-gray suit. Despite his advanced age, he sat ramrod straight.

Davenport leaned over the rail between them and whispered into McCarthy's ear. The Saint didn't speak and instead gave a slight nod. Despite the stuffy atmosphere, McCarthy appeared unfazed. In fact, Cassandra did not notice any perspiration on his face.

Cassandra glanced again at Hanson and Janka. She guessed Janka was six inches taller, and his hard eyes glared at her. While he made an intimidating appearance, she would rather run into him, than Hanson, in a dark alley.

A thin, middle-aged woman with glasses and dark-brown hair entered the courtroom. "Hey, folks. I'm terribly sorry about the conditions in here. The AC isn't working, and we're not sure how soon it'll be fixed. Please be patient, and Judge Ogden will be out momentarily."

Clayton Ogden would conduct the hearing, not Edward Gradisher! The news hit Cassandra like a professional boxer landing a right cross to her jaw. She had appeared before the judge a few times and had found his rulings erratic. She also thought he had the legal mind of a sixth-grader.

Ten minutes passed, and everyone in the courtroom seemed to be melting except for McCarthy. Cassandra emptied a water bottle yet still felt drained. She was somewhat thankful her jacket concealed the pond of sweat forming on the back of her blouse, but she also had the urge to strip to her underwear, even in court, to feel cooler.

Not a moment too soon, the bailiff in the corner announced, "All rise! Court is now in session, the Honorable Clayton Ogden presiding."

A man in his early sixties entered. His black robe covered his stocky frame and contrasted with his thick white hair. His bulbous nose and the reddish hue of his face reinforced Cassandra's suspicion that he had a drinking problem. Months ago, during a meeting in chambers, she had smelled alcohol on his breath.

Ogden ambled to the space between his bench and high-back leather chair. He squinted and made a quick scan of all those present.

"Good morning, everyone!"

"Good morning, Your Honor," all those in attendance said in unison.

Ogden smiled. "Oh, and good morning to you, Bo. It's been a little while."

Davenport nodded, and Cassandra heard Mike let out a groan. She knew what Mike knew. The judge's personal greeting to defense counsel indicated there was a distinct possibility the hearing wouldn't go well. Nevertheless, she believed if she gave her best presentation, Ogden would still order Parkhurst held without bail.

Ogden took his seat, followed by all others. He reached under the bench, and a moment later, Cassandra heard an electric fan's faint whirl.

"Let's get started," Judge Ogden said. "Would the defendant and his attorneys be so kind as to rise and take their places at the podium."

Davenport and Parkhurst made their way, but Hayworth remained seated. Ogden's failure to give an admonishment surprised Cassandra.

The judge cleared his throat. "Mr. Davenport, your client is charged with one count of aggravated assault, one count of aggravated battery, and one count of false imprisonment. How does your client plead?"

Davenport grabbed his suspenders and puffed out his chest. "My client pleads not guilty to all counts, which I might say are ridiculous and beneath even the miserable reputation of the district attorney's office."

Davenport's posturing bothered Cassandra, and she wondered why the judge did not tell the pompous windbag to shut his mouth and stop wasting time. There was already too much hot air in the courtroom.

"I might add, Your Honor, this whole situation has been totally blown out of proportion. Mr. Parkhurst was engaged in rough but consensual sex acts. There was absolutely no crime of any kind."

Cassandra rose. "Your Honor, if I may?"

"Proceed, Counselor."

"The defendant lured the victim to his vacation rental home and threatened the poor woman with a knife. The defendant was about to forcibly handcuff her to the bed and beat her without mercy when officers arrived on the scene. Therefore, the charges are wholly appropriate."

"Uh-huh," Ogden said. He put his right elbow on the bench and his chin in his right hand. "Are the parties prepared to discuss bail?"

"Yes, Your Honor," Cassandra said.

"Of course, Your Honor," Davenport bellowed.

"Very well. Please proceed, Ms. Morgan."

"The defendant should be held without bail," Cassandra said confidently, "because he poses a danger to the community. Last weekend, he engaged in serious and violent conduct, and he has two arrests for assault in New York City. In the alternative, the defendant is an extreme flight risk, which is another reason to deny bail. He probably lives in New York, and this alone means he's a flight risk. In addition, we aren't aware of a fixed address. He previously gave the police an alias and a false address, and he has used other aliases, which further show deception and a risk of flight. There is one other matter, may I?"

The judge waved his right hand and then dropped it on the bench.

"The defendant is under investigation for multiple murders. We are awaiting DNA results, and once received, we'll have enough evidence to directly connect him to one murder victim. If the defendant is indeed a serial killer, there's no doubt he poses a danger to the public. Further, given the ongoing investigation, he has every incentive to flee to avoid facing the death penalty."

The judge had no visible reaction and instead motioned for defense counsel to proceed. He then leaned into his chair and made full use of his armrests.

Davenport again grabbed his suspenders. "Your Honor, this is nothing short of outrageous! Correction, 'outrageous' is a gross understatement. The prosecution is making wild accusations without a shred of proof." He waved both hands in the air. "Her case is very weak, and she resorts to the worst smear tactics imaginable. This is wrong!" he barked as he pounded the podium. "It's also clear Ms. Morgan engaged in gross misconduct prior to my client's arrest. She sent her personal goon to attack Mr. Brody Robertson, a bartender at Rousseau's, one of our finer establishments. Mr. Robertson had no choice but to falsely identify my client so he could save his own skin."

Even though Cassandra made no visible reaction, Bo Davenport's accusation caused a moment of panic. She asked herself how he had discovered the incident at the bar and realized she had a major problem on her hands. If Philip LeMay were told about Davenport's accusation and determined it was the truth, her current employment would end, and her bar license would be in jeopardy. At least she had spotted no reporters in the gallery before the hearing had begun.

"What the hell?" Mike whispered.

"It's just Bo being Bo," she whispered back.

Upon hearing Davenport's accusation, Judge Ogden frowned. "Counsel, please save it for a future hearing. Given your reputation, I'm quite certain you'll be filing a motion to suppress in short order."

Davenport leaned on the podium and waved his left fist. "That and a motion to dismiss. I might further add–"

"No, you may not. Not now," Ogden calmly said. "Please stick to the issue of bail."

Davenport appeared flustered, and Cassandra suspected it was more of his courtroom theatrics rather than genuine emotion.

"As you please, Your Honor," he said, as he wiped the sweat off his brow with his handkerchief. "There's not even the slightest sign that my client poses a danger to anyone. There's also no question Mr. Parkhurst should be released on a reasonable bail amount. He also agrees to supervision, even though it's wholly unnecessary."

Cassandra rose again. "Your Honor, I object to defense counsel's trashing of the district attorney's office. He's making the same outlandish statements he's repeated time and time again without any merit. What does he consider reasonable bail, ten thousand dollars?"

Ogden did not flinch and shifted his eyes to Davenport.

"We're agreeable to more than reasonable bail, Your Honor. In fact, we propose an excessive amount to meet the prosecution halfway. My client's uncle, Mr. Conor McCarthy, is willing to post 1.5 million dollars in cash. Mr. Parkhurst will also submit to an electronic ankle monitor. If our fine parish doesn't have the proper equipment and can't pay for it, Mr. McCarthy will foot the bill and kindly donate it. Pending trial, my client will live in the Garden District in the home of Mr. Justin Scarborough, Mr. McCarthy's dear friend and business associate."

Ogden appeared deep in thought, at least for him, and rubbed his chin with his right hand.

"Your Honor, may I respond?" Cassandra asked.

"No, thank you. Your position on bail is quite clear."

Ogden put down his right hand. He stared at the ceiling and drummed his right-hand fingers on an armrest. Cassandra felt more impatient than usual thanks to the gradual increase in temperature.

With his eyes still fixed toward the ceiling, Ogden proclaimed, "The defendant's request for bail in the amount of 1.5 million dollars with electronic monitoring is fair and reasonable, and it is so ordered. We're adjourned."

Cassandra was shocked by the ruling. She wanted to leap to her feet and raise a strenuous objection. However, she knew the judge would give no consideration to her complaint, and if she protested too much, he would hold her in contempt and perhaps throw her in jail until the next morning.

Ogden rose from his chair and shuffled out of the courtroom. Cassandra was so upset she could barely control herself, yet was still rational enough to know she should not make any derogatory comments. If any court personnel overheard her while Ogden was no longer present, they would report back to him, and that would not bode well for any future hearing or for her future in general. She instead touched Mike's left arm and said, "Let's go."

Cassandra hustled out of the building and into the nearby parking lot, where the conditions were even worse than inside. On an ordinary day, the sweltering heat sucked the life out of her, but this time, anger and scorn kept her going. Once Cassandra and Mike were inside her Mustang and the doors were closed, she started the engine and turned the air conditioner to the maximum, but the almost instant rush of cool air could not calm her.

"Damn it!" Cassandra said as she slammed the steering wheel. "What the hell was that idiot Ogden thinking? You know what's going to happen? Parkhurst will bolt. Just wait, he'll do it. Why the hell did Ogden order his release?"

"Well," Mike said with a sigh. "He and Bo Davenport are friends. They belong to the same country club, where they've eaten lunch together many times."

"That's just terrific!"

"Yeah, I know. I'm not thrilled about it either, but there's not much we can do about it."

Cassandra's eyes focused off into the distance for a few seconds. She then turned her head toward Mike. "Maybe there is. Why don't we investigate The Saint's business associate? What was his name, Scarborough? If we find something on him, he would be an unfit sponsor for Parkhurst, and that would give me grounds for a new bail hearing."

Mike shook his head. "I already know plenty about Scarborough. Among other things, he's a silent partner for a series of strip clubs in Louisiana and Texas. More than once, the one in New Orleans was under investigation for prostitution and drug trafficking, but there's never been enough for an arrest. Here's some more good news: Scarborough's also a friend of the district attorney. He makes contributions to LeMay's campaign fund, and good old Phillip probably reciprocates in one way or another."

"You're certain about Scarborough and the DA?"

"Very."

"This is seriously wrong." She smacked her steering wheel again. "To hell with it. I'll still ask LeMay for permission to appeal the bail order."

Cassandra continued to fume as she considered her options. She could not force Ogden to recuse himself and could not convince any other judge to remove him from the case, not over something as supposedly innocent as he and Davenport being fellow club members. She also couldn't use LeMay's association with Scarborough to her advantage if their relationship appeared legitimate on the surface. At present, she didn't have the time to look below the surface and discover the size of the iceberg.

Chapter 39

Cassandra returned to the district attorney's office and nodded to colleagues as she passed them. She didn't know whether they were aware of the morning's hearing and didn't care. She kept moving toward Philip LeMay's corner office and approached Constance Segal, his executive assistant, a pale, stocky, middle-aged woman with dyed-red hair. Cassandra didn't understand how Segal could be in a good mood all the time. Nothing seemed to bother her, and as far as Cassandra could tell, she was not a drug user.

"Good morning, Connie. I need to speak with Mr. LeMay about this morning's hearing. Could you check to see if he's available?"

"Of course! One moment, please." Segal bounced out of her chair, entered LeMay's office, and returned seconds later.

"He can see you now."

"Thanks," Cassandra said with a fake smile.

"Have a great day."

Cassandra entered LeMay's spacious corner office, which had room for his leather chair, a desk, two guest chairs, a couch, a small table, and four more chairs, all of which were better quality than typical government furniture.

LeMay sat at his desk while fluorescent lighting cast down upon his bald head and stocky frame. He wore reading glasses and seemed to be reviewing paperwork.

With trepidation, Cassandra announced her presence. "Good morning, Mr. LeMay."

"Morning. Please have a seat," he said coldly. He removed his glasses and set them on his desk. "It's the Parkhurst case, correct?"

"That's right," Cassandra said as she sat. She noticed LeMay wore an expensive gold watch, possibly a Rolex or a Cartier, either of which was cost-prohibitive for a public servant.

"No need to give me the details because I sent Armstead to observe. You must've not seen him in the back row. The little bastard told me you didn't argue forcefully enough, but that's his jaded opinion. I'm aware of the bad blood between the two of you, and I can't agree with him. Even if you pressed your arguments more, it wouldn't have made a difference."

"Thanks." In her mind, she swore at Armstead.

"He also told me something rather disturbing. Bo Davenport accused you of strong-arming and threatening the life of a bartender."

Cassandra nervously laughed and gave a dismissive wave. "Oh, come on. You know that blowhard. He makes one wild accusation after another, and Judge Ogden didn't buy it."

"Uh-huh," LeMay said with a serious look. "I hope that's all it is, just Bo being Bo. You've pushed the envelope a time or two, but never that far."

"Right, of course." She felt guilty for telling another lie and feared during a preliminary hearing, Davenport could put Robertson on the stand and make a big stink for the media. Even if LeMay did not believe Robertson, he would get upset with her for tarnishing his office in the eyes of potential jurors and, even worse, in the eyes of potential voters.

"Getting back to the reason I'm here," Cassandra said. "Here's the bottom line… Ogden really screwed up by releasing Parkhurst on bail. You know and I know he's a serial killer, which means he needs to remain in custody. So, I want to appeal the bail order."

LeMay flashed a sardonic smile and leaned back in his chair. "You realize this office rarely questions bail determinations, since we have to appear before the same judges time and time again."

"I'm aware of the policy, but this is an extraordinary case."

LeMay stared at her. "It is, but we have to examine the matter from the perspective of Ogden and the appellate court. We believe Ryan Parkhurst is a serial killer. However, as of this morning, we don't have the evidence to support our opinion. Ogden based his decision on the evidence at hand, which only concerned assault and false imprisonment. Since a trial court judge has wide discretion over bail, the appellate court won't second-guess him, given what we presently have."

Cassandra opened her mouth, but before she could speak, LeMay held up his right hand.

"You got lucky Bo Davenport suggested a high bail with electronic monitoring," he said. "Without it, Ogden probably would've freed Parkhurst on a much lower amount."

"Sure, and it doesn't matter. We really need to keep him in custody until we get the DNA results."

LeMay glanced at the ceiling and clenched his jaw. "I'm not some damn fool who fell off the turnip truck. I get it, and based upon *the evidence*, we don't have a good basis for an appeal. End of discussion, period. Anything else?"

"Yes, sir. This case will require considerable manpower. I'm requesting you appoint another ADA as second chair."

"You're putting the cart before the horse. If and when we have enough evidence to charge Parkhurst with murder, I'll assign another prosecutor. I'll even let you pick your partner. You'll get all the resources you'll need, but as of right now, we don't have a murder case."

"I understand," Cassandra said through clenched teeth. She needed another prosecutor to counter Parkhurst's legal team, which she anticipated would grow. On the other hand, there was no point arguing because she knew she could not change LeMay's mind.

"Good." LeMay's mood brightened. "As long as you're here, let's go over possible murder charges. If there's a DNA match between Parkhurst and the material found under Amy Nguyen's fingernails, you'll have the green light for murder in the first degree and the death penalty. All evidence for the other murders is circumstantial, correct?"

"Correct."

"What about attempting to gather something more?"

Cassandra thought he had lost his mind. "How are we supposed to do that?"

LeMay frowned and exhaled through his nose. "Do I have to spell it out for you? Prior to the bail hearing,

Parkhurst had to report his permanent address. Well, did he?"

"He listed an apartment in Manhattan."

"There you go," he said as he held up his right hand. "Ask NYPD to execute a search warrant on that location. They can look for evidence of travel to New Orleans shortly before the murders, phony IDs, and anything else relevant. Who knows? He might've brought home the victims' clothing as souvenirs."

"But what if the address turns out to be bogus?"

"Seriously?" LeMay shook his head. "If the address is phony, file a motion with Judge Ogden. Providing a phony address should be grounds to revoke bail, and you might get what you want."

"Oh, I see your point. Thank you." She kicked herself for not having the idea first.

"You're welcome. Why don't you move back into your old office? Please close the door on the way out and tell my assistant I'm not to be disturbed."

Chapter 40

Two mornings later, Detective Scott Langford called from New York. "We executed the search warrant on Parkhurst's apartment shortly after 6 a.m. and found nothing."

"No evidence connecting him to a crime?" Cassandra asked.

"No, absolutely nothing. The apartment was empty, no furniture, no phone, no dishes, nothing. It was obvious the place had been thoroughly cleaned, not a speck of dust. Also, someone had poured bleach down the bathroom sink and down the shower drain."

"You're kidding?"

"I wish I were. We spoke to the neighbors before they headed to work. A couple of them saw movers hauling away furniture on Sunday morning, and someone spotted a moving van in the parking garage."

Cassandra's frustration level rose. "I'm sure they weren't real movers. It was probably The Saint's men."

"Probably."

Despite her disappointment, her mind raced and focused on the next step. "Detective Langford, I've already chewed up a lot of your time, and I'm asking for a little more. Could you draft a declaration detailing what happened?"

"Give me an hour, and I'll send it by email attachment."

Cassandra didn't need to give a further explanation to Langford, a well-seasoned detective. She would draft a motion for bail revocation, and his statement would be the supporting proof. In the motion, she would argue Parkhurst's associates tried to obstruct justice by hiding evidence. Parkhurst could do the same or worse if allowed to remain out of custody pending trial. She expected defense counsel would claim Parkhurst's friends cleaned out the apartment as he faced an extended stay at a home in New Orleans. However, based upon her past experiences, she reasoned the judge would see through such an argument, despite his association with Bo Davenport, as he loathed dirty tricks. He would revoke bail, no doubt about it.

Since it had been a couple of years since Cassandra had drafted a motion to revoke bail, she conducted legal research on her computer in her regular office. She was taking notes when she heard a knock on her office's doorframe. She looked up and had never seen Mike with such a serious expression, as if his levity and joy of life had been snatched away from him.

"Don't kill the messenger," he said with his hands raised.

She tossed down her pen, anticipating more bad news. "Now what?"

"Parkhurst disappeared."

"What! How the hell did that happen?"

Mike shook his head and exhaled in apparent exasperation. "Yeah, I know, I know. I was shocked too. Parkhurst had the electronic monitor on his ankle, and Scarborough's house has plenty of security cameras. A live feed was sent directly to us. The cameras weren't pointed at the house, but they should've seen someone leaving the property."

Cassandra groaned. "I don't like the sound of 'should've.'"

"Yeah. Parkhurst cut off the ankle monitor, and it triggered an alert. Before anyone could get to the house, he jumped over a wall and got into a black sedan. A couple of kids saw it happen."

"Did they get the license plate number?"

"No. We looked at where Parkhurst climbed over, and it's in a blind spot between two cameras. I'm sure it's not a coincidence. Don't worry. We'll get him back."

Mike's assurances had no effect on her because if The Saint were behind his nephew's escape, his vast resources would allow him to keep Parkhurst well hidden. He could also supply Parkhurst with yet another identity. She doubted he would ever return to New Orleans, even though he could not control his thirst for brutality and murder. Somewhere, sometime in the future, the police in another city would discover a battered and brutalized body. Then another. Then another.

By the day's end, Judge Ogden had issued a warrant for Parkhurst's arrest. Many law enforcement agencies began searching for him, including the New Orleans Police Department, NYPD, the FBI, and the US Marshals. At the FBI's request, Interpol issued a Red Notice, alerting the world as to Parkhurst's fugitive status.

* * *

Three days after Parkhurst's escape, Cassandra met Mike and Tyler in the trailer behind police headquarters.

"Can you two keep this meeting really quiet?"

"Sure," Mike said while Tyler nodded.

"As you know, there's been rumblings about the district attorney being corrupt for some time, and I think I've seen some evidence of it. He always wears expensive clothes and a gold watch, which are a little too much for someone on a public servant's salary. There are also his ties to Scarborough. LeMay told Donnie that an aunt died and left him three houses, but I'm not buying it. So, would you be willing to investigate his financial situation?"

Mike chuckled. "We nab Parkhurst again, *and* we take down a sitting DA before I retire. Hell yes, I'm in."

Cassandra focused on Tyler. "What about you?"

He shrugged. "Guess so. Since there's not much to do for the Parkhurst case, Mike and I'll probably be pulled back to vice. We can investigate LeMay on the side."

"Good. Please keep me in the loop, and don't tell Donnie anything. I trust him, but he frequently talks to LeMay, and he might say something or act differently somehow and arouse suspicion. Don't report anything to your chain of command, and don't put anything down on paper, at least not right away. If you did either one, word of your investigation could reach the chief of police, who's friends with LeMay. If you find anything, contact the FBI."

"We might get in trouble for that," Mike said.

"Do you care?"

He smirked. "Come to think of it... no, not really. What are they going to do to me, make me retire? Tyler?"

"I doubt we'll get into trouble. If the DA's corrupt, the top brass would look really bad if they tried to shut down the investigation."

* * *

For several days following Ryan Parkhurst's disappearance, law enforcement made extraordinary efforts to locate him to no avail, as if he had vanished into thin air. No one could determine whether Conor McCarthy had been behind his disappearance or whether he had engineered it on his own.

Chapter 41

Three weeks after Ryan Parkhurst disappeared, the crime lab informed Cassandra that Parkhurst's DNA matched the DNA from the skin and blood cells found underneath Amy Nguyen's fingernails. The chances the cells belonged to someone else were one in one billion. Cassandra could now charge Parkhurst with murder, which wouldn't matter as long as he remained a fugitive, and there were still no leads regarding his location.

Later the same morning, her cell phone rang.

"This is Lieutenant Roy Abernathy with the Jefferson Parish Sheriff's Office," he barked. "Is this Morgan?"

"Yes, it is."

"I'm at the storage facility off Highway 90 in Avondale. You need to get your sorry ass down here *right now!*"

The man rotten attitude irked Cassandra, and her temper flared. "What'd you just say?"

"You heard me."

"Does this have anything to do with Ryan Parkhurst?"

"Wow, you must be a genius! Why else would I call you?"

Cassandra then heard a click.

"What a jackass," she said to no one. She considered calling his sheriff to complain, but it could wait. She first wanted to see what awaited her in Avondale.

Once Cassandra stepped outside, a massive wave of heat and humidity overwhelmed her, and she began to sweat during the short walk to her Mustang Fastback. She climbed into her vehicle and grabbed her sunglasses. Her Mustang then roared to life.

* * *

Forty minutes later, Cassandra arrived at the storage facility and found the nearest parking spot. As she left her car, she was again enveloped in the unrelenting heat. The area felt like a steaming jungle without the amazing surroundings. Cassandra glanced above and noticed storm clouds forming, which provided little relief during the suffocating Louisiana summers. She grabbed a water bottle and cursed to herself because she had forgotten to bring an umbrella.

Cassandra walked past six or seven police vehicles and towards the storage units. In the distance, several individuals gathered, including a six-foot-five Caucasian with a lantern jaw, brown cowboy hat, black T-shirt, and brown cowboy boots. To the left of him, the roll-up door to a smaller storage unit was open. When Cassandra was about twenty feet away, the man spotted her. He towered above her and glowered down at her as she approached.

"Are you Morgan?"

"Yes, I am." Cassandra came closer. "Are you Lieutenant Abernathy?"

"Where the hell have you been?"

"Back off!"

"What?" he said as his eyes bugged out.

Cassandra imagined no one had ever challenged him like that. She moved to within four feet of him and stared into his eyes. "Back. Off. Ever hear of traffic? I had to deal with two accidents."

"I don't like your mouth!"

"Too bad. Now, do you want to bitch and yell at each other while the sun beats down on us or what?" She looked to the left and then walked toward the storage unit. Inside, the crime scene photographer, a diminutive African American, took pictures.

"Wait a minute," Abernathy said. "Don't go in there yet. Let him finish."

She turned to face him. "Why am I here?"

"Brett Duncan, the dumbass manager, said a guy named Shawn Murphy rented this storage unit for several years. He always paid an entire year's rent up front and in cash. Guess who he looks like?"

Cassandra didn't need to give an answer.

"When Parkhurst's face appeared on the news, the dumbass thought he looked familiar, but he was too stupid to make the connection. After Parkhurst didn't pay his last bill, Duncan checked out the unit. He probably wanted to see if there was anything worth stealing, and–"

Abernathy looked over Cassandra's shoulder. "You're done?"

She glanced to her right and saw the short and slender man give a thumbs-up. He was also drenched in sweat.

"You'll need to take more photos after we've dusted for prints," Abernathy told him. "The guy should've been here by now. If his sorry butt isn't here in five minutes, I'm going to fire his ass."

The photographer gave a brief wave and walked away.

Abernathy then redirected his attention to Cassandra. "Morgan, go ahead, but don't touch anything."

I know that. I'm not an idiot, she said to herself.

Once Cassandra stepped inside, she took off her sunglasses and let her eyes adjust to the dimmer light, which a bare bulb provided. Inside the storage unit, the heat and humidity were the worst she had ever experienced, as if an invisible entity was using the air to squeeze every bit of moisture out of her body until she expired from dehydration.

A 55-gallon oil drum stood in the back of the storage unit. Along the right wall was a workbench with two drawers and two shelves above it. A rope, two sets of handcuffs, a roll of duct tape, and a red scarf sat on top of the bench.

Cassandra became fixated on the scarf because it was probably the one that was used to strangle Jane Doe 1. She had to restrain herself from grabbing and examining it for missing fibers, the ones that were imbedded in Jane Doe's neck, so as not to contaminate a critical piece of evidence.

Cassandra broke her singular focus to examine the rest of the workbench before the surrounding conditions overcame her. Bras and panties had been placed on the two shelves: seven sets on the top shelf and six on the bottom. Cassandra concluded the underwear belonged to the serial killer's female victims, plus one extra set. She turned toward the storage unit's door, and Abernathy was standing a couple of feet past it.

"We have twelve female victims and thirteen sets of underwear," she said. "One more corpse must still be out there somewhere."

"Guess again. The last one is in there," he said as he pointed to the oil drum. "She was sealed inside. Duncan opened the lid before he called 911. If you want to take a look, I'll hand you a pair of gloves."

"No thanks. How long has she been in there?"

"Don't know. Since she was sealed up, decomposition didn't naturally occur. She mummified instead."

"Any idea as to her manner of death?"

Abernathy scoffed. "Do I look like I'm psychic? You'll need to wait for the autopsy."

"I take it she's nude, and you have no clue who she is."

"You're half right. Take my pen. Stick the point behind the front edge of the left drawer and slide it open."

Cassandra guzzled her entire water bottle and then went back inside. She placed the tip under the drawer and eased it forward. She then observed a Kentucky driver's license for Kathy Munson.

Cassandra surmised Munson was not the last victim. She had been Parkhurst's first triumph, at least in his mind. He had kept the corpse and the driver's license to better preserve the memory of his first kill, but had determined stuffing bodies in drums and storing them was too inconvenient. Killing a groundskeeper and dumping Jane Doe 1's body in a family mausoleum also created too much work. Thus, he turned to tossing away his victims throughout the parishes surrounding New Orleans.

Cassandra walked out of the storage unit and stood in front of Lieutenant Abernathy. "We'll need to speak with Kathy Munson's relatives and subpoena her phone and credit card records to figure out when she disappeared."

He scoffed again. "That's your problem, not mine. We'll process the scene and the body, and you can deal with the rest. I'm sick and tired of your serial killer murdering whores and dumping them in my jurisdiction."

"So am I, and they were young women with their whole lives in front of them." Cassandra pointed her right index finger at him. "You need to remember that." She took two steps toward the storage facility entrance and stopped. She spun around, looked up, and glared into his eyes. "And by the way, if we ever meet again, can the attitude, or I'll have your balls for lunch. Do I make myself perfectly clear?"

Abernathy's face turned red. "What the hell did you just say?!"

Cassandra ignored him. She turned around and donned her sunglasses as she walked away.

Chapter 42

During the summer months in southern Louisiana, the skies could be clear and blue and then, one hour later, a thunderstorm. Rain could drench everything in seconds and pound so loudly on a roof that a tourist would fear its collapse.

As Cassandra drove back to the office, a storm hit her with full force. Rain slammed into her car in torrents, rendering the windshield wipers almost useless. Even though the safer course of action would have been to pull to the side of the road and wait for the rain to relent, Cassandra refused to yield.

She contemplated her next move. She could now charge Parkhurst with several murders but still needed more evidence. Despite the conditions inside the storage unit, perhaps the Jefferson Parish crime lab would find Parkhurst's fingerprints or the victims' DNA on the underwear.

Cassandra then addressed the elephant in the room: Parkhurst was still missing. Until someone apprehended him, everything else was irrelevant. She realized no one had tried contacting Conor McCarthy, aka The Saint, to convince him to hand over his nephew. Even if McCarthy was not responsible for his escape, she was certain he knew where Parkhurst was hiding.

Cassandra considered her career. Once the criminal proceedings resumed, Parkhurst's defense team would again accuse her of ordering Elroy Dupree to attack the bartender at Rousseau's. If they managed to convince Judge Ogden, he would become upset, but he wouldn't throw out the case. No one on the bench would give that big of a break to a serial killer. The district attorney could fire her, however, and the state bar could revoke her law license. After balancing the risks and rewards, she decided the consequences to herself were far less important than bringing Parkhurst to justice.

Cassandra couldn't bark at her boss like she did to Abernathy. LeMay wouldn't listen if she did, and he'd probably suspend her. She would instead approach him with a lighter touch, yet she was uncertain it would work because she had little practice with one. She hoped LeMay would conclude it was time for a Hail Mary pass and would allow her to confront McCarthy.

* * *

When Cassandra arrived at the district attorney's office, she found the always cheerful Constance Segal was not around. So, she let herself into LeMay's office, where he was at his desk and on the phone, ending a call. He glared at her with a frown as he hung up the phone.

"Can I sit down?" she asked.

LeMay motioned for her to do so. "You're a sight. What have you been doing, playing inside a sauna while fully clothed?"

"Close. I was at a storage facility in Avondale, where Parkhurst kept memorabilia of his victims."

LeMay's eyes widened. "Run that by me again?"

"Parkhurst rented a storage unit under an alias, where he kept the bras and panties of his victims. He also kept a corpse in an oil drum."

LeMay was speechless.

"The authorities in Jefferson Parish are processing the scene. I doubt we'll find evidence of Parkhurst or the victims' DNA on the underwear, but maybe we'll get lucky."

"Uh… right," LeMay said. "What a sick bastard! Wait for the processing of the recently found evidence and then we'll consider charging options. Since we still can't tie most of the murders to this parish, the attorney general will probably assert jurisdiction, and I'm sure I can convince him to appoint you as the lead prosecutor. The AG will probably assign one of his people as second chair. Would you be fine with that?"

"Absolutely," Cassandra said enthusiastically.

"Now, we really need to locate Parkhurst again."

She nodded. "Right, and I have an idea. I bet his uncle knows where he is. With your permission, I'd like to fly to New York and speak with McCarthy in person. Perhaps I can convince him to disclose his nephew's whereabouts."

LeMay gave another one of his sardonic smiles. "Do you really think he'll give up his own kin?"

"It's worth a shot. When McCarthy was present in court, Parkhurst faced relatively minor charges compared to several murders. If we lay out the details of his crimes, maybe he'll help us out of moral outrage."

LeMay shook his head. "You've been out in the sun too long. McCarthy made a living as a contract killer, which means murder's nothing to him."

"But there's a reason he's nicknamed The Saint. It's his moral code, which probably includes respecting all women. Torturing and murdering them is the complete opposite."

"He won't believe you because it'd cut too much against the grain. No matter what you tell him, he'll never accept that his beloved nephew is a complete psycho. That means it's not a good idea to go half-cocked to New York. We can alert the law enforcement community that Parkhurst is indeed a serial killer, and he'll become a higher priority. Shoot, I wouldn't be surprised if he made the FBI's Ten Most Wanted list. One day, he'll be apprehended again. There's no way he can hide forever."

"But we should try every avenue to find him, including talking to his uncle."

LeMay's facial muscles became tense. "There you go again, losing perspective." He leaned back in his chair. "You need to take some time off."

Cassandra blinked twice. "Is that an order?"

LeMay clenched his jaw. "It was only a suggestion. However, if you want it that way... fine, it's an order. You're a spoiled child who can't take no for an answer, and so I'm giving you a time-out. Starting tomorrow, consider yourself on vacation for the next two weeks. Just be glad it's with pay and not without." His facial muscles relaxed. "Maybe this job is getting to me, and I need a few days off too. I know you need downtime to clear your head. Go visit your parents or take a road trip."

"Okay." Cassandra knew if anything else came out of her mouth, LeMay would suspend her without pay or fire her. "Can I leave now?"

LeMay gave a quick wave of his right hand. "See you in two weeks. If Parkhurst is captured before then, you can return earlier."

She was halfway to the door and then turned around. "I forgot to tell you something. You might get a call from the Jefferson Parish Sheriff. Lieutenant Abernathy was being a royal pain to me, and I chewed him out."

"Abernathy? Really big guy, wears a brown cowboy hat?"

"That's him."

LeMay chuckled. "Yeah, he's a pain in the ass, and I'm sure he deserved it. Please close the door on your way out."

Cassandra returned to her office on the other side of the building. She turned on her portable stereo and inserted a CD of Mozart's chamber music. LeMay's decision perplexed her.

Why not have a simple conversation with McCarthy? she thought. What would be the worst thing that could happen? He won't kill me. If he refuses to cooperate, the only "harm" would be the cost of my air travel, a hotel room, and other minor expenses. Big deal.

Cassandra continued to fume, and the music didn't have a calming effect. After a few minutes, she turned it off. "This isn't right. This isn't right," she said to no one. She bolted out of her office and headed for the empty trailer behind police headquarters. Using her cell phone, she placed a call to Detective Scott Langford in New York City.

"Hello, this is Cassandra. There's been a break in the case."

"Oh yeah? You nabbed Parkhurst again?"

"Not yet, but we now have a lot more evidence against him. I'll brief you in person later."

"You're coming here?"

"Uh-huh. I'm flying out tomorrow. I want to show The Saint photos of his nephew's handiwork and explain why we know he did it. Does he care about women being tortured and murdered?"

"Ah… I'd never given it any thought. I guess it's worth a try, and he might give up Parkhurst's location, if he knows it."

"Where can we reach McCarthy?" Cassandra asked.

"He owns an Irish social club and eats lunch there every Thursday. When you fly in tomorrow, I'll pick you up at the airport. Just let me know if it's JFK or LaGuardia."

"Are you sure?"

"Of course," Langford said. "If you arrive early enough, you can have dinner with my wife and me and then bring me up to speed."

"Sounds great. See you tomorrow."

Chapter 43

Brooklyn, New York

Two days later, Detective Langford drove Cassandra through busy streets toward the Bay Ridge neighborhood. For the fifth time in quick succession, she considered how to approach Conor McCarthy. He would not be warm or charming, and thus, she reasoned any attempt to engage him on a personal level would be a wasted effort and could offend him. Older men with stern personalities, including judges, did not bother or intimidate her, and career criminals never fazed her. However, The Saint was another matter, as he seemed beyond the law's reach, a legendary hit man who imposed his will through his presence and reputation. She was uncertain she could maintain her composure in front of him.

Cassandra didn't want to further obsess over a potential meeting with McCarthy. So, she turned her attention to Langford, who focused on the traffic in front of him. She finally realized why he had looked so familiar. With his distinguished nose and mustache, he reminded her of a great uncle who had passed away about ten years previously.

"Hey, thanks again for letting me stay in your guest bedroom," Cassandra said. "It'll cut down on my expenses."

"You're welcome," he said awkwardly. "Aren't you getting reimbursed for the trip?"

"Actually… I asked the DA for permission to travel, and he said no."

Langford groaned. "I didn't need to hear that."

"Sorry. Are you going to get in trouble?"

"Me? Of course not, but I'll have to report it to my lieutenant. We won't inform your boss, but if he calls and asks about you, we can't lie to him." Seconds later, he said, "And we're here."

Langford pulled to the curb alongside a busy four-lane road, two in each direction. Businesses filled the first floors lining the street, while the second and third floors apparently contained apartments. Cassandra left the vehicle with her satchel and stood in front of a plain white building with no windows and no sign. A small Irish flag next to the front door gave the only hint of what was inside.

Cassandra bent over to speak to Langford through the open passenger side door. "This is it?"

"Yes," he said. "It's a private club, members only. In his retirement years, McCarthy has become a creature of habit, and he should've just finished his lunch by now. You need to go alone so that he might be more receptive. He's not too fond of the NYPD, and he certainly knows who I am. I'll be waiting for you in the restaurant across the street." He pointed to a building with a blue awning above the first floor. "Just remember, you'll be in his place, and you must play by his rules. Be respectful at all times."

"I'll do my best. Will anyone be listening in?"

Langford smiled. "Are you asking if the place is bugged? No, it's not. McCarthy forbids talking business in his social club, which means there's no justification for a wiretap. Good luck."

"Thanks."

Cassandra closed the passenger door and stepped toward the building's entrance. She opened the front door and then another padded with green leather. As she walked in, she was transported to another place and time. The city noise disappeared, and an unfamiliar instrumental tune filled the air with a melody similar to songs by Frank Sinatra and Tony Bennett. She observed green leather booths and square tables with green, high-back leather chairs, enough seating for about seventy people. White linen covered all the tables. She also noticed the absence of a bar, which reflected part of The Saint's moral code: no alcohol consumption. Antique fixtures attached to the vaulted ceiling provided adequate lighting.

Cassandra spotted McCarthy, in a dress shirt and yellow-tinted glasses, seated in a back booth along with two other elderly men. Finished plates of food and water glasses filled their table. Tommy Hanson and Lazlo Janka sat at a table, but they didn't notice her.

A tall, older man in a black suit and tie was positioned behind the maître d' stand by the inner door. He gave a thin and disingenuous smile.

"May I help you, madam?"

"Yes, please. I'm Cassandra Morgan, and I'm with the district attorney's office in New Orleans." She removed a business card from her satchel and handed it to him. "I'm requesting the opportunity to speak with Mr. McCarthy for a few minutes."

"One moment, please." He turned and tapped on a metal portion of the maître d' stand. He then raised his right hand.

Hanson peered in their direction. Upon seeing Cassandra, he motioned to Janka, and they marched to The Saint's booth. McCarthy flicked two fingers, which prompted his guests to excuse themselves and head down a hallway to the right. Meanwhile, the maître d' stood next to Cassandra and held out his right arm at a low angle, indicating she should proceed no further.

Hanson leaned forward and whispered to McCarthy, who remained icy calm. The Saint nodded once, and Hanson whispered again. McCarthy flicked two fingers, which resulted in Janka returning to his seat, and Hanson buttoning his jacket and striding toward Cassandra.

He stopped within four feet of her. "Mr. McCarthy will see you at his residence tomorrow morning at 9:30. The meeting will last no more than ten minutes. Don't be late and come alone."

"Uh, thank you," she said awkwardly. "Where does Mr. McCarthy live?"

Hanson scoffed. "Look at a map." He then returned to his table.

The maître d' gave another thin smile and opened the inner front door. "This way, please."

Cassandra was uncertain how to react. She would have her meeting but on McCarthy's turf, which would create a more intimidating atmosphere. She forced a smile to the maître d' and departed. Once on the sidewalk, she noticed the restaurant with the blue awning and walked to the nearest intersection, which she briskly crossed. Upon entering the restaurant, she noted the interior's worn blue booths and heard bacon crackling in the kitchen. Langford sat alone in a small booth, nursing a cup of coffee.

"That was quick," he said as Cassandra slid into the opposite side.

"Yeah. McCarthy wouldn't speak to me right now. I have a meeting with him tomorrow morning at his house. Any idea where it is?"

"Uh-huh. He lives in Todt Hill on Staten Island. I'll take you there."

"One of his men told me to come alone."

"I'm sure he did."

Chapter 44

The next morning, Cassandra stood in front of Conor McCarthy's residence with her satchel in hand. Through an eight-foot-tall wrought-iron gate, she saw a three-story Mediterranean villa covered in natural stone and a three-tier castle fountain sitting in the middle of a small, sculptured garden. A circular driveway encompassed the garden from one gate to another further up the street. The driveway made a slight right toward a two-car garage, which appeared tiny compared to the rest of the residence.

Cassandra pressed the buzzer next to the gate and noticed a security camera above it.

"Yes," a rough voice said over the intercom.

"Good morning. I'm Cassandra Morgan, and I have–"

The intercom cut off, and a moment later, she heard a buzz. The gate slowly swung open in the home's direction. With trepidation, she moved toward a massive double door comprising of more wrought iron and frosted glass. Just as she reached it, Lazlo Janka, the thug with a dark ponytail, opened the right-side door.

"Come inside," he said with a sneer.

Cassandra nearly froze when she noticed a bulge on the left side of Janka's jacket, which meant he was carrying a pistol. Nevertheless, she entered the massive foyer with a ceiling rising above the second story. An ornate chandelier hung from above, and light-gray marble covered the floor. Sweeping staircases containing the same marble and wrought-iron railings wrapped around both ends of the foyer. While the room's opulence impressed her, fear remained more prominent in her mind.

Cassandra followed Janka to the foyer's other side, where he stopped and ordered, "Wait here." He took his place four feet to her right and held his hands behind his back. She scanned her surroundings to distract herself from Janka's imposing presence. To her left, there was a dining room with an extra-long table and sixteen chairs with elaborate carvings. The hallway before her led to a glass back door, through which she saw part of another garden.

Tommy Hanson, the walking tank, came out from the hallway to the right. Cassandra noticed a similar bulge of a firearm underneath his jacket's left side, which reinforced her fears.

"He's ready," he said to Janka.

Hanson led her down the hallway with Janka right behind. The doors to other rooms were closed, and family photographs hung on the walls.

When they reached the end, Hanson opened the door to a private study, where McCarthy sat silent and attentive in a brown leather chair. He wore a three-piece suit and his usual glasses. His hands were clasped and rested on an oversized antique desk. Two wooden, antique chairs were in front of it. A built-in oak bookshelf lined the left wall. Behind its glass were a large wedding photo in an elegant silver frame, a metal model of the Brooklyn Bridge, many old books, and a bronze sculpture of a lion. A ticking antique clock was hanging on the wall behind him.

Hanson stood between McCarthy and the bookcase with his hands apparently clasped behind his back. Janka remained at the door, standing in the same position, which made Cassandra feel trapped.

"Please sit down," Hanson commanded.

She complied and placed her satchel on the hardwood floor. She forced a smile. "Thank you for seeing me," she said nervously.

Tick-tock.

McCarthy remained silent and motionless.

Here goes nothing, she said to herself. "Mr. McCarthy, this is why I came to see you… A serial killer has claimed the lives of fourteen people, one man and thirteen women. The women lived elsewhere and– and came to New Orleans on the weekends to work as prostitutes. They were lured to various vacation homes, where they were tied down, beaten, burned, and strangled to death. I– I'm sorry to inform you that it was your nephew who committed these horrific acts."

Cassandra swallowed and waited for someone else to make a comment. The only sound she heard was the antique clock's ticking. Except for an occasional blink, The Saint did not move a muscle. She did not even detect visible signs of breathing.

Tick-tock, tick-tock.

Cassandra took a deep breath and continued. "Under multiple aliases, Ryan Parkhurst rented, uh, vacation homes at the same time as the murders. DNA underneath the fingernails of one murder victim is a match to his DNA."

She again waited for any reaction from McCarthy.

Tick-tock, tick-tock.

"Your nephew rented a storage unit in Avondale where… where he kept one victim in an oil drum and the underwear of all his female victims."

Tick-tock.

"The police have made great efforts to locate him since he fled and went into hiding. I'm… now respectfully asking for your assistance in locating him."

McCarthy remained stone-faced and silent.

Tick-tock, tick-tock, TICK-TOCK, TICK-TOCK.

"I brought copies of some photos and reports for your review."

Cassandra grabbed her satchel and retrieved a two-inch-thick manila folder. She then removed six 8½ x 11 photos from the folder, each one showing the body of another victim. She lined them in a row on the desk facing The Saint.

"If— if you please give me one moment, I'll explain each photo and the evidence in detail."

As she removed more photos, McCarthy's head turned toward Hanson. She noticed and froze, uncertain what she should do. The Saint's head returned to its original position. He placed his hands on the desk for support and rose to a standing position. Hanson took a step back to allow him to pass, and Janka slid behind Cassandra's chair. The Saint then shuffled out of the study and down the hallway.

"We're done," Hanson said.

Cassandra stared at him in disbelief.

"No way Ryan is a serial killer," he said more forcefully. "We're done. Get up!"

Cassandra jumped in shock and then grabbed her satchel. She put the strap over her shoulder and stood. Without a word, Janka escorted her through the hallway and out the front door. The entire time, she heard Hanson's footsteps behind her. Once outside, the front gate swung open. Upon reaching the property's edge, she realized she had left the manila folder and its contents in the study. She turned around.

"Excuse me, uh, I left—"

Hanson whipped his right hand across his body and grabbed the pistol in his shoulder holster, which caused her to shudder in terror.

"Move," he commanded.

Cassandra couldn't speak. She turned toward the gate and was afraid Hanson would shoot her in the back. She wanted to run but could barely put one foot in front of the other. After reaching the sidewalk, she turned around and watched the gate close while Hanson and Janka marched back inside. A wave of depression and hopelessness replaced her fear as her last chance to bring Parkhurst to justice vanished.

Chapter 45

Mid-May 2019
North Hollywood, California

Rebecca returned to her apartment exhausted after a twelve-hour day at the law firm. She tossed off her shoes and fell onto her couch. She was hungry but too tired to cook. She closed her eyes and was starting to doze off when her cell phone rang.

"Hello, Rebecca," said a familiar hoarse voice.

"Hi… Wait a minute. How did you get my cell number? And this isn't a collect call. I hope you're not using a contraband phone. I don't want you to be written up right before your parole hearing."

Nick chuckled. "Thanks for your concern, and the phone call's sort of legit. Wally Sims, one of the guards, is letting me use his cell, and he tracked down your number. I'm in the law library, and no one else is around. So, we can talk freely."

"Isn't the guard breaking the rules?"

"Let's say bending them because he owed me a favor. We had a real nutcase in our cell block who was constantly talking about stabbing Sims. Since he's one of the better guards, he didn't deserve it. It was obvious this nut had a serious mental health issue, and I alerted a psychiatrist. After an evaluation, he was transferred to Vacaville, where they can better treat him."

Despite all she had heard, the potential for violence in prison still amazed her. "Good thing you took care of it…

Hey, we should mention it during your parole hearing. You just did another good deed."

Nick scoffed. "No way. Others would see me as a snitch. If word gets out while I'm still here, which it will, I'll have a target on my back."

"But you didn't just help the guard. You helped the other inmate get the care he needs."

"Doesn't matter. A rat is still a rat."

Rebecca sighed. "Okay, we won't mention it."

"Thanks. Did you know the board postponed my hearing from this Thursday to the same time Thursday next week?"

"What! Are you sure?"

"Absolutely. Maybe they mailed your letter to the wrong address. I got mine."

"Did they tell you why it was postponed?"

"Of course not. That would be too much of a burden for the precious board. Can you still make it?"

"I think so. I'll double-check tomorrow morning. I'm sorry you couldn't finish your story during my last visit. I really needed to get back to the firm for a meeting."

"Did you make it?"

"Barely." She should have gone to bed, but curiosity got the better of her. "Do you have the time to tell the rest?"

Nick chuckled. "All I've got is time."

Chapter 46

Early September 1999
New Orleans, Louisiana

Cassandra sat on her couch in her one-bedroom apartment and held a shot glass filled with Southern Comfort, the third of the afternoon. Her other hand gripped a television remote control, which she used to surf the channels, while she dwelled on what had transpired and what could have been.

If her trip had been successful, LeMay would have discovered she had flown to New York without permission. He would have reprimanded her, but could not fire the hero responsible for returning Parkhurst to custody. Otherwise, he would have suffered too much political blowback.

However, Cassandra had been unsuccessful, and if LeMay learned of her trip, he would fire her for insubordination. She doubted another government agency or a private law firm would hire someone who could not follow the rules. She had no desire to start a solo practice, though, as too much time would pass before enough money came her way. In the meantime, she wouldn't have enough savings to cover all her bills, including the loan payments for her '69 Mustang.

Cassandra considered calling her ex-boyfriend to reconcile, even though she knew it wouldn't matter. He had been polite yet emphatic when he ended their relationship. Looking back, she now understood he had tolerated too many missed phone calls and too many plans pushed aside for her career. She had no close friends to call and didn't want to discuss her present situation with her parents. So, she sat alone with a shot glass.

Her cell phone rang, and despite her apathy, she answered the call.

"Hey, this is Tyler."

"Yeah, okay."

"Where are you? Someone said you're on vacation. Why didn't you tell us about it?"

Cassandra groaned. "It's not a vacation. LeMay forced me to take two weeks off. Long story. What's up?"

"Sorry about that. Mike and I discovered a bank account in the name of LeMay's deceased mother. Social Security checks are still being deposited into it, and someone routinely makes withdrawals. Three guesses who's doing it."

Despite the alcohol in her system, her mind cleared. "Interesting. The Feds can prosecute him for Social Security fraud, which is probably a felony, and an indictment alone might force him to resign. Anything else?"

"One of LeMay's bank accounts had many suspicious deposits, and we're digging into them."

"Good. He's probably been in the back pocket of a few crooks."

"Probably," Tyler said. "The FBI's now on board, and they're looking into The Saint's connections to New Orleans. As Langford told us, McCarthy owns a company that provides security for the riverboat casinos. Over the past five years, three guards have been arrested, and each time, LeMay intervened and ordered the charges to be dropped."

"Sounds promising."

"Yeah," Tyler said. "When are you going back to work?"

"Soon, assuming LeMay hasn't figured out a way to fire me."

Chapter 47

On Saturday morning, Cassandra was asleep when her landline rang. The noise startled her, and she noticed it was dark outside. After the second ring, she reached for the phone and knocked over the now mostly empty Southern Comfort bottle. She watched a few drops of liquid spill onto the carpet. After the third ring, she answered.

"Hello?" she said and then coughed away from the mouthpiece.

"Get to Pine Grove by no later than 6 a.m. and continue west on LA-16," a male voice ordered.

"To where?"

"You'll figure it out, and you'd better not call anyone else. Come alone or you'll regret it."

"Where's Pine Grove?"

"Look at a map."

Cassandra heard a click, ending the call. Her head hurt from another hangover as she tried to process what she'd been told. The clock on her dresser read 4:20, and she wondered who would call her so early in the morning. She pulled herself up to a sitting position, and a moment later, she suddenly realized it was Tommy Hanson. Goosebumps formed on her arms, and she felt a chill all over.

Cassandra ran her fingers through her auburn hair and tried to concentrate. She stumbled out of bed and headed to the bathroom sink. After flicking a light switch, she splashed water on her face and stared into the mirror. She had a significant problem. A brute who worked for a notorious assassin wanted to meet her at an unknown location. Even though she did not want another encounter with Hanson, she believed she had no choice. She kept a couple of old maps in a closet and would study them after she got coffee into her system. She traipsed towards the kitchen while the dull headache persisted.

Cassandra flicked another light switch and saw a pristine map of Louisiana lying on the countertop. Someone had broken into her residence while she was sleeping! Her hands trembled as she slowly unfolded the map. Someone, probably Hanson, had used a black Magic Marker to circle Pine Grove, a tiny town northwest of New Orleans and close to the Mississippi border. She was uncertain she could make it there by the imposed deadline.

Cassandra's heart pounded and the dull headache intensified, compromising her ability to think in a logical and straightforward fashion, and her hands were still shaking, which did not help matters.

She paced back and forth in the living room and considered calling Donnie, Mike, or Tyler, despite what Hanson had told her. She opened the kitchen drawer where she kept her cell phone, and saw it was missing. Her mind raced. *Did I make a call from the couch or the bedroom?*

Cassandra frantically searched the living room and found nothing. Next, the kitchen and the same result. She darted to the bedroom and ransacked the dresser. She rifled through her bedsheets and removed them completely. The cell phone was not under the bed, in the closet, or in the bathroom. In her panic, she concluded Hanson must have stolen it when he'd left the map.

Cassandra wondered if Hanson bugged her landline. She then shuttered over what would have happen if she made a call. Hanson probably never bluffed and neither did his employer.

Cassandra then considered whether The Saint wanted to assassinate her in Pine Grove. However, if he wanted her dead, someone could have killed her while she was sleeping. Perhaps The Saint wanted to dispose of her in a more remote location, where her body would never be found.

Cassandra dashed to the bedroom to get dressed. For a strange and unknown reason, she felt compelled to pull back a curtain and peek out a window. In doing so, she noticed a black Chevy Suburban parked across the street, which stuck out like a sore thumb. The driver's side window rolled down to reveal a fair-skinned man wearing dark sunglasses, even though it was well before dawn. He stared at her and pointed towards the front of his vehicle, indicating she had to get moving. She gasped.

Cassandra closed the curtain and feared if she did not act as Hanson had instructed, the man in sunglasses would break into her home and slaughter her. As fast as she could, she threw on underwear, a gray Tulane T-shirt, jeans, socks, and tennis shoes. No time to brush her teeth or drink coffee. Besides, she no longer needed a caffeine boost. She scrambled to the parking garage and jumped into her Mustang. As she exited the building, she scanned for the black Suburban, but it had disappeared.

Cassandra drove as fast as she dared while her mind raced. She worried a police officer would pull her over and write her a ticket, which would waste too many minutes. The officer would ask why she was speeding. If she told the truth, she would sound like a lunatic, and he could take her into custody for an evaluation. If she lied and the officer detected it, he would continue his interrogation and waste even more time. She worried about getting lost or getting into an accident and missing the rendezvous. She also wondered whether ending up in a hospital would be a better option than what awaited her.

Every few miles, Cassandra glanced in her rearview mirror in search of the Suburban, which never reappeared. She also pondered alternative destinations, including Seattle, her hometown, or anywhere else far from McCarthy's reach. She could run to the FBI, but she was uncertain they would believe her. The federal witness protection program was not an option because she reasoned it was only for persons who testified against crime lords. As of now, Cassandra had nothing to offer. She needed a security detail, but no one had made a direct threat to justify one. So, she continued on the path laid out for her.

Chapter 48

Just before six in the morning, Cassandra arrived in Pine Grove, where the sun was about to cross the horizon, and the local residents were still asleep. She passed through the town's center, consisting of a post office, three small businesses, and a white church. Just as she was leaving the town behind, she spotted a crow in the road about one hundred yards ahead. Cassandra slowed to give the crow enough time to fly away. Instead, it stared at her and refused to move. She became unnerved and swerved into the opposing lane to avoid hitting it by a wide margin. She returned to the westbound lane and stopped. She looked behind her, and the crow had vanished. After a few more panicky moments, Cassandra continued on LA-16, a two-lane road lined with pine trees on each side.

Half a mile later, she came to a church with red-brick walls and a white steeple near the northeast corner of an intersection. Another black Suburban imposed itself in front of the church, closer to the road. A man with blond hair, a black suit, and dark sunglasses stood next to the vehicle. His unbuttoned jacket revealed a pistol and a shoulder holster. The man stared at her and pointed to the side road.

Cassandra made a right turn and was so distraught she had difficulty controlling her vehicle. She drove down a narrower two-lane road and passed open fields and scattered homes. At another intersection surrounded by pine trees, she found another man in a suit and dark sunglasses standing next to a third Suburban. This one held an AR-15 semi-automatic rifle, which he pointed to order a slight left turn. Just before she did so, she looked in her rearview mirror and saw another black monster on wheels approaching from behind, probably the first or second SUV she had encountered.

After the turn, a pine forest encroached from both sides, as if the trees were ready to pounce on Cassandra's vehicle. She again glanced in the rearview mirror and saw two black monsters following her. She made a bend to the right and came upon a clearing. To the left, an abandoned ranch-style house was falling apart about one hundred feet from the road. Most of its exterior paint had faded away, and plywood boards covered its windows. The surrounding trees cast shadows that formed double-sided serrated blades.

A black Ford F-150 pickup truck blocked the road fifty feet past the house, forcing Cassandra to pull into the abandoned home's long asphalt driveway with weeds growing through its many cracks. She trembled as she parked and feared this was the end for her. The two Suburbans parked behind her, blocking her exit.

Through her rearview mirror, Cassandra saw the drivers exit their SUVs. The man closer to her held a 9 mm semi-automatic pistol in his right hand and strode toward her Mustang. His dark sunglasses could not conceal his even darker expression. When he reached the passenger-side window, he bent down and tapped on the glass with his weapon.

"Get out," he said calmly.

Cassandra trembled and slowly exited her vehicle. She did not make any sudden movements out of fear of reprisal. The same man pointed the pistol toward the road.

"Over there," he said.

She somehow managed to reach the road's edge. The men moved to her left and took positions ten feet away from her with their firearms in plain sight. The black pickup's driver stepped out with an AR-15 in his hands. Then she heard another vehicle approaching. She turned her head to the right and saw a black limousine with tinted windows. When it stopped, its back bumper was six feet past where she stood.

Lazlo Janka came out from the passenger's side rear door with anger and hate in his eyes. He stepped toward Cassandra and stopped a foot past the rear bumper. She noticed a bulge underneath the left side of his brown sports jacket. Tommy Hanson exited the limo from the driver's seat. She saw bulges on both sides of his black jacket, and his face was red and tense.

Hanson opened the driver's side rear door, and The Saint stepped out, stone-faced and in a three-piece suit and yellow-tinted glasses. He moved toward the rear of the limo, and Cassandra heard each step as it crushed her soul. Hanson marched to the trunk and opened it, revealing Ryan Parkhurst lying inside with his hands and ankles bound with rope. Parkhurst's gray suit was dirty and torn, and the right side of his face was bruised, bloodied, and swollen.

Hanson lifted Parkhurst out of the trunk and threw him to the ground. He landed with a thud and moaned in pain. His right hand was limp, indicating a fractured wrist, and cigarette burns were present on his left hand. He coughed twice, and blood trickled out of his mouth. Hanson didn't bother to close the limo's trunk.

Parkhurst tried to rise and face his uncle, but Hanson grabbed his neck with one hand and forced him to his knees. Janka removed a small pipe from his jacket. He swung it and connected with Parkhurst's thigh, who wailed in pain and collapsed to the ground.

"No more. Please, no more," he whimpered.

Janka took a step back, and with his right hand, removed a 9 mm pistol from the holster on his left side. He raised it to Cassandra's head, forcing her to stare into the face of death.

"Over here," Hanson directed.

Parkhurst moaned on the ground.

Cassandra turned her head to see another 9 mm pistol in Hanson's left hand. He held the barrel and reached out to her.

"Take it."

She could not move.

"Take it now!"

Cassandra heard Janka rack a round. She finally pushed herself to grab the weapon in Hanson's hand. Since she had no strength, the gun and her hand dropped to her side. Hanson then removed a .45-caliber pistol from his left holster and aimed the gun between her eyes.

Parkhurst rose to his knees and turned to face The Saint, who only stared and remained still. He clutched his bound hands together and begged, "Please, Uncle. Don't kill me! Please!"

McCarthy did not react, and the three other armed men, the drivers of the SUVs and the pickup, stood as silent witnesses.

"Shoot him!" Hanson ordered, as he kept his pistol trained on Cassandra's head.

"No, please don't," Parkhurst said. "Uncle, no! I don't want to die!"

"Shoot him in the head now!" Hanson said as he cocked his gun.

Parkhurst cried and bowed his head. Cassandra raised the pistol and held it with both hands. Once she extended her arms, the muzzle came within two feet of Parkhurst's head, but she couldn't open fire.

Hanson took a step forward and put the muzzle of his firearm to her temple.

"Do it!"

Her heart pounded the hardest it ever had in her life, and she could do nothing except remain frozen in fear.

"Now or you're dead!"

Cassandra pulled the trigger. A deafening sound rang out. The bullet slammed into the back of Parkhurst's head and exited through his jaw, along with a spray of blood. He fell over, and the left side of his face hit the asphalt. The ghastly scene should have horrified her, but she was too petrified to react. She let her arms fall to her sides, and the pistol remained in her right hand.

Janka squatted next to Parkhurst, a deep frown on his face. "He's still breathing." He then stood and backed away.

"Shoot him again!" Hanson said, still pointing his weapon at her. Janka did the same with his pistol.

Cassandra again raised the pistol and pulled the trigger. Another deafening sound rang out. The second bullet drove through Parkhurst's right temple and exited below the left eye, along with another spray of blood. She dropped the pistol and suddenly felt extremely vulnerable and alone. She concluded she was going to be the next one to receive a bullet in the head.

Hanson continued to aim his gun at her. Meanwhile, Janka holstered his weapon and retrieved a pair of plastic gloves from a pants pocket. After slipping them on, he removed a clear plastic bag with a ziplock from another pocket. He bent down, grabbed the barrel of the pistol Cassandra had used to shoot Parkhurst and dropped it into the bag and closed it. He then stood and placed the bag into the limo's open trunk.

"Remove your T-shirt," Hanson said.

Cassandra could not move.

Hanson tapped her head with his gun. "Remove it now!"

She took it off, revealing her bra. Hanson ripped the shirt away with one hand while continuing to point the firearm with the other. The Saint remained still while Hanson tossed the shirt to Janka. The man standing near the black pickup placed his AR-15 inside the truck and moved toward the limo's trunk.

Janka stepped toward Parkhurst's body and swiped the bottom of Cassandra's shirt against what was left of his face. Janka then returned to an upright position and stepped toward the limo. The other man reached into the trunk and removed a clothes hanger and a piece of cardboard. He and Janka put Cassandra's shirt on the hanger and slipped the cardboard inside so the blood on the front did not touch the rest of it. Janka again reached into the trunk and pulled out a plastic suit bag. He put the shirt inside, tossed the bag into the trunk, and closed it. The other man returned to the black pickup.

Hanson kept his gun trained on Cassandra. "Here's the situation," he said. "The gun you fired belongs to you. You might not think so, but it's registered in your name, and your fingerprints are on it. After you shot him, you checked him to make certain he was dead. In doing so, you accidentally got his blood on your shirt. If anyone sees this evidence, you have a big problem, understand?"

Cassandra's entire body trembled.

"Here are your choices. One: You can keep your mouth shut, leave the state, and never return. If you choose this option, the gun and the shirt will never see the light of day. Two: You can refuse to leave, and you'll be facing three murder charges. One for him and two for more sympathetic individuals who'll be killed with the same gun. Who will they be?" He shrugged. "How about your parents? Don't they live on Woodlawn Avenue in Seattle?"

Hanson put his face within inches of Cassandra's and stuck the firearm's barrel in her ear.

"Or three: You can open your big mouth. If you do, no matter where you are or how hard you try to hide, I... will... find you. Before I'm through, you'll be begging me to kill you and end your pain. Got it?"

Cassandra continued to tremble and said nothing.

"Good," he said.

The Saint turned around and stepped into the black limousine with tinted windows.

"You need to leave now," Hanson said as he walked backwards toward the driver's door. "The local sheriff will receive an anonymous tip in exactly twenty minutes. There's one other thing."

Hanson reached into the side of the driver's door and retrieved a cell phone. He tossed it in Cassandra's direction, and it landed in a pool of Parkhurst's blood.

Hanson slipped into the driver's seat as Janka climbed into the rear compartment on the other side. The three other men entered their respective vehicles. The two Suburbans backed out of the driveway and onto the road, facing the way they came. In doing so, they only missed Cassandra by two feet. She was so petrified that she did not flinch. They then took off at an accelerated pace.

Hanson put the limousine in reverse and used the driveway to make a three-point turn. Once he had backed out, the right passenger-side door was three feet in front of Cassandra. The corresponding window rolled down to reveal Janka, The Saint, and... Phillip LeMay. As the window rolled up, the limo sped off with the black Ford F-150 right behind it. They drove into the distance, and Cassandra dropped to her knees, put her head in her hands, and wept uncontrollably.

Chapter 49

Mid-May 1999
North Hollywood, California

Rebecca was horrified at what she had heard. She guessed she would not sleep well and dreaded the forthcoming nightmares. The ending of Nick's story was inconsistent with everything she had read. According to those sources, the local sheriff had claimed he had gone to the abandoned house on a hunch. He and Parkhurst had exchanged gunfire, and the sheriff had fatally shot him. Rebecca acknowledged his story could have been false. Nothing she had read provided any details to support his hunch, and no one had questioned the sheriff's version of events.

"That's it," Nick said. "I know it's awful, but I never promised a happy ending."

"'Awful' is an understatement. Why'd you tell me the story?"

"I have my reasons."

She rolled her eyes. "Not good enough."

"You'll figure it out."

"Fine," she said with a sigh. "Why was Cassandra forced to flee the state?"

"She had to leave because she was LeMay's biggest threat. Even if she couldn't officially lead the investigation against him, she was the driving force behind it. LeMay knew her tenacity and determination, and she wouldn't stop."

"But she was gone, and the investigation continued."

"Right, but McCarthy was working on a deal behind the scenes. The US Attorney in New Orleans had political ambitions and wanted to run on an anti-corruption platform. LeMay would've pled guilty to Social Security fraud, and the US Attorney would've grabbed some headlines. No one else would've been charged. If the case had dragged out, it would've continued well past the next election, which wouldn't have been good for anyone."

Rebecca got off the couch and stood to stretch her legs. "But when the public became aware of the fraud, LeMay committed suicide."

"Well... not exactly. That was the official story, not the real one. Tommy Hanson killed him and made it look like a suicide."

Rebecca's mouth dropped open. "What? Why?"

"Tommy didn't know about McCarthy's plan. He thought LeMay would cut a deal with the Feds and rat out everyone else, including his boss. So, he secretly traveled to New Orleans and eliminated him."

"Did The Saint find out?"

Nick groaned. "Oh yeah. He was really pissed and didn't want LeMay's death coming back to him. Tommy was lucky he wasn't killed. McCarthy instead threw a few bucks at him and ordered him to go away, far away."

"Besides LeMay and Parkhurst, was Tommy responsible for anyone else's death?"

"Yeah, there were a few others."

"How many?"

"I'd rather not say."

Rebecca wanted more information but would not push Nick. "What happened to Donnie and Mike?"

"Nothing. They retired. Don't know what happened after that."

"What about Tyler?"

"He got frustrated and quit. Not sure why, and no clue where he went."

"What about the first victim, Jane Doe 1, the one found in the mausoleum? Was she ever identified?"

There was no answer.

"Nick?"

"Yeah… Still here. They never figured out who she was."

"Didn't they put a sketch of her face on the news or something like that?"

"Yeah. They hired a… forensic anthropologist. I think that's what she was called. They gave her Jane Doe's skull. She created a face out of modeling clay, and they showed it on the news. I'm surprised you never saw a picture of it on the internet."

"How do you know I searched for stories on the Crescent City Killer?"

Nick gave a light chuckle. "Isn't your entire generation surfing the internet and playing on their cell phones?"

"What happened to Cassandra?" Rebecca asked.

"Not sure. She left in a big hurry and changed her name to Sandra Colton, which wasn't much of an alias. Colton is her mother's maiden name."

"Look, I'm not trying to be mean or anything, but how do you know all the details? You mentioned private conversations between Cassandra and Donnie, and you knew Cassandra's thoughts. You couldn't have known everything."

"What the hell? You think I made the whole thing up?" Nick asked in a hostile tone.

"No, of course not. I'm just wondering about the details."

"Whatever," he said in his normal voice. "I had reliable sources, and the most significant parts of the story were accurate. For some of the minor stuff, I filled in the details to make it more interesting, and they were consistent with their personalities."

Rebecca was uncertain what to believe. "Okay," she said, "I get it.

There was silence on the line. Images of Nick's story continued to flash in Rebecca's head, and she feared the last portion would haunt her forever. She questioned what she would have done if she had been in Cassandra's position and could not come up with an answer.

Rebecca didn't know what to say next. Part of her wanted to interrogate Nick to determine the source of his information. Another part of her recoiled over the thought of learning anything more. Even if the first part was the stronger one, any further questions would have to wait.

"Anyway," she said. "We have the parole hearing very soon.

Nick smirked. "Yeah, I know."

"Yes, of course. Please make certain you tell the truth during the hearing," she said. After a moment, she added, "This means no exaggerations or made-up facts."

"Yeah, yeah," he said dismissively.

"No, not 'yeah, yeah.' Let's do everything the right way, okay? See you next week."

Rebecca sat in front of her laptop on her small dining room table. She accessed the internet and ran a search for "Sandra Colton attorney." Without reading anything else, she clicked on the first link, which was for an article in a newspaper she did not recognize, *The Oregonian*.

> Local Law Professor and Community Leader
> Passes Away
> November 14, 2018
> Sandra Colton, Lewis & Clark Law School
> constitutional law professor and founder of

an alcohol and drug counseling support group for female professionals, died yesterday after a brief battle with pancreatic cancer. She was 54. "We lost a great colleague and an inspiration to so many," said–

Rebecca closed her laptop as she could not bear to read any more.

Chapter 50

Rebecca arrived at the state prison ninety minutes before the hearing with the parole board because she wanted to go over Nick's testimony one more time. In an attorney visit room, she reviewed his case again. His convictions for manslaughter, assaulting a police officer, and assaulting a prison guard were all egregious offenses. On the other hand, Nick had obtained two degrees in psychology and had assisted inmates in different ways. He also attended church services. Rebecca was cautiously optimistic about the hearing and laughed to herself. At first, she wanted Nick to remain in prison, but now she was rooting for him.

After about fifteen minutes, Rebecca heard two sets of footsteps, which she guessed belonged to Nick and a guard.

"Stick around, man. It won't take much," an unfamiliar male voice said.

A wiry Latino in his late twenties stepped into the doorframe. His appearance frightened and intimidated Rebecca, as gang tattoos covered his hands, arms, neck, and the top of his shaved head.

"You Rebecca Holt?" he asked, revealing his crooked teeth.

"That's me," she nervously said. "Who are you?"

"A friend of Nick's. He told me to deliver a message."

Confusion entangled with her fear. "What do you mean? We're supposed to meet before his parole hearing."

"Nah. It was last week."

"What! Are you sure?"

The inmate flashed a lopsided smile. "Yeah. Heard all about it. Nick really fucked up, said all kinds of stupid things. When they said he wasn't gettin' out, he went off. He threatened an old lady and tried to rush her. Fuckin' stupid, man."

Rebecca was flabbergasted. "That's not like him, not at all."

He shrugged. "That's what I heard, and he's gonna catch another case."

"What's that?"

"He's gonna get smacked with another charge and do more time."

"I– I don't understand. Why'd he do it?"

"Dunno. Fuckin' stupid."

"Please tell Nick I want to see him right now."

"Nah," the inmate said with a smirk. "Nick said you're fired, and he told me to give you this." He raised his right hand, which held a white business-size envelope. He moved to the table's edge and remained standing.

"What's inside?" she asked.

"Dunno. Nick said you can't read it until you get back to your office. Promise?"

"Yeah, okay."

He dropped the envelope onto the table and left the room.

* * *

Still flustered, Rebecca walked out of the prison with her satchel over her right shoulder and the envelope in her left hand. She was upset. Nick had wasted so much of her time, and she could not understand why he had betrayed her.

Once Rebecca entered her vehicle, she stared at the envelope, wondering what was inside. She wanted to rip it open, but instead honored Nick's request, even though he did not deserve it. She tossed the envelope on the front passenger's seat and glanced at it every few minutes while driving to Downtown Los Angeles. Some partners at the firm would blame her for what had happened, and perhaps they would not give her credit for the time she spent on Nick's case. If so, she would need to make up for it with more long and tedious hours.

Rebecca regretted accepting the assignment and thought in hindsight, when Patterson offered her the chance to represent Nick, she should have fabricated an excuse. She could have said, "I'm sorry, Mr. Patterson. I can't do it. I had an uncle who was murdered, and I can't even sit in the same room with a killer." It could have worked, although she could never bring herself to spin such a fairy tale. Many lawyers made good liars, but she was not and did not want to become one.

When Rebecca returned to her office, she groaned at the sight of a foot-high stack of paperwork sitting on a corner of her desk. A handwritten note on top said:

> *Review and be ready to discuss during tomorrow's meeting at 2:00.*

Rebecca sighed as her bad day became even worse. "Review" meant analyze in extensive detail. She would need to work until midnight and a few hours the following morning to be ready for the grilling during the meeting. No amount of money or prestige was worth this kind of abuse.

Rebecca let her satchel drop to the floor and then tossed Nick's envelope onto the desk. She fell into her chair and closed her eyes for a moment. On some level, she dreaded opening the envelope, yet she suspected things could not get any worse. She opened her eyes, ripped it open, and removed a folded sheet of plain white paper. She unfolded it and gasped as she read two handwritten lines:

> *My name is Thomas Jay Hanson.*
> *Jane Doe 1 is Samantha Montgomery from Aurora, Colorado.*

The note shocked Rebecca so much she had to read it again to make certain she had read it correctly the first time. The page then fell from her hand onto the desk, and she could only stare at a wall. Moments later, her mind cleared, and she was mad at Nick for lying about everything prior to owning the bar.

Rebecca then realized everything else Nicholas Malone/Tommy Hanson had said made sense. He knew so much about the Crescent City Killer and the investigation because he had read the file Cassandra had left behind at McCarthy's home. LeMay could have discussed the case with McCarthy, who then told Tommy.

Rebecca also realized Nick/Tommy had not given his honest opinion about the parole board granting his release. He had never wanted parole, as he felt guilty over his criminal conduct, most of which had gone unpunished. Perhaps telling the serial killer story had been the only way he thought he could redeem himself.

Rebecca thought about Samantha Montgomery, aka Jane Doe 1. For the past twenty-five years, her family must have wondered what had happened to their daughter or sister. She shuddered at the possibility Samantha could have borne a child who had grown up without a mother and not known why.

She realized there was a significant impediment to informing Samantha's family. Disclosing Nick's note would violate attorney–client privilege, an ethics violation the California State Bar did not take lightly. She considered passing the information to the police in New Orleans or Aurora without revealing how she received it, but doubted anyone would believe her. Wild conspiracy theories about the Crescent City Killer filled the internet, and she also imagined many crackpots had called the police with their own delusional tales. With no context, the police would give no consideration to her report.

Rebecca shifted her eyes to the stack of paperwork on her desk. Despite little desire to touch it, she had no choice. She scoffed as she remembered what Nick had told her: too much work and too little enjoyment of life, quit now. Easy for him to say.

She did not hear the knock on her door.

"Rebecca?"

Nothing.

"Rebecca?"

She adjusted her line of sight and saw Carter Patterson standing in the doorway.

"Are you all right?" he asked. "You look as if you're in a daze."

"I'm fine. I've just been thinking for the past couple of minutes."

Patterson raised his eyebrows. "Oh really? Your assistant told me for at least the last forty minutes, you've been staring into space. I take it the parole hearing didn't go well."

"You could say that."

"What happened?"

She looked away and sighed. "Malone lied about the hearing being postponed, and it went forward last week. He intentionally made a bad impression and got denied parole."

"Why would anyone do that?"

Rebecca's eyes shifted toward the paper in the middle of her desk.

Patterson grabbed the page. He read it and gasped. "Oh dear." Without looking back, he felt for the chair behind him and sat down. "Oh dear. This explains a lot." He set down the note. "Do you believe him?"

"Yeah… I guess so," she said flatly.

"How did he know Jane Doe 1's name?"

She simultaneously gave a smirk and frown. "He probably beat it out of Parkhurst. I wish we could inform Samantha's family about her death and give them some closure, but…"

"Yes, yes, of course. It's a shame, a real shame. I'll give it some more thought and run it by Goodman, our ethics expert, although I doubt we can mention it to anyone."

Both attorneys sat in silence for about a minute.

Patterson then rose from the guest chair. "You've had a terrible day, and it's not even noon. Why don't you go home and decompress?"

"Yeah, right." She glanced at the pile of papers and back to Patterson.

He grabbed the note on top. "'Review by tomorrow at two.' This is for Vandemere?"

She said nothing.

He dropped the note and held out his hands to the side. "I'll talk to him."

She scoffed. "He won't care."

Epilogue

Mid-August 2019
San Diego, California

Three months later, Rebecca parked her Honda Civic at the end of a strip mall and peered at the blue-and-white sign for RTM Sports Bar & Grill. A banner announced, "Monday Night Madness Starting September 9." She was in the right place and was dressed in a dark-blue T-shirt and faded jeans. She also had pulled her ponytail through the strapback of a Padres baseball cap.

Rebecca entered the bar, and as expected, she saw several flat-screen televisions. Two elderly men sat at a table and stared at an 82-inch Samsung. All the other seats were empty, which was no surprise, as it was about three in the afternoon. A young Latina with an hourglass figure, long, flowing burgundy hair, and large brown eyes stood behind the bar. At least twenty beer bottles, each a different brand, were in a row behind her. Above the bottles hung a framed photo of three middle-aged men. The ones on the left and right were Latino. The one in the center was Caucasian and had a shaved head.

"May I help you?" the bartender asked with a pleasant smile.

Rebecca pulled up a barstool. "Miller Lite, please."

"On tap or a bottle?"

"On tap."

"Are you going to the game tonight?" the bartender asked as she poured.

"Huh?"

She handed over the full glass. "You're wearing a Padres cap. Are you going to the game?"

"Uh, yeah," Rebecca lied. She took a sip of beer.

"Nice to see your support for the home team, even though it's another down year. Did you leave work early?"

Rebecca gave a wide smile. "Nope. I quit my job last week, and I'm going to find something better."

The bartender smiled. "Good for you!"

"Thanks. Nice place. How long have you been open?"

"About six months, and we're doing great. Even on weeknights, the place is packed. That's what happens when three cops open a bar. They invite their buddies on the force to the grand opening, and word gets out."

"That's great," Rebecca said. "I noticed the picture behind you. Are those guys the owners?" She took another sip.

The bartender looked behind her, and her face lit up. "Yep. That's Rodolfo, Tyler, and Manuel. Rodolfo and Manuel are my uncles." She turned back. "And I've known Tyler forever. He's practically family."

"That's nice. Are all three still on the force?"

"No. Uncle Rodolfo and Uncle Manuel retired to open this place. Tyler needs about two more years to retire with full benefits. He doesn't mind because he loves being a motorcycle cop. My uncles encouraged him to become a detective, like they did, but Tyler never bothered. When he's not on the job or working here, it's hard to get him off his bike. He just loves to ride, and I can't blame him, you know."

"Sure. How much do I owe you?"

"Four bucks."

Rebecca removed a twenty-dollar bill from her right front pocket. "This is the smallest I have."

"No problem, but the cash register out front is jammed. I'm waiting for Uncle Rodolfo to fix it. I'll be right back with the change." The bartender exited through a back door.

Once she was gone, Rebecca retrieved a folded envelope from her right back pocket. It was addressed to "Tyler Winfield." She placed the envelope underneath her glass and made certain his name was visible. The note inside read:

> *Tyler:*
> *I'm an attorney who's recently represented Tommy Hanson. He's currently incarcerated in a state prison under another name. Please don't try to find him.*
> *Do you remember Jane Doe 1, one of the Crescent City Killer's first victims? She was found in a family mausoleum. Tommy told me her name is Samantha*

Montgomery, and she's from Aurora, Colorado.
Please inform the police in New Orleans and Aurora
so they can confirm her identity. Samantha's family
needs to know what happened to her and have some
closure.
Sincerely,
A friend

Rebecca left the sports bar before the bartender returned.

Acknowledgments

Charles A. "Charlie" Wiegand III was a New Orleans native and a walking encyclopedia of the city and southeast Louisiana. He was also a mentor and a great friend. I had several discussions with Charlie to create more authentic settings for this novel, and whenever I talked to him about anything, it was always very enjoyable. Sadly, Charlie passed away at the age of 77.

I must thank Erik Empson, Polly Phipps-Holland, and Tarek Salhany with The Book Folks for all their assistance and patience. Polly had great suggestions for improving the storyline, and I wish I had thought of them first. I also appreciated Erik, Polly, and Tarek tolerating my personality quirks.

My wife, Carolyn, is a violinist, and she picked the classical music mentioned in the novel, and my daughter, Caitlyn, provided the words to describe it. Caitlyn also helped me create the chapter concerning Donnie Green's backstory and other paragraphs that were critical to the storyline. In addition, I discussed potential character names with Carolyn, Caitlyn, and my sons, Michael and Andrew.

Retired editor William Greenleaf, author Brad Chisolm, and author Claire Kim provided several tips and advice. Kay Bruce and Dean Emeritus Ronald Phillips of Pepperdine read an earlier version of the manuscript and provided their input. Jerry Rishe read both earlier and later versions. Michael Lysecky and retired Pepperdine law professor Daniel Martin gave edits and suggestions.

Finally, I must recognize Mark Becker, a lifelong family friend, architect, and real estate developer. Mark assisted with the description of three residences, the Broussard family's home in St. Charles Parish, the creole cottage in the Garden District, and the colonial cottage in Lakeview. The Broussards' home was based upon the Oak Alley Plantation, which was featured in the movie *Interview with the Vampire* and during an episode of *Leverage: Redemption.*

If you enjoyed this book, please let others know by leaving a quick review on Amazon. Also, if you spot anything untoward in the paperback, get in touch. We strive for the best quality and appreciate reader feedback.

editor@thebookfolks.com

www.thebookfolks.com

More fiction by the author

PROTECTION RACKET

When a hot-shot, womanizing lawyer is found murdered in his office, a female co-worker is indicted for the crime. Her parents call on David Lee from a rival firm to clear Amanda's name and defend her at trial. Falling for his attractive client, David will dig deep to prove her innocence, but there may be more to it than first meets the eye.

Available January 2025.

Other titles of interest

THE OTHER DETECTIVE
by James Davidson

Days before World War Two, Polish detective Johann Tal is called out to investigate a brutal murder. A couple have been discovered dead in Danzig's dockyards, and a policeman's bloodied uniform found next to them. Many years later, another detective is called out to a different murder. If the two cases are linked, it spells serious danger.

FREE with Kindle Unlimited and available in paperback!

THE DEVIL'S ARTIST
by Iain Henn

When a massive wreck on the interstate kills several people, a mural in Seattle that seems to glorify the disaster creates outcry. However, upon discovering that the painting was created days before the event, criminal investigators are baffled. Are they dealing with a psychic artist, or someone who played a role in the incident? Soon other murals appear, and the race is on to stop further tragedy.

FREE with Kindle Unlimited and available in paperback!

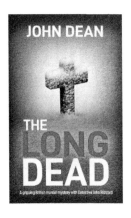

THE LONG DEAD
by **John Dean**

When a routine archaeological dig turns up bodies on the
site of a WWII prisoner of war camp, it should be an open
and shut case for detective John Blizzard. But forensics
discover one of the deaths is more recent and the force
have a murder investigation on their hands.

FREE with Kindle Unlimited and available in paperback!

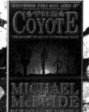

Also by Michael McBride

NOVELS

Ancient Enemy
Bloodletting
Burial Ground
Fearful Symmetry
Innocents Lost
Predatory Instinct
Sunblind
Vector Borne

NOVELLAS

F9
Remains
Snowblind
The Event

COLLECTIONS

Category V

MICHAEL MCBRIDE

THE COYOTE

A THRILLER

FACTOR V MEDIA

For Dani

Special Thanks to J.G. Faherty, Gene O'Neill, Norman Prentiss, Gord Rollo, William C. Rasmussen, Jeff Strand, Linda Walter, my family, and all of my loyal friends and readers, without whom none of this would be possible.

They say your blood flows from the earth, but in my experience they're wrong. Blood flows to the earth. Whatever gifts it bestows, it always takes back in spades.

DAY 1

tash hema

e:'ed

There are people who believe that the memories of our ancestors flow through our blood in much the same way animals inherit migratory instincts from theirs. In my opinion, beliefs like that breed victims, for not all of our antecedents figured out how to truly live, but every single one of them found a way to die.

ONE

Hickiwan District
Tohono O'odham Nation
Arizona

September 9th

I was sick of the heat long before I boarded the plane at Denver International Airport. Turns out I had no idea what it truly meant to be hot. They call it an Indian summer, but never in front of me. The same way people probably tiptoe around African-Americans on Black Friday. I'm not that sensitive to the whole politically correct vibe. I didn't get to choose my bloodline any more than I got to pick my parents. It would have been nice to have known them, though, but that's neither here nor there. People die all the time. Fact of life. Nothing you can do to stop it. You start dying the moment you're born. The problem is that from time to time people get a little help along the way. And that's why I was out here in the middle of this godforsaken desert, roasting alive, wondering if it was possible for my sweat to actually boil.

That, of course, and the color of my skin.

"I don't like the way they're looking at me."

"You get used to it. Don't take it personally."

I picked up a rock and hurled it at the nearest buzzard, which merely flapped its massive wings when the stone struck the saguaro cactus beneath it. The others just sat there on their perches with their bald heads and their beady little eyes. They obviously knew the score.

"Shouldn't they be circling overhead, waiting for us to collapse? This strikes me as sheer laziness."

"Out here in the desert, you learn in a hurry not to waste your energy. Any physical exertion costs you hydration, and once you start losing water, there's no way of getting it back."

I figured the Border Patrol agent was being overly dramatic. After all, that's what locals do. They get to piss first to mark their territory when the Feds are called in. This guy was just encouraging me to hold mine a while longer, but, believe me, I had no intention of saving mine for drinking down the road. Not once we reached the crime scene. I was going to piss all over it when we got there. Metaphorically, of course. The way those vultures were still eyeing us, I didn't see any harm in saving my fluids for later use. You know, just in case.

The Sonoran Desert was vastly different than I expected. When I hear the word desert, I think of sand dunes stretching from one horizon to the other. I imagine camels and mirages and women dressed like belly dancers. This, however? Well, this was a lot like the rest of Arizona, only hotter.

We ascended from a wash filled with mesquites—which somehow qualified as trees, despite having more in common with cacti—onto a steep, rocky slope riddled with yuccas and prickly pears and cholla. Fortunately, it was too hot for the snakes to be out basking. At least that's what the CBP agent told me. His name was Blaine Randall and he looked more like he belonged in a sweater with Greek letters and a plastic cup of keg beer in his hand than out here in his forest-green uniform with a baton on one hip and a Heckler & Koch P2000 .40 caliber semi-automatic holstered on the other, but I wanted to believe him. I *really* wanted to believe him. I've never been a big fan of legless life forms, especially the venomous kind that strike just because they feel like it.

We must have looked the pair: a WASP in dusty paramilitary fatigues leading a Native-American in L.L. Bean hiking gear and a blue FBI windbreaker slung over his shoulder across uninhabitable land over which their forefathers had long ago fought and died. To be fair, I'm also half white, but tend to be mistaken for Hispanic. Maybe I should incorporate something cool and distinctly native into my name so there's no confusion, like Lou Diamond Phillips. As far as names go, I could have done a hell of a lot worse than Lukas Walker, but something like Luke Sky Walker would really sing.

By the time we crested the ridge, only to find ourselves at the foot of another, even steeper embankment, Randall's green and white Ford Explorer was little more than a sparkle on the dirt drag that cut a straight line through the creosotes and palo verdes.

"What were you doing all the way out here?"

"My job."

"You know that's not what I mean."

"I was cutting sign. You know, tracking? That's what I do. It's not like we sit on our asses in air conditioned rooms watching monitors all day. We're out here in trucks that can't get to half of the areas we need to reach, so most of the time we're on foot. Alone. Outnumbered. And in the middle of a goddamn war zone."

"I hear you. Beirut and Sarajevo don't have anything on Middle of Nowhere, Arizona."

The agent stopped on the rugged path in front of me. I meant to push that button; just maybe not as hard as I actually did. I could almost see his quills bristle underneath his uniform. He took one deep breath, then another. When he finally turned around to face me, he was calm and composed. Not impulsive. Not emotional. His hands were open at his sides, not clenched. Randall might have been a man capable of violence, but he was not, by nature, a violent man.

Trust me. I know all about violent men. That's my job.

"Now seems like a good time to clear up a few common misconceptions," Randall said. "The media portray us as a kind of Gestapo; racist thugs in green cruising the desert, abusing the illegals, and then dumping them across the border. Here's a little peek behind the emerald curtain...There are three hundred seventy-six miles of border in Arizona alone. We at Ajo Station are responsible for sixty-four of those, thirty-six of which are completely unfenced and indefensible wilderness areas. We have more than seven thousand of a total of forty-five thousand square miles of desert to patrol, including Organ Pipe National Monument, the Barry M. Goldwater Bombing Range, and the entire Tohono O'odham Reservation. This whole section of the state was designated a High-Intensity Drug Trafficking Area by the Department of Justice. We estimate an average of three thousand undocumented aliens cross through here every day and we pick up maybe a third of them. That's a thousand arrests a day. Over the course of a year, that's more than twice the size of the Allied army that took Normandy on D-Day. That alone qualifies as an invading force."

I studied his facial expressions and mannerisms through the course of his tirade. That's kind of my thing. Some people are born with the ability to sing or run fast or throw hard. Me? I was born with a hypersensitive BS meter. The mouth may be capable of deception, but the body is not. For someone trained to detect even the smallest lie, the body is an open book. Micromomentary facial expressions, nervous tendencies, eye movements, voice inflections, speech patterns, diaphoresis. Maybe I can't precisely read them all, but I can definitely tell when they're at odds with the words. I'm the guy you don't invite over for a friendly game of poker or ask to be your wingman at the bar. I catch all the signals. The problem is that there are people out there who don't give off normal signals like the rest of us. They're called sociopaths, and so completely do they believe their own lies, the all-encompassing web of deception they weave around their daily lives, that even when they lie, for all intents and purposes, they're telling the truth. There's no little cricket chirping in the backs of their skulls to let them know what they're doing is wrong. Their reality is fluid. It's whatever they determine it to be from one moment to the next. And they fascinate the hell out of me.

Randall's face was still red and he was breathing hard, but he appeared to have gotten it out of his system. I had learned everything I needed to from him. Every investigation begins with a seemingly infinite number of suspects. The first person who needs to be crossed off the list is always the person who discovered the crime, which, in this case, was simple enough. I could have done without the lecture, though. At least out here under the blazing sun. Lesson learned. Next time I confront someone, I'll do so indoors with the AC blasting. Don't let anyone tell you I can't adapt.

"Sorry." I held up my hands in mock surrender. "I tend to lack diplomacy when I'm on the verge of being cooked alive."

Randall stared me down for a few seconds, then nodded and mounted the path once more. His posture and the tension in his shoulders suggested that he was suitably placated for the time being, but I wasn't likely to garner that invitation to dinner I'd been angling for. I supposed I'd survive. After all, I hadn't been entirely forthcoming with him from the start. I find it's always best to hold back every last bit of information you can, should you later need something with which to barter. And when it comes to capital, information is king. It also doesn't hurt to let people think they know more than you do. That way their responses remain unguarded.

Which was why I didn't tell Randall that I'd been thoroughly briefed on the situation on the way down here. Best to let him keep the upper hand as long as possible. Or at least let him think he had the upper hand. Anything he inadvertently betrayed would only add to what I already knew, and this was definitely a world apart from the one in which I lived.

Down here, drug trafficking organizations, or DTOs, run just about everything. They've organized all of the smuggling. Everything from cash to drugs and guns to illegals. Heck, they control immigration better than we do. They have whole networks of human smugglers called coyotes, and their pollero minions, bringing load after load of UDAs across the border every day, charging two to five grand a head and then abandoning their clients in the middle of the desert at the first sign of *La Migra*, the Border Patrol. They have foreign nationals actually paying for the right to carry fifty-pound bales of marijuana across forty miles of the harshest terrain on earth and more lining up for the chance. There are more than twenty different gangs, often working in conjunction, moving that merchandise in the city of Phoenix alone. They, in turn, bought weapons that they shipped back across the border with the remaining profits to arm the growing narco-insurgency, which already had both the man- and firepower to roll right over the border onto American soil and lay claim to a network of highways that reached into the heart of every city in the country.

While the chief function of the Border Patrol was still to round up and deport UDAs, every time an agent approached a group of migrants in the desert, he ran the risk of being gunned down or overwhelmed by superior numbers. There was no way of knowing whether the agents were walking up on a party of dehydrated illegals dying from the heat and in desperate need of BORSTAR aid, or a pack of bandits whose haul of weed and methamphetamines was stashed off in the mesquites until the guns appeared in their hands. Even the innocents whose lives were saved by the CBP agents wouldn't rat out their coyote guides because they knew that once they were healthy enough to be bussed back to Nogales or Sasabe, they just needed to save up the money to hire a new coyote to take another crack at the American dream. And if they couldn't find a way to earn the money, there was always a DTO willing to let them risk their lives hauling drugs bound for our schools.

Needless to say, finding human remains out here wasn't an entirely unusual experience. Between centuries of pioneers and migrants and bandits, the Sonoran was positively littered with bones. What made this situation unique, and thus necessitated the presence of someone like me, was the nature of the crime. They needed me specifically because this whole area was situated on a political and racial landmine. We were within the borders of the United States and yet on sovereign Tohono O'odham land, and the media were just licking their chops at the prospect of the powers that be tripping over their own largely ineffective policies. If details somehow managed to leak to the press, here I was, a minority of O'odham descent, a federal agent essentially investigating other more publicly loathed federal agents, and I had a face the cameras absolutely loved. That I was exceptional at my job didn't really factor into the equation.

By the time Randall finally stopped walking, I was starting to think those vultures might have been prescient. I was drowning in my own sweat, yet, at the same time, I was thirstier than I'd ever been in my life. My lungs were made of paper sacks and my skin felt like tanned leather. There were so many cactus needles in my socks that I winced with every step and my shirtsleeves were damp with blood from the stinging lacerations inflicted by the cruel hooks of the mesquite branches. I was seriously debating how thirsty I would have to get before I went for Randall's throat and sucked his blood, when he turned around and, with a flourish, gestured toward the base of the stratified red rock escarpment, which rose from the crest of the mountain into the cloudless sky.

I whistled appreciatively.

"I was really hoping you'd be impressed."

Randall shook his head as he turned away, but I saw that flush of pride on his face.

Had he been able to read mine, he would have seen that I wasn't so much impressed by his discovery or the lengths to which the killer had gone to display the blood, but by the sheer volume the miraculous human body was capable of holding.

TWO

At the scene of any murder, the blood told a tale to those who knew how to listen. There were crime scene investigators who could read the various spatters and stains, who could tell you exactly how many blows or shots or slashes a victim had received and from which angle they had been struck and with what velocity they had been delivered. I was not one of those people, nor did I wish to be. I chose to focus on the living and finding a way to hold them accountable for their crimes against the dead. But even I could clearly see that the killer had attacked with great speed and savagery; however, while the victim had obviously suffered, his or her death hadn't been unnecessarily protracted.

High-velocity spatters climbed the stone wall and streaked the hardscrabble path. They were a seemingly impossible dark red against the rust-colored rock and sand. There were various amoeba shapes where the body had been left to bleed out from at least two distinct wounds, while the unknown subject, or unsub, took his time leaving his calling card on the stone wall.

It had been painted twenty feet tall in the victim's blood using the paw of a medium-size canine as a brush, as evidenced by the wisps of fur and nail marks around the telltale pad prints, and confirmed by the initial investigatory team.

"Pretty morbid, if you ask me," Randall said.

I didn't, but people always let you know when they're ready to talk and it was generally a good idea to let them.

"Walk me through it."

"Like I said, I was cutting sign. The coyotes and polleros are essentially just like any other smugglers. When they find a shipping lane that works, they keep using it until we eventually figure out a way to block it off. Traveling through the mountains offers a hell of a lot more cover than wandering across the flat desert and their trails aren't readily visible from the air. Not to mention the fact that we can't easily patrol them like we can the drags. But once they've been using a route for a while, it starts to get paved with trash. These UDAs just toss off their extra layers of clothing or throw down their food wrappers and water bottles. Thing is, with as little rain and wind as we get through here, all that stuff pretty much stays where they drop it."

"And you were following one of those trails?"

"Not that day. We'd actually just busted one up on the other side of the mountain, so when word gets back to the coyotes on the other side of the border, they have to alter their shipping lanes on the fly. And considering the risks involved, they generally send their pollero underlings—"

"The wannabe coyotes."

"Yeah. The chicken wranglers. Makes you feel all warm and fuzzy about humanity, doesn't it?"

"So you were searching for one of these alternate routes."

"Found one, actually. I couldn't have been more than four hours behind her, in fact."

"Her? The crime scene report said it was impossible to conclusively identify the victim without more than a sample of blood. They couldn't even confirm the sex without the presence of the hCG hormone."

The CBP agent beamed.

"I was following her tracks. Size six to seven. Canvas Keds knockoffs to be precise."

"How can you be sure they belonged to the victim and not the killer?"

"Please. I had to have been following them for more than a mile. They led right here and stopped. There's no way the killer wiped his tracks leading away from the scene but didn't have the foresight to wash his trail leading up to it."

"How do you know the killer 'washed' his trail?"

"When you've been out here for any length of time, these things stand out like neon signs. I could tell the prints I was tracking were roughly four hours old because the soil under the turned gravel was still darker than the ground around it, but not as dark as the stones I turned over myself. That means the walker passed through closer to sunrise than midnight, but before the temperature started to rise again. It was about seven in the morning when I found them and the footprints had been crossed by insect tracks. The bugs only come out right before dawn, before the heat really kicks in. And the generic Keds are a common choice for the female immigrants since they're cheap, have reasonably durable soles, and they're available at a huge markup at any of the stores in Altar, where the majority of the UDAs go to hook up with coyotes.

"The exit tracks are even easier. After trying to keep up with all of the new trends, like tying carpet or foam blocks or tire treads or fake animal tracks over their shoes, it's almost amusing to come across the old tried-and-true brush-off."

"With a tree branch?"

"Mesquite branches specifically."

"How can you tell that?"

"Look over there. See where it looks almost like someone raked the sand really softly? That's from the barbs on the mesquite branches. They generally aren't quite that clearly defined. They only look like that in this case because—"

"He used them like a sled to simultaneously drag the body away and obliterate his tracks."

Randall tapped his sunburned nose.

"You're catching on."

"So what can you tell me about our unsub?"

Randall's smile faltered.

"He came across some poor migrant girl out here alone in the desert, saw his opportunity, and took full advantage of it. Happens all the time. You'd be surprised how many women we pick up who claim—"

"This wasn't a crime of opportunity. The unsub was already waiting out here. He knew exactly what he was going to do. He sat right up there on that ledge where he couldn't been seen until it was too late, then he jumped down behind her. He grabbed her by the hair, pulled back her head, and cut her throat from right to left. Then he laid her body down on the ground right here and used the wound in her neck to paint the pattern on the stone. When he ran out of blood, he had to cut her lower abdomen open over here to get at the last of the unclotted blood.

"The attack was carefully planned and precisely executed. This man was in control the entire time. He demonstrates the classic signs of a sociopath, the Alienated Type specifically. He shows no remorse for the act of killing. His victim was merely a substrate he utilized to deliver his message. Nor did he deliberately inflict more pain than was absolutely necessary. He killed her with the first cut, and in the quickest manner possible, which demonstrates a measure of compassion."

"How do you know it was a 'he' and not a 'she'?"

"More than ninety percent of all serial killers are male. That aside, it takes a tremendous amount of force to cut through so many layers of skin, cartilage, and muscle to even get to the great vessels. Far more than you might think. And to do so in one swift motion? We're talking about a person with significant upper body strength, especially to be able to do it with one hand. Besides, women tend to exhibit less emotional restraint, especially when it comes to an act as intimate as murder. No, the evidence here suggests that the murder itself had absolutely nothing to do with the selection of the victim. He didn't know her personally. She merely served the purpose of helping to create a message to which we have no choice but to sit up and pay attention."

"A smiley face? Seems kind of like he's sending a mixed message to me."

"That? That's not the message. That's just him having a little fun at our expense. Thumbing his nose at us, if you will. We haven't found the real message yet."

"We had guys all over this place. There's nothing else out here. We'd have found it if there was."

"You're missing the point."

"I'm very good at what I do. I don't miss anything."

"The real message is with the bodies. When we find them, we'll find the message this guy is going to great lengths to deliver."

"What do you mean...*bodies*?"

"Come now, Agent Randall. Tell me you didn't think this was his first?"

He looked over at the dried blood on the red rocks. I watched the comprehension dawn on his face as the color drained from it.

"Like you said, thousands of *undocumented* aliens come through here every week. There's no record of who they are, where they come from, or where they're going. For all intents and purposes, they don't exist. There's no one to immediately miss them and no one to go looking for them. Heck, how many Juan Does are sitting in the cooler at the Pima County Medical Examiner's Office waiting to be ID'd. Most of these people don't even have dental records. Do you really think he didn't select them for that very reason? They're the perfect choice of victim for a sociopath honing his craft. He's just stepping up his game now, a game he wants to play with us."

"So you're saying—"

"You've got a hunter on the refuge, warden." I clapped him on the shoulder and started back down the trail. "Somewhere out here in this forty-five thousand square miles of desert is a serial killer who's been doing this for a long time now without anyone noticing."

THREE

My memories of my parents are yellowed and faded by time. What were once full-length videos in my head are now scattered snippets. Most have become just lifeless photographs. Time is a thief that takes only what's near and dear to us, the things to which we cling so tightly we assume they can never be pried from our grasp, and yet one day we open our hands to find them gone. We wonder how we allowed such a thing to happen and cling even tighter to the few precious memories that remain, memories we commit to our very being, to our unconscious mind where time can't find them, even if we can only visit them in our dreams.

I never really knew my parents, at least not as a boy grows to know them. My spotted memories are captured inside the glimmering prism of youth, which tends to lend truth to lie and lie to truth. I remember my mother humming to me while she gently traced her fingertips around my eyes and I slowly drifted off to sleep. I remember her cutting the crusts off of my bread and wiping her hands on a dish towel. I remember waking to the sound of her laughter, and, ultimately, to the sound of her tears.

My father was a military man, through and through. He believed in his country. He believed in his ideals. He believed so deeply that when the Air Force demanded he up and move his family, he immediately asked "How far?" I was born at Kadena Air Base in Okinawa, and by the age of two had lived in three different states and three different countries. By third grade, I had attended five different schools, the last of which was in Kaiserslautern, or K-Town, Germany. I remember that clearly, because that's where we'd been stationed when my father was shipped off to Iraq for Desert Storm, and that was where I was awakened by the sound of my mother crying the night she learned he had died.

My mother was never the same after that. Whatever memories I have of her after we moved to Colorado aren't the kind I try too hard to recall. I know it was cancer that claimed her, but she had started to follow my father the moment the Scud missile obliterated the fuselage of his F-15. I choose not to believe it was because she loved me any less, just that he had been her reason for living and I was a manifestation of that love, not separate from it. By the time we committed her ashes to the sky with my father's, I'd already been living with my maternal grandparents for nearly two years, the longest I had ever lived in any one place.

My grandfather had retired from the Air Force a full colonel in his early fifties in order to live the life his earlier sacrifices had afforded him. He had also been my father's commanding officer when he inadvertently introduced him to the daughter he had hoped would never live the life of a military wife as her mother had. I know he loved my father, yet, at the same time, I'm sure he hated him for taking his daughter from this earth. He didn't blame him, though. At least I don't think so. My grandmother did for a while, but my presence helped her get past it, for to despise him was essentially to despise me, since I was half of him, and I wore the better part of that half on the outside. And she would have thrown herself in front of a truck before ever thinking such thoughts.

They weren't my parents, nor did they pretend to be. Still, they devoted themselves to making me happy and helping me build a future. A future which, unfortunately, they had never been destined to share, but one for which I will eternally be in their debt.

My paternal grandparents were a different story. I could only assume that my father had parents. I mean, we all had to come from somewhere, right? He never spoke of them though, and when I asked about them his eyes would cloud up and he kind of vanished into a world inside himself. I figured if they were still alive, they'd try to track me down. I *was* their grandchild after all. By the time I was old enough to look for them, they had already passed. In fact, they weren't buried far from where I was now. Assuming they were indeed the right Billman Hilarion and Wavalene Maria Walker. I pretty much stopped looking once I found their obituaries. There was really no point in attempting to learn any more about them considering they were dead to me long before they died, or, rather, they had never actually existed. Nor had this reservation, which apparently my father had left the moment he was able and never once looked back. Like my grandfather, ever the pilot, used to say, "The future's on the horizon, not in your slipstream."

I knew precious little about that half of my heritage. Truth be told, I had never really cared. Not because I didn't get curious from time to time, but because for whatever reason it was my father's cross to bear, one he had elected not to bequeath to me. Now here I was, sitting in my pool Crown Victoria outside the tribal police station on a street my father must have intimately known as a child, soaking up every last bit of the air conditioning before I again braved the god-awful heat.

The thermometer on the in-dash readout said it had dropped to a mere one-hundred-five and I could feel the warmth radiating from the closed window. The faded asphalt wavered as a primer-gray pickup materialized in the distance like a mirage. It blew past fast enough to rock my car on its suspension. I glanced at my rearview mirror and saw that the bed was brimming with dark-skinned men, women, and children, crammed one on top of the other.

I opened the mirror application on my iPhone and tilted it so I could perform a quick crust check of my nostrils. It wasn't an actual mirror, obviously, but rather a forward-facing camera that was looking at you even as you were looking at it. I'd love to say I was above a certain level of vanity, but the way I saw it, you were the one who determined how other people would judge you. The last thing you wanted was to cede the upper hand before the first words came out of your mouth.

With a sigh, I reluctantly opened the door and climbed out onto the gravel parking lot. The searing heat hit me squarely in the chest and I inhaled fire into my lungs. How anyone could endure this climate on a daily basis was beyond me. By the time I passed the second-hand cruisers—which looked like early nineties model Caprice Classics handed down by another department whose logo still showed through from beneath the tribal seal—and entered the station, I was ready to trade my soul for a tall glass of something even remotely cold. What I found was all of the humidity that had somehow been sucked right out of the arid region.

A ceiling fan turned overhead and a window-mount swamp cooler chugged from behind the unmanned front counter, blowing little more than the rapidly evaporating hot water. I felt like I'd walked into a gym locker room. Beads of sweat rolled down my back between my shoulder blades. Maybe I should have just called from my car. After all, this was just a simple notification to let them know I would be actively conducting an investigation within their jurisdiction, one that required neither their assistance nor consent. I was just about to turn around when I heard the clomp of footsteps on the hollow wooden floor and a large man appeared from the office door at the back of the room.

He wore a tan uniform with the Great Seal of the Tohono O'odham Nation on the shoulder and a badge on his chest. I say wearing, but what I really mean was bursting out of. The collar threatened to cut off circulation to his head, which sat on a triple ring of chins, and his belly hung over his belt to such a degree that his shirt couldn't possibly remain tucked in. He had jet-black hair and dark, hooded eyes, which glittered with an intelligence belied by his sloppy appearance. It looked like he'd lost an argument with his razor. There were small nicks and cuts all over his jaw line and neck.

He stopped mid-stride and turned to face me. He looked me up and down for a long moment, then slapped the files he'd been carrying onto a desk at the back of the small squad room. The phone on the desk rang, but he paid it no mind.

I watched his face, zeroed in on his eyes, but for the life of me, I couldn't read him, which was a unique and somewhat disorienting experience for me. He must have read the expression on mine, because he placed his fists on his hips and cracked a crooked smile.

He said something in a language I didn't understand. The words were blunt and halting and delivered with an almost singsong rhythm.

I shook my head.

"It's about time," he said in English. "We've been expecting you."

FOUR

"You've been expecting me?"

"We were expecting you about a month ago. That's why I said it was about time."

"A month ago?"

"Suddenly there's an echo in here?"

"I'm at a loss."

"You're a fed, right?"

"Special Agent Lukas Walker. FBI."

"And you're here because of the report I faxed to the Phoenix office last month…"

He pantomimed a rolling gesture with his hands like he was trying to coax the rest of the story out of me.

"No. I haven't been briefed on your report. I'm here on an entirely different matter." I smiled. "Why don't we start over?"

"I think that would be for the best."

I flashed my shield, leaned across the front counter, and extended my arm over the logbook.

"Special Agent Lukas Walker. FBI."

"Chief Ray Antone. Tribal Police."

He shook my proffered hand and discreetly wiped his palm on his trousers. Like I could help it. It had to be a hundred and twenty degrees in here.

"So if you aren't here at my request," Chief Antone said, "then why *are* you here?"

I walked slowly from one side of the entryway to the other, checking out the small adobe structure. The walls were thin and cracked. There were points where the grid pattern of the chicken wire framework showed through discolored patches. The laminate desks were chipped and mottled with cigarette burns. The overhead fluorescent tubes hummed and flickered. The computers on the desks were bulky old Gateway PCs. Against the rear wall, behind the desks, were rows of dented file cabinets incapable of closing with all of the paper poking out, framed pictures of the new Tribal

Council Building I passed on the way here, and a faded painting of the tribal seal on the wall above a fancy stainless steel coffeemaker. The sunshine outside was attenuated by the accumulation of dust on the windows.

It was exactly what you would expect from an underfunded tribal police station in the middle of nowhere and it looked as though great care went into the perpetuation of that image. After all, I had seen the craftsmanship of the council building and figure whoever did that job undoubtedly had an exclusive contract and could have done a better job patching the walls in here with his feet. I could also see the bulge of a smart phone in the chief's front breast pocket. This was a man willing to let people think him primitive and incompetent in order to gain the initial advantage, but not at the expense of his taste for a good cup of coffee.

I liked him already.

That didn't mean I was ready to concede that advantage, however. And I still hadn't figured out how to read him. A man accustomed to the daily maintenance of such an elaborate lie undoubtedly knew what he was doing.

"Why do you think I'm here?"

"Who died?"

"Why do you think someone's dead?"

"I've got a reservation crawling with drug runners, a twelve-year-old granddaughter who thinks she's twenty-two, and my sciatica's acting up something fierce. But you're right…I've got nothing better to do than verbally spar with you, so I'll play along. If you were investigating trafficking, you'd be part of a task force and wouldn't be able to go anywhere without your ATF gorilla escort. If the problem was the gangs moving out onto our land, they would have sent someone of Hispanic descent. The only reason that I can think of for a handsome young buck with native blood like yourself to be out here is if there's the potential for media involvement and the boys back in Washington don't want to end up with a racial issue on their hands. You're obviously educated and the fact that you don't have a partner attached to your hip suggests a certain amount of autonomy, at least in the field. And I know the federal government doesn't trust anyone. So that means you're working closely with important people who can't be bothered to waste their precious time on actual physical investigative work. They trust you well enough to serve as their eyes and ears, but you also have the law enforcement skills to potentially bring permanent resolution to the situation. So I ask you again, who died?"

"I was hoping you could tell me."

"You're just trying to piss me off now, aren't you?"

I smiled. I still couldn't read him, but I had gained the upper hand in the situation. It wasn't much of an advantage, though. Not yet anyway.

I removed a manila envelope from under my jacket and set it on the counter between us. Antone looked up at me and I nodded. He opened the envelope and slid out three pieces of paper. Each was a photocopy of a digital picture forwarded to my office three days ago from the Border Patrol station in Ajo via the Phoenix office. The first was of the cliff side itself for locational triangulation, the second of the ground where the victim had bled out, and the third was of the smiley face painted on the wall.

Antone studied each in turn, then stacked them, straightened them on the countertop, and slid them back into the envelope. Without a word, he handed the pictures back to me, turned, and walked away from me into the office from which he had emerged when I arrived. A moment later, he appeared with a file folder in his hands. He held out the file and stared expectantly at me. I failed to read the expression on his face as I took it from him. I opened it and slid out a stack of reports, beneath which was a series of digital photographs.

"This is what I sent to the Phoenix Bureau a month ago," he said.

There was a picture of another mountain from a distance, then one of a trail running between two steep red rock walls. A classic bottleneck. I didn't see the blood spatters on the path until I turned the page and viewed the detail shot. The final three pictures were all of the twenty-foot design painted on the rocks in the victim's blood.

"That's Fresnal Canyon, about twenty miles south-southeast of here."

When I glanced up from the pages, I couldn't hide the surprise on my face. We were on a level playing field again, at least for the moment. And then he took the advantage back.

With a vengeance.

"Damned if you aren't the spitting image of your old man, but I'll bet you must hear that all the time."

FIVE

The Tohono O'odham Nation is the third largest Native American reservation in the country. The forty-five hundred square miles of desert land is divided into eleven geographical districts, which are governed by a council and an elected chairperson. The better part of its traditional land was acquired in the Gadsden Purchase of 1853 and then bisected by the now hotly contested Arizona border. Once known as Indian Oasis, the city of Sells changed its name in 1913 to honor Cato Sells, whose name in the O'odham language means "tortoise got wedged." It serves as the capital and government seat and houses roughly three thousand of the twenty thousand total O'odham, which kind of explained why I didn't have to look especially hard to find the police station.

The whole town was smaller than the subdivision in which I lived with my grandparents. I tried to imagine how I would have felt had my neighborhood been overrun by thousands of immigrants every day, some armed and toting drugs on their backs, others starving and dropping dead in the hills. I tried to imagine armed federal agents cruising the streets and Blackhawks beating the air overhead, day and night. Then I tried to imagine being impoverished and roasting alive on top of it all, a citizen of a country largely oblivious to my daily suffering and yet entirely separate from it, isolated from blood relations on the other side of an invisible line and unable to visit for fear I would never be able to return again.

And, ultimately, failed.

Not that I lack the imagination, but because the entire situation is far outside of my realm of comprehension. All I know is that even putting myself in that fictional position in my mind made me uncomfortable. I felt helpless. I felt hopeless. And I felt angry.

But angry enough to kill?

That was a line in the sand that took a certain kind of individual to cross, one already predisposed to sociopathic tendencies. And at this point I couldn't even be sure our suspect pool consisted of the twenty thousand O'odham. Any person from any state could have driven down here for a hunting expedition, and any bandit willing to smuggle drugs and potentially shoot federal agents couldn't be placed above killing for pleasure.

I was no better off now than I had been when I stepped off the plane this morning. Worse, actually. At least had we taken my car we could have enjoyed the modern convenience of air conditioning. The chief's squad car was like a sauna. He smirked every time I toggled the AC switch. I was starting to think of it as a stick I used to poke the midget who lived under the hood, prompting him to blow his rank breath through a straw and into the vents.

This kind of heat does strange things to your brain, as I was coming to learn. I saw lakes on the horizon, but we never seemed to reach them as they poured off the edge of the earth. I was saving the last two sips of my bottled water for when I needed them most, even though I knew they were evaporating by the second. My mouth was filled with the salty taste of my own sweat and the greedy passenger seat was soaking up every drop I wasted. I had a Beretta Px4 Storm .40 caliber under my left arm, there was a sawed-off twelve-gauge Remington bolted to the console between us, and Antone had a Smith & Wesson M&P .357 magnum semiautomatic in a holster under his right. I considered myself an even-tempered and level-headed individual, but a part of me really wanted to draw any one of those three and paint that smug grin of his all over the interior.

I hadn't risen to the bait he had dangled in front of me back at the station, but I knew it was only a matter of time. Eventually, I would stop deluding myself, and, in doing so, would sacrifice every advantage I currently held, which really only boiled down to the fact that my badge was bigger than his.

"Fresnal Canyon's just up there." Antone nodded toward the towering red rocks up the rise and to our left. "That mountain over there. Kind of looks a little like a top hat? That's Baboquivari. *Waw Kiwulik* in our native tongue. It is the most sacred of all places to our people."

That he had said "our" and not "my" didn't escape my notice. Sure, a part of me was curious. Who wouldn't be? I knew next to nothing about this half of my heritage, but I wasn't in any kind of mood to be drawn into this world right now. At least not while I had a job to do.

Antone went on anyway, despite the fact that I tried to appear as though I hadn't heard him. I stared out the window to my right, watching the creosotes and palo verdes fly past through the cloud of red dust that accumulated on the glass, and somehow inside of the car, as well.

"There's a cave below the peak. That's where I'itoi lives. He's our mischievous creator god. When the world was first born, he led the Hohokam, from whom we descended, up from the underworld and to the surface. His home is within that cave, deep in the heart of a maze. Visitors to the cave must bring him an offering to guarantee their safe return."

"I guess our victim must have forgotten to bring along an offering for this mischievous god of yours."

"Don't be too quick to lay this at the feet of I'itoi. There are many gods of mischief out here in the desert."

"Probably ought to look into getting that problem taken care of."

"You mock me, but you don't know the desert. Coyote is the most mischievous trickster of all, and it's thanks to the ineptitude of *your* policies that we have so many coyotes running amok out here."

"Touché."

"If it weren't for NAFTA and the sudden influx of cheap American corn, these people wouldn't need to risk their lives braving this heat in search of minimum wage—"

"If your reservation didn't offer them unmolested passage, they wouldn't be risking their lives braving this heat."

"I do not condone the smuggling of illegal substances on my reservation, humans included. I don't want drugs in the hands of my children any more than you do. But you try telling a rancher who gets a two thousand dollar annual treatise stipend from a government that claims ownership of his land that he can't feed both his starving animals and his family. You try telling a single mother she's going to have to leave her home in search of a job or subsist on the paltry sum the casino pays out once a year. These men come in here with cash money, and a lot of it at that. They throw it around like they have more than they could ever want.

Heck, what's the harm in letting a man store some things in your barn when he's willing to pay you five grand a month? Or how about that single mother who suddenly meets a nice man who's willing to take good care of her and her children and all she has to do is look the other way from time to time? This is our daily reality. The law—my law, your law—doesn't exist out here. When it comes right down to it, these smugglers are a whole lot less intrusive than the damn green and white Explorers tearing up our land and the war choppers thundering over our homes and sweeping their spotlights across our windows all night long. But you wouldn't know about things like that, would you? How could you possibly understand?"

His face was flushed and he was breathing hard when the cruiser coasted to a halt on a widened stretch of the shoulder.

I can honestly say that for the first time I was thankful to climb out into the heat and did so the first second I was physically able.

Surprisingly, it felt like it was starting to cool off. It might even have dropped below a hundred. I wouldn't have bet my life on it, but even if it was all in my head, I was grateful for the illusion.

The arrow-straight dirt road shot back toward the wavering horizon, where the blood-red sun was preparing to slink off into oblivion. The leaves of the bushes looked like they were on fire. To the east, the Baboquivari Mountains rose abruptly from the flat terrain, giant red rocks that made me somewhat nostalgic for the Garden of the Gods back home in Colorado. Shadows had even started to form behind some of the taller formations and in the steep canyons. And over it all lorded Baboquivari Peak like the angry fist of a dictator, somewhere beneath which the god who led my ancestors from the underworld sat inside of his maze, rubbing his palms together and plotting mischief.

Leave it to Chief Antone to kill my rising spirits.

"Don't get too excited about the falling temperatures. All that means is the snakes and scorpions are going to start coming out to hunt. And, believe me, they're going to be hungry and pissed off."

"I know exactly how they feel."

Antone smirked, mounted what appeared to be a trailhead, and struck off toward the mountains. I followed, but at a reasonable distance. I figured it was probably best to let him take the lead, considering he was the one who actually knew where we were going. That, and he was a bigger target for the rattlesnakes to strike.

Don't let anyone tell you I can't be considerate when I have to.

SIX

Antone was remarkably lithe for such a large man. He scaled those hills and trails like he was part mountain goat. Granted, he held onto his belt with one hand the entire time to keep his pants up, but we made excellent time and reached the canyon itself before sunset.

I had to marvel when I turned around and stared off across the desert and the miles of seamless sand and rolling hills that stretched off into eternity. Everything glimmered with an almost ethereal red glow. There was a strange beauty to the landscape that was perhaps enhanced by the inherent danger of it. I felt somehow triumphant, as though I had both bested it and been accepted by it. As though I had survived some sort of trial by fire, the reward for which was a momentary glimpse behind the veil, a peek at the gentle soul lurking beneath the deadly exterior.

Antone clapped me on the shoulder. I glanced back to see him nodding to himself with an almost wistful smile.

"We're burning daylight," he said, and led me deeper into the advancing shadows, which had begun to fill the canyon like floodwaters.

The scuffing sound of our footsteps echoed back at us from the canyon walls, which grew steeper and taller until they nearly blocked out the sky. Skeletal shrubs grew from the cracks in the rocks and tufts of wild grasses and ambitious creosotes and sage fought over the pockets of sand where the occasional ray of light reached the ground. A ribbon of sand suggested that a trickle of water had flowed through here somewhat recently, and the rocks were marked with old water lines from the sporadic flash floods. There were a ton of footprints, one of top of another, moving single-file into the mountains. Trash and shed clothing were heaped against the rocks in some places, dropped right onto the ground in others. I saw weathered burlap sacks and crumpled wads of duct tape from the massive bricks of marijuana smugglers carried on their backs. I heard the rattle of diamondback tails more often than I would have liked, but never actually saw one. An owl hooted, a forlorn mooning sound, and bat wings whistled overhead. Stars materialized from the blue sky as the black of night encroached from the east.

My sweat cooled and then froze. I had goose bumps, which was a divine sensation after allowing my body to maintain such a high temperature for so long. Crazy to think that it was probably still in the mid-eighties. The air was crisp and dry. I felt alive in a way that I hadn't before. It was almost as though I'd reached some sort of truce with the earth and we'd both agreed to a ceasefire, largely because the constant battles had gone on for so long that we'd forgotten who started the war in the first place.

Or maybe I was just mentally and physically exhausted and in desperate need of sleep.

"Just up ahead." Antone was wheezing, but showed no outward sign of slowing. "Past the fork."

"Why the rush?"

"You'll see."

Two thinner canyons merged ahead of us at a large stone formation that looked almost like a giant coyote in profile, sitting on its haunches with its snout raised to the sky. Its legs were eroded and discolored. Sand and desiccated weeds had swept up its back. Its rear end led to a narrow passage that wended to the right into the shadow of Baboquivari Peak. Antone led me down the opposite fork, which was even narrower. Ancient petroglyphs were barely visible on the stone walls where time and the elements had conspired to erase them, smoothing designs that must have been etched by hands as old as the Sonoran itself. The walls lowered to the point that I could see the cacti and brambles lining the edges, at least where there was enough dirt to take root. Other stretches were lined with rocks perched so precariously it was a miracle they didn't fall on our heads.

I recognized the trail from the crime scene photographs, and I knew exactly where we were when the bottleneck formed ahead of us. The canyon had veered to the left as we walked, funneling us to the north. I could see just the upper crescent of the setting sun to my left, framed by two tall stone formations. It shined between them and through a crevice in the canyon wall in such a way that it cast a spotlight onto the giant faded smiley face.

"He knows this area intimately."

"That's why the rush. You needed to see it like this. It wasn't just meant to be viewed. It was meant to be viewed at this precise moment."

I stared at the massive design. The blood had dried and flaked away in sections, but the image was still more or less intact. I could even still see the ovular impressions of the pads on the canine paw the unsub had used as a brush. It was similar to the one I had seen earlier, only missing the strokes that showed the hint of the circular shape of the head, as though the picture became one step closer to completion from one instance to the next, chronologically speaking. I couldn't find any corresponding Native American symbology, nor was there any modern societal correlation. I felt as though there were a deeper meaning I just couldn't quite grasp. A tip of the tongue kind of thing. All I could say with any certainty was that not only was the killer thoroughly enjoying himself, he had every intention of continuing to complete his design unless we figured out a way to make him stop.

I heard the crunching sound of footsteps and whirled, my Beretta already drawn and sighted on the source of the noise. Three people rounded the bend. I nearly drilled a hole through the forehead of the first and another through center mass of the second before my mind caught up with my instincts. The man in the lead wore his shirt tied over his head and jeans that were more dirt than denim. His shoes were mini porcupines of cactus needles. The woman to his right looked like she'd picked out her best blouse and blue jeans for a picnic in the park, but they were now ripped and tattered. She wore sandals that had obviously once had heels and her feet were caked with a crust of blood mixed with sand. The third figure was a young girl who couldn't have been more than twelve years old. Her tears had dried in muddy smears on her cheeks and her hair was a nest of tangles. Her pretty white dress was shredded and filthy, her bare legs scraped so deeply in some places that they were going to have to be stitched closed when the dirt was eventually irrigated from the wounds.

All three froze and stared at me with wide eyes. The man reached behind him and cautiously drew the girl out of the direct line of fire.

I slowly lowered my pistol and slid my finger off of the trigger.

A curious expression crossed the man's face, one I read as a series of conflicting emotions in rapid succession: fear, confusion, acceptance, gratitude. And then he and his family were gone.

Neither of us had known the other party was there. I could have gunned them all down and no one would ever have known.

"They don't understand how far the journey is," Antone said. "They're led to believe that it's just an afternoon hike after they're dropped off at the border. Little do they know it ends up being closer to four days across the sweltering desert. The coyotes keep their money and consign them to their fates."

I imagined the look of surprise on some poor migrant's face as he or she rounded the corner into the deep shade of the canyon only to find death waiting with a glimmering blade.

"They mostly travel at night," Antone said. "The smart ones, anyway. When the sun goes down and it's cooler. And they're impossible to track through these mountains after dark, even if you know these hills like the back of your hand."

I turned in a complete circle, but didn't see what I had thought I would. The canyon walls had to be at least twenty-five feet tall. A jump from that height was an unnecessary risk, and someone crouching up there would be clearly silhouetted against the sky. The killer would be better concealed down here in the shadows.

I found where he had waited about thirty feet deeper into the canyon, on the far side of the bottleneck. It had been easy enough once I located the nearly invisible scratch lines where the unsub had swept away his tracks. Interestingly, he had dragged the victim's body deeper into the canyon, in the opposite direction of the trailhead. I lost the brush marks under a riot of migrant footprints within a few feet.

"What's farther up there?"

"More of the same. What you're really asking, though, is how did he get the body out of here?"

I nodded and switched on my penlight, but it did little to combat the advancing darkness. Without a full battery of spotlights, we wouldn't be finding, let alone following, any tracks tonight.

"Coyote is the master of deception. If anyone knew his tricks, he would undoubtedly find his paw in a snare."

I stared up at the moon as it took form in the sky.

I'd been approaching this from the wrong angle.

The smiley faces.

The canine paw.

Our unsub fancied himself a trickster. There was undoubtedly even deception involved in the creation of that illusion. If I was right, there was nothing even remotely amusing about the message he was attempting to deliver. Nothing at all. And we would only learn more about him when he chose to reveal it, when he completed the design he had started, despite the fact that every single one of us knew what the design would look like when it was completed.

Or did we?

Somewhere in the distance a coyote yipped and bayed at the same moon.

"I'm done here," I said, and struck off back toward the car.

SEVEN

I was already formulating my report—which I would deliver via private videoconference directly to my Special Agent-in-Charge, Thomas Nielsen, when I reached my pool vehicle—as I walked down the trail toward the chief's car. My SAC was a good guy, as far as agents in his position went, but he was a lot more politically motivated than most. I don't know whose chair he had set his sights on; all I knew was that he didn't intend to remain in his for long. Denver wasn't New York or Los Angeles or Houston, but it wasn't a backwoods posting either. Nearly the entire front range of the Rocky Mountains fell under our jurisdiction. Phoenix could have made a legitimate argument for this being their case since it was in their backyard, but Nielsen would never have allowed it. In this case, I was his golden ticket. If my face ended up on the evening news, you could wager a vital organ that Nielsen's would be right there beside mine. He had pulled out all the stops on this one. He had a native—albeit half-breed—O'odham with an excellent track record working a high profile case with the full tactical support of a dozen federal agencies and the backing of the brain trust back at Quantico.

I'd never worked directly with Behavioral before. They'd profiled a few unsubs for task forces I was a part of in the past, but I'd never really brushed shoulders with them. If I even got to now. It was a distinct possibility that Nielsen would usurp that role, too. I was curious to see how they worked, though. My formal training was minimal, at least compared to most of the profilers with their multiple doctorates. The majority of what I've learned has been in the field. I have a B.S. in Cognitive and Developmental Psychology from the University of Denver, but rather than pursuing a doctorate, I had elected to join the FBI. Or, as I like to say, I was seduced by the dark side. I wasn't the kind of guy who could tolerate being cooped up in an office, nor was I the kind to spend my weekends in seminars or lectures.

And it turned out I really enjoyed carrying a gun and a shield.

Field work was even more fun than I had initially thought it would be. I loved the hunt. I lived for the chase. It was a game played on an open field with no rules and only our opposing wits as our allies. The only problem was the stakes involved. The longer we played this game, the more people died. And that, in my mind, was an unacceptable outcome. The time had come to put an end to this game.

Unfortunately, unless I got lucky, someone else was going to have to die first.

If they hadn't already.

Again, I was happy enough to let Antone take the lead. The visibility was decent since the moon was nearly full, but I figured there was no harm in letting the chief pick the way down the trail for me. If he went down, I'd know where not to step. I didn't own enough suits to sacrifice a decent pair of slacks like these.

The chief stopped dead on the path in front of me. Before I could ask why, I smelled it, too.

We had company.

The faint aroma of cigarette smoke. Hand-rolled, not domestic. Sweet. I could see the faint glow of a cherry downhill as the smoker took a drag, momentarily casting an orange glare over the Ford pickup truck against which he leaned.

Antone shook his head and started down the path again, his momentary burden noticeably lifted. He glanced back over his shoulder as we neared, a crooked grin on his face. Again, it was an expression I couldn't quite decipher, but I was starting to establish a baseline.

There were actually two men waiting for us when we arrived. They'd parked right behind the chief's cruiser, canted upward on the slight slope. The taller of the two dropped his butt, ground it into the dirt, and stepped away from the pickup. He was tall and slender and clad nearly entirely in faded denim, from his well-worn jacket to his open shirt and his jeans. The leather of his boots had paled to the color of dust and he wore the brim of his Stetson low, hiding his face in shadows.

The other was shorter and stockier, but even from afar it was apparent he was an impressive physical specimen by the slope of his shoulders and the taper of his waist. He hopped down from where he sat on the tailgate and rolled what sounded like a bottle deeper into the bed. He wore a checked flannel shirt open over a tight white T-shirt and even tighter blue jeans. A long, dark braid snaked out from beneath his cowboy hat.

Whoever they were, the chief obviously didn't perceive them as a threat. He approached them with his guard down and his fists on his hips. I thought I saw a smile form in the shadows lurking under the brim of the tall man's hat.

"How did I know we'd end up running into you sooner or later?" Antone extended his arm and shook the tall man's hand. "I guess word travels even faster than I thought around here."

"It does when the FBI rears its ugly head on our reservation. People go straight into panic mode thinking we're about to find ourselves in the middle of another Pine Ridge situation." He turned to face me. "Finally decided to show up, I see."

"Roman and his boy here were the ones who found what I just showed you," Antone said. He pronounced it Row-mahn. I couldn't help but think that made it sound pretentious.

"I figured I would look you up when it was a good time for me, rather than waiting for you to track me down when it was convenient for you. And I was curious. Can't fault a guy for that, can you?"

"Thought you'd catch a glimpse of the FBI's token Injun?"

His smile grew even wider. There were flecks of tobacco along his gum line.

"Like I said, can't fault a guy for being curious."

I heard the scuffing sound of boots from my left and felt the weight of Roman's son's stare on me. I turned casually to find his eyes fixed directly on my face. I nodded, but solicited no appreciable reaction whatsoever. I turned back to his father.

"Anything you want to tell me about the nature of your discovery?"

"Nothing I didn't already tell the chief."

"What were you doing up there when you found the crime scene?"

"Hunting."

"Hunting what?"

"Little of this. Little of that."

"Get anything that day?"

"It had been a fairly productive hunt, all in all."

"I assume you have an alibi for the time of the murder."

"Tell me when that might have been and I'd imagine I could scrape one up."

"Without a body, you can't fix time of death," his son said. I turned to find him still staring directly at me. I think he might even have advanced a step, but I couldn't be completely sure. This "boy" had to have been in his mid-thirties. I would have initially guessed lower based on his physique. Up close it was apparent that he wore his age in the lines around his eyes and the corners of his mouth. There was something oddly familiar about him, but I couldn't quite place it. His face was devoid of expression, save for the slightest twinkle of what I read as both amusement and hostility in his eyes. Or maybe merely distrust. "So there's no way you can pinpoint a date, let alone a time for which an alibi would be necessary."

"What do you know about the body?"

"Only that there wasn't one."

"And what do you think might have happened to it?"

"A lot of things can happen out here in the desert. Could have been a coyote dragged it off—"

"Coyote?"

He was about to say something else when his father cut him off.

"Whole desert's thick with them. We don't know any more about the body than you do, I'm afraid. We'd have told the chief if we did."

I glanced back at the son. He was still staring at me, but he had distanced himself enough that he was no longer in my personal space. The way the moonlight hit him made him look like someone I knew, but, for the life of me, I couldn't figure out who. There was something so familiar about his face that I was almost certain I had seen him somewhere before. It was the eyes. Something about his eyes—

He caught me looking and turned away to face the desert.

"Anything at all out of the ordinary you might remember could end up being important," I said to the father. "Don't hesitate to call the chief. He'll know how to reach me Mr....Sorry, I didn't catch your name."

"Walker," he said. "Roman Walker. And this is my son, Ban."

EIGHT

To say it was surreal standing in the home in which my father grew up would have been an understatement of titanic proportions. I felt like I had crossed over into some parallel universe where the father that was my father had never been my father, but some stranger who wore his skin and lived a completely different life.

I'm the kind of guy who needs to be in control of any given situation, which, in this case, was like trying to walk straight up a wall. I simply had to resign myself to the fact that I'd fallen down the rabbit hole and do my best to land on my feet. I had an investigation to conduct and could ill afford any sort of distraction, let alone one of a personal nature.

Despite my earlier gripes, I was fortunate to have ridden with the chief to the canyon. The long ride back to the station had granted me the opportunity to sort through my thoughts. And staring out into the desert at night—with the pitchfork saguaros lording over the sand and the sky so clear I could almost imagine reaching right up and grabbing the stars—did wonders to help me find something resembling a moment of clarity.

I don't know why I hadn't expected to encounter blood relations while I was here. It was naïve to think that my father's parents were his only physical link to this reservation. Considering he never talked about them, why in the world would he mention an older brother? Maybe there would have come a time when my father explained the situation to me, maybe even brought my mother and me out here to see where he was from. Maybe that had always been his intention and he simply ran out of time in the end. We all make plans for the future without seriously contemplating the fact that we could be struck by a car or diagnosed with some terminal disease or vaporized by a Scud missile the very next day. I may not have known my father as well as I would have liked, but I had known him well enough to understand that he wasn't a man willing to run forever. He was the kind who faced his demons, one way or another. Just on his own terms. Or at least that's the way I choose to remember him, the way I choose to be myself.

I could compartmentalize when I had to. The commitment to maintaining two lives—one professional and one personal—had been a prerequisite for joining the Bureau, especially as a field agent. The problem was that in this case, I had yet to determine where to draw the line between them. I don't believe in cosmic forces or serendipity or even coincidence. I couldn't ignore the fact that my uncle and cousin, who previously hadn't even existed in my wildest dreams, were the first to find the scene of a murder that was always meant to fall into my lap. Not because fate or destiny or some mystical shaman decreed it, but because I was the only logical choice for the assignment based on who I was and the skill set I possessed.

I had delivered my report via my laptop in my Crown Vic in the parking lot of the station after Antone dropped me off on his way home for the night. I think I did a reasonable job of appearing in control of the situation. I obviously hadn't been in a position to pass along anything resembling an actual development, but Nielsen had become somewhat detached himself after learning of the second similar case that had never made it onto our radar. It could have been easily misplaced or overlooked or dismissed out of hand. Things like that happened all the time. We needed to confirm that one of those scenarios had happened, though. Otherwise the spotlight of suspicion fell squarely onto the chief and, to a lesser extent, my newfound kin.

It hadn't taken very long to locate Roman's truck after that. I maybe cruised a dozen different roads before finding it parked in the dirt driveway of a small adobe house with nothing but open desert stretching away from it into the night. If I had any chance of seizing the advantage, if there even was one to seize, I needed my arrival to be totally unexpected.

I must have been really losing my touch. Roman had been sitting in a wooden rocker on the crumbling concrete pad that served as a front porch when I arrived.

"This one here is your daddy and me when he was maybe eight and I was ten." Roman pointed at one of roughly fifty framed pictures tacked to the cracked adobe wall. We were in a narrow hallway that separated the two bedrooms from the main living area, which itself was little more than an extension of the kitchen. In a way, the tiny house reminded me of every family housing unit on every Air Force base around the world. "That was the day I taught him how to shoot my twenty gauge."

I stared at the two young boys, one who had grown up to be my father, the other a complete stranger. It was obvious the children were related, but looking at the man beside me now, I had a hard time believing my father would have looked anything like him. This man was *old*, for starters. A quick mental calculation placed him in the neighborhood of sixty. The father from my memory had never aged beyond his early thirties.

There were pictures of the boys everywhere. Some were in black and white, others in faded color. The clothes looked mostly homemade and both boys had worn their hair long clear up until the point when they'd been able to braid their locks back over their shoulders. I don't think I ever saw my father with hair more than half an inch long. I found myself smiling at the boys, who always smiled right back. They were happy children. Their smiles reached their eyes. I couldn't help but wonder what possibly could have happened to drive a wedge between them.

And then we passed from the pictures of the boys to those of their parents and the seemingly countless generations of theirs. These were people who didn't smile for the camera and appeared largely annoyed by its mere presence. I won't say the wives looked fearful of their husbands, but they certainly weren't overjoyed to be in such close proximity, especially as the timeline went further and further back. The most recent portraits were something of an enigma though. There were plenty of inconsistencies from one to the next, perhaps as the nature of their relationship changed. The man made every effort to appear hardened, but I could tell it was merely a suit of armor he wore. The woman's eyes twinkled with life until, abruptly, whatever spark animated them fizzled.

"Those are your grandparents. Our parents. It really is too bad you never got to meet them. And they never got to meet you."

"They didn't even know I existed."

Roman turned and looked at me long and hard. His expression was one of contempt. At first, anyway. And then it softened to one of sympathy.

"I want to show you something."

He led me down the hallway and ducked into the room on the right. It was obviously the master, and it was a room in transition. The bed and coverings must have belonged to my deceased grandparents. As had the majority of the furniture. The clothes in the antique wardrobe and the majority of the prints and tapestries hanging on the walls reflected tastes I attributed to my uncle, who had moved into this house after his parents had been committed to a kind of assisted living arrangement that sounded more like a hospice to me. He stopped before a tapestry with the logo of the Arizona Diamondbacks.

"I always wanted to play pro ball," he said, as if that explained anything, then yanked on the decoration, sending pushpins flying. "I didn't have the heart to take these down."

I managed not to gasp, but just barely. There was no hiding the surprise on my face, though.

There were pictures thumb-tacked to the wall.

Pictures of me.

NINE

Most of the pictures had been clipped from newspapers I immediately recognized. Others were actual photographs snapped from afar.

I didn't know what to say. I couldn't even seem to remember how to breathe.

All of them were of me. My picture in the Rocky Mountain News when I won the science fair in eighth grade. Another from the Denver Post during my hockey days in high school. My commencement photo. An interview I did for the college paper. And there were snapshots. Everything from my high school to my college to my academy graduation. Pictures of me smiling and laughing with my friends and grandparents, entirely oblivious to the ones who had journeyed all the way from this reservation so as not to miss my special moments.

"Why didn't they ever say anything to me? I would have—"

"Would have what?"

"I don't know. I never had the chance to find out."

"It was a sore spot between my parents. My mother was the one who took the pictures. My father never approved." I recalled the pictures of my grandparents, of the grandmother whose eyes were alight with joy and the grandfather whose eyes reflected his love for her, but at the same time, a solemn commitment to his duty. And, later, the physical toll their emotions had inflicted upon each other. "He and your daddy didn't part ways on the best of terms."

"Why's that?"

"Because Rafael committed the one sin for which my father couldn't forgive him."

I scoffed. My father couldn't have sinned at gunpoint.

"What could he possibly have done that was so bad?"

"He left."

Roman shrugged and turned away. I caught a glimpse of the anger and the hurt on his face before he did. Everything may have transpired a lifetime ago for me, but the wounds were still fresh for him.

His boots clomped on the floor as he walked back out into the hallway. I turned to follow him and stopped when I saw the framed pictures sitting on the dresser. They were of a woman who wasn't in any of the portraits in the hallway. She was a beautiful woman, the kind who maintained her natural beauty as she grew old. Time had aged the portraits but not the woman herself, stranding the colors and the clothing in an era so long ago I couldn't even recall it.

I looked up when Roman leaned around the doorway.

"Ban's mother?"

His eyes flared with fire. Quickly. So fast I could have blinked and missed it. And then it was gone as though it had never existed.

"Those aren't for your eyes," he said, and ushered me from the bedroom.

I didn't force the issue. I had seen the woman's physical expression in Ban. My cousin. He had her mouth and her nose. These people were strangers to me. Whatever might have transpired between Roman and her was none of my concern.

I studied the pictures of the family I'd never known on my way back into the main living area. I tried to commit them to memory, because I wouldn't be coming back. There was nothing for me here. I took comfort from the fact that despite whatever may have happened, my paternal grandparents had cared for me, if only from a distance. This world might have been a part of my heritage and, to some degree, my past, but it wasn't my future. We all have our ghosts, and my father had left his here. I had no intention of making them my own.

"Offer you one for the road?" Roman said. He closed the refrigerator door with a single bottle in his hand before I even replied.

"Thanks anyway."

He popped the cap and started drinking while he walked across the living room toward the front door. It was a room at odds with itself. Aged adobe walls with surround sound speakers mounted to the cracks. A hand-planed mesquite table with a fifty-one inch flat screen on it. A wicker chair with a beaded design next to a leather La-Z-Boy recliner. Frayed woven rugs. A laptop on the end table. A Blu-Ray player balanced on a chipped and faded ceramic pot.

My phone vibrated in the front pocket of my pants. That was never a good sign. Especially not at eleven at night. I kept my thoughts from betraying me on my face.

"Thanks for the hospitality," I said.

"It was nice to finally meet you. I loved your daddy. I see a lot of him in you."

I tried to smile, but had to settle for a curt nod.

"I'm sorry I didn't get a chance to talk to Ban. Wish him my best."

"I'll tell him you asked after him. He's night security at the Desert Diamond Casino if you find yourself up that way. He's not the trusting kind, but he's got a good heart. Probably do you both some good to have a few words before you leave."

"We'll see what the future holds. It wouldn't surprise me if we ran into each other again."

I stepped down onto the porch. A scorpion skittered away from my shoe. When I looked back, Roman opened his mouth as though about to say something, then closed it and nodded to himself. I smiled and nodded back. I knew all about regret.

He closed the door, sealing off the strip of light that had spilled onto the driveway.

I climbed into the Crown Vic, slid my phone out of my pocket, and checked the number of the missed call. I didn't immediately recognize it. I had to drive all the way back into town before I was able to hold a signal long enough to check my voicemail.

The call had come in more than forty minutes ago. It must have been just floating out there in the atmosphere, waiting for me to catch a signal long enough to come through. Two more messages had been delivered since.

By the time I finished listening to the first, I had turned right on the main street through town and pinned the gas. Before the second ended, I had the brights on, the speedometer flirting with eighty, and gravel pinging from my undercarriage. I saw the lights on the horizon shortly after finishing the final message.

This wasn't good news.

This wasn't good news at all.

DAY 2

tash go:k

me'a

The Emergency Medical Research Center of the University of Arizona, in an effort to educate the public about the dangers of crossing the Arizona-Sonora border, developed a formula to determine the incidence of heat-related death. At ninety degrees Fahrenheit, there's a twelve percent probability of death should a walker set out across the desert. At ninety-seven degrees, that risk more than doubles. At a hundred degrees, the chances of individual survival plummet to sixty percent.

The average temperature in the Sonoran Desert in July is one hundred and four degrees.

TEN

Baboquivari District
Tohono O'odham Nation
Arizona

September 10th

I arrived at the same time as the dogs. There were two CBP SUVs parked facing the hillside, their headlights illuminating a game trail that wended up into a forest of heavily needled cholla and prickly pears. I parked between them and left my brights on. The top of the rise was crowned with a massive stone formation reminiscent of a medieval fortress. To either side of it, the jagged hills were a serrated blade aligned against the night sky. I could see the flicker of flashlights moving through the brush.

I opened my door and was assaulted by the sound of barking. The canine agent had the rear doors of his truck open and was unlatching the cage doors for a pair of large dogs that looked like a cross between a German shepherd and a wolf. One was jet-black, the other mottled brown and gray. Both had teeth that looked sharp enough to tear through a meaty thigh and jaws strong enough to snap bone. Had I not worked with units like this in the past, I would have been positively terrified by their apparent ferocity, but I knew these dogs were partners with their handlers in the truest sense. They went home with him at night and quite possibly even slept in the same bed. When they were in the field, though...

"Special Agent Walker."

I flashed my badge at the handler, who didn't even look at me. He was a wiry man with large ears and a long face. He wore his green CBP ball cap so low over his brow that I couldn't see his eyes. According to his name badge, my friendly new pal's name was B. Sykora.

"Stay behind me," he said. "Keep downwind at all times. Don't cross the tracks or you'll confuse the scent. Don't even think about trying to pet either of them. These dogs are trained to go for the groin or the throat if they sense that I'm threatened in any way, so don't try to approach me. If I tell you to do something, you do exactly what I say the moment I tell you to do it. Are we clear?"

I smirked and rolled my eyes.

"You had me at 'trained to go for the groin.'"

He sighed and shoved past me.

"Come on down, Pookie," I heard him whisper as he lifted down the black one. The other one hopped down on its own. He had them leashed and headed up the path in a matter of seconds. Sykora ran with them like the third dog in the pack. It was everything I could do to keep a visual on them. I don't know what kind of animal cut this path, but it was definitely thinner than I was. My sleeves kept snagging on the cholla needles and it felt like I had impaled my feet on spikes. I kind of hop-ran sideways through the hellish landscape until the headlights faded behind me and I had to use my penlight and the occasional bark to guide me uphill toward the point where I had seen the flashlights when I arrived. At least that fortress-rock served as a decent landmark.

The very second I exited the field of cacti, I pulled off my shoes and started plucking the needles out of my socks. I had whole chunks of cholla on the bottoms of my shoes where the thick needles had been driven clear through the soles. The pain was fierce, but tolerable. The itching, however, was something else entirely. I felt like I had ants crawling under my skin as I scrabbled up the slick talus to where the path wound back behind a cluster of saguaros and entered a shallow, sloping canyon.

I didn't know exactly where I was, but I had a general idea. This was the northern portion of the Baboquivari Mountain Range, near the point where it began to taper back into the rolling desert hills. I was roughly twenty miles east-northeast of Sells, ten miles south of I-86, and fifteen miles north of the crime scene Antone had taken me to mere hours ago. The site the CBP agent had shown me this morning was now forty-some miles southwest of here. If there was any significance to the geographical arrangement, I couldn't see it.

The path led deeper into the canyon, down the eastern slope of the mountain. I could hear the echo of voices, but couldn't make out the words. Flashlight beams glowed from around the bend.

The dogs started to bark. Hard. Frantic.

The voices became excited and I heard a shout and the clamor of footsteps.

I broke into a sprint and nearly barreled into a CBP agent as I rounded the bend. Had he been faster on the draw, he would have put a peephole in my chest before I shoved my badge into his face. He was jumpy and wired and his eyes stood out from his pale face like there was something pushing on them from behind.

"What's going on?" I asked.

"Dogs caught a scent."

More staccato barking. A crackle of static from the radio on the agent's hip.

"*Just a group of wets.*"

I recognized Sykora's voice.

"*Someone else call it in,*" a different voice replied. "*You keep those dogs moving, Brant.*"

"*If there's anything out here, we'll find it. We just have to start over again.*"

I inwardly cursed and blew out a long breath.

"You were the first on the scene?" I said.

The agent nodded.

"Walk me through it, Agent…" I held my light on his name patch. "…Reynolds."

"I was cruising the Venganza Drag when Oscar seventy-four went off."

"Oscar seventy-four?"

"Oscars are the buried sensors we plant in the desert. When they detect motion, they send a signal back to the station and dispatch relays the call to the nearest unit. They're numbered sequentially. I was the closest patrol. Roughly Oscar sixty-seven or so. Since I couldn't have been the one who set it off, we knew it had to be a bunch of wets." He glanced up at me. "Undocumenteds, I mean." A nervous smile. "So I drove out to the Oscar and found their tracks crossing the drag. We call them drags because we drag a grate along them to wipe out all of the tracks."

"I know what a drag is."

"Okay, okay. So I found their tracks. They crossed the drag walking backward. I mean, like that would fool anyone. Who in his right mind would leave the 'States and risk his life crossing the desert to get *into* Mexico, you know? It didn't take a genius to know they were going to try to cut across the mountains to get to the Amnesty Trail and I-86—"

"Amnesty Trail?"

"That's what they call it. They even print maps of it down there. The idea is that if you follow the landmarks all the way up the trail to the highway, there'll be a lookout posted in the hills to radio one of the drivers who cruise up and down the highway all day to pick them up and take them to a safehouse in Tucson or Phoenix."

"And you know where this trail is?"

"Everybody does."

"And you don't just close it off?"

"We patrol it. We don't have the manpower to just sit on it. Besides, most of the trail's on the res and those guys like us on their land even less than the UDAs."

He totally missed my point, but I didn't have the time to debate it.

"So you drove up to the lot here to cut them off."

"Right. They were moving up the eastern side of the mountains, so they wouldn't be able to see my headlights if I stayed on the western slope. We've all used this canyon as a shortcut before. I was just cutting through when I heard something up ahead. Sounded kind of like someone chewing really loud. Kind of anyway. So I got out my light, drew my gun, came around the bend, and bang! Right there in front of me is a mangy old coyote. Just sitting there licking the rocks, totally oblivious to the fact that I'm standing there with a light and a gun pointed right at him. I didn't want to shout and spook the UDAs. I mean, Lord knows if they're packing AK-47s. So I kicked a rock at the thing and it turned to face me like I wasn't even a threat. Its eyes flashed in the light and I saw that its muzzle was red. I took another step and it finally bolted off into the night. Another couple of steps and I turned my light onto these rocks over here..." He led me another five paces and lighted up the canyon wall with his flashlight. "...and this is what he was enjoying the hell out of licking."

I was right. This smiley face appeared to be slightly more complete than the last. The only real difference I immediately noticed was the shape of the nose and the fact that it pointed in the opposite direction.

The blood still glistened where the coyote had been lapping at it. The remainder had dried, but not to the point of flaking. My best estimate placed the time of death at roughly twenty-four hours ago. Two nights following the Border Patrol's discovery of the previous scene. The night before my arrival. The timing couldn't be coincidental. Not after such a long gap between the previous two, assuming there weren't more out there we hadn't found yet, which at this point, felt like a fairly large assumption. It was possible the unsub was dissociating and the murders were going to start coming faster and faster until we stopped him, but I was inclined to think not. The painting was meticulous, the strokes perfectly controlled, emotionless. Even less blood had been spilled on the path. It was the exact same *modus operandi*. Clean slice across the neck from behind, right to left, an arterial arc on the opposite wall. Two puddles where the victim had bled out, one from the neck and the other from the abdomen. It was almost surgical in its precision. Minimal suffering. An almost compassionate execution. He painted on the wall, then dragged the body off into the mountains once more on a travois improvised from branches that obliterated his tracks behind him. There was nothing to follow beyond the strokes of the leaves and the thin stripes of the hook-like thorns. He was still in control. At least of himself.

The most pressing problem now was that he'd identified his adversary—the FBI in general, and me specifically—and had decided to raise the stakes and aggressively take me on, head-to-head. This wasn't a case that was going to drag on indefinitely. He had directly challenged me to stop him. I knew exactly how this would end if I was able to, but the part that scared me was I had no clue what the consequences might be if I didn't.

I shivered despite the warmth of the night and stared out over the valley to the east. The Amnesty Trail. An endless stream of victims. Infinite places to hide. The American Dream. The Valley of Death.

The killer had announced his presence and declared his intentions. If word traveled as fast as Chief Antone thought, by now the killer already knew I had declared mine.

The blood would flow again.

Soon.

My first order of business had to be figuring out who was the weak link in the chain of information. Who at the CBP had let it slip that the FBI was being called in? Was the killer an agent or just someone who monitored their communications? At this point, it was my only real lead, assuming the unsub hadn't gotten sloppy and left something for the crime scene unit to discover, and the sooner I started chasing it—

A chaos of barking. Down the wash and to the right.

The crackle of static from Reynolds's hip.

"*They've got something,*" Sykora said, his words barely decipherable over his frantic dogs. "*It's a clean scent. Go on guys! Get...*"

I was at a dead sprint before the communication trailed off behind me, streaking straight toward the source of the barking.

ELEVEN

I passed the group of UDAs the dogs had first found. They seemed content just sitting there, passing around a water bottle one of the agents must have given them, waiting for their eventual arrest and deportation. After several days in the miserable desert heat, I'd imagine I'd be looking forward to an extended stretch in an air conditioned detention center with some warm food, too. Especially if I was about to get a free bus ride back to my family.

I hustled down the path as fast as I could, slipping on the loose gravel, sliding on slickrock, plowing through thorny bushes and dodging cacti. The barking grew louder and I could see the glow of flashlights through the mesquites at the bottom of the first valley. The dogs were going nuts. The agents were shouting. There were at least three distinct voices. Beyond them, about a mile farther down, an Explorer bounded down off of the drag and made its way up to the trail in our direction before the topography forced it to stop. The sound of the car door slamming echoed through the night. I was maybe twenty feet from the line of trees when the barking abruptly stopped.

I drew my Beretta, held my penlight beam parallel to my sightline, and approached in a shooter's stance. I could still hear the voices, but they were softer, muffled. I pressed through the sharp branches, using my shoulder to shield my face from the thorns. They latched right into the fabric like fishhooks and tore on their way out. I heard spiders the size of my hand scuttling across the detritus away from me.

I found the agents at the bottom of a dry creek bed, where presumably water had once flowed but now only creosotes grew from the rocky soil. One of them was down on a knee, shining his light on a flat river rock with what was definitely a small spatter of blood on it. Not much really. Maybe a drop the size of a dime smeared across the length of the stone. Without the dogs there was no way we ever would have found it. I heard them thrashing through the shrubs about thirty feet to my right.

The agent rose and openly appraised me. He looked like I imagined Wilford Brimley must have in his early fifties, with the kind of mustache that appeared to wear him as an accoutrement rather than the other way around. He inclined his head and grunted. I'd dealt with enough grizzled veterans to know that his expression meant that I had been reluctantly accepted as long as I was helpful and didn't step on any toes. I hoped my return nod purveyed the message that as long as he stayed out of my way, I wouldn't be forced to shoot him. I figured he got the gist when he glanced at my Beretta.

The other agent was off to the side, talking into his two-way with his back to me, whispering so that he couldn't be overheard by either of us. I tapped him on the shoulder and relived him of his radio when he turned around.

"This is Special Agent Lukas Walker," I said into the microphone. "I need you to check and see if there was any unexplained Oscar activity last night."

"*I can't do that without a direct order from my supervisory agent*," a woman's voice said.

I glanced back at the man from whom I had borrowed the two-way, read his face, and peeked at his left hand where it rested on the hilt of the club tucked into his belt.

"The killer could be out here with me and your husband right now."

A long pause.

"*Give me just a second*," she finally said.

I don't think it even took that long.

"*No unusual or unexplained activity last night. Only confirmed patrol vehicles on established routes.*"

"And there were no long or unnecessary delays from one Oscar to the next?"

"*Not without documented arrests. Is that what you documentaries needed?*"

"Yeah," I said. "That's what I needed to know."

That wasn't at all what I wanted to hear, though.

I passed the radio back to the agent and slowly turned in a circle.

The unsub knew this area. Knew it like the back of his hand. Knew it so well, in fact, that he knew exactly where all of the

Oscars were and how to circumvent them without setting them off. He knew how to beat the east-west drag system. He knew not only how to remove the body from the scene of the crime, but how to get it to a vehicle of some kind and out of the area without leaving a single telltale track. He knew everything that I didn't. Fortunately for me, that narrowed the list of potential suspects down to a much more manageable number. I was going to have to be exceptionally careful how I approached it, though. The unsub was definitely wired into the system.

The barking stopped.

All three of us turned in unison and looked to the south.

I bolted straight toward where I had last heard the dogs, charging headlong through shrubs that tore at my clothing and dodging others that would have done serious damage to me at that speed. I couldn't hear a blasted thing over my own ruckus, save for the distant hoot of an owl and what I could have sworn was the howl of a coyote. I burst from the mesquite thicket with the majority of my skin still attached to my bones, stumbled up a short rise, then skidded down a slick slope lined with scree. I barely stopped in time to keep from impaling myself on a flowering nopales cactus the size of a tree with pads like dinner plates. I skirted it and heard a sound so incongruous with the situation that I couldn't initially place it. It was the sound of…laughter?

On the other side of the nopales, the dogs were running in wild circles, first one way, then the other. Noses to the ground, tails in the air, they wheeled around the small clearing, sniffing creosotes and sage and cacti and the ground, nearly colliding with each other while their handler sat on the ground between them. Sykora was laughing so hard he was crying. There was dirt on the tip of his nose. He looked up and saw me and started to say something, but ended up laughing even harder. He held up a handful of damp earth. Whatever the overture was supposed to mean, I obviously didn't get it. The expression on his face didn't fit with the laughter. It was one of both frustration and…admiration?

Sykora wiped the tears from his cheeks with the backs of his hands and managed to climb to his feet. The dogs continued to run aimlessly around him until he steadied them with a single gesture of his hand. One sat to either side of him as he held out the dirt again. I stared at him blankly, waiting for an explanation. Frankly,

I had been starting to wonder if he'd found himself a button of peyote when he sniffed the pile in his hand and offered it to me again. His laughter trailed off. I realized I was undoubtedly looking at him with the same befuddled expression as the dogs.

"Go on," he said. "Take a whiff. Tell me that's not absolute genius."

I leaned forward and was hardly within a foot of it when I smelled a foul stench and quickly recoiled.

"For the love of God! What the hell is that? It smells like piss!"

Sykora started laughing again, but stopped abruptly when he saw my face. That was one of the great things about being able to interpret facial expressions; I could also deliver them with the kind of precision that made them impossible to misread, even for someone who spent the majority of his time with animals. Even the dogs must have recognized the expression that suggested thrusting urine into the face of a man with a semi-automatic pistol dramatically shortened one's life expectancy into the range of…oh…seconds.

"That's exactly what it is," Sykora said. "Coyote urine to be exact."

"You can tell the species of animal by the smell of its pee?"

"I train tracking and rescue dogs for a living. I have whole shelves in my garage lined with bottles of urine. Tell me you wouldn't find little details like that important if you knew you could end up off on your own and about to stumble blindly into a mountain lion's den?"

I couldn't fault his logic.

"What did you mean by genius?"

"Don't you see?" He held up the handful of earth again and shook it. I think we'd reached the point in the conversation where we both recognized that he'd been holding the dirt-urine longer than absolutely necessary. He hurled it off into the shrubs. "He had the urine with him. He knew we'd have a canine unit. Not only did he cover his tracks, he confused his scent trail. The urine is so concentrated that the dogs can't smell anything else over it. We're going to have to go back, find his scent again, then try to pick it up out there in the open desert. That's if we're lucky. Between all of us and the arrival of the crime scene unit, we've undoubtedly destroyed whatever scent trail was once there. This guy knows exactly what he's doing. He even sprayed the urine in what looks like a spiral pattern to get the dogs running in circles. Chasing their own tails. Get it?"

I shook my head.

"Then go back and start again. We need any lead we can possibly get."

"Do you really think someone smart enough to think of using coyote urine to fool the dogs would be careless enough to leave anything resembling a trail leaving this clearing?"

I shot him a look that said he had about three seconds before I shot him with something else. Whatever else he might have been, Sykora was not a stupid man. He and his dogs vanished back in the same direction from which we had come at about the same time the other agents finally arrived. The younger version of Wilford Brimley crinkled his nose.

"Coyote bitch," he said.

Apparently you could also tell the sex of an animal by the smell of its piss. There was a whole world of urine intricacies out there to explore. I was totally missing out on all of the fun.

It wasn't until that moment that I realized just how out of my element I truly was. I was going to have to modify my approach if I had any hope of catching the unsub. He wanted us to catch him, but not yet. Not until he'd completed his grand design and delivered his message. And he wanted to have a little bit of fun at our expense in the process, namely by demonstrating his superiority by outthinking and outmaneuvering us. He knew the established law enforcement protocols, both federal and tribal, and had spent much time planning clever ways to subvert them.

I walked away from the other agents and crested the adjacent ridge. The Sonoran Desert stretched away from me into the darkness, past where the agent was picking his way uphill with his flashlight, past his car with its headlights staring blankly in our direction, and all the way to the unmarred eastern horizon.

He was out there right now.

I could feel it.

Coyote is the master of deception. If anyone knew his tricks, he would undoubtedly find his paw in a snare.

The King of Lies.

You mock me, but you don't know the desert. Coyote is the most mischievous trickster of all, and it's thanks to the ineptitude of your policies that we have so many coyotes running amok out here.

The Killer.

I had a Beretta Px4 Storm .40 caliber under my left arm, there was a sawed-off twelve gauge Remington bolted to the console between us, and Antone had a Smith & Wesson M&P .357 magnum semiautomatic in a holster under his right.

The Coyote.

Somewhere in the distance, an animal I was beginning to revile yipped and howled at the moon, its voice echoing off into eternity.

TWELVE

A serial killer is defined as someone who kills three or more people in a timeframe of greater than a month with a cooling-off period in between. Conservative estimates suggest there are between thirty-five and fifty serial killers at-large in the Unites States at any given time. Some theorize a more realistic estimate places that number between one hundred and one hundred and fifty. That's roughly the same amount of American-born hockey players currently in the NHL. Who do you think you have a better chance of running into on the street?

I've worked a grand total of five cases involving serial killers. That's almost one a year. The first was the kind that didn't garner a whole lot of attention. Not at first, anyway. I was fresh out of Quantico and part of a task force composed almost exclusively of local law enforcement agents. My partner and I were essentially sent in to act as an FBI presence. You know, as a show of support. After all, we weren't entirely convinced we were dealing with an actual serial killer. Considering the crimes had been committed right there in our own backyard, it seemed prudent to at least pretend we cared until we could either dismiss the situation or assume authority over it. At that point, we were only looking at two murders with similar, although not necessarily identical, MOs. Both involved dark haired women in their early thirties who had been strangled with some sort of ligature and dumped at construction sites in the northern part of downtown Denver, where gentrification was in full swing. It wasn't until a third was discovered in the carcass of the Gates rubber factory that we knew for sure.

Fortunately, the victim hadn't gone quietly. The killer had been identified using a tissue sample scraped from the back side of her right upper incisor, which brought us to the residence of a man named Lester Frye, who worked for the staffing agency that provided night security guards for the construction sites. As such, he'd been at the periphery of the investigation from the start, just close enough to realize when we were about to nail him. We found him with his big toe in the trigger guard of his shotgun and the bedroom ceiling of his apartment painted with blood and gray matter.

Our involvement might not have been what brought resolution to the case, but my preliminary, informal profile had been spot-on and my then-Assistant Special Agent in Charge Nielsen had rewarded me by getting me a small, largely observational role on the Boxcar Killer task force. By the time I was handed the assignment, five bodies had been discovered in freight cars along the main north-south railroad route from Wyoming through Colorado and all the way down into New Mexico. The only connection between the victims was the nature of their deaths: blunt impact to the base of the occipital bone with enough force to sever the spinal cord. Internal decapitation, they called it. No other physical or sexual violation, despite the fact that they'd all been discovered completely naked. My task had been to track the credit card activity of the victims both prior to and after their deaths. I had taken it a step further, though. I had isolated the final transactions of the victims on the established dates of their murders and utilized the various security cameras at nearby ATMs, street lights, and inside the stores themselves to establish what the victims had been wearing, the only thing the killer had taken from them in addition to their wallets. Three of those cameras—one each in Cheyenne, Fort Collins, and Pueblo—had also captured an image of the same man following them from a distance. Facial recognition software did the rest.

Andrew Stanton, a fifty-three year old railroad engineer who'd been out of work since the economy started to founder, had been downsized by the very freight line on which the bodies were discovered. We picked him up at the Burlington Rail Station in Casper, Wyoming, wearing a dress and makeup belonging to his most recent victim. Apparently, he'd been using whatever cash the victims had been carrying to purchase tickets, dressing in their clothing so no one would recognize him, and simply riding from one end of the line to the other and back again, essentially living on the trains since he knew no other life.

My ingenuity garnered me a larger role in the task force investigating the Drifter, a name I never really found fitting. To me, that moniker made him sound like a man who traveled the country, searching for the place where he belonged. I envisioned him as looking a lot like James Dean in *Rebel Without a Cause* based solely on the name, which was a preconceived stereotype I had to fight against the entire time. In actuality, the Drifter was a rather plain looking man named Dennis Howard, who fashioned homemade rafts he could set adrift on the Mississippi River. He just strapped the bodies of his victims to the undersides of these floating heaps of junk and trusted the mighty river to eventually destroy them and bounce the corpses along the bottom, one of which ended up as far south as Natchez, Mississippi. Considering he lived and hunted in St. Louis, that was no small accomplishment. Lord only knew how many others were still tangled on the bottom or buried in the silt or washed up in any number of vast marshes.

Had his MO been to drown them, we might never have found him. Instead, he took his victims to an abandoned factory that used to process bone meal for pet foods, where he butchered them in an insulated dry storage room that had accumulated a layer of crusted blood on the floor so deep we couldn't even find the bottom with a hammer and chisel. The victims had inhaled the lingering particulates, which forensics had been able to scrape from their sinuses, tracheas, and lungs. Since they were dead before submersion, they never breathed the water into all of those ordinarily air-filled recesses. Had he not kept their eyes, we might never have convicted him.

The fourth was the crown jewel on my resume, the feather in my professional cap. I had initially started investigating the case on a hunch. Five housewives had been reported missing from the southern suburbs of Denver over a six month span. Wives leaving their husbands wasn't uncommon. Nor was leaving without taking any of their belongings with them. Women walked away from their lives and started from scratch with their lovers every day. None of the women had left behind children. A history of infidelity was essentially impossible to prove. And if the police tried to track down every wife who left her husband, they wouldn't have any time left to give speeding tickets. What first caught my eye was that in each case the husband had filed the formal missing persons report immediately following the end of the twenty-four hour waiting period. All of the reports had been filed on Saturday evening, which meant that all of the women had left them late in the afternoon on a Friday. Records indicated that all five husbands had called the police and pretty much every emergency assistance agency and nearby hospital multiple times. In each case, the wife had left behind her car, everything she owned, including her purse, and a husband who, upon interview, failed to set off my facial BS detector. Each of the husbands, to a man, was convinced that his marriage was in excellent shape, there were no problems with fidelity, and he would be willing to do anything within his power to bring her back.

Without any proof of foul play, my only option was to talk to the neighbors, who pretty much corroborated what the husbands had said. One in particular, a busybody I was confident I'd caught about a half a bottle of wine into her evening, suggested that the woman across the street might have run off with the UPS man. She said she sure as hell would have. Apparently, he'd had some pretty muscular arms, over which she had drooled while he was leaving the house carrying a large box back to his truck. A call to the main UPS hub had confirmed that no delivery or pickup had been scheduled for that address, nor were they missing any trucks from their fleet. The man on the phone had chuckled about the muscular arms comment. It turned out that was a trait fairly common to men who delivered heavy packages for a living, believe it or not, but he did invite me down to interview the drivers who worked the southern routes. One of them, a ruggedly handsome guy named Rich Meyers, had proffered his hand and looked me in the eye and I had known right then and there that he was my man. It had been written all over his face. Not guilt or fear or regret, but a smug kind of pride. Not arrogance, per se, more like the expression of a cat that knew for a fact there were no canary feathers around its mouth and it had hidden the bones where no one would ever find them.

We did, though.

A search warrant served with a battering ram later and we found the remains of all five women, each in a different meat freezer in his garage. He'd been so proud of himself that he told us all of the details, about how he had been delivering to these women for months; how they had looked at him like he was a piece of meat; how he had rushed through his earlier deliveries and hurried back to their houses as his final stop of the day; how he had smiled and offered to carry the big, seemingly heavy package inside for them; how he had knocked them unconscious with a blow to the head and carried them back out to his truck in that big, formerly empty box; how he had dropped them off in his garage, locked them inside their new homes, and rushed back to work to punch out right on time. The bloody smears and claw marks on the undersides of the lids validated his story. The other things he told us he did to them upon his return are buried in the back of my mind, for those are words I choose never to relive, the expressions I never want to see again, the fates I wouldn't have wished upon my worst enemies.

That was just over a year ago now. The case that had made me, that had helped carry Nielsen into the SAC's office, that had brought me out here now.

This was now case number five. This was no longer a scenario where having a good looking native man—one still riding a modicum of celebrity in the press—to trot out in front of the cameras when they showed the bloody smiley faces was the main point of my continued presence. This was now officially the third murder perpetrated by the same person with the same MO. There had been a cooling-off period between the first two, followed by a period of acceleration.

I had no choice but to declare it official.

I was up against a serial killer.

He had identified me as his adversary.

And with this victim, he had declared war upon me.

A war I was no longer entirely certain I could win.

THIRTEEN

The sun was already rising by the time I reached my car. It was a good thing it had been dark when I arrived at the scene. If I'd had a better look at the maze of cacti, there's no way on this earth I would have attempted that route, let alone at a sideways run with only my penlight to guide me. It was a miracle I wasn't slowly bleeding to death from a million puncture wounds. A brighter man than I was would have taken one of the paths that wound around the cactus field on the way back. That brighter man would have been repeatedly struck by the thousands of diamondbacks I could hear shaking their rattles as they emerged from their dens to bask on the flat red rocks. That brighter man had probably at least figured out where the nearest emergency medical assistance could be found, though. I bumped that task to the top of my list, right below having a little chat with Chief Antone.

His words still troubled me. As did that fact that he was left-handed and in each instance the killing stroke had been delivered from behind, right to left. That in itself wasn't proof that the killer was left-handed, but it was somewhat damning evidence. The problem was that we'd already established that the evidence couldn't be trusted. If our unsub fancied himself the mythical trickster of lore, then nothing could be taken at face value, especially now that he'd demonstrated how meticulously every detail had been plotted.

The red desert shimmered under the red sun as it crested the red mountains behind me. The dust that rose from my tires glittered red in my rearview mirror. Even with the AC going strong, I could feel the heat starting to take hold of the world without through the window. I didn't need to glance at my in-dash thermometer to know that the sun wasn't even all the way up and it was already pushing a hundred degrees. Today promised to be even worse than yesterday. Between the deadly heat, the brutal landscape, and the venomous creatures, I couldn't fathom how anyone would actually choose to live here. The thought of starting my day in a pool of sweat, shoving my feet into slippers the scorpions had claimed during the night, and stepping out onto my porch to find a rattlesnake coiled around my morning paper was about as much as I could bear. It was no wonder my father had left this miserable place at the first opportunity. You couldn't possibly get any farther away than the Air Force could take you. And this was about the only place on the planet where they could never send you back, at least not now that the Cold War was over and the Barry M. Goldwater Bombing Range was decommissioned, leaving behind craters and bunkers and the husks of tanks and live munitions to collect dust for future generations of our vaguely hominid mutant descendants to unearth and study.

Don't let anyone tell you I can't be every bit as nostalgic as the next guy.

I came across the chief's cruiser by accident. He was turning onto the main drag from the north as I was coming in from the east. I followed him all the way to the station and pulled into the gravel lot beside him. He sat in his car, staring at me through the window for several long moments with an expression I couldn't interpret on his face. It took me a minute to realize he was waiting for the dust to settle so he didn't get a big mouthful of grit. By the time we got out of our cars, a filthy skein had settled on my windshield that I was more than grateful not to have in my lungs. It made me wonder how much had already accumulated in there over just the last twenty-four hours. I tried not to think about the fact that people died in sandstorms not from being pelted by grains or buried under dunes, but by drowning. Technically, asphyxiation by sand. As an Air Force brat, I learned all sorts of interesting trivia that would probably never do me much good as a game show contestant. Unsurprisingly, most of it seemed to have something to do with strange and unique ways to die. I guess when you're in the business of killing, it pays to learn a little about the craft.

Heat stroke, for example, is a nasty way to go, especially considering you remain cognizant of your ultimate fate the entire time. In a nutshell, your body sweats to lower your internal body temperature in essentially the same manner as an evaporative cooler, but that sweat costs you fluids, and there's a finite reservoir from which to draw. Once that reservoir is exhausted, your body starts to wring it out of you at the cellular level. The blood keeps it as long as possible in an effort to maintain the flow to your brain, largely at the expense of your limbs and viscera. You stop forming urine, but continue to amass toxic byproducts your kidneys can no longer filter. You stop producing saliva, so you can no longer swallow or even wet your tongue, which begins to swell inside your mouth. You stop generating tears, so there's nothing to cleanse the dust from your eyes or lubricate your lids enough to blink. The sun burns your eyes, causing a ghostly reddish-white cataract to form, robbing you of sight. Your lips blacken and split, letting you keep the pain, but not the blood. Consciousness comes in waves. There are the hallucinations and then there is death, either of which is vastly preferable to the searing pain that exists in between. Eventually, your body can no longer combat the external forces, allowing your core temperature to rise beyond your physical threshold. Past 102. Past 104. Past 106. Your body ceases to function. Whatever control you once held over your physical vessel fades into memory. Some people have been known to peel off their clothes, fold them neatly, and fall dead mere steps away. Others try to swim down into the ground in search of water or cooler sand and end up half-burying themselves. Still others are found with their mouths sealed shut by cactus needles from attempting to eat the pads in a misguided effort to steal the moisture they were designed to hoard. And there are some whose momentum just carries them forward until they're dead before they hit the ground.

The distance from my car to the front door of the station was only fifteen feet, but all of those thoughts went through my head during the walk. I didn't care if the water came out of the tap orange with rust, I was going to drink the hell out of it at the first opportunity. Maybe I could spontaneously evolve some sort of hump to contain a little extra while I was at it.

The expression on my face must have been common around these parts, because I could definitely tell Antone was enjoying a good smirk at my expense.

Deciphering that expression wasn't a victory to write home about, but it was a small victory nonetheless.

"You look thirsty enough to drink piss," he said. "There's a water cooler in the back office."

I looked squarely at him and tried to divine exactly what he meant by that, what he knew. And just like that I was back to square one.

"Okay, okay," he said. "So we refill the container from the tap, but at least it's cold. Do you have any idea how much it costs to get a Deep Rock delivery all the way out here?"

"Surely any driver would be thrilled to make the trip, if only for the scenery."

I ducked into the office and filled one of the plastic cups stacked on the desk by the cooler. The others had names scribbled on them in black marker. Apparently, these weren't designated single-use. Or maybe Louis and Olivia just really liked their cups. The tank made a blurping sound as it filled the cup. I pounded the first one and took the second back out with me.

"Looks like you enjoyed some of the scenery last night yourself." Antone was leaning over one of the desks with his back to me, but I could hear the smile in his voice. I glanced down. My pants looked like they'd been attacked by some great quilled creature. Loose threads dangled from a hundred different puckers in the fabric and there were several small tears through which you could see the scabs on my skin.

"Let me guess...you found another one of our friend's smiley faces, am I right?" He peered back at me with one eyebrow cocked. "I assume my phone number must have slipped your mind. It's kind of hard to remember, what with one nine and two ones and all."

"Your powers of observation are impressive. You must have a great mind for details."

He stepped away from the desk, which apparently belonged to my eco-friendly, water-drinking pal Officer Louis Abispo. I guess when your entire existence is predicated upon land that's been hotly contested for centuries, it pays to head off any potential confusion. Even the fax machine had Louis's name on it. The curled fax Antone had just torn off the heat printer didn't. It had a lot of blurry words and a series of photographs of the canyon wall at which I had been staring in person only a few hours ago.

"We have an arrangement with Ajo Station," he said.

"And here I thought you'd tapped into some mystical shamanistic powers."

I watched the anger flare in his eyes. Just a quick spark, but it was something. I figured a dig at his heritage would expose the chink in his armor. That infuriating smirk was back on his face a heartbeat later.

"Let's take a ride," he said. "There's something I want to show you."

FOURTEEN

Don't let anyone tell you I can't adapt on the fly. I learned from yesterday's mistakes. After taking a few minutes to change into a pair of jeans and hiking boots, I donned my blue FBI windbreaker and matching ball cap, and got into my car before the chief could object. I had that air conditioner cranked up so high I had to put on my sunglasses just to be able to keep my eyes open against the ferocious arctic winds blowing from my dashboard. I had loaded my hump and had the plastic cup I had reappropriated from the station half-full in the cup holder. I was ready for whatever the morning might bring.

"Turn right up here," Antone said. He was sitting in the seat beside me with his eyes closed, seemingly perfectly at peace with the world. His jowls jiggled as the car jounced from the pink asphalt onto the gravel road. "Now just keep going straight."

We were heading due south with the mountains lording over us to the left. I could see Baboquivari Peak at the furthest extent of my vision to the southeast and thought about that mischievous creator god of ours leading the Hohokam up from the underworld. I imagined crawling through dark tunnels from the heart of the earth, emerging to find myself in this almost Apocalyptic desert wasteland, and then turning right back around again.

"What's so funny?" Antone asked.

I glanced over to see that he hadn't even opened his eyes. Saguaros flew past behind him like pitchforks raised in defiance of the sky. He smiled and I went back to navigating the straight road. Now that I had satisfied my physiological need for water, my next order of business was tracking down some coffee. The monotonous landscape and the buzz of the tires and the rhythmic vibration of the suspension reminded me of just how long it had been since I last slept.

"Stop here."

I coasted to a halt at an intersection in the middle of nowhere. The east-west road led straight into a deep valley between mountains to my left and the horizon to my right, where a rooster tail of dust trailed what I assumed to be a vehicle.

Antone opened his eyes.

"Freshly grated," he said. "Perfect timing."

The engine made a ticking sound as it idled. I could feel the dust settling on my skin as it snuck in through the vents. It formed a dry paste on my tongue. For a moment, I nearly thought about switching off the AC. Can't win for losing, I suppose.

"Waiting for the roadrunner, Wile E.?"

If he caught the coyote reference, it didn't show on his face.

The cloud of dust kicked up by the distant car faded into the eastern horizon beneath the wavering sun.

"Turn left here," he finally said. "No. Not on the road. Into the desert itself."

I hesitated for a second or two before cranking the wheel and rocking over the gravel shoulder and into the sand. Branches and bushes scraped the sides of the Crown Vic with loud screeching sounds and I suddenly realized why Antone hadn't put of much of a fight. It was a pool car, anyway. I wasn't going to lose any sleep over it.

"Keep the drag to your right." He reached toward the dashboard. For a moment I thought he was going to kill the air, forcing me, in turn, to kill him, but his hand stopped over the portable VHF transceiver/scanner. "May I?"

I nodded and he clicked on the radio. He dialed in a frequency I quickly recognized as belonging to the Border Patrol. Their lingo and radio chatter were unique among all law enforcement agencies. And you could always count on the agents out in the field to have music blaring inside their SUVs. Beneath the snippets of conversation, I could clearly hear both Metallica and Bruno Mars, which, interestingly, didn't mesh as poorly as one might expect.

"What are we waiting for?"

"You'll see."

The desert bumped past beneath us. I had to slow the car to maneuver around clusters of cacti and piles of stones. I could hear cholla skeletons raking the undercarriage. I had to use the windshield wipers to clear the glass of dust, which was seeping into the car and settling in a coating thick enough that I again thought about my lungs and the fun-filled prospect of asphyxiation.

"See that big saguaro up ahead? The one kind of standing out from the top of that hill with all of the palo verdes?" I nodded. It was maybe a few hundred feet ahead and slightly to the left. "Stop when you get right up to it."

I had no idea what he intended to do, but he was definitely starting to try my patience. I don't have many inherent character flaws, at least that I'm willing to admit, but the few I have are probably worth at least a casual mention. I'm physically averse to the sound of a person chewing with his mouth open, I can't stand people who try to talk to me during sporting events, I would love nothing more than to shoot out the tires of people who drive too slow in the left lane, and I absolutely despise people who waste my time. If I had my way, these would be capital offenses that fell somewhere on the spectrum of severity between presidential assassination and mass murder. If Antone didn't get to the point in a hurry, I was going to sentence him to the long walk home, and we all know how that would end now that it was pushing a hundred-five degrees.

I rolled to a stop and put the car into park. The hell if I was killing the engine, though. Not while there was still Freon to abuse.

Antone lifted the transceiver out of its charger and opened his door. The heat raced in and buffeted me from the side like a runaway truck, nearly knocking the wind out of me.

"You coming or what?" Antone said, and closed the door.

I was thinking "or what" sounded like the better option, but I opened my door anyway and climbed out into what felt like an oven. Glass is made from superheated sand, as everyone knows. Sand has reflective properties similar to the facets of gemstones, which serve to both conduct and repel light and heat. The ambient temperature might have been a mere hundred-five, but with the added heat radiating from the ground, it had to be pushing one-fifteen. I could feel the rubber soles of my shoes starting to melt. The sweat came so hard and fast it gave me the chills. My chest felt as though there was a midget sitting on it. My vision momentarily wavered.

And it wasn't even noon yet.

Antone crested the rounded knoll and stood on top of a rock that looked like a tortoise shell. The saguaro stood a solid five feet taller than him. I shoved through the sharp shrubs and climbed up beside him. Cacti grew from the crevices in the rock and I'm pretty sure I didn't want to meet the diamondback that shed the monstrous length of desiccated skin tangled in the prickly pear by my right foot.

"You listen." Antone passed me the two-way. "Tell me what you hear."

There was a lot of activity. It sounded like one unit was chasing a group of UDAs toward the highway while two more converged on a different group northeast of Lukeville. A park ranger in Organ Pipe blurted something about shots fired and a panel truck tried to barrel straight through a barricade at the edge of the reservation. The dispatcher was positively frantic trying to coordinate backup units and air support. It was mass chaos on a scale the likes of which I'd never imagined. It sounded like a battlefield out there, and yet from where I stood I couldn't see another living soul, let alone any indication that we weren't the last two people on the planet.

"What am I supposed to be hearing?"

Antone smirked, hitched his pants, then crouched at the base of the saguaro. He brushed aside the leafy branches of a palo verde and looked up at me expectantly.

"They plant these in features of the landscape they can readily identify from a distance, like this big old cactus here."

I didn't see what he meant at first, not until I squatted down beside him. There was a lump in the soil from which an antenna stood like a willowy sapling.

I listened to the chatter again, then looked from one horizon to the other before letting my gaze settle on the chief.

"We're sitting right on top of an Oscar and dispatch didn't relay the alarm to a field unit."

Antone's smirk broadened into a smile. He stood and reached into the front pocket of his pants. He pulled out a sleek black box roughly the size and shape of a radar detector. A series of lights ran down one side; a row of switches on the other. Four rubber-capped antennae were screwed into the very top of it. I stared at the lone red light glowing on its face.

"A hundred thirty bucks at Radio Shack," he said, waving it in front of me. It was a portable digital GPS/five-band signal blocker, the kind of thing people used in movie theaters and classrooms and at all sorts of events to make it impossible for the jerks to ruin their experience by yammering endlessly through it. The kind of device favored by conspiracy theorists everywhere to prevent the government from triangulating their location using the microchips implanted in their brains or teeth or wherever. "The Oscars function just like any other remote transmitter. They generate an RF signal that's amplified by the cell towers and relayed to a receiving station. And I just jammed the signal with the push of a button."

He beamed and switched the red light off.

The response was immediate.

"*Oscar Nineteen? Oscar Nineteen?*" the dispatcher's voice crackled from the static.

"*Unit three-two-six responding,*" another voice cut in. "*I'm maybe ten miles out.*"

"Might want to straighten your tie, Special Agent Walker," Antone said. "We're about to have company."

He started back down the hill toward my car.

I looked past him at the horizon, where I could already see the cloud of dust rising from the road once more.

FIFTEEN

I dropped the chief back off at the station and drove out of town. I needed time to think. The portable signal jammer changed everything. The Coyote, as I had come to think of him, could travel through the desert with relative impunity, as long as he was able to prevent the Oscars from radioing in his location, but that still left two glaring problems.

First...his tracks.

If he was traveling by car, he would still leave tire tracks. And he couldn't cover any significant distance on foot, least of all with a corpse in tow, without leaving at least one recognizable print. Even if he was avoiding the main roads and driving through the open desert, someone would have noticed something. With so many CBP vehicles routinely patrolling all of these drags and the almost superhuman tracking skills the agents possessed, I found it hard to believe there was a single one among them who would miss tire tracks like the ones I had left when I drove off the road with Antone. You could probably see my trail from orbit. Throw in the fact that the air space was closely monitored by radar due to all of the drug trafficking and there was no possible way he could have flown in. Not to mention the predator drones with their thermal sensors flying sorties over the desert. How could one man possibly beat them all?

And second...where were the bodies of his victims? Or maybe a better question would be what exactly was he doing with them? I got that he was leaving a message. What further use could he have for the remains after leaving his cryptic design? Deep down, a part of me suspected there was more to the message than what I'd seen so far. More than the eventual completion of the smiley face. I couldn't help but think that the victims themselves had a role to play in the killer's endgame, but, for the life on me, I couldn't imagine what.

I wished I could run a few thoughts past Nielsen and through the guys at Behavioral. I still hadn't determined where the information was leaking yet, so I couldn't trust anyone, especially since I was dealing with someone who not only knew how the specialized law enforcement protocols worked, but someone who was technologically adept enough to circumvent every countermeasure we had in place. For all I knew, someone with that kind of skill could pluck all of our communications out of the ether and break our encryptions in his head.

I had thought I was driving aimlessly until I found myself parked across the street from the house where my father had grown up. Maybe subconsciously this had always been my destination. Like I really needed a distraction. Or perhaps that's exactly what I needed. Who knew? I was just about to drive off again when the front door opened and Roman stepped out onto the porch. It was a long driveway and I was about two hundred feet away, but the Crown Victoria wasn't the invisible, anonymous vehicle the federal government must have envisioned when it signed the contract with Ford. I might as well have had a siren mounted on the roof.

Roman cupped his hand over his brow to better see my car with the glare on the hood and roof, then raised his arm in greeting.

Nothing I could do now. I turned down the driveway and drove right up to him. He stepped back inside and closed the door before the dust could enter the house. I sat in my car until the dust settled. He emerged onto the porch at the same time I climbed out of the driver's seat.

"I had a hunch you'd be back," he said.

"That makes one of us."

He grinned and ushered me inside with a sweep of his hand. I guess there was a part of me that hoped something of an echo of my father might still reside here, something through which I could feel closer to him, if only for a short time, but nothing like that existed here. This was a stranger's house. This man was a stranger to me. There was nothing to bind me to this place, nothing to link me to my past or foretell of my future. And yet I found myself inexorably drawn to it. A behavioral geneticist would argue that blood seeks blood, that I inherently recognized a "sameness" in my uncle and that my senses identified a biological similarity in hormones or pheromones or the smell of his sweat or any number of invisible traces. A psychologist might say I felt orphaned and isolated and was attempting to create a sense of wholeness to fill the void left by the deaths of my parents when I was so young. I just knew that I needed to be here right now, whether I was led here by my brain or my instincts. There was some deep-seated answer I needed to find for a question I didn't even know how to pose.

Roman stood back while I walked a circuit of the room, again studying the contradictions in furnishings. The collision of modern and traditional was a train wreck that made me uncomfortable on a primal level, as though there were a war being waged just out of sight.

"You want to know why your father left," he said.

I nodded. Maybe it was as simple as that.

Roman sighed and sat down in the La-Z-Boy while I continued to pace the small house, perhaps feeling like a tiger in a cage as my father once must have. A wistful smile settled onto his face.

"Rafael and I were inseparable, you know. We did absolutely everything together from the time we could crawl nearly until his eighteenth birthday. That was when things started to change. We went from playing football and going hunting every day to barely speaking. I'm a big enough man to admit my role in our falling out. Not a whole lot of good that does me now. I think Raffi knows that, wherever he rides the wind now."

I stepped into the hallway and looked at the boys. They had been happy as only children can be. They knew nothing of pain or suffering and each new dawn brought the promise of excitement and adventure. Perhaps a part of me was envious, maybe even a little jealous, for by the time I reached the age of the boys when they started to braid their hair, I had been forced to confront the worst thing in any child's life, regardless of his age. I lost both of my parents, the threads that tethered me to the world. As far as I was concerned, they died on the same day; I just had the opportunity to say a long goodbye to my mother as she wasted away.

"You have to understand…this was a different time. This was the early eighties and the threat of nuclear war was real. Especially out here. The ground shook nonstop from the bombing range. Day and night. Boom-boom-boom. Dust filling the air. It felt like the end of the world. As far as we knew out here, it was just a matter of time before we went to war with the Commies. There were all sorts of people moving down here and digging up the desert building bomb shelters. Survival camps. Pseudo-military groups. Propaganda out the wazoo. And your daddy got it in his head that he needed to be the one to do something about it."

I moved on to the pictures of my grandparents: one whose face was alight with life and the other who desperately wanted to join her but felt the pressure of his responsibilities and traditions. I wished I had known them.

"Look at this from our perspective. The O'odham are a proud people. We've been here since before there was a United States, since before the first white man ever set sail on the ocean, since before anyone started keeping track of time. We might be citizens of your country, but we are first and foremost members of the Tohono O'odham Nation. Our responsibility is to our families and our people. To our way of life. To the perpetuation of our sacred traditions. My father and those of his generation viewed the Cold War as someone else's problem. The white man's problem. We all knew the Commies wouldn't launch their nukes because we would launch ours. Mutually assured destruction. It was all political posturing, a stalemate. So why did we need to throw our hat into the ring? Rafael felt differently. He said we all have a responsibility to freedom, without which the O'odham Nation would be absorbed and our way of live destroyed forever."

As the pictures aged, so did the people in them. These were serious men and women from a more serious time. When more children died at birth than not. When starvation was a real threat. And when people still carried the memory of their land being sold by people who didn't own it, and them right along with it.

"Your daddy and mine were too much alike. That was what it came down to in the end. Both of them treated responsibility like a religion. They swore an oath to it and lived and breathed its tenets. The only difference was they prayed at different altars. When Raffi came home from school one day and said he'd decided to join the 'Forces, there was so much yelling you could have heard it all the way from the Rio Grande. I was going to the community college and working construction at the casino, but I was still living here. I remember it like it was yesterday. I was sitting right over there by the hearth. Eating black beans. Strange the things you remember. Raffi walked right in with his head held high and told my father that he was getting married and signing on with the Air Force."

That caught my attention. He didn't meet my mother for at least another two years.

Roman glanced over his shoulder. I caught his expression as he caught mine. He looked like a man who'd tracked mud into someone else's house. He hadn't meant to let that slip. He recovered quickly and turned away once more.

"The very next day he disappeared for close to a week. Came back with his head shaved and news that he'd been in Colorado. He'd enlisted in the Air Force and would only be around until the end of the summer. Your grandfather told him there was no reason to wait that long. Your daddy agreed. Your grandfather disavowed his very existence and your father turned his back on his people. My parents were never the same after that. I don't think my mother ever forgave my father for chasing Rafael away. I don't think he was ever able to forgive himself either. Those were some dark days, and I was more than happy to find my own place right after that."

I tried to position myself so that I could see the expression on Roman's face when I asked the question that was eating at me, but he stared straight through me and into another time and place.

"What happened to the girl my father was going to marry?"

"She met someone else and moved on with her life. I think she was always haunted by his ghost, though. First love and all that. Hmph. We were all just kids back then."

"He was your brother. Why didn't you ever track him down?"

"I loved him, but I had nothing to say to him. He turned his back on me too, you know. Don't make him out to be some kind of saint."

There was an edge to Roman's voice. The same edge I had heard the night before in his bedroom. The edge that told me it was time for me to leave.

He continued to stare off into memory as I stood there in front of him, caught between the present and the past.

SIXTEEN

After I left Roman sitting in his chair, I made the eighty-minute drive into Tucson to buy a small refrigerated unit that plugged into the cigarette lighter of my car and a full case of Arrowhead water. I was hoping to expense it, but at this point I didn't care in the slightest. It was odd…two days ago I looked at bottled water as a scam perpetrated by greedy corporations hoping to make money off of a product that was essentially free to them and refused to contribute any of my money to their coffers. On principle. Today, I viewed it as emergency medical intervention, the potential difference between life and death. I also got myself a big, greasy, sloppy burger. That was a luxury I simply couldn't pass up. Nor was the two hour nap I took in the back seat. I was hoping not to have to use the signal jammer I picked up at Radio Shack, but better to have it and not need it than to need it and not have it. By the time I headed back out into the open desert, I felt like a new man. I was refreshed, mind and body, and I had gained something of a new perspective.

I was approaching this case from the wrong angle. I was following the unsub, allowing him to lead me to his ultimate message. Instead, I needed to be proactive. If I was correct in my assumption that his goal—at least his first goal—was to complete the smiley face design, then I already knew his figurative destination. Rather than waiting for him to get there, I needed to head him off at the pass. There was something we had obviously overlooked at the crime scenes. The Coyote had used urine to obfuscate his trail for one simple reason: if we'd been able to follow it, it would have led us directly to him. It was often the most simplistic logic, the kind employed by children, which led to the greatest discoveries. I needed to go back to the beginning and start all over again.

Something my grandfather used to say kept playing over and over in my mind.

Show 'em the left and bring the right.

It was a fighting metaphor. Distract your opponent with some left-handed jabs so he doesn't see the knockout blow you're about to deliver with your right coming.

I couldn't help but think that this was exactly what the Coyote was doing with the smiley faces; distracting us with a grand design to prevent us from uncovering his true goal. I had a sinking feeling in the pit of my stomach that whatever it was had to be far worse than I could imagine.

I ended up driving through Sells on my way to the crime scene Agent Randall had shown me yesterday morning, the second chronologically. It was a different place in the heat of the day. School must have just let out. There were children kicking a soccer ball in a dirt field, others playing in the parking lot of a nameless restaurant serving what smelled like spiced beef, beans, and tortillas from buckets on folding tables. There were families eating and laughing together, sitting in the beds of their pickups or on the hoods of their cars or at the picnic tables I could barely see through the condensation on the inside of the front window behind the servers. I smiled as I drove past. They were so busy enjoying themselves that no one even looked in my direction.

That wasn't entirely true.

There was one person toward the side of the lot. His eyes were locked on my car the entire time. The T-shirt under his flannel was brown with dirt and grime. As were his jeans, which had bloody handprints smeared across the thighs. Rattlesnake skins hung from what looked like an artist's easel beside him, over which they'd been stretched to dry. The innards of the snakes were laid out before him like long sausages or already chopped up in the bucket next to his cutting block.

I nodded to him despite the tinted glass and watched in my rearview mirror as he stared at my car until he vanished from sight.

I had a hunch my newfound cousin Ban wasn't quite as happy to see me as my uncle was. And based on the way I had left him, I didn't imagine I would be getting an invitation to the Walker family reunion this year. Or any other.

I sensed overt hostility there that I couldn't quite rationalize. I won't pretend I understand anything about reservation life. I get the fact that my father violated some unwritten code. I know that his decision to leave was a betrayal on many levels, but there was something else that no one was telling me. I could see it in their eyes. They were keeping something from me, something that still bothered them, even so many years after my father's passing. Considering I was a stranger and I couldn't imagine any of them gave a rat's ass about my feelings for them or anyone else, I couldn't think of a single good reason not to just hit me squarely in the face with it. It didn't help that I was a federal agent either. I must have embodied pretty much everything they hated in a single package that looked just like any of them.

While the anger in my cousin's eyes was understandable, I was having a hard time interpreting his facial expression. It was almost as though he wasn't wearing one at all, as though he had a permanently bland affect, an emotional void. I was going to have to look into that. Not necessarily because I cared about him or about mending fences on my father's behalf, but because in much the same way as Chief Antone, he was an enigma to me.

I was still pondering the way he had stared at me through the car window, as though he could actually see me through the dark tint, as I picked my way higher along the treacherous path Randall had guided me up for the second time in as many days. I was so lost in thought, in fact, that I didn't notice I wasn't alone until I heard the skitter of pebbles.

I suppose a normal person's response to an unexpected noise is to look up and evaluate the situation. I drew my Beretta and aimed it at the source.

Two men burst from behind a clump of cholla and sprinted away from me.

Blue jeans and cowboy boots. Dirty button-downs with fake pearl snaps. Hair wet with sweat.

Immigrants.

I jerked my finger out of the trigger guard before I shot them both in the back of the knee.

The woman who had been killed here had never stood a chance.

I stepped around the cholla and found myself staring down the sightline of my pistol into three dirty faces, the whites of their wide eyes a stark contrast to their filthy skin. They were just kids. The oldest was a boy who couldn't have been more than eighteen years old. The girl he cautiously eased behind him and out of the line of fire appeared to be a few years younger. The third was a mop-haired boy who couldn't have been more than twelve or thirteen. He started to cry.

"La Migra?" the older boy said. He stared me up and down and then repeated the words. "La Migra?"

I shook my head slowly back and forth and lowered my weapon.

The older boy's expression metamorphosed from terror to bewilderment to understanding in the span of a heartbeat. I could only continue to stare as they leapt up from the ground where they'd been cowering and ran right past me. I stared down at the bloody needles of the dead cholla clusters on which they'd been kneeling as they raced toward the open desert in the same direction as the older men who had abandoned them to their fates.

I hoped that I hadn't just done the exact same thing.

I heard the scrabbling sounds of their shoes on the gravel and rock, the clatter of talus as they slid downhill, the scraping of the mesquite branches across their clothing, and then a hollow *thump*. Then another. And another still.

I turned and looked downhill, to where the loose scree slid down into the yellow weeds at the edge of the mesquites. The branches still swayed where the children had shoved through and into the dry creek bed. I never took my eyes from that spot as I slipped and slid and skidded down. I pushed through the now-still branches and weeds that tangled around my ankles, stomping the ground as I went.

Stomp.

Stomp.

Stomp.

Stomp.

I hopped down into the sandy creek bed and turned around. I could see the signs of their passage. The bent and broken branches. The trampled weeds. The collapsed edge of what was once a rocky bank. I stared at one point that didn't look quite right for a long moment, then raised my foot and stomped on it.

Thump.

I did it again.

Thump.

I dropped to my knees and brushed at the sand and gravel, but they didn't move. I could have sworn I smelled a trace of urine. I swept my hands to either side until I found the straight edges of what appeared to be a large square board and fully exposed them. I dug my fingers into the dirt, grabbed one edge with either hand, and lifted it upward. The board came away with minimal resistance. It was only an inch thick and about two feet tall by two and a half feet wide, but it was large enough to conceal the mouth of the tunnel that led down into the earth.

SEVENTEEN

Everyone knows about Pavlovian or Classical Conditioning. Whenever Pavlov fed his dog, he would ring a bell. Eventually his dogs began to salivate at the mere sound of the bell. A specific physiological reaction had been conditioned in response to an external stimulus. Another, lesser know facet of this psychological concept is generalization. You let a boy pet a rabbit and every time he does, you scare the hell out of him by clanging two pipes behind his head. In time, he grows to fear not only the rabbit, but every other furry white animal. Even a fur coat. A specific reaction to a general stimulus. Further down the chart you come to odor generalization, which is an unusual phenomenon wherein your brain conditions itself with a kind of sensory memory. It remembers the worst thing you've ever smelled and categorizes it as such so that whenever you smell something really dreadful, your brain interprets that scent to be the classically conditioned odor of memory.

In my case, it was the scent of a stagnant warm-water slough in the San Louis Valley marshes. My grandfather took me duck hunting there about twenty years ago and, I kid you not, the smell that belched out of the vile black mud when I slogged through it in hip waders was like burying my face in a fat man's crack after he ate a ton of chili seasoned with sulfur, and inhaling deeply when he passed damp wind. Ever since, I haven't been able to smell cabbage soup, a park trash barrel, a gym locker room, or enter a port-o-potty without their rather ordinary scent generalizing into that flatus-bog odor.

Until today.

The horrific stench that came from the dark hole in the earth was worse than anything I had ever encountered. This one was going to be with me for the rest of my life, I was certain. It was how I imagined the asphalt might smell after driving by the same dead dog on the side of the highway every day for an entire sweltering summer, watching the fur rot off and the flesh putrify and the scavenger birds pick at it and the insects dissolve it, hoping someone would come along and scrape it up, and when no one ever did, finally pulling over with a spoon and trying to do it myself. I was going to miss that fat man and his sulfur-chili, because after this, that was going to be a fond childhood memory.

The flies didn't seem to mind, though. I could hear the echoing drone of their contented buzzing coming from the depths, beyond the range of my penlight.

If this was my reward for not shooting those undocumenteds, I was going to need to have a little chat with the man upstairs about his incentive plan.

I pulled my shirt up over my mouth and nose and bit it to hold it in place. A couple of deep breaths proved that the smell had already invaded my sinuses and there was no way of evicting it now, so I resigned myself to breathing through my mouth. I held out my Beretta and my penlight and slithered into the hole behind them.

The tunnel was barely wide enough to accommodate my shoulders. There was no way I would be able to turn around. If I ran into trouble, I was going to have to back blindly out. Fortunately, whoever had constructed it had put some serious thought into its design. There was rudimentary cribbing made from scrap wood supporting irregular plywood remnants. Based on the texture and the color of the wood, it had been down here for years. At least I knew the sand and rocks weren't going to collapse on me and bury me alive with this rotten stench.

The dirt floor was scarred with scratches I was now easily able to identify as the thorns of mesquite branches. There were coarse ridges that suggested the tunnel had originally been dug with a collapsible shovel or spade. They hurt my elbows and knees, but at least they provided some traction.

My beam caught up with the black flies, casting shadowy blobs across the rock wall where the tunnel appeared to terminate. They grew larger and larger as I neared. Their buzzing grew louder and louder. I'd been wrong to think the smell couldn't get any worse. It somehow amplified itself with each wriggling movement I made until the ground vanished beneath my arms and I found myself staring down into a small cave roughly the size of a refrigerator box. At least I could rise to my hands and knees, which made locating the mouth of the tunnel opposite me even easier. I had to swat the bloated flies out of my face as I advanced deeper into the earth. Eventually, this second tunnel opened up into another cave where I found the source of the smell and the flies' delight. There were broken mesquite branches in the corner, their withered leaves and thorns crusted with blood. Beside them were wadded balls of Saran Wrap that were a sickly shade of black and positively covered with flies.

He had dragged the body in here, removed it from its travois, wrapped it in cellophane to contain the smells of decomposition and putrefaction, and left it down here for some length of time— presumably the duration of the physical investigation—before coming back to retrieve it. That's why we had lost his trail so easily and had been unable to pick it back up. There hadn't been one to follow, at least not at that time. And he used the same urine trick to conceal the hidden hatch. For all I knew, he could have been sitting down here in the darkness with it that entire time. Hell, he could still be down here…right…now.

I rose to my feet and turned slowly around. I was in a natural formation roughly the size of a walk-in closet, with smooth stone walls that leaned inward toward each other and met about a foot above my head. Ancient petroglyphs had aged to nearly indistinguishable impressions. There was another tunnel up near where the rocks formed a pinnacled ceiling. I shined my light up into it to make sure the way was clear, and then hauled myself up into the confines. Again, I found myself nearly wedged in there as I squirmed farther into the mountain. I figured I had to be somewhere under the stone wall upon which the second smiley face, chronologically, had been painted.

I won't pretend to be a geologist. I know nothing about the different kinds of rocks beyond the fact that sandstone crumbles, granite is hard and gray, and limestone is smooth and subject to the erosive forces of water. Whatever this was, it was red and smooth and had been channeled by forces far older and stronger than man.

The passage wound to my right and then started a steady ascent. I saw occasional smears of bodily dissolution. This was the path he had used to remove the remains.

My pulse thundered in my ears. My erratic breaths echoed back at me from the stone walls. I could barely see my gun ahead of me. I could be wiggling right into some kind of trap and I wouldn't know it until my spirit was looking back down at my lifeless corpse.

And then, abruptly, the tunnel ended.

I managed to roll over onto my back and directed my penlight upward. A natural stone chute of sorts led straight up. It took some doing, but I worked my way to standing and shined my light over the walls. There were what almost looked like small recessed shelves leading up into the darkness. Perfectly designed for one hand and one foot to either side. I worked my way upward until I ran out of up and shoved another wooden slab out into the fresh air, which, even though it was superheated, felt absolutely divine as it washed over me, filled my lungs, and cleansed my sinuses of the smell of festering death.

I climbed out, blinking, into the blinding light and sat on the edge with my legs dangling back down into the shadows. The wooden slab had been adorned with a stone that made it almost invisible. You would have to know what it was to distinguish it from the surrounding rocks, from the cracks between which all sorts of blossoming cacti grew. Massive red rock formations rose all around me. From where I sat, I could no more see the surrounding desert than anyone out there could see me. I was about to start climbing up the rocks to figure out exactly where I was when I caught the reflection of the sun from something metallic beside me. A thin, coiled wire poked out of the ground at the edge of the hole. I pinched it between my fingers and pulled on it, exposing its length all the way to the base of a prickly pear, where a small radio transmitter had been fitted into a crevice near its roots.

A tiny red light blinked on the face of the black box.

The Coyote knew I was here.

EIGHTEEN

There was no time to pat myself on the back. The moment I triggered that transmitter, I had accelerated my adversary's timetable. He wouldn't have equipped a beacon like that unless by finding that cave I was closing in on him. While that in itself was an encouraging thought, I still didn't have any idea who the Coyote was. The only new knowledge I had added to my woefully sad stockpile were the facts that he knew things about this desert that few, if any, other people did; he'd been planning this for what had to have been years; and his shoulders couldn't have been much broader than mine. And he was strong. Dragging a body was more difficult than one might think. We were talking about a minimum of a hundred pounds of dead weight, no pun intended. Probably more. And somehow pulling it behind him while he squirmed on his belly, then hauling it up and out of the earthen tube.

I debated calling in a crime scene response team from the Phoenix office to scour the cave and the egresses from it, but I knew they wouldn't find anything useful. The Coyote had planned this too meticulously to be careless when it mattered most. He had anticipated someone finding his hidey-hole at some point and surely took all of the proper precautions to keep from leaving prints or shedding trace evidence. They wouldn't have found anything beyond the victim's unmatchable DNA in the tunnel he had used to exit the warren either. If I was correct and he had dragged the remains down the western face of the rocks, there was nothing in which to leave a footprint and the wind was blowing right across the mountainside, scouring it of even the dust that coated damn near everything else on the reservation. And there wasn't a track of any kind in the surrounding desert as far as I could see.

I wouldn't be able to sit on these findings for very long, though. If I didn't make some significant headway on my own— and soon—I was risking charges of my own for withholding evidence. I refused to let this go out over the open airwaves where the Coyote would be able to track all of our movements as we negotiated every little investigative step with all of the overlapping law enforcement agencies on the reservation. Not yet, anyway.

The Coyote had considered every variable I could think of, at least at the first scene. I was hoping I would have better luck at the others. I couldn't afford to give him any more time to go back over the crime scenes. After all, if he followed the same pattern, it was a distinct possibility that the third body was still on site, which was why I was streaking across the desert as fast as I could, racing a rooster tail of dust and the Border Patrol agents who would undoubtedly be converging on the site once they found my tracks. The radio frequency jammer was only going to buy me enough of a head start to have a little quality alone time, so I was going to have to make it count. The last thing I wanted was for someone who could be the leak, or even the killer himself, to intrude upon the scene and spoil whatever slim chance I had of discovering something new.

I easily recognized the fortress-rock from miles away and found the turnaround at the base of the field of cholla without much difficulty. The small dirt lot, if it indeed qualified as such, was littered with tire treads and footprints and trash. Identifying any new tracks would be a hopeless proposition. I could only pray the crime scene response team had taken more care higher up.

I killed the bottle I was drinking, tossed it to the floor on the passenger side, and grabbed another from the tiny cooler. I shoved it into the pocket of my windbreaker and stepped out into the afternoon sun. It felt as though there was no distance between the sun and me at all. I had my Beretta in my hand and was sprinting up the winding path, heedless of the needles raking my jacket and the rattling sounds coming from seemingly all around me, before I even formulated a plan.

How much time had elapsed since I triggered the alarm beacon? An hour maybe? Ninety minutes? What could he have accomplished in that amount of time and what agenda had I unwittingly set into motion? I had no backup and no one I could fully trust, and I knew with complete certainty that more blood was going to flow. Soon. I could feel it in my bones.

And I still didn't have the slightest idea of how to stop it.

I burst from the path, scrambled up the slope, rounded the fortress, and dropped down into the canyon. The smiley face was still exactly how I remembered it. The blood was still clumped in the sand on the trail. A length of police tape hung listlessly between the stone walls. I figured after the CRST finished gathering evidence, all caution would be thrown to the wind. I wasn't disappointed. There were footprints everywhere. I few Styrofoam coffee cups and plastic water bottles. Cigarette butts. It didn't matter. I had the advantage of knowing what I was looking for this time, assuming he hadn't dramatically altered his MO. And I sensed that he hadn't. With as much time and effort as he had invested into the first, I saw no reason to suspect he hadn't put even more planning into this one.

If I was right, he had chosen these locations because of whatever underground features already existed or he'd been able to excavate while hidden from view by the canyon walls. After all, each of the murders had taken place in a mountainous location despite the countless miles of open desert, rolling hills, cactus fields, and dry washes with ample hiding places in between. No, the location was every bit as important as the message, and I needed to figure out why.

I stomped straight down the trail through the narrow canyon. I stomped all the way down into the trees. I stomped right up to the point where I had found Sykora laughing himself to tears while holding a handful of piss-dirt. I could still faintly smell the lingering ammonia odor of the coyote urine as I stomped around the spiral pattern and continued upward toward the crest of the same hill upon which I had stood last night until I heard a muffled *thump*.

I took a step backward and stomped on that point again.

Thump.

The dirt that had blown over the wooden square shivered. I needed to be even more careful this time. A smart man anticipating his impending capture might try to booby trap the lid of the hatch. A brilliant man would play his game right up until the final hand was dealt. I was about to find out what kind of man I was up against.

I brushed the sand away from the edges until I revealed all four sides. Rocks and gravel and even a small cactus had been affixed to the lid of the hatch with some sort of clear epoxy. So much care had been taken in its construction that I could barely discern it from the surrounding ground, even on my hands and knees. I cleared the sand and pebbles from around it, searching for wires or electronic devices of any kind, but found nothing.

For a full minute, I just knelt there staring at it. Finally, I opened the bottle of water, took a long swig, then poured the remainder around the seams of the hatch. No electrical hissing or sparks. Just the sound of water trickling down into the earth.

"No time like the present," I said out loud.

I hoped no one had heard. That would have made a lousy epitaph.

I lifted the slab slowly and carefully in an effort to detect even the slightest resistance from underneath. Once I had it high enough to peer below the hatch, I was able to confirm that there was nothing attached to it and set it off to my right.

The stench that erupted from the hole in front of me struck me like an uppercut, obliterating the generalization of the previous odor. I guess I should have considered myself fortunate to have found the other one first so I wouldn't have had to relive this gut-wrenching smell twice. I barely had time to cover my mouth and nose before I lost my lunch. I had greatly enjoyed that burger the first time, but figured I probably wouldn't so much the second.

The tunnel into which I now stared had originally been dug by an animal of some kind. The burrow was rounded and angled down under the rock formation that covered it. It was roughly the size of the previous one, but curved deeper into the hillside mere feet down. I shined my light inside. Shadowed forms scuttled away from the beam. For the life of me, I couldn't remember if a scorpion's sting was lethal and really didn't want to find out, but I was running out of time. I took a deep breath of the relatively clean air, then dove down into the vile darkness and the mud of my own creation, following my light and my pistol past the bend and into a warren approximately the size and shape of the interior of a Volkswagen Beetle.

Above me was the coarse underside of the massive red rock. Several strands of roots trailed from the cracks around it. The walls had been scraped by what appeared to be generations of coyote claws. At least I thought they were coyotes. They could have been medium-size dogs. I mean, without their heads and legs, the half-dozen carcasses could have belonged to just about any sandy-furred canine species. Their remains had been in the process of consumption and decomposition for quite some time. The bones had been picked clean, save for the greasy yellow adipose layer that still clung to the fur draped over the skeletons, which rippled with unseen critters scurrying around beneath. They made clicking and crunching sounds, and I could have sworn I even heard the muffled buzz of a rattle, but I was in no hurry to find out what inhabited the carcasses. At least now I knew where the Coyote had gotten his paintbrush-paws. I had no idea what he had planned for their heads, though. At least, not yet.

I didn't initially see the opposite egress from the den behind the heap of carcasses. I imagined the Coyote chuckling at the idea of me crawling over the infested remains. I was going to take a little extra pleasure in taking him down for making me.

Crawling over the remains without sticking any of my body parts into the mess or disturbing the creatures inside of them was an almost superhuman feat, but I somehow managed to do it and slithered into the hole behind them. This one featured the same makeshift cribbing as the last, built from scraps and remnants. I assumed the killer had stolen them from various building sites, but I couldn't prematurely rule out the possibility that he actually worked in construction. The wood here was newer than the last instance, for whatever that was worth. I hadn't gone twenty feet before the tunnel suddenly ended in a natural rock formation reminiscent of a wide chimney. The faintest hint of light arched down from high above, glittering with motes of dust, while only darkness waited below.

I couldn't believe I was even thinking about attempting this.

I holstered my pistol, bit the penlight between my teeth, and pulled myself out over the nothingness. Sand and pebbles slid over the rim and clattered to the ground seconds later. I braced my forearms against the smooth rocks to either side, arched my back, and pressed my knees and toes against the far side. Progress was maddeningly slow as I inched downward, turning my head from side to side and up and down in an effort to visualize my surroundings. Ancient petroglyphs shaped like palm prints had been scored into the walls, along with various animals and stylized hybrids I couldn't see clearly enough to identify. The recurrent native symbology wasn't lost on me. It could be significant, yet, at the same time, it could also be meant to deliberately mislead.

Just when I thought I would never reach the bottom, my feet touched solid ground and I collapsed to my hands and knees. All of my muscles seemed to be trembling at once and I was confident I'd peeled the skin off of my back, elbows, and knees. I hoped I wasn't going to have to go back up the same way because I flat out didn't have it in me. Fortunately, it only took a minute to find the way out. Just enough sunlight leaked through the cracks around a large stone that I could tell it didn't quite fit perfectly. It also allowed me to see the starburst of blood from where the body had been dropped down the chute. The rocks beside and above the makeshift egress had been braced with wood and epoxy to hold them in place. I rolled the center stone outward and recoiled from the sudden influx of sunlight. I blinked until I could see again, then crawled out into the murderous heat. I hadn't realized how cool it had been underground until I emerged.

The tripwire sparkled to my right, but it no longer mattered that I had triggered it.

From where I crouched, I could see the point where the east-west drag terminated against the mountain. Right where the Border Patrol agent had parked last night before starting uphill on foot. All someone needed to do was back up to the end of the gravel road, haul the body out, and throw it—

Brush marks on the sand in front of me. The side-to-side trails of leaves being swept back and forth to cover prints. They were faint, but they were fresh.

I leapt to my feet and followed them at a sprint. They led down the hill and around a stand of cacti and onto a flat stretch of desert spotted with creosotes and sage and palo verdes that had grown to the size of trees. And that was where the trail ended. There was a splotch of blood still aggregating in the dirt and what looked like the print from the back of a hand and wrist. A wad of foul cellophane was tangled in a creosote.

No more brush marks.

No footprints or branch marks or thorn scrapes or tire tread.

Nothing at all.

The ground leading away from me almost looked like someone had taken a leaf blower to it, scattering the sand and flattening the weeds and erasing any sign of passage.

I had been so close.

So close…

NINETEEN

By the time I again scaled the hill and reached the crime scene, there were a handful of CBP agents waiting to greet me. Perhaps greet was the wrong term. There was a whole lot of shouting and waving of pistols, but we eventually got things straightened out and all walked backed to our respective cars with the sun setting ahead of us across the desert.

Having spent the majority of my life on the front range of the Colorado Rockies, I was so accustomed to what others might call majestic sunsets that I rarely even noticed them anymore. The sun set behind the snow-capped peaks every night. That was just kind of what it did. I hoped the people who lived here didn't take this one for granted, for this was one of those things you had to see to believe. The way the red sun seemed to waver on the distant horizon, spreading a glow the color of the flesh around a peach pit across the rolling hills, was positively breathtaking. Or maybe it was merely the way the temperature was plummeting and the fact that I no longer felt like I was in immediate danger of dropping dead that lightened my spirits. Whatever the case, something in my brain had finally seen fit to give up a decent idea of how to proceed. The only problem was I wouldn't be able to do anything about it until the morning, which left me with the whole night to kill.

Hopefully, that wasn't the Coyote's plan, as well.

The CBP agents had been about as courteous as one would expect from civil servants. They thanked me for wasting their time and encouraged me to find just about anywhere else on the planet to be. One especially helpful fellow even suggested about the only place that might be hotter than this, which made me feel a whole lot better about not telling them what I had found at either of the crime scenes. There would come a point when I would have to, but not yet, and not like this. This was still my game to play and, fortunately, they hadn't searched my car and found my signal jammer beneath the driver's seat, so I still had the ability to play it.

As far as they knew, I had no knowledge of the Oscars, which left them with the impression they would still be able to monitor my movements while I traveled relatively unimpeded. And I had learned that the batteries lasted less than four hours with continuous use. The guys back at Ajo Station were probably racking their brains trying to figure out how my car had just suddenly appeared on top of one of their Oscars in the lot and would have their tech guys going over the preceding units in the series to check for malfunctions. I, on the other hand, simply needed to pick up some more batteries.

I was surprised to find the streets of Sells all but deserted upon my return. After witnessing so much activity earlier in the day, I kind of figured there'd be at least some sort of night life, but I was sorely mistaken. The daytime apparently allowed the community to perpetuate an illusion that vanished with the setting sun. This was an occupied zone. The only cars on the streets were the green and white Border Patrol Explorers. They cruised slowly through town with their spotlights directed between houses and buildings. The agents driving them couldn't possibly have stared me down any harder if I'd had illegals clinging to my roof and hanging out of my open trunk. I turned on my scanner and listened to them call in my license plate and the make and model of my car each time I passed a patrol, although it was hard to hear with the insane amount of radio activity.

If I thought what I'd heard earlier with Chief Antone was chaos, this gave a whole new definition to the word. There were multiple dispatchers coordinating so many different units on so many different frequencies that I couldn't even begin to keep them straight. A Blackhawk streaked past overhead, so low it rattled my windows. Its spotlight snapped on as it traced the street all the way to the edge of sight, where I saw several shadows break cover and sprint off into the night. Two Explorers raced past me on either side, their sirens blaring. It was hard to fathom that I was still in the same country as I had been two days ago. This felt like a military state, and I supposed that was exactly what it was. I couldn't help but wonder what it might have been like before the simultaneous invasion of the narco-insurgency and the para-military forces of the country to which the sovereign Tohono O'odham Nation was forced to swear its allegiance. It was hard to believe that the construction of a great wall along the US-Mexico border could be any worse than this. I tried to imagine how different the course of my life might have been had my father been awakened by the sounds of warfare in the street outside his home rather than the distant rumble of bombing that heralded the end of the world, while at the same time closing off my mind to thoughts of the children trying to sleep behind the shivering windows of the houses lining what should have been quiet rural streets.

I found a twenty-four hour store that reminded me of a pawn shop on East Colfax in Denver. It was an adobe structure with bars on the cracked windows and a hand-painted sign over the door that was stenciled with oddly inflected O'odham words, beneath which it read simply "Always Open" in English. I was able to load up on batteries and jerky and even a cold four-pack of Red Bull. There was a coffee pot full of black tar and a sign above it that declared it free for law enforcement officers. Judging by the expression on the face of the cashier behind the wire-reinforced glass at the back of the store, I had a pretty good hunch how he felt about the law enforcement community as a whole and figured that no matter how much I loved coffee, I would never need it that badly. He was looking at me like I'd deflowered his sister in front of him on prom night and then followed him home and asked for an introduction to his mother. There was something else in his eyes, though, something that led me to believe he was stroking the freshly oiled barrel of a shotgun under the counter and just praying for the opportunity to use it. I slid the cash through the pass box and told him to keep the change, if for no other reason than to expedite my departure.

Don't let anyone tell you I've lost touch with the common man.

I changed the batteries in the car, switched on the jammer, and listened to the chaos on the scanner all the way out to the second crime scene, which was technically the first chronologically. It was the one to the southeast along the Baboquivari Range, where Antone had introduced me to my biological uncle and cousin, who had found the first smiley face in the shadow of Baboquivari Peak, beneath which our creator god, I'itoi, lived deep in his maze. I was starting to think there was some significance to the myth, some symmetry between the underground from which the Hohokam had been led to the surface of the earth and the tunnels the Coyote had excavated to stash his victims.

Like I said, I have a hard time trusting the notion of coincidence. I found it strange now, in retrospect, that Chief Antone had told me that legend on our way to the site. Stranger still his initial reaction to my arrival at the station. *It's about time. We've been expecting you.* Like he hadn't just been awaiting the arrival of a federal agent...

He'd been waiting for *me*.

I had a harder time finding my way to this crime scene than either of the previous two, which gave me the opportunity to test my recognition of rattling sounds in the dark and introduced me to both a gila monster and a banded kingsnake. Or was it a coral snake? At least it was cooling off rapidly enough that both reptiles were sluggishly working their way back to their burrows. I couldn't remember if it was the kingsnake or the coral snake that was venomous, but it had been a long enough day already without having to find out.

When I finally identified the right canyon and followed the correct fork, I just sat there on a rock across from the design, staring up at the faded smiley face for the longest time. The blood was flaking off in some spots, already completely gone in others. There was something about it that just wasn't right. I couldn't pin down what any more than I could explain why. The lines were too carefully formed. Their incompleteness somehow seemed complete, for lack of a better way to describe it. Everything about it seemed precise, and yet the design itself appeared as though it wasn't meant to. The eyes could have been depicted in any number of ways. Why slanted lines? Why one longer than the other? Why did the nose look like it did: an angled straight line and a curved underside? There had to be some significance to it, to its precise lack of precision. Why was it painted onto the stone rather than on the ground? Why was it so large when it was on a stone face you couldn't see from a distance, only when you were standing directly before it? Was it meant to imitate a primitive petroglyph? Was that why the lines themselves were seemingly so stylized? Did the Coyote intend to use a native motif to help purvey his message or in order to point the investigation in the wrong direction?

It was obvious that Chief Antone and Roman and Ban Walker all knew more than they were telling me and it was starting to really get under my skin. It was high time we all put our cards on the table, but I needed to gather more information before I was in a position to confront them. If I was right about my plans for the morning, I would be in a position to do so tomorrow.

It was already shaping up to be a banner day.

I stomped around for a while, but that proved unnecessary in the end. I was starting to get a feel for what I was looking for. It wasn't an identifiable track per se, but rather the utter and complete absence of them that led me to the egress. Maybe I didn't have the skills or the experience to do what the CBP agents did and maybe I never would. All I knew was that I could tell the difference between the surrounding sand and the stripe that looked like it had been smoothed with a leaf blower. It didn't hurt that it led straight up to a hole in the hillside like a red carpet the killer had rolled out just for me. I don't know if I had missed the hole before because I hadn't been looking for it or because it had been concealed the last time I was here. I didn't suppose it mattered much considering it had undoubtedly been scoured of any potential evidence like the others. I figured I'd just perform a cursory search to satisfy my own curiosity and hopefully figure out what was troubling me about the physical crime scenes, this one in particular. It was something about the smiley face, which, the longer I looked at it, the less I truly believed that someone who had spent so much time planning these crimes would go to such extreme lengths to deliver such a seemingly benign and meaningless message. I mean, what did he hope to accomplish? The Smiley Face Killer wasn't much of a moniker if he was angling for notoriety or his story on the big screen. And why use the coyote motif on top of it? There were too many contradictions and coincidences. I was obviously missing something crucial that would serve as the domino that would make the entire row topple in sequence.

The hole itself was halfway up a steep slope covered with wild grasses, cacti, and irregularly-shaped red rocks that appeared to have been arrested in a perpetual state of avalanche readiness. Despite first impressions, they were deeply lodged in the mountainside and allowed me to climb over them so as not to have to do battle with the omnipresent cholla and prickly pears. It didn't take long to make my way to the hole, which appeared to be a coyote burrow, just like the last. At least it had the appearance of being excavated by claws rather than any manmade implement. From where I was now, I could see where the canyon opened onto the desert, and a slice of the flatlands that stretched away into the infinite darkness. This had to be his back door. It would have been too visible by the standards he'd already set forth to be the main entrance. If I hadn't lost all sense of direction, the crime scene itself was maybe twenty-five feet uphill and a hundred feet to the northwest. His primary point of egress couldn't be too far from there; I just hadn't been able to identify it in the dark.

Of course, there was always still a chance I was wrong and I was about to disturb a pack of starving mongrels by sticking my head right into their midst. At least that would make for a better smell than I anticipated in any of the other scenarios that played out in my head.

The stench that wafted from inside the hole removed any doubt as to what was or what might once have been inside. I was going to have to remember to pick up some Vicks at the very next opportunity. Or maybe I'd be better off just lopping off my own blasted nose.

I gave the rim a cursory inspection, then lowered myself to my belly, held my penlight and my gun in front of me like before, and squirmed into the earth. I advanced slowly. Cautiously. If I were going to set a trap for someone, this is where I would do it. I couldn't think of any other reason he would have left his back door standing wide open, assuming that was indeed what had happened. The scratches from the branches he had dragged through here were nearly indistinguishable from the marks made by the claws that carved this tunnel, but I was coming to be able to see these things with the kind of clarity that I wouldn't have thought myself capable of mere days ago.

My entire body wasn't even all the way into the horizontal shaft when it bent sharply to the right and out of sight.

I paused and listened.

A blind corner was the perfect place for some sort of booby trap. It was an opportunity that was almost too good to pass up. Based on the narrowness of the tube and the sharpness of the turn,

I would essentially have to wiggle the majority of my torso around the bend before I would be able to raise my head far enough to clearly see the way ahead of me.

The only sound was the harsh echo of my breathing.

I guess it all boiled down to how badly I wanted this guy and to what lengths I was willing to go to catch him. When I looked at it like that, there really was no decision to be made at all.

I wriggled forward and around the bend as fast as I could. The hell with it. By the time I was able to see ahead of me, I was halfway to the end of the tunnel, a dark oval through which the beam of my penlight diffused into a weak golden aura. I could hear the buzzing of flies and another sound that I couldn't quite place. I was nearly to the den itself when my light fell upon the object resting on the ground just across the earthen threshold. It was a small burlap pouch with a leather cord threaded through the material and cinched on top. The fabric was black with what could only be blood. It was positively alive with flies.

Just sitting there where I couldn't possibly miss it.

Where I had been meant to find it.

I heard a kind of swishing sound beneath the drone of the flies.

I exhaled slowly to steady my nerves. I was either going to have to set down my penlight or my Beretta in order to grab it, and I honestly didn't much care for either option. In the end, I decided neither was acceptable and managed to toss my penlight backward and close enough to my face that I was able to manipulate it into my mouth. I tilted the beam as well as I could toward the satchel and dragged it closer, into the tunnel and out of the den. A tug on the leather cord and the bag opened wide enough that I could pinch it by the crusted underside, invert it, and dump the contents—

"Oh, God..."

TWENTY

I don't know what I had expected to be inside the satchel. I guess I didn't ever really stop to think about it. Maybe a part of me just assumed it would be something like a finger or a toe. Maybe a few of each. It was a decent size bag. Something meant to taunt or torment me, some way for him to show me he was in charge, but nothing at all like what fell out. In fact, it took several beats for me to recognize exactly what they were. They looked almost like little ceramic balls glued together, side-by-side in ascending size, crusted with blood. A T-shaped knob of bone protruded from the broad end of each.

They were rattles.

The realization hit me at the same moment I heard the sweeping sound again. Closer this time. I shoved myself backward with every last ounce of strength as a dark shape streaked past my face and struck the dirt wall beside me. It wasn't a sweeping sound. It was hissing. In context, I clearly recognized it now. My sudden movement had set off a frenzy in the coyote den. Hissing and thrashing sounds echoed from the warren. As rattlesnakes, they were born in a bad mood that could only be enhanced by lopping off their tails and throwing them down into a strange den that smelled like death warmed over.

I dropped my penlight, which shined deeper into the tunnel, illuminating dark shapes slithering across the threshold behind the one that had missed me. It had already recoiled and reared up into striking position. The nub of its tail stood straight up as it vibrated. The thing had to be as wide around as my forearm. Fortunately, I still had my pistol and the damn snake was so big it made an easy target. I squeezed the trigger. The diamondback unraveled and whipped backward into the darkness beyond the light's reach at the same moment the thunderclap of the report swatted me upside the head. I'd swear I saw the other snakes strike at the ruined reptile as it flew past, but I was backing around the bend in such a hurry that I didn't stick around to find out for sure. And I was more than happy to let them share their venom with each other instead of with me.

I felt my feet drop over the outside edge as another shape sliced across my field of view and past my face, so close I could smell it. The deafening report in such close quarters had thrown off my equilibrium and made the tunnel appear to turn clockwise around me, but I was still able to squeeze off another shot that hit the snake while it was recoiling to take another strike at me.

And then I was out of the tunnel and into a darkness so much lighter it was like daytime in contrast. I tried to stand, tried to run, but only managed to send myself toppling over a large rock and tumbling down the hillside. For several seconds, I felt like I was being bludgeoned with baseball bats and then I was flat on my back, gasping for air I couldn't quite seem to catch. The image of rattlesnakes firing out of the mouth of that hole and raining down on me got me crawling. The air finally broke through and I gasped and lunged to my feet. The ground teetered beneath me as I staggered away from the hillside and finally collapsed onto a sage bush that felt like a pincushion, but was vastly preferable to the nopales beside it.

I don't know how long I lay like that, just draped over the shrub with the imagined sound of rattles shaking in my head. When I finally rolled off of it and onto the sand, I started to laugh. I laughed harder than I had in a long time. I laughed so hard I'm sure there were a dozen migrants crossing the Sonoran who dove into the nearest hiding place at the sound of my dawning madness. The Coyote had known I was nipping at his heels and tried to eliminate me before I caught up with him. And he had wanted me to know his true identity right before I was struck repeatedly by a half-dozen rattlesnakes. He wanted me to wonder why he did it as I stumbled through the desert, the venom coursing through my blood, stealing the sight from my eyes while the pain became unendurable. Or maybe he thought I'd never make it back out of the tunnel. Regardless, he had taken a risk in doing so, a gambit that was going to blow up in his face.

I rolled over onto my back and looked up the slope to where the mouth of the hole was limned by the beam from my lost penlight.

"I'm coming for you," I said, and pushed myself to my feet.

I spent nearly the entire walk back to my car plucking cactus needles from my hands and arms by the light of the moon. I waited until I reached my car before prying the large ones from the left side of my face and neck with the aid of the mirror app on my cell phone. The last thing I needed was to leave bits embedded under the skin or create any ghastly puckered scars. Besides, I had a little extra time to play with.

The Coyote thought I was dead.

It was only a matter of time before he learned the truth, but for now, I essentially had my own personal jammer that would allow me to sneak up on him. And I was going to enjoy every second of it. I wanted to see the expression on his face when he realized that he had failed, that I knew who he was. That I had beaten him. I wanted to memorize the expression so I could recall it whenever I chose. I wanted it to be the last thing I saw at night before I drifted off to sleep and the first thing I saw before I opened my eyes in the morning.

This was personal now.

I guess it always had been, and I needed to know why. It made sense that if I was going to figure out the answer to that question, Why was the best place to start.

The town of Why, Arizona was actually the location of Ajo Station, despite being ten miles south of the town of Ajo. It sits just to the west of the Tohono O'odham Reservation and north of Organ Pipe National Monument, twenty-five miles straight up Highway 85 from Lukeville and the Mexican border at Sonoyta. Prior to 9/11 and the subsequent commission of the Department of Homeland Security and the U.S. Customs and Border Protection Agency, the town boasted a whopping population of roughly one hundred and its sole claim to fame was the Y-shaped intersection where Highways 85 and 86 merged. At the time of its founding, state law required all city names to have at least three letters, thus the über-creative Why. And now that the Arizona Department of Transportation had caved to safety concerns and convention and rebuilt the intersection into a more traditional T-shape, disappointed tourists now had to content themselves with a peek at the unrestrained bedlam that was Ajo Station and blow their money at the Desert Diamond Casino east of town.

I made the drive in thirty-five minutes flat, despite the lights and sirens that were positively everywhere as I neared town. There were Explorers literally bursting with undocumenteds. The station itself might as well have been equipped with a turnstile for all of the arrests coming in and transport buses heading back and forth from any number of overflowing detention centers, where the illegals would simply plead guilty to save time and be shipped back across the border, only to try their luck again.

Even this close to midnight, the level of activity was positively insane. Blackhawks thundering past overhead, their spotlights scouring the desert. Headlights bounding through the hills. The scanner was going nuts. Whatever they were paying their dispatchers, it wasn't enough. They made air traffic controllers sound like Ben Stein. I couldn't imagine there was an insurance company on the planet that would sign any of them to a life insurance policy with a suicide payout.

The casino itself was sleepy by comparison. It was really little more than a Vegas-themed truck stop. The real magic happened at the main Desert Diamond Casino outside of Tucson, where I heard it rumored that John Mellencamp frequently performed, sans Cougar. This place wasn't even open twenty-four hours. Probably even had clocks. It had that vibe of sweaty desperation about it that made me not want to touch anything for fear of contracting some form of terminal depression. I could positively taste the haze of cigarette smoke all the way from my car, where I sat trying not to scratch at the itchy spots from which I'd recently removed the cactus needles.

There was a steady stream of traffic, primarily interstate truckers, through the self-serve bays. A good number had already bedded down for the night in the dirt lot around the side of the casino. I didn't have to sit there for very long to realize that the women coming and going from the cabs weren't carhops. I'd imagine they probably weren't legal residents either.

The convenience store slash restaurant was well-lighted and relatively vacant. There were a couple of heavyset men at the counter and another perusing a wall of magazines. The rotund woman at the register also capped off the coffee, walking back and forth from one to the other in a continuous loop that had surely worn a trench into the floor.

The casino side was the diametric opposite. It was dark and smoky and all sorts of sirens flashed and lights flared from the rows of slot machines I could see through the front glass doors. A uniformed security guard stood sentry just inside the right door and out of sight. He magically appeared to admit anyone who neared. I didn't figure my cousin Ban would be so easy to find and I wasn't disappointed. I still needed to approach this the right way, though. I couldn't afford to give up my advantage.

By the time I stepped out of my car, the security guard was already in the open doorway, staring straight at me. It appeared as though I wasn't the only one doing a little surveilling. I opted for jeans and a T-shirt and left my jacket and cap in the car, but the damage was already done thanks to my conspicuously inconspicuous Crown Vic. He smiled as he ushered me inside and led me down a long row of slots to a small doorway concealed in the wall. Another guard, who wore the air of supervision as heavily as the gut hanging over his belt and onto his lap, was seated behind a desk upon which sat a dozen flickering monitors only he could see. He stared expectantly up at me from a fleshy face that appeared to hang from the bones of his face like a big gob of snot. The name badge on his chest read: J. Armandiriz, Chief of Security.

I smiled.

He didn't.

Great. I was going to have to do this the hard way.

I reached for my badge jacket, but he waved me off.

"No need."

"I'm sorry?"

"The rooms are in the back. Just head through the door behind the blackjack table and find the first open room. One of the girls will be in short—"

"I'm afraid there's been a misunderstanding here. I need—"

"I know all about your needs. Spare me the song and dance. We're closing up in half an hour and I have a fun-filled night of hosing the drunks out of here ahead of me. So just get back there and—"

Turns out I wasn't the only one who could read expressions. This joker was a little slow on the uptake, but he managed to get the gist of mine just fine. I watched his change from surprise to alarm to sheer terror in the time it took me to reach across the desk and grab him by the hair. I had a hunch he was the kind of guy who wasn't going to run off and tattle on me. I bounced his head off of one of the video monitors and sat down in the chair across the desk from him. Pleasantries out of the way, I got right down to business.

"Here's the deal: I've had a pretty rotten night and I'm all out of patience, so I'll make this so simple that even you can understand it. I'm going to ask some questions. You're going to answer them. If you do so, I'll walk out of here and you can go back to doing whatever it is you do. If you don't, I'm going to drag you out of here by the scruff of your flabby neck and drop you somewhere out there in the desert where you can wipe your fat ass with cactus pads for all I care. If you repeat a single word of what transpires here, I will descend upon you with the wrath of God and shove that cereal box badge of yours straight down your throat. Have I made myself perfectly clear?"

A trickle of blood rolled down his forehead. I watched his Adam's apple rise, then jiggle as he swallowed a knot and whatever pride he might have thought he possessed up until that moment. I think he might have tried to speak, but I was able to read his face well enough without verbal confirmation.

"And I expect whatever cut your taking off of these girls'…labors…to go back into their pockets as a bonus so they can move on a little faster."

That one hit him like a blow to the gut. He just had one of those faces that made you want to keep hitting him. Fortunately for him, I had a more pressing engagement.

"Where's Ban Walker?"

The expression on his face was one of utter confusion. I knew right then and there that I was wasting my time, valuable time that I simply didn't have.

"How the hell should I know? I haven't seen that guy in probably two years. Not since I had to let him go."

"Why?"

"He was an arrogant prick. Thought he was better than all of the rest of us just because he'd worn the colors of the green Gestapo for all of about thirty seconds. Like his shit don't stink, right?" His eyes had been doing their best to avoid mine, but they latched on when he finally caught up with the situation. His cheeks flushed with what could have passed for the return of his confidence. "I always knew there was something wrong with that guy. What did he do?"

"I just need to talk to him."

"No. No. There's more to it than that. You're federal. He's done something really big."

"Do you still have some way of tracking him down?"

"Don't you think I'd be smart enough to trade that information if I had it?"

"Honestly?"

"Screw you. Don't think just because you got that big old badge that you can treat me like something you scraped off your shoe. You think you're the only fed who comes in here? I probably knew more agents than you do. And don't think for a second that any of them would be happy to hear that you're threatening their free…entertainment."

"You really want me to come back here, don't you?"

"No." He smiled. "I want you to get the hell out of here."

He leaned forward and rested his chin on his pudgy fists. He cocked his head first one way, then the other. I don't think I've ever seen an expression that smug on another human being.

I rose to leave. There was nothing for me here. I had learned everything I was going to, which amounted to somewhere between jack and squat. I turned and headed for the door, uncertain exactly how the confrontation had turned on me. Maybe I just needed to work on my people skills.

"You look just like him, you know," Armandiriz said to my back.

And there I had my answer.

"What did you just say?"

"It's the eyes. You guys have the exact same eyes."

If you've never seen a three hundred pound man flip backward over his chair, I highly recommend it. An overhand right to the bridge of the nose works quite well, especially if you swing hard enough. And I guarantee it'll knock that smug grin right off of his face and onto yours.

Don't let anyone tell you I don't know how to loosen my tie and have a little fun from time to time.

DAY 3

tash waik

wuhi

The term sociopath is considered antiquated and has been replaced with the formal medical diagnosis of Antisocial Personality Disorder. Kind of takes away the element of personal accountability, I say. 'Don't blame me, I have APD.' Funny how the staggering increase in violent crime over the last fifty years coincides with the integration of psychology into the mainstream, isn't it?

TWENTY-ONE

Sells District
Tohono O'odham Nation
Arizona

September 11th

For every action there is an equal and opposite reaction. Take punching a three hundred-pound slab of humanity hard enough to send it flipping head over heels. Or heels over head, as the case may be. The consequences, while not entirely unanticipated, are always worse than you expect at the time.

When you think about the logistics of essentially punching a side of beef with enough force to knock it off the hook from which it hangs, you realize you would have been better off just drawing your sidearm and shooting it. Physics further dictates that force travels in a straight line. For the behavioralists who claim that mankind wasn't born with the propensity for violence and instead that it's a conditioned response to negative external stimuli, I offer proof to the contrary. The human arm is one of nature's strangest and most force-resistant designs, trailing only the rock, the tree trunk, and the mammalian leg. An arm is constructed with the ability to form a compact club at its most distal end. That club is mounted on a long, whip-like fulcrum that attaches to the trunk roughly three feet from the origin of the imparted force. It is designed to impact with the knuckles of the second and third digits, the index and middle fingers, respectively. From there, the force of the blow—in this case, an overhand right—travels up the lengths of the second and third metacarpals, which further distribute that force between the eight carpal bones and then the two long bones of the forearm, although primarily the thicker radius. It's then further absorbed by the humerus, which is the longest and strongest bone in your body next to the femur. From there it passes into the heavily muscled shoulder girdle and dissipates into the thorax. All so you don't end up breaking your hand when you hit someone.

That doesn't mean it won't still hurt like a mother, though.

I drove with my left hand and rested the knuckles of my right on a cold bottle of water in my lap. Cold being a largely subjective term like pain, which was definitely winning the battle between the two. As much as I had enjoyed punching Boss Nass at the time, I regretted it even more now. Not necessarily because it hurt like a mother, as I'm sure I've mentioned, but because it was diverting my focus from the task at hand. It also exposed a chink in my armor that until now I didn't realize I possessed. I've always been able to draw a firm line between the personal and the professional, despite the fact that I take my job very personally. This one had hit too close to home, though. Too close to a home I hadn't lived in for a long, long time, but a home filled with unresolved feelings nonetheless.

Despite what anyone might say about him, I am my father's son and I take great pride in that fact. I may not have known him as well as I would have liked, but I knew him well enough to know that he placed loyalty and honor and service above all else. He believed in his ideals and believed to the very end that they were worth fighting and, ultimately, dying for. Maybe a part of me wishes he had placed me before his ideals. That he would have recognized a boy needs a father worse than a largely forgotten war needed a largely forgotten hero. I guess I understood that in his own way he had. We can't always choose the way our parents love us. Which, I suppose, serves as the sad war cry of the abused child, too.

The irony is not lost on me.

The comparison to the man I was convinced was the Coyote cut me to the bone. I'm not blind. I couldn't help but see the physical similarities between us, the parallels between our lives. He was a few years older, but we had essentially been born at the same time. I had been raised in a different world, though. He was born here and stayed here. His was the life that could have been mine had my father bowed to tradition as his had before him. And as his brother had, as well. I had been raised in a large house on a large lot in an upscale suburb by people who pretty much devoted the last quarter of their lives to raising their grandson as if he were their own son. My cousin had been raised apart from the outside world and largely in a position to resent it for past wrongs perpetrated by a government that no longer existed in the same form. While I had gone to a prestigious prep school and an even more prestigious college, he had been shown a route from a single communal school straight through community college and into a job force that existed to serve the community. I had joined the FBI and received the best law enforcement training in the entire nation. Where I had been taught to hunt out in the real world, where rules applied. He had been trained by the Border Patrol, and, by extension, the very same government, to hunt in a lawless land where none of the traditional rules applied. He had seen the pictures of my successes accumulating on the wall in his family's homestead, seen me living essentially the same life, only on a grander scale. He had known about me while I hadn't even looked hard enough to learn of his existence. I wasn't responsible for the path he had chosen, but I wasn't entirely blameless, either.

This case had always been destined to fall into my lap and he had known it from the moment the idea first crossed his mind. This was his challenge to me, the gauntlet he had thrown at my feet. Me vs. him. Mano a mano.

Blood on blood.

But that wasn't the part that bothered me the most. The worst part was the realization that our roles could easily have been reversed, were it not for the random nature of fate.

The impartation of force.

We had both chosen the same straight line of impact, yet here we both were now, two irresistible forces on a collision course with one another, hunting on the reservation of our ancestors, which had already tasted the blood of countless generations of our forebears. And before this was over, it would taste even more. One way or the other. I could feel it deep in my very being…

That had always been his plan.

I just couldn't understand the sheer ferocity with which he hated me. There had to be something more, some reason above and beyond living a lifetime in the shadow of a cousin who had no idea he was even casting one. I was the kind of guy who tended to take a rattlesnake striking at his face a little bit personally. Maybe it all boiled down to the fact that Ban and I were both just really sensitive, touchy-feely kind of guys.

I'd been so distracted by my thoughts and the pain in my hand and the furious itching on my face and neck that I didn't at first appreciate the subtle inquiries of one of the dispatchers over the scanner until a note of panic crept into her voice. I turned up the volume in an effort to isolate her thread from all of the others, which, while every bit as frantic, had some semblance of control to them. This woman's voice reflected concern of a more personal nature, something entirely outside of her normal work routine. And I wasn't the only one who noticed it. The background din faded significantly as field agents turned down their stereos and limited their communications to the bare essentials. There was an electricity crackling from the underlying static that I couldn't quite define. A palpable tension, a sense of expectation, a mounting potential. The kind of energy that ripples through the air moments before the thunderheads crest the mountains and the grumble of thunder rolls down through the valleys.

"Unit one-one-eight respond. One-one-eight respond! Damn it, Matthews! Respond!"

"Talk to us, dispatch. What's going on out there?"

"Two-six-eight. Zero-seven-five. You both should still be close to the Destruya Drag, correct?"

"Zero-seven-five. Fifteen miles south."

"Two-six-eight twelve miles north. What's going on over there, Teri?"

"I lost one-one-eight between Oscars fourteen and fifteen."

"What do you mean...lost?"

"He radioed in brush sign across the drag at twenty-three fifty-three."

I looked at my clock. The glowing green numerals on the dash read 1:14 a.m.

"Visual confirmation of target?"

"Negative. He elected to track on foot."

"Fifteen on the Destruya is the wash at the base of Mt. Vainom. When did he fall out of contact?"

"Last check-in was oh-oh oh-eight. He failed to make the oh-one hundred."

"He could have been right on top of the wets and had to go silent."

"He would have clicked to acknowledge. You know that. You all know that."

"What was his last communication?"

"He said the sign led northwest into an arroyo before he lost it, that it just stopped right there in front of him and he was going to have to try to pick it up again. Must have backtracked on him, he thought. Probably saw whatever coyote was in there marking his territory. He said something about it smelling like a whole pack in heat up there..."

Her words faded and the ground seemed to drop out from under me. I glanced at the clock again.

1:16.

Unit one-eighteen had radioed in sign at 11:53. It had taken him fifteen minutes to reach the point where the trail terminated. And he had now been out of contact for sixty-eight minutes. The closest unit was a twenty-minute drive and a fifteen minute walk away. One hundred and three minutes. Nearly two hours, when all was said and done. That was more than enough time.

Way more than enough.

I pinned the gas and launched the Crown Vic across the desert toward the jagged ridge of the Baboquivari Mountains, which I could barely see on the distant horizon.

We were already too late.

TWENTY-TWO

Time passed like an out-of-body experience. I barely remember racing my headlights down dirt roads I could hardly see for the dust. Saguaros firing past my windows like shadowed mile markers. Gravel pinging from my wheel wells with machine gun rapidity. Sliding sideways through turns and righting myself in the open desert. Branches screeching through the paint job. Only having the vaguest idea of my destination until I saw the distant convergence of sirens and headlights and the clouds of dust from their passage rising up to blot out the stars. Arriving to find Explorer doors standing ajar and light stretching out onto the bare dirt. Flashlights jouncing across the wash, appearing and disappearing through the branches of the mesquites and cottonwoods. Barely having the presence of mind to put my car into park before I jumped out into the night and barreled through the darkness with my Beretta in my hand. Trying desperately to keep the flashlights ahead of me in sight while simultaneously negotiating the rugged terrain and keeping my skin from being flayed by the thorns and the cactus needles. Feeling the ground shake as a Blackhawk streaked across the sky toward the mountains, luring me onward with the sweep of its spotlight. The continuous arrival of lights and sirens behind me. The shouting of agents. The barking of dogs.

Under any other circumstances I would have marveled at their fluidly coordinated response, especially when you take into account the vastness and remoteness of their patrol zone. But it was like showing up for the fireworks on the fifth of July.

The show was already over.

I had expected both escalation and acceleration from the Coyote, yet I never imagined anything like this. Taking down a Border Patrol agent in the field would make him public enemy number one for the more than three thousand agents roaming the deserts from Southern California through Eastern Texas, who tended to take the death of one of their own almost as personally as the act of avenging him. This wasn't a nameless, faceless immigrant who no one would ever notice was missing. This was a man with a name and a face and a badge that guaranteed the full resources of the federal government would be at the disposal of those in pursuit of his killer.

The Coyote had signed his own death warrant.

And maybe that was exactly what he wanted. The powers-that-be could only keep a lid on this situation for so long, but what could he possibly hope to accomplish by gaining so much attention? A serial killer made a pretty lousy martyr.

The staggering wind generated by the chopper blades buffeted me as I entered a narrow valley of sorts. The steep slopes to either side were grassy and spotted with clumps of cacti, yuccas, and creosotes, which grew from bare gaps in the red soil where scree had slid down the mountain through the eons. A dry creek bed a mere half-foot wide meandered between the trunks of palo verde trees. There was all sorts of trash and discarded clothing heaped under their bowed branches, and it was obvious even to a novice like me that this was a fairly common layover point for undocumenteds attempting to sneak through the Baboquivaris.

I had to shield my face from the blowing sand and branches as I passed from the arroyo into a narrow canyon where the soil and grasses gave way to sheer red rock. The golden spotlight jiggled across the ground ahead, guiding me around a bend and to a spot where I finally caught up with the other agents at the convergence of two even narrower canyons, one of which led nearly straight up a series of stone ledges to where I could see the Blackhawk attempting to hover. One of the agents had his free hand pressed to his ear and was shouting into his two-way. I couldn't hear a word he was saying over the mechanized thunder, but his face was scarlet with the exertion. The other was staring at the stone outcropping another ten paces ahead of me and to my right, his sidearm drawn and pointed uselessly between his feet. The expression on his face was one of utter disbelief, as though his brain had yet to sift through the myriad emotions to settle on just one.

I tried to wave off the chopper, but it made no outward sign that it had seen me. Or maybe the pilot simply didn't care. They were blowing away whatever evidence may once have existed.

That was the problem with working any sort of crime against a law enforcement officer of any branch; his brothers-in-arms were prepared to go to any lengths to find the perpetrator and carry out their own brand of justice, even if it meant trampling every law they upheld through the normal course of service. I couldn't fault them for it, though. Were our roles reversed, I would have undoubtedly felt the same, but this approach was counterproductive, especially considering how small the Coyote's lead was on us now. He had to still be out here in the desert somewhere, and if they wanted retribution to be served, they needed to get the hell out there and find him.

"Give me that!" I shouted and took the transceiver away from the surprised agent before he could object. I depressed the button and shouted into the microphone. "Get that chopper out of here! You're destroying the crime scene! If you want to actually do something useful, sweep the desert to either side of this mountain for any sign of where he might have had a vehicle waiting. If there isn't one, then that means he's still up here with us somewhere! And get us some more goddamn backup and an emergency response team in case your guy's still alive up here!"

I shoved the radio back into the agent's chest. I could have interpreted the rage on his face from space. The Blackhawk banked away and took its light with it, stranding us in darkness, but at least it was a darkness bereft of wind and noise.

"You want to help your guy? Suck it up and do your job. He could still be out here somewhere. And so could the man who came after him, so get your head in the game!"

The professional in him tempered his emotions and grudgingly nodded. He stepped away and clicked on his flashlight. I could hear him taking control and radioing his other units to set up a firm perimeter and gather all of the necessary investigative teams as I walked toward where the other agent still stood, staring slack-jawed at the canyon wall. I don't think he'd so much as breathed since I first saw him.

I commandeered his Maglite—a six-inch mini professional-plus LED model that produced a beam every bit as powerful as that of the old two-foot billy club model—from his utility belt and shined it up at the design painted on the wall. The blood was so fresh it glistened. There were spots where rivulets of blood still trickled from the carefully constructed lines. The paw prints were so fresh and clear that it almost appeared as though they'd been made by a living coyote, which, I guess, in a sense they had, because the Coyote was the master of deception and continued to prove it.

This design was different. It broke the pattern. It wasn't a continuation of the previous design. It wasn't the more completed construction of the smiley face I had expected. This one was unique. This one was meant just for me. To mock me. This was his way of showing me and everyone around me who was running this show.

And, up to this point, that most definitely wasn't me.

This changed everything.

I stared at the design painted in the Border Patrol agent's blood and allowed myself a moment to seethe before I again mastered my emotions.

I turned and walked away. I still had a tunnel to find around here somewhere with Lord only knew what waiting for me inside.

TWENTY-THREE

Fortunately, the agents on the scene were so preoccupied with their designated tasks that I was able to wander off on my own without drawing any unnecessary attention to myself. They were undoubtedly all happy I wasn't anywhere near them anyway. My presence would only complicate the mission of vengeance upon which they had all embarked. And it didn't help that the customary interagency distrust was in full swing, and not just from their side. Besides, the majority of them had already scattered to the four winds. From where I stood on a crest of rock overlooking the desert to the east, I could see at least a dozen different sets of headlights bounding through the sand. A pair of Blackhawks had already swept the area around me and the immediate vicinity and were now working their way toward the horizon. Thus far, they'd found exactly what I thought they would.

Nothing. Nada. Zero. Zilch.

This may have been a dramatic escalation, but it hadn't been haphazardly executed. This had been the plan from day one. I was just struggling to grasp Ban's reasons for bringing the might of the Border Patrol into a situation it would have been happy enough to avoid.

I had to keep thinking of him as the Coyote. I couldn't afford to humanize him, to allow myself to make some sort of personal connection to him. He was a killer, a sociopath whose blood may have come from the same pool as mine, but who was nothing like me. Parallels and physical similarities were all we had in common. That, and the fact that each of us intended to destroy the other. There was no other possible outcome.

This most recent message really pissed me off. I wanted to storm back down there and tear the canyon wall apart with my bare hands. A winking face. For Christ's sake. He had shoved a stick right into the bee hive and enraged the honey bear in the process.

Forget the design, I was going to tear *him* apart with my bare hands.

I turned away from the desert and headed back around a tall spire of rock that looked like a serrated knife blade from the distance, slid sideways through a crevice in the northeastern face of the mountain, and found myself in a small circular clearing nearly completely enclosed by walls of red rock. There were faded petroglyphs all around me, carved so long ago that even the sparse amount of rain and wind that penetrated the enclave had nearly erased them. Perhaps that was part of the personal message the Coyote was trying to deliver to me. I simply wasn't in the mood, though. I'd had enough of his games and it was time to put an end to them once and for all.

It stood to reason that his entryway couldn't have been far from the killing zone. I couldn't think of any other reason for there to have been so much coyote urine near the design, especially considering he'd used it to cover the end of his trail in the past. The dogs had been all but useless in close proximity to the site and had led their handler on an escapade across the Sonoran that had ultimately brought them right into the midst of a group of walkers bedded down in a gully, waiting for what had to sound like World War III to end. No one noticed me slip off the beaten path, haul myself up the rock steppes, and cross a ledge bordered by a sheer drop to where I now stood. It was the perfect place for a man to work undisturbed for hours on end, where no one would see him excavating earth day after day from afar. I was starting to understand him, and I was reaping the rewards of my patience.

The hole was at the base of the southern side, approximately one hundred feet due north of the winking face. He obviously hadn't hauled his victim up the rocks and across that narrow trail, so this had to be where he had emerged following the killing. From here, he could have headed north toward the distant Baboquivari Peak or to the east or the west through one of the narrow valleys or canyons. His brush mark tracks led from this clearing to the edge of a slope carpeted with wild grasses and prickly pears, where they vanished completely. There were leaves and broken branches around my feet. He'd snapped them from the trees nearby and had them waiting right here for him when he emerged with the body. Thus, I was confident in my assertion that the Border Patrol agent's remains weren't inside, but I knew my adversary well enough to know that the warren wasn't empty. Whether he thought I was dead or not, too much planning had gone into this plot to take any chances. At least the agent from whom I had commandeered the flashlight hadn't come looking for it. I was going to have to be completely inside the tunnel before I turned it on. Those choppers might have been far off now and the patrol vehicles scattered across the desert, but if any one of them by chance saw my light, I was going to have a hard time explaining exactly what I was doing and the reason I had withheld information from them. Plus, angry agents crawling through dark, tight spaces in pursuit of a fellow agent's murderer tended to shoot first and ask questions later.

I stared down at the boulder I had rolled away from the orifice. This tunnel hadn't been burrowed by a coyote. This one bore all the telltale chop marks of a spade or a shovel. I could see the wooden cribbing from where I stood. He had known where he was going when he started to dig, which justified my earlier assumption that he had extensive knowledge of the area's geology. I looked around the edge for wires or a transmitter. Nothing. I listened for the sound of anything inside. Silence. Of course, just because I didn't hear a rattle didn't mean I was safe in that regard.

I was stalling and I knew it.

We were nearing the endgame. I could feel it. There was no more time to waste.

Leading with the Beretta and the Maglite as I was now accustomed, I squirmed into the darkness. I flipped on the light the moment I was able and saw that the tunnel ended only a short distance ahead of me. The edges of the opening were jagged where he'd been forced to chisel through solid rock to reach the surprisingly large cave. The lower rim was scarred in straight lines where ropes had bitten into the stone. It didn't matter if he had used the rope to haul himself or heavy equipment up and down since I didn't have one, nor did I have the ability to track one down.

I wiggled my torso out over the nothingness and shined my light downward. The smooth stone floor had to be fifteen feet down. Two and a half times my height. Definitely feasible. But I was going to have to holster my sidearm, pocket the flashlight, and drop down into the pitch black. If there was a better option, I couldn't see it. I shined the beam throughout the cave, but accomplished little more than moving the darkness around. I rolled over onto my back, shoved my pistol into the holster under my left arm and the Maglight into the right pocket of my jacket, and maneuvered myself toward the hole. It took some doing, but I twisted and turned in such a way that I ended up hanging from the lip by my hands, my feet dangling roughly seven feet above the ground. Dropping from this height wouldn't kill me, nor would I probably break any bones. A sprained ankle would seriously hamper my style, though, so the moment I let go and felt the earth strike the soles of my feet, I was already flexing my knees and hips to absorb the impact and rolling to dispel the momentum. In one motion I really wished there had been people around to witness, I rolled to my feet, crossed my arms over my chest, and simultaneously drew both the Beretta and the flashlight.

I turned slowly in a circle, evaluating my surroundings.

The cave itself was nearly the size of a single-car garage, with an irregular roof to one side, domed to the other. The petroglyphs on the walls were remarkably well preserved, despite the thick layer of dust adhering to them. There were no shadowed forms crouching against the walls, strange burlap sacks on the ground, or slithering forms composed of darkness and fangs. Besides the pile of scrap wood from the cribbing in the corner and the smear of blood across the rock floor, there wasn't a damn thing—

I froze when I saw it.

A quick reflection from the deep shadows up and to my right.

My heartbeat thundered in my ears. A million potentially shiny objects, all of which were easily capable of doing serious bodily harm, raced through my mind in the time it took me to raise the beam to the small alcove about eight feet up, where I saw just about the only object in the world I didn't imagine.

It was a digital audio recorder.

Small. Handheld. Spatters of blood had dried to black blotches and smears. I stared at it for several moments before I finally decided "screw it," tucked my hand into my sleeve, reached up and brought it down. I pressed the largest button, which I assumed would be the one to make it play. The recorder started to hiss. From beneath the hissing came a scraping sound. It grew louder and more distinct until it defined itself as footsteps. The tread was heavy and natural. Maybe a little hesitant, but not overly so. A clattering sound; the recorder shifting location, perhaps into a pocket. Rustling. Static. The footsteps again. Closer. Slower.

Whoever was walking toward the recorder sensed something was amiss.

Another footstep. Another.

Stop.

More clattering.

"*Hola, amigos. Estan arrestados.*" Hello, friends. You're under arrest. After days in the brutal heat, that was often enough to get the undocumenteds out of their hiding places with their hands on their heads.

There was a note of concern in the agent's voice. Concern, but not fear.

A muffled footstep. Another.

The crackling sound of gravel trickling across stone.

The rush of wind.

A thud.

A scrabbling, scraping sound.

A grunt.

A clatter.

A high-pitched gasp.

A wet splatter.

A gurgle.

Another thump.

Thrashing.

A footstep. Strong, confident. Another.

Heavy breathing. Exertion of some kind.

A tearing sound.

Fabric.

More tearing sounds.

Flesh.

The difference between them was distinct. It was a sound I knew I'd never be able to forget as long as I lived.

I stood there in the darkness listening to the killer dip the coyote paw into the sopping wound, take a step toward the canyon wall, and slap it onto the rock. Over and over. Listened to the faint scratching sounds of the dead animal's nails on the rock. I listened to it beyond the point where he tore away more clothing and slashed open the gut. Then I listened to the damp slapping sounds some more. There will always be a part of me standing in that dark cave listening to the gruesome scene, as life was transformed into death, and death into a meaningless message meant only for me. To think that a boy had been born and raised, had lived and loved, had walked the earth for however many years, only to meet his fate in a slot canyon in the form of a winking face.

If that's not proof of the frailty of the human condition, then I don't know what is.

I listened until all was said and done and I was alone in the silent darkness, hardly even able to make myself breathe. Then, with a muffled crumpling sound and a click, it was all over. Mercifully. I felt the warmth of tears on my cheeks. The dispassionate nature of the deed was almost a posthumous insult to the victim, a violation even more repugnant than dipping a coyote's paw into the wounds, as though the man's physical vessel were no more than a mere paint can. I looked at the readout to confirm that I had listened to the only file, then put the recorder back up on the ledge.

I think I would have preferred the rattle-less diamondbacks.

It didn't take long to find the tunnel he must have used to drag the body in here after ending the recording. I wasn't looking forward to crawling through another tunnel covered with the victim's blood and dripping with copious amounts of coyote urine, but right now, I just really needed to get the hell out of here. I felt dirty and sick to my stomach, as though the very air inside the cave had absorbed the Coyote's evil and it was leeching into my pores.

It was time to end this nightmare.

Permanently.

TWENTY-FOUR

I was waiting in the parking lot of the Tohono O'odham Community College when the first cars started to trickle in. I had managed to change clothes and wash my hands and face, but I still felt tainted by the night's adventures. I could only imagine how I must have looked. Or smelled. Not that I really cared, mind you. At this point I was of singular focus and I'd be damned if I wasn't going to find exactly what I was looking for inside.

It struck me at the second crime scene, before I even set off for the casino, that no man, no matter how long he had lived here or how long he had spent exploring the desert, would have the kind of precise geological knowledge that the Coyote possessed without some form of outside assistance. The kind of assistance that the United States Geological Survey supplied to anyone who had the gumption to get off his ass and look for it. The kind of assistance that was readily available to every federal agency, or for an agent trying to fly under the radar, or any private individual at just about any library on the face of the planet. Which was why the moment I saw the elderly woman approaching the doors to the college library with a set of keys in her hand, I was jogging straight up the walkway toward her.

The library itself wouldn't rival most public branches I've been in. The law library at DU was probably at least twice the size of this one by itself, but I only needed to look at one thing, and I would have wagered a vital organ that they had it.

The librarian greeted me with a smile, despite the fact that I was a stranger creeping up behind her with the stench of death seeping from my pores. She had one of those faces that was a fulfillment of her aging process, not merely the result of it. She was warm and open and her smile was the kind I associated with freshly baked cookies. She was large, but wore the weight well. And for some ungodly reason, wore a shawl even though it had to be in the mid-nineties already. I believed in making snap judgments about people. They'd saved my life on more than one occasion. This was one of those rare people who reminded me why I do some of the horrible things I do. Right about now, that was exactly what I needed.

And she was helpful to boot. She could have led me straight to any number of geological surveys and topical maps, the kind bound in musty binders like carpet samples or rolled up in long dusty tubes. Instead, she took me down an aisle lined with books on archeology and anthropology that smelled of field use and to the reference room through the back door. She sat in front of one of the Gateway computers, which must have come as part of the donated set in the police station, and blew through a series of prompts and menus with the speed of a teenage hacker on Mountain Dew and methamphetamines.

"I have to be able to keep up with the kids these days," she said in answer to the question I hadn't posed. That way of thinking obviously didn't extend to her wardrobe, but, then again, mine was starting to date me as well. She glanced back at me and smiled. "Can't let them think they can do all of their learning on Wikipedia, you know." She winked. "Here's what you're looking for. Kind of a popular subject lately."

She rose from the chair with the grace of a woman half her size and gestured for me to take it.

"How so?"

"You aren't the first to come looking for these maps. How do you think I knew exactly where to go?" She patted me on the shoulder. "It's nice to see so many people taking an interest in their heritage. Won't be long before it's entirely assimilated. Did you know only ten percent of our youth can speak our native O'odham language?"

"What's that about our heritage?"

"The Hohokam, of course. They are our roots. They are the ones Elder Brother brought up from the underworld with him."

"Elder Brother?"

"I'itoi. Elder Brother. The Pima call him Se:he. He also graced us with the gift of the Himdag, the guidelines that allow us to remain in balance with nature and the world around us. He is the Man in the Maze. You see his design throughout the southwest. You even walked right underneath it when you entered the library." She winked again. She was one of those few people who could pull it off. "It seems to me you have a whole lot more research to do before you even begin looking for the mystical underworld of lore."

"Who else has been looking?"

"A good number of people. Mostly students, although I suspect they're looking for some things the smugglers might have hidden. You know..." She leaned forward and whispered conspiratorially. "...drugs."

I nodded sagely to let her know that I appreciated the gravity of her statement.

"I'm hunting for something altogether different."

"Oh, I understand. A handsome, clean-shaven young man like you? I wouldn't have pegged you for a criminal. I'm sure you're looking for the same thing as Chief Antone, aren't you?"

"The chief looked at these maps, too?"

I tried to keep the surprise out of my voice, but she caught it. She now appraised me with a skeptical eye. Her smile dimmed and the deep lines of age advanced in its stead.

"I knew your father, you know," she said, and turned away. "Trouble followed that boy like a coyote. Always nipping at his heels. You're just like him, aren't you? You've got that good in you—I can see it—but you've got that coyote following you too. Kindly don't bring it in here with you. We have enough coyotes of our own. A whole nation full of them anymore."

And just like that, her smile returned.

"Rafael was always one of my favorites. He was curious about every little thing. Always wanted to learn what was out there beyond the desert. He and that brother of his. Roman. Two peas in a pod they were. Shame they let something so silly get between them. I cried when I heard he'd moved on from this world. I always knew he'd end up dancing in the sky." She dispelled the sadness from her voice with a sigh. "I'm just glad you finally decided to investigate your roots."

I smiled at her. I didn't know what to say. Obviously, telling her that I had little interest in a culture that seemed strange and alien to me was the wrong thing. I was simply on information overload. The chief already investigating the sub-Sonoran geology. My father and trouble nipping at his heels. Students looking for buried cartel caches. An obscure creator god who kept cropping up out of the blue. Elder Brother. It was my father's elder brother whose son was out there right now, killing people on the open desert and absconding with their bodies.

And here I had thought I was the one nipping at the Coyote's heels.

I heard voices from the front of the library.

"Let me know if you need any more help." She placed her hand on my arm and I had the urge to place mine on top of it. "I hope you find what you're looking for."

I nodded. The sincerity in her voice rendered me speechless. Maybe there was a part of me that felt as though something was missing from my life, a void I had attempted to fill with my work. Friedrich Nietzsche said that if you gaze long enough into the abyss, the abyss gazes also into you. Every time I turned my eyes inward, I found the Coyote looking back at me.

She was nearly out the door before I found my voice.

"How did you know who I was?"

She smiled and winked.

"You have your father's eyes."

And then she was gone, leaving me alone with the computer and a maelstrom of thoughts that positively made my head spin. I had to focus on the task at hand, though. And right now that task was tracking down a serial killer who was lurking somewhere out there in the mythical underworld of the Hohokam.

I plugged my USB drive into the computer and began downloading the information as I scrolled through it. There were several different types of map. From the simple two-dimensional topographical to the three-dimensional digital elevation models and everything in between. While both would undoubtedly help in my search, it was the ancillary material that was of the utmost importance. Landsat 7, a polar, sun-synchronously orbiting satellite controlled by a joint effort between the USGS and NASA, was equipped with specialized instrumentation that allowed it to provide more than mere superficial imaging. The ground-penetrating radar was capable of mapping up to sixty feet beneath the surface with surprising accuracy, while the magnetometer analyzed and mapped the composition of the strata based on discrete magnetic properties distinct to every kind of soil and rock. In essence, one showed you where to find the underground cave you were looking for; the other showed you where to dig in order to reach your destination via the route of least resistance.

A cursory glance essentially proved my theory. The mountains were pretty much riddled with subterranean formations, while the open desert was essentially solid earth beneath the sand. It wasn't much, but it was nice to finally be right about something.

I pulled the storage device and slipped it back into my pocket. I could download the maps onto my laptop without arousing any suspicion and further evaluate them away from prying eyes.

But first, there were a couple of people I needed to track down.

I exited the research room and walked straight toward the front door. The librarian was busy helping people at the main counter while a girl I assumed to be her student aide unpacked her backpack and clipped on her name badge.

I stopped in the foyer and stared up above the front door toward the pinnacle of the vaulted ceiling. Nestled into the inverted V was a round textile woven on a loom by hands that had undoubtedly turned to dust long ago. It was created in the yellows and reds and browns of the Sonoran sands themselves. A red stick figure stood in the mouth of a large circular maze that reminded me of those old plastic party favors you had to tilt to guide the miniature BB into the slot in the center.

I'itoi. Elder Brother. We meet at last.

I glanced back to find the librarian watching me. She smiled and nodded.

I returned the gesture and pushed through the glass doors into dry air that felt as though it had been superheated in a blast furnace.

TWENTY-FIVE

Chief Antone's car wasn't in the lot at the station when I arrived, so I sat across the street and waited for a few minutes. I watched Louis of the plastic cup working at the closer of the two desks and a woman I assumed to be Olivia manning the phones at the front counter while several people I didn't know milled around the lobby. They both looked harried, but that was the status quo at every police station around the world. The difference was written in the impotent expressions on their faces and the way they repeatedly glanced at their watches. They had expected some sort of help that had yet to arrive. I figured the chief had probably belatedly heard about the craziness of the previous night and was out at the crime scene now. He was undoubtedly pretty upset with me for not passing along the news as soon as I heard it. As far as I was concerned, that made us even. I had a few choice words to share with him about the research he had done that could have been extremely beneficial to me had he not kept it to himself. And I wanted to know why he had done so. He was hiding something and I intended to find out what it was.

I figured I had some time to kill before the chief returned, so I decided I would pay a call on my good old Uncle Roman. This whole I'itoi thing wasn't sitting right with me. It could be entirely coincidental, but I'm sure I've made my views on that subject perfectly clear. Somehow that myth was connected to this case and the Coyote had made sure to point it out at every turn with the metaphorical recreation of the ascension of the Hohokam from the underworld and the petroglyphs. And who had led them but one mischievous creator god they affectionately referred to as Elder Brother.

Roman was sitting out on the porch, smoking, when I turned down his driveway. I pulled in right behind his truck, leaned across the seat, and popped the passenger side door for him without waiting for the cloud of dust to settle.

"Let's go for a ride," I said.

Roman walked straight to the car and climbed in, his face devoid of expression. He had a bottle of Coors Light in his hand, despite the early hour. He didn't say a word. He just closed the door and reclined the seat so that he had room for his long legs. His braids had begun to fray and the skin on his face had noticeably paled. I recognized stress when I saw it.

I also recognized guilt.

I headed back down the driveway and turned right, away from Sells.

"How long have you known?"

He was silent for a long moment before he finally spoke.

"I didn't know. Not for sure anyway."

"Why didn't you tell me?"

"I was hoping I was wrong. You know? He's my son."

I waited for him to elaborate, but he said nothing more. Not for another five miles or so down the gravel road into the open desert. There was a little white cross staked to the side of the road. The flowers strung around it were withered and desiccated.

"Turn right here."

I didn't have to ask why. We both knew where we were going.

I slowed and turned onto some sandy ruts that hardly qualified as a road. I could see the foot-shaped impressions in the matted brown grass of the center stripe where walkers had jumped over the ruts to avoid leaving clear prints. A stratified butte stood off to my left in the distance, a constant reminder of a long gone age when this land of sand and sun had been under the sea. The western horizon was ridged with the Ajo Mountain Range where Randall had led me to the second crime scene. In between, there was a whole lot of nothing. Pitchfork saguaros. A ribbon of mesquites and naked cottonwoods marked the passing of a vaporized stream. A ridge like the vertebrae of a skeletal snake from which cacti and yellow palo verdes grew. A glimmer ahead and to my left; a reflection of the sun from the manmade object I was sure was my destination.

I watched it grow larger as we neared until it took form from the sand. It was a formerly white mobile home painted a mottled reddish-brown with dust. There were tumbleweeds tangled in the skirt. Piles of rocks marked where animals had tried to tunnel under it. The wooden front porch leaned toward the stairs leading up to it. An old television antenna dangled over the side by its wires. I could faintly see orange curtains through the dust on the windows.

I coasted to a stop twenty feet from the front porch and waited for the dust to wash over the car from behind. We sat in silence with the engine idling. I studied the trailer home while he stared blankly out the passenger side window.

"We used to live here together. Once upon a time. Just the two of us. Seems like so long ago now. I haven't been out here in probably close to a year."

"He lives here alone now?"

"Last I knew, anyway. Ever since my parents died and I moved into their house."

"Where did he live before that?"

"Had a place in Why for a while. Another in Sells. Did a spell down in Lukeville. Across the border in Sonoyta. I don't know exactly what he was looking for, but he never did find it."

"Why didn't things work out with the Border Patrol?"

"How long do you think any O'odham would last with a gang of thugs like that? They treat us like dogs. Worse. Like we're somehow the enemy. Like it's our fault these traffickers are abusing our land and forcing them to be out here protecting us. Like we're weak for not protecting ourselves."

I nodded. What could I say?

I opened my door and climbed out. The day was strangely quiet. I couldn't hear a single car engine or airplane. No rustling of the breeze through the shrubs. It was as if the world itself had stopped turning.

Roman closed his door and walked around the hood to join me.

"You still have the key to that thing?"

He patted the front pocket of his jeans in response.

"Mind opening her up?"

Had he declined, I could have obtained a search warrant without much difficulty. I also could have just kicked the door in, but I would have had a hard time explaining that with a witness standing right here next to me.

He probably figured it was best to just open it up and be done with it. Or maybe he was curious himself. I suppose Frankenstein had been fascinated by the monster he had inadvertently created, too.

Roman's footsteps echoed from beneath the wooden stairs and porch. Rusted nails creaked in their moorings. The keys jingled as he found the right one and slid it into the lock. He turned the key until it made a clicking sound.

"Okay." I drew my pistol. "Step away from the door."

He nodded and backed up against the railing. I knew there was no one inside, but that didn't necessarily mean it was empty. I sighted down the Beretta, took hold of the latch with my left hand, threw open the door, ducked to the side, and pressed my back against the trailer.

The door banged against the opposite side of the frame and shivered back toward me.

No gunshots. No explosions. No shouting. No snakes. No nothing.

Just a smell that told me no one had lived here in quite some time.

It was dark inside, save for the thin strip of light that slanted across the room from the open doorway. My shadow stretched across carpet worn bare in spots and thick with dirt and dust. I eased cautiously across the threshold, leading with my pistol, and toggled the light switch with my elbow. Once. Then again.

Nothing.

Fortunately, I was becoming accustomed to this scenario and drew the Maglite from my pocket. I shined it backhanded into the room with my left, braced my right forearm on top of it, and advanced into the main room.

I took in my surroundings as quickly as possible.

A half-wall to my right. Beveled rails. The kitchen beyond. Single doorway to my left. Bathroom. Hallway. Dark room at the very end. Bedroom. Doorway to the right of it. Presumably another bedroom. No sign of movement.

Buzzing sound. Flies?

The smell. Something rotting. Garbage, not decomposition. Spoiled food.

Definitely flies. Crawling on the refrigerator, swirling over the sink.

Another step. A creak from the floorboards. I exhaled slowly to steady my nerves. Glanced back at Roman on the porch. Elder brother was the wild card. I didn't like him behind me with the unknown ahead.

The furniture: threadbare and old. Seventies-style fabric. Wood showing through the armrests. A recliner chair with broken springs. Coffee table; chipped lacquer, stained with rings. Television; dark, small. No pictures hanging on the faux wood paneling. Cobwebs draped from the ceiling, meeting at the broken light fixture. Back window, boarded and braced with an empty bookcase.

Another step. *Creak.* Hollow space below.

Glance back. Roman still on the porch, nose crinkled. His expression: revulsion. Resignation.

Turn back to the kitchen. Sweep the light. Patina of dust and grime on the table. Two chairs, duct-taped vinyl. Linoleum floor, orange and gold, peeled away from exposed, water-stained wood near the sink. Brimming with rusted pots. Two more steps. Roiling cloud of flies. Cupboard beneath open, overflowing trash can, the source of the smell. Cross into the kitchen, sight down my pistol from left to right. Clear. Cabinets closed; too small to hide inside anyway. Refrigerator—*squeal*—ugh. Rotten mold, cheese. A puddle of lettuce, fruit? Grape skeleton. Slam the door closed. Turn around.

Roman standing in the main doorway, silhouetted against the brilliant daylight, hand over his mouth.

Walk quickly across the living room. Kick in the half-bathroom door. Grime-stained sink. Toilet open. Cracked mirror. The door struck the inner wall, rebounded, closed again. Move on.

Hallway. No pictures. Crevices in the ceiling. Broken fixture. Glass shards from the shattered bulb on the carpet.

Bedroom to the right. Boarded window. No bed. Bookcase in the corner. No books. Closet door, open. Empty.

Hallway again. Glance back. Roman in the entryway. Turn away. Two more steps. Kick in the main bathroom door. Plastic tub, cracked, ringed with grunge and rust. No head on the shower. No curtains or rings. Sink. Medicine cabinet, triangular shards of broken mirror lining the edges of the face, reflecting my flashlight beam. The smell? Christ. Nothing I want to see.

Back out. Peek over my shoulder. Roman in the main room, looking around as though walking into an unfamiliar place.

Master bedroom. Mattress on the floor. Stained. Crumpled sheet. Pillow, no case. Brown bottles. Scorpions skittered across the room toward the open closet, vanished into the shadows. Dark, imitation walnut paneling, chipped and faded. Crumpled plastic dropcloth in the corner. Black and crusted. Smell of rot. Not garbage this time. Decomp. Light fixture, gone. Nothing but wires. Spider webs; hairy occupants the size of my hand.

Step into the room.

Creak. Creak.

Stomp on the floor.

Thoom.

Hollow.

Glance back at Roman, his eyes awash in shadows, tears glistening on his cheeks.

Creak. Creak.

Chase away the darkness in the closet with my light.

Creak. Creak.

Bare shelf. Two wire hangers on the rack. One plastic. Zero scorpions.

Creak. Creak.

Edge of carpet, curled up in the corner. Smell of decomp stronger.

Creak. Creak.

Glance back. Roman, out of sight. Damn it.

Closet again. Stomp.

Thoom.

The floorboards shuddered underfoot. Stomp the curled carpet in the back corner. No crunching or squishing sounds. Grab the carpet, yank it back.

The smell hit me so hard I had to cover my mouth and nose with the bend of my left elbow. A gap in the floorboards. Easy enough to slide to the side with my foot, exposing the dark area beneath the trailer and contained by the skirt.

I shined my light down there and the brown scorpions raced away, clicking and clacking.

Even though I had a good idea of what I would find, I was unprepared for what I saw.

"Christ..."

TWENTY-SIX

I heard a creaking sound behind me, spun around, and nearly shot Roman right in the chest.

He shielded his eyes from the flashlight beam and I read it on his face. He knew what I had found. There was no surprise or alarm, merely a blank expression that told me everything I needed to know. This was a man whose worst fears had just been realized.

"You knew about this but did nothing to stop it?"

Roman shook his head.

"I didn't know. I just always suspected that there was something…wrong with him. Something broken inside of him that I couldn't fix. I tried to be his father, tried to love him like a father is supposed to…"

"He led you to the scene of the first crime, didn't he? No one had found it, so he led you there. His own father. He led you there so you could discover his work and report it."

"We were hunting, same as always. He didn't lead me anywhere. I just walked up on it. Saw it there…on my own…"

"What could you possibly have been hunting out there in this godforsaken desert?"

"Anything. Everything. Doves. Rattlesnakes. Coyotes. Jackrab—"

"What about people? You ever hunt human beings out there?"

"Never, God damn it!"

"What's the difference between actually doing it and turning a blind eye and allowing it to happen?"

"I told you! I didn't know!"

"You're his father! You should have known! You should have been able to stop him!"

The expression on his face was one of sheer and unadulterated hatred.

"What gives you the right?"

He stormed back down the hallway, his footsteps pounding on the hollow floor all the way into the main room and out onto the porch.

I turned my attention back to the hole in the closet floor. The wood was aged where it had been cut. I didn't know enough about the aging process of wood to estimate how long ago it had been sawed. Not that it really mattered in the grand scheme of things. I think I was just looking for any little thing I could find to postpone the inevitable. I'd never really had much direct interaction with scorpions, but it still wasn't something I looked forward to experiencing. I could have happily lived my entire life without ever seeing one in person, let alone braving the living carpet of them crawling around beneath me in the darkness. At least they didn't like my light. I was going to have to buy something nice for the agent from whom I had borrowed it. Right now, it was just about my favorite thing in the whole world.

Don't let anyone tell you I'm not hopelessly sentimental.

I leaned over the edge and shined my light under the house once more. Only a few scorpions had crawled back out into the open, where I had hit them with my beam before, and they scuttled out of sight pretty much immediately. The desiccated carcasses of their brethren were scattered everywhere.

I was really not looking forward to this.

I sat on the precipice and let my legs dangle. The heat and humidity wrapped around my ankles and feet like a wet blanket. It had been a while since anyone had opened this hatch to let it breathe, which definitely worked against me. The smell could have at least had the opportunity to dissipate a little. I pointed the beam directly beneath me, waited to make sure that nothing was going to come crawling or slithering out, then dropped down onto the dirt in a crouch. I shined the light in a circle around me as fast as I could to prevent being overrun. I could hear clicking and grinding sounds all around me in the darkness. Fortunately, whatever was making them seemed content enough to leave me be. That didn't necessarily mean that I was comfortable crawling deeper under the house and away from the lone egress, but there was no other way I could examine what I had seen at the edge of the flashlight's reach from above without actual physical proximity.

Flies buzzed at the periphery of the beam above a dark hole in the ground. There were only a few of them. After all, there wasn't much left for them to eat. The scorpions appeared to have consumed all of the flesh before turning on each other. The bones protruding from the pit were old. They'd been absolved of flesh long ago. All that remained now was a rust-colored discoloration and the black knots where the tendons had rotted from the inside out. If I were to wager a guess, those at the very top had to be at least six months old. Maybe more. I didn't have any desire to dig down there through the remains to see how many there were or how old the ones at the bottom were. It was enough for me to know that there were so many, the majority still mostly articulated. By all appearances, the bodies seemed to have just been hauled down here in one piece and hurled into the hole. I saw no obvious signs of either acute or prolonged violence, no fractures that had yet to begin the process of healing. Nor did I see any rumpled plastic like I had in the bedroom above me. Only a sheet of warped plywood he must have used as a cover until the deep pit, which must have once seemed ambitious, started to overflow.

I tried to picture the Coyote living a single floorboard away, while scorpions and snakes feasted on the decomposing flesh, while generations of flies lived and bred and died, only to be replaced by the maggots that picked up where they left off. Falling asleep on that stained mattress listening to the buzzing and clicking. Plotting how to get his next victim to hurl down into the stinking pit with the others. Why even bring them back here when he could simply leave them in the desert for the carrion birds? It was the only part of the act that felt even remotely intimate. There almost seemed to be a disconnect between Ban and his victims that I couldn't quite explain, as though he hadn't known them in life and had no desire to make the effort in death. Their bodies were refuse. He lived exclusively for the hunt. That was the only thing that mattered. So why was he now trying to send a message? What could he possibly have to say that would justify so much senseless killing?

If he had kept trophies, he had obviously taken them with him to wherever he was now. There was nothing here; no mementos of any sort. This was now just an abandoned trailer in the middle of nowhere he had once used for the disposal of bodies. And he had obviously found a new home now, someplace where there were now the bodies of at least four victims to keep him company.

All I had accomplished here was proving what I already suspected. He had been killing people out here for a long time and no one had been the wiser. How many other pits like this were out there? How many smiley faces had we already missed? For all I knew, the desert could be painted with them and the Coyote could be sitting around a pit the size of the Grand Canyon already nearly filled with corpses.

I looked down at the tangled mass of bones, at the lives stripped of their humanity. Somewhere out there mothers and fathers, brothers and sisters, and sons and daughters were lighting candles and saying prayers for the safe return of these poor souls, hoping that wherever they were they were happy and alive. Soon enough the truth would set in, if it hadn't already. These were the lost and never-to-be-found. These were the forever unidentified. Even after this discovery was turned over to the locals, these remains would just be shuttled off to the Pima County Medical Examiner's Office/Forensics Science Center to wait for eternity with the hundreds of others that were found in this very desert every year. Maybe a few of them would be identified from photographs loved ones sent to their various consulates, pictures of missing persons smiling their biggest smiles in hopes that such precious captured moments would suffice in lieu of dental records. This was the closing of the circle of life, down here in the darkness, where their ribcages now provided shelter for the very animals that had consumed their hearts.

These people meant something to someone, whether or not they did to their killer. They had mattered. They still mattered.

If only to me.

I was the one upon whom they counted to bring their murderer to justice, or, failing at that, to avenge them.

There was nothing more to be learned down here. I crawled toward the hole in the bedroom closet and climbed back up into the trailer. The front door was still standing open as I had left it. I stepped out under the blazing sun, for once grateful for the dryness of the heat.

I stood on the decrepit porch and used my cell phone to anonymously report the trailer to the ME's office directly to keep the call from being traced back to me too quickly. Between the Border Patrol and the FBI, there would be agents crawling all over this desert like ants at a picnic, but I still couldn't fathom why that would be a positive development for the Coyote.

I watched my father's elder brother through the windshield of my car as I spoke. He had his face buried in his hands. I had to admit there was a part of me that wanted him to look up so I could see an expression of shame or remorse, maybe even regret, something to let me know that he recognized the evil he had brought into the world. Something other than the emotional distance he had already shown me, the same emotional distance I felt toward his son and him.

My blood.

My family.

It frightened me how very much alike we were.

TWENTY-SEVEN

"Where's his mother?"

Neither of us had spoken since we left the trailer. I'd imagine both of us wanted to burn it down, but for different reasons.

"None of your business."

I recognized his tone. It was the one he used to end a conversation. I truthfully didn't care whether he wanted to talk or not, nor did I care if I pissed him off in the process. He wasn't the only one who was in a vile mood.

"She leave you? Is that it?"

"You're walking a thin line. Blood or not, you're still an outsider here."

His cheeks flushed with anger, but he kept his eyes straight ahead, on the road. He was trying his best to keep his expression studiously neutral. I'd been doing this for so long that I could see the cracks forming before he even realized there was the possibility that they might. And the more he protested, the more I started to think that whatever happened to her had some bearing on what was happening here now.

"Was that her in your bedroom? The pictures on the dresser?"

His lips whitened as he tightened them against his teeth. I didn't have to see his hands to know they were balled into fists.

"There are some things that aren't any of your business. Things that were never meant to be your business. You can run all over this reservation, saying and doing whatever you want, but this subject is off limits. Especially to you." I slowed the car as we neared the turnoff for his driveway. The tactic was transparent. "Just let me out anywhere through here."

"Was it another man? Did she run off and leave you with the kid?"

"Stop the car. Let me out."

"Did she recognize the fact that her own son was a monster, is that it?"

"I'm warning you. I don't care what kind of badge you carry."

"Did she sense the evil in him and decide she'd sooner—"

I didn't see the punch coming. I heard the crack, tasted copper on the back of my tongue, and the next thing I knew we were barreling through the desert, tearing up creosote and cacti and heading straight toward his house in a cloud of dust. I stomped the brake and the car skidded sideways to a halt. Before we were even fully stopped, Roman was climbing out the door.

"She died," he shouted through the closing door. I watched him walking away until he turned and pointed at me. I could barely hear him through the car door, but his expression alone would have sufficed. "Don't you come back here again! Ever!"

And with that, he vanished into the settling cloud of dust.

I stretched my jaw and rubbed at the spot where he had belted me. His fist had connected with the curvature of my mandible, just beneath my right earlobe. I might have seen it coming in time if he'd swung with his right. It didn't matter. I was man enough to admit that I'd had it coming. I knew I was pushing too hard and I'm sure my words had been barbed, but I was angry and I needed to take it out on someone. I know he wasn't responsible for murdering those people, nor was he directly to blame for the actions of his son. I wanted to hurt him because he could have stopped Ban. He could have intervened before it ever reached this point. Maybe Ban could have even received help. As it stood now, if he wasn't killed out here in the desert, he would end up riding a needle. Of course, after murdering a federal agent, he wouldn't survive his first night in prison.

I sat there a while longer, watching the dust settle like snow onto my windshield and hood. It turned the blazing sun an orangish color while the sky appeared to fill with ash. Finally, I reversed the car and backed toward to road, dragging branches and whole uprooted bushes with me. The scraping sounds that came from under the car made me grateful this was a pool car and not my personal vehicle. I backed right out onto the main road and stared at the trail of destruction I had left in my wake. The branches under the hood had nearly erased the tire tracks. There was a thought on the edge of my consciousness, like a tip-of-the-tongue kind of thing, but I couldn't quite grasp it. Something about the way the brush marks obscured my trail struck a chord.

It would come to me eventually. When I was ready.

I put the car into drive and headed back toward town. The last shrub had just shaken loose from my undercarriage when the first Crown Vic blew past me in the opposite direction at close to ninety. Two more whipped past right behind it, so fast that the wind from their passage nearly buffeted my car onto the shoulder. The ME's office must have called the Bureau first. I watched for brake lights in the rearview mirror, but none of them so much as slowed. I guess I should have been thankful for the desert camouflage that now disguised my vehicle.

There was that elusive thought again, but I still couldn't catch it.

I focused again on the road. I had enjoyed spending time with my uncle so very much that I figured now would be a wonderful time to have a little chat with Chief Antone. Why waste a perfectly rotten mood on myself when I could share it with someone as deserving as the chief? I understood the hypocrisy of being angered by the fact that he was keeping information from me, but, damn it, I was a federal agent. It was in my job description.

The police station looked pretty much the same as it had earlier, although things seemed to have calmed down in the interim. The aura of panic had faded to the more manageable bedlam I associated with most rural station houses. And still the chief's cruiser was nowhere to be found. Maybe his absence was nothing out of the ordinary. Could have even been his day off for all I knew. Besides, tracking him down might not be such a terrible thing. It gave me the opportunity to see him in his element, or at least his element, whether he was in it at the time or not. There was something about him that still didn't sit right with me.

Who was I kidding? It was downright maddening.

It took all of about thirty seconds to pull his home address from my computer. I was there in ten minutes flat. He lived in an old adobe home not unlike the one in which my father had been raised. It was the same color as the dust that trailed my car and apparently utilized the same repairman as the police station. The cracks in the adobe showed through the discolored patches from a hundred feet away as I turned down his dirt driveway. Brown juniper shrubs lined the rutted drive. A nopales cactus sagged to my right, the pads black and eroded. Generations of tumbleweeds had aggregated against a ramshackle picket fence enclosing what I assumed passed for a front yard, although it was little more than a rectangular slice of the same desert that stretched away from me to the distant horizon.

I parked beside the fence and watched the curtains through the front windows while I waited for the dust to settle. I climbed out and walked toward the gate, which was ordinarily held closed by a frayed length of rope, but now clapped open and closed on the gentle breeze that had arisen from the southwest. The rusted hinges squealed when I opened it and passed through. The front porch was a faded wooden number that had been built over a crumbling concrete pad. The planter boxes on it contained potting soil that had dried to a pale gray and spilled through the cracks in the pottery. There was a cholla carcass beneath the window to my right, over which hung the bleached skull of a bull, and a dead row of sage along the fence line. Considering the cacti and shrubs grew naturally around here, it must have taken some doing to kill them off. The entire house gave the same impression of carefully tended decrepitude as the police station.

All except for the upper rim of the satellite dish I could barely see over the corner of the roof.

I understood why the chief cultivated such an image for a police station servicing a largely impoverished tribe, especially when it came to dealing with external agencies, but I couldn't come up with a single good reason why he would go to such lengths when it came to his personal domain, unless there was something inside that he was trying to hide.

I knocked on the front door, which was about the most solid feature of the entire façade. I didn't expect anyone to answer and wasn't surprised when no one did. I peeked through the gaps between the curtains, which revealed nothing but the horizontal blinds behind them.

I knocked again and waited.

Antone had mentioned a twelve year-old granddaughter, but this house showed no indication that she lived here. He hadn't said a word about a spouse or the child that had spawned the granddaughter or even if he or she had any siblings. I hadn't thought to ask, primarily because I flat-out hadn't cared at the time, but that knowledge would have served me well right about now.

I knocked again, harder this time.

It didn't look like anyone was home; however, the last thing I wanted to do was surprise a terrified housewife or latchkey kid and take a shotgun blast to the gut. Unfortunately, I just didn't have the time to screw around. I didn't know where Antone was and I really didn't want to be inside his house when he returned.

I stepped down from the porch, crossed the yard, and wandered around the side of the house. There were more dead junipers and a couple of dead pines with bark ravaged by beetles. The back of the house looked marginally better than the front. A bent aluminum screen door, without an actual screen, opened onto a small deck that contained a single lawn chair and a half-dozen empty ceramic planters. The chair was the anomaly. The metal still shined and the cushions were in good shape. There was little more than a patina of dust on them, which was easily enough brushed off before I sat down in the chief's chair. Like the coffee maker at the station and the satellite dish, this was the indulgence that shattered the illusion. I imagined Antone sitting just as I was now, staring off to the west across the rolling desert to where the sun would set behind the distant mountains. A stratified ridge rose from the sand and creosote a couple of miles away. Beyond it, I could see the roofline of an outbuilding. Or at least what looked like the roof of a manmade structure from this distance. Two faint parallel tracks wound around the shrubs and cacti toward it.

I stood again and rapped on the screen door. Thirty seconds later I had it propped against my back and was working the lock with my rakes. I knew what I was doing crossed a line. Anything I found inside—if there was anything to find—would technically be inadmissible in a court of law, but I wasn't trying to make a case against the chief. Anything he might be doing that he shouldn't be was surely small potatoes. He wasn't the Coyote. I was certain of that, but I needed to know why he was investigating the natural underground formations at the same time the Coyote was using them to facilitate his killing spree. Like I said, I don't believe in coincidence. The chief was definitely keeping something from me and hiding it behind the guise of helpfulness.

A rake pick is about the easiest tool to use when it comes to getting through any standard keyed lock in a hurry. It's pretty much just a slim metal rod with a snake-shaped curvature at the end. The standard tumbler lock is composed of a series of spring-loaded mechanisms called pin stacks, each of which is made of two pins, one on top of the other, a key pin and a driver pin, respectively. When the properly cut key is inserted into the lock, the teeth create the right amount of tension on the key pins to force them upward until the bases of the driver pins align at what's called the shear line. That's the point where the lock disengages and the key can be turned to open the door. A rake essentially takes the place of the teeth of a key. All you have to do is run it back and forth inside the lock until you get all of the pins to "hang" at the shear line, apply a little tension, and…voila.

The back door popped open, just a crack.

I slid the sleeve of my windbreaker over my hand and used it to open the door. I went in fast and low, drawing my flashlight with one hand and my pistol with the other.

No shotguns roared or terrified women screamed. There was no sound at all, save for the metronomic ticking of a clock deeper in the house. I waited for nearly a full minute, listening to the *tick…tock…tick…tock* while beads of sweat trickled down my spine between my shoulder blades, then started into the house.

TWENTY-EIGHT

I entered via a kitchen that smelled of black beans and peppers. I backhanded my flashlight, aligned it with the sightline of my Beretta, and examined my surroundings. The dishes in the sink had been rinsed but not washed. The counters were cluttered with random cooking utensils. My flashlight beam reflected from a stainless steel industrial coffee maker that ground the beans, drew the water directly from a tap connected to the sink, and brewed whole pots at a time, on demand. It probably cost more than the bulky old microwave and the avocado-colored refrigerator and stove set combined. There was a table buried under newspapers. Three of the four chairs were heaped with boxes of files.

An arched doorway granted access to the great room. The curtains were not only drawn and blinded, but draped with heavy blankets so as not to admit a single ray of light, or, more likely, to prevent anyone outside from seeing what Antone was doing. The furniture had been shoved against the walls to clear space for a series of folding card tables in the middle of the room. They were plastered with maps. The very same maps I had viewed at the library, only these had been enlarged and laminated and were positively covered with markings from red and black grease pens and ringed with stains from the bottoms of mugs of coffee. There were circles and Xs and arrows and notes scribbled so hurriedly that I couldn't decipher them. The television was an eighties model and the stereo had a record player. Both were buried under so much dust that I wondered if Antone even knew what they were. A Remington twelve gauge leaned in the corner behind the front door.

I followed the hallway back toward the bedrooms. The walls were lined with framed pictures, just like Roman's. They featured a much younger, and much thinner, version of Antone. I hardly recognized him. His facial expressions were genuine and transparent, not guarded and indecipherable as they were now. He had been happy; the lines on his face reflected laughter, not worry.

And it was readily apparent that he loved both of the women in the pictures with him. One was presumably his wife, the other the daughter who carried parts of both of them in her face. Her mother's long black hair and slender nose. Her father's large dark eyes and once-prominent jaw. Her mother's wide, toothy smile that showcased the upper gums. I watched her age backward as I walked, regressing from a young woman to a teen to a toddler. There was another picture at the end of the row, arranged almost as an afterthought, or perhaps, instead, to be interpreted as separate from the others. It was of the daughter and a child with her eyes, but the smile on her face was forced. She couldn't have been more than eighteen and her youth conflicted with the weight she carried in the bags beneath her eyes. From there, the pictures metamorphosed into the granddaughter alone, but none of them beyond the age of four or five. If she was now twelve as Antone had said, then there was a good chunk of time missing, a good chunk of her life.

The pictures on the opposite side ranged in age from pastel to manila and bronze to black and white. I recognized a little of Antone in some of the people, who were every bit as serious as my own lineage had been, although they didn't seem to be featured with the same prominence. I didn't know what to make of that. There was one picture in particular that caught my eye. It was offset from the others as though it bore some significance to whoever had hung it. There were two children, a boy and a girl, sitting astride a piebald horse on only a saddle blanket. I didn't recognize Antone at first. He'd been a scrawny thing, even at what appeared to be eleven or twelve. The girl behind him was a few years younger and wore the kind of blissful smile only a young girl who had yet to be touched by the realities of life could wear. I recognized her immediately, even so far back through the prism of time. I had seen her before. With a much older Antone and in the face of her daughter. This was Antone's wife. They'd been together in some form or fashion since before they were even teenagers. They'd perhaps even lived their entire lives together.

I felt a great sense of sadness at that realization. It was obvious that she didn't live here, and yet a part of her still haunted this place. The aura of loss seemed to radiate from the house itself.

A wife who wasn't around anymore. A daughter who no longer sent pictures, even of her child. A man for whom their absence was a palpable entity within his home, a man with a secret that involved the hidden geological world beneath the desert. A man who appeared to be singlehandedly trying to keep Folgers in business.

There was something here. I could feel it. Something that played a role in the chief's involvement in this case.

I nodded to myself and resumed my search.

The bathroom off the hallway smelled of ammonia and the shower curtain was opaque with mildew. I drew it aside to reveal a freestanding tub with a ring of grime and rust. There was a shaving kit and a lone towel that looked like it had already been subjected to several uses. I opened the medicine cabinet and glanced at the contents. A crumpled tube of toothpaste and a flattened brush. Deodorant and cologne. A shelf full of bottles and prescriptions: acetaminophen, ibuprofen, amoxicillin, terbinafine, sertraline, onabotulinumtoxinA, lorazepam, ondansetron, loperamide. There was even a bottle of Anacin, which I didn't even realize was still on the market. The top shelf was reserved for another toothbrush, a hairbrush, a bottle of perfume, and an ornamental jar of what appeared to be potpourri. It had to be Antone's wife's shelf, although a woman utilizing a shelf she would need a ladder to reach seemed more than a little impractical. I closed the cabinet and moved on down the hallway.

I opened the door to the smaller of the two bedrooms, which was a dusty homage of sorts to the daughter. It looked as though she had just walked out of it one day and never returned, but her parents had left it in precisely the same condition in case she decided to return and resume the life she had abandoned. There was a sadness to it that suggested an element of guilt and a desperate kind of hope to which it was almost hard to bear witness. I closed the door again and followed my flashlight beam into the final bedroom.

The master was another shrine, this one to the woman I recognized as Antone's wife from the pictures in the hallway. Her portrait was framed with dark wood that had been hand-carved into an intricate flowered pattern, which must have taken countless hours to complete, and draped with red velvet sashes. It rested on a small table in the corner in a half-circle of white candles in glass holders. Dried flowers adorned the walls surrounding it, beside which several newspaper articles had been tacked. They were a part of the display, and yet ultimately apart from it. The kind of discordant arrangement one could only associate with a law enforcement officer, and one who bore the weight of the words. The clippings were crumpled and yellowed and at odds with the elegance of the shrine.

I rounded a bed that didn't appear to have been slept in for quite some time and stepped over a mess of dirty clothes on my way across the room. My light illuminated the face of a woman who hadn't aged beyond her early fifties. Her eyes were bright and carefree, her smile completely lacking any kind of self-consciousness. The lines on her face suggested that the expression hadn't been feigned for the camera. That was just who she was. A woman who envisioned a future beyond the horizon, one with a husband with whom she had been in love since she was just a child. Not one that could be summarized in a handful of paragraphs by a woman who had never even known her.

Desert pursuit turns deadly

Sandra Talbot, Arizona Daily Star

TUCSON — A local woman was involved in a collision with a truck being pursued by a Border Patrol vehicle after allegedly running a checkpoint on I-86. Eyewitness accounts suggest the truck, a newer-model Ford F-250, was traveling at great speeds across the open desert when it launched from the shoulder and struck a Nissan Sentra traveling westbound on the interstate. The driver of the Sentra, Eloise Maria Antone, was airlifted to the University of Arizona Medical Center in Tucson, where she was pronounced dead on arrival.

The driver of the truck, Ignacio Mendez, a Mexican national wanted on trafficking charges in Texas, was also admitted to the UMC with various injuries, purportedly of a non-critical nature.

Following his treatment and release, he will be remanded into the custody of agents from the Department of Homeland Security and transported to the Central Arizona Correctional Facility, where he will await the filing of formal charges and subsequent hearings.

According to a press release issued by the DHS, the truck driven by Mr. Mendez contained more than thirty bricks of marijuana with an estimated street value of nearly three-quarters of a million dollars. The bricks had been welded inside the frame of the vehicle beneath the rear seats of the extended cab.

"This marks another small victory in the war against the cartels," said Supervisory Border Patrol Agent Neil Rivera of Ajo Station. "Although I think we can all agree that the price we paid in this instance was too high. No loss of American life is acceptable."

Mrs. Antone, 52, a former tribal councilwoman and professor at the Tohono O'odham Community College, is already the twelfth civilian casualty in the war on drugs this year in Arizona alone. She was a lifelong resident of the former Papago Indian Reservation, a two-term Vice-Chairwoman of the Sells District, and author of scholarly works about the history of the Tohono O'odham and the Hohokam peoples. She is survived by her husband Raymond Antone, an officer with the tribal police, and a daughter and granddaughter.

The other articles were the standard follow-ups. Human interest pieces featuring Antone's wife, the agent—whose name was withheld, for obvious reasons, at the request of the DHS— who had been chasing the truck that took her life, the impact on the reservation as a whole, and one article with a quote from Antone himself, then a mere officer yet to assume the mantle of chief.

"This is our daily reality down here. The rest of the country needs to be made aware of the war being fought on American soil. The cartels must be stopped and held accountable for their crimes, whatever the cost. Even if I have to do so by myself."

They were the words of a man obsessed, or maybe possessed was a better word. Antone had taken on a mission, a crusade against an enemy that washed across his native homeland on a tide of humanity. I knew a thing or two about obsessions. They were the kind of all-consuming passions that could ultimately lead to a downward spiral of self-destruction. A man could become so consumed that he forgets about the things in his life that matter most. He forgets about the grieving daughter in his pursuit of the forces that robbed them both of her mother. He forsakes sleep for caffeine in order to extend the hours of productivity in the day. He allows his property to become a shambles for there's no time to tend to it, if he even notices its deterioration. He decides to strike at the enemy by searching the underground caves the traffickers use to store their caches of drugs and firearms, which places him in the mountains at night...

Smack-dab in the middle of the Coyote's hunting grounds.

TWENTY-NINE

I sprinted back into the main room and shined my light on the maps. I needed to figure out where Antone had gone last night. The topographical map appeared to be the central focus of the arrangement. The markings on it were clustered in wavy lines running from north to south, following the course of the mountains. It didn't take long to figure out Antone's system. He utilized the various Landsat sonographic maps to find the underground caves, compared them to the three-dimensional elevation models, then charted them on the topographical map. The locations of the caves were marked with black circles. Those he had apparently already investigated were crossed out with large Xs. Some were red, others black. Beside the red ones were numbers and abbreviations scribbled in a hand I couldn't easily read and didn't have the time to waste trying. Right now I was of singular purpose.

I needed to find Antone.

There didn't appear to be any rhyme or reason to his approach. Maybe he was following hunches or tracking the known movement of drugs. Maybe he was evaluating the features based solely on size. I didn't have the slightest clue. But I did have a very bad feeling about this.

Antone obviously hadn't come home last night, nor had he gone to work this morning. Based on what I had witnessed at the station, I was also reasonably confident that he hadn't called in either. I already knew that the Coyote had been in the Baboquivari Mountains last night and I was willing to gamble that he was still somewhere up there. I don't believe he would have attempted to cross the open desert with the corpse of a Border Patrol agent while his fellow officers were converging from all points on the compass. There simply hadn't been time. No, he was still up there somewhere, and if Antone had come into contact with him, he had done so up there in the Baboquivaris.

I narrowed my search to the north-south stripe of circles to the east of Sells and the south of I-86, which cut across the reservation from Why to Tucson. There had to be a dozen circles already, seven of them crossed out in black, four of them in red.

And one that had yet to be crossed out one way or the other.

I grabbed the corner of the map, tore the whole thing off the table, and blew through the house. The screen door banged from the back of the house as I burst from the kitchen, hurdled the porch railing, and dashed around the side toward the driveway. I was in the Crown Vic and screaming backward in a cloud of dust toward the main road in a matter of seconds. I nearly shot right across it before cranking the wheel, pinning the gas, and rocketing to the east.

My best guess was that I was about twenty-five minutes out if I really pushed it. From there, it was still going to take time to pick my way up into the hills and find the entrance to the underground cave. I could only hope that the larger features Antone was investigating would be easier to find than the ones the Coyote had been using, which thus far had apparently been too small to warrant Antone's scrutiny. Regardless, if there was a chance that Antone was still alive somewhere up there, I was going to need any and all of the help I could get, damn the consequences.

I grabbed my cell phone and called the police station. Officer Olivia Benally answered before the second ring in a panicked voice that confirmed my suspicions. I had just identified myself and started to express my concerns when she interrupted me.

"They found the chief's cruiser."

"What? Who did?"

"Ajo Station called maybe twenty minutes ago. One of their agents came across the chief's car abandoned out off the Malvado Drag near Diaz Peak. There was…there was—" She nearly lost it before blowing out a long exhalation to compose himself. "There was blood inside the car."

"Diaz Peak? Isn't that in the Ajo Range? That can't be right. There's no way—"

"Look. I told you everything I know. Louis is on his way out there now and I have to coordinate things from my end while running the entire department by myself. If you want anything more, you're going to have to call Ajo."

She hung up on me, but there was nothing more to say anyway. Everything about this situation was wrong. I could feel it in my bones. I clicked on my scanner and it exploded with voices, so many I couldn't immediately pick out a single identifiable thread, but there was no mistaking the rage that crackled from the voices of the agents and the grim determination with which the dispatchers directed them. I imagined the majority of these agents were the same ones who had been up all night scouring the desert and were now running on anger and adrenaline fumes. They wanted the man who killed their brother-in-arms, and they wanted him all to themselves before any outside agency could intervene.

I slowed the car and pulled to the side of the gravel road. The Baboquivari Mountains rose ahead of me through the front windshield. I glanced up at the rearview mirror. Nothing but seamless desert all the way to the horizon, beyond which I could imagine Blackhawks thupping over rugged hills crawling with agents on ATVs and on foot. Two different mountain ranges on totally opposite sides of the reservation.

The engine ticked as the dust washed over the car from behind and settled onto the hood.

The radio chatter was frenetic. Every agent within a hundred miles must have converged upon the area when Antone's car was discovered with blood in the interior. You could probably drive a convoy of semis bursting with drugs straight through the heart of the reservation and no one would notice or care.

I peered again through the sheen of dust on the windshield, then up at the rearview mirror. There was no sign of movement as far as I could see in either direction.

I had been certain that the Coyote was still in the Baboquivaris and the map on the passenger seat beside me all but confirmed that Antone had gone up there, as well. Curse Antone and his infernal signal jammer or every move he had made during the night would have been documented by the Oscars.

Windshield.

Rearview mirror.

Windshield again.

My left foot tapped restlessly on the floorboard.

Show 'em the left and bring the right.

Windshield.

Rearview mirror.

Windshield again.

I looked down at the laminated map beside me, then toward the point where the Baboquivaris merged into the southeastern horizon, not far past the top hat-rock of Baboquivari Peak itself.

The voices from the scanner provided a ruckus that made it nearly impossible to think.

Windshield.

Rearview mirror.

Windshield again.

Coyote is the master of deception.

Before I even realized I had reached a decision, I was speeding straight ahead with the Baboquivari Mountains growing larger in front of me by the second.

THIRTY

It felt like it took me forever to find the right spot. Not because I couldn't read the topographical map, but rather due to the challenge of selecting the right east-west drag to get me there. I had turned down several that necessitated U-turns while I navigated the desert with my eyes glued to the proper arrangement of peaks and valleys. When I did finally follow the correct route, it led me straight up into the foothills to a rutted road that guided me on a circuitous course even higher, until the terrain became more than the Crown Vic could overcome and I was forced to coast backward to a point where I could park in a copse of ironwood trees. The canopy might have offered shade, but it did little to spare me from the heat. The moment I killed the engine and the AC stopped blowing, the heat closed around me like a fist.

I tucked a bottle of water into either pocket of my windbreaker, rolled up the map, and donned my cap to keep the sun out of my eyes. I was already sweating through my shirt when I climbed out of the car and looked uphill toward the rugged peaks lined with cacti and palo verdes, which grew straight from the scree and steep escarpments that would dictate my path.

I took a long pull from the first bottle and pocketed it again. It had to be well over a hundred, but at least there was a breeze blowing at my back. I debated taking off my jacket. My skin was dark enough that it didn't immediately burn; however, the lightweight fabric allowed for a small amount of convective cooling from my sweat that I wasn't ready to sacrifice.

There was still the distinct possibility that my hunch was wrong and I had consigned myself to a wild goose chase. I guess there was only one way to find out for sure. I was only a few feet from my car when I saw fresh tire treads in the dirt. Someone had recently parked here. Someone whose car was limited by a clearance and suspension similar to my own. The vehicle had tires of similar width, too.

I knelt and studied the ground. There was a circular smudge from the toe of a shoe where someone would have stood and pivoted on one foot in the process of sitting down in the driver's seat. The pressure had rolled over a pebble that revealed a crescent of dirt that was slightly darker than the rest around it. The print had been made before sunrise, but not my much.

And it was the only one.

At least I knew I was in the right place. The rest of the footprints had been erased in a circle around where the vehicle had been parked as though with a leaf blower, just like I had seen at the third crime scene. I didn't have to look far to find where the air-swept path led upward toward a crest of rock shaped like the bow of a ship breaking through the mountainside.

And now I had a decision to make. I could either call this in and attempt to convince a highly motivated army of Border Patrol agents that they were looking in the wrong place or I could strike off and risk any number of bad outcomes on my own. Regardless, if my assessment of the situation was correct, Antone was already dead.

I stared uphill for a long moment before I finally started walking. I didn't even glance back at my car, where the scanner still rested in the charger on the console. I was on my own. As I had always been meant to be.

The lack-of-tracks trail guided me only so far before vanishing, although I could still see the occasional signs of recent passage in the slightly matted clumps of wild grasses and in the bent and broken branches of the palo verdes. The only thing I could tell with any kind of certainty was that whoever had returned to the vehicle and driven it away hadn't been dragging a makeshift travois as he had in the past. The placement of the footsteps was cautious, but not overly so. As though whoever left them had no objection to someone following his trail if they were good enough to find it, and yet at the same time was careful enough not to leave a single track with enough definition that it could later be identified and matched to him. I found this interesting and somewhat unnerving. I could only assume that suggested the killer intended to walk free when all was said and done, which was either a symptom of an overdeveloped ego or implied a different kind of resolution to the endgame than I envisioned.

I paused whenever I found anything resembling shade and drank from the rapidly warming water. It's amazing how quickly your body temperature rises in response to the environment. I was in good physical shape, but I could barely go a quarter-mile without starting to feel like I was sweating out more fluid than I was retaining. I couldn't imagine the prospect of attempting to cross forty miles of desert in extremes like this. I think I would have rather taken my chances swimming across the entire Gulf of Mexico.

At least I was working my way up into sharp valleys that appeared to be deep enough to offer some respite from the merciless sun. I did appreciate the fact that the rattlesnakes clung to the cover of the shrubs and were kind enough to warn me when I got too close. I was starting to get used to them, anyway. I didn't mind them nearly as much when they weren't striking at my face.

I picked up the trail at the mouth of a red-rock canyon barely eight feet wide before losing it altogether. It was more of a crevice than a canyon really, like the two neighboring mountains were in a constant state of flux, moving apart in increments of inches per century. The uneven ground offered bare stone upon which to tread without leaving a print, at least not one that I could detect. If I was correct, I was nearing the destination Antone had marked on his map. The biggest foreseeable problem was that I was still going to have to find the entrance to the cave. And this arroyo formed a perfect bottleneck, the kind for which the Coyote had already shown a fondness.

I drew my pistol and waited. A hawk cried as it circled over the foothills behind me. A sudden gust of wind caused pebbles to trickle down the rock walls from somewhere above.

I dropped the map on the ground and unrolled it with my foot. Yeah, I was in the right place. Somewhere on the far eastern side of this gully. I nudged a rock onto the map to hold it in place and advanced cautiously in a shooter's stance.

The air in the arroyo was perfectly still. A feather would have fallen like a lead weight. The sound of my breathing echoed back at me from the narrowing walls. A ribbon of sand navigated the rocks underfoot where seasonal dribbles flowed. I was starting to think that I had chosen the wrong route. The rock walls constricted and it almost looked like the passage terminated in front of me. I was nearly to the terminus when I recognized it for what it was: a sharp bend to the right. Branches and random detritus had accumulated in the junction. I was just about to step over them so I could peek around the corner to my right when I heard a sound.

I stopped dead in my tracks and listened as hard as I could.

It sounded like waves washing against a beach, a slow repetitive shushing sound, but that obviously couldn't be the case. Considering the complete absence of airflow, it couldn't be the wind either. I thought about the rattle-less diamondbacks and ruled them out just as quickly.

Gravel skittered down the stone wall to my left. I glanced up to see a buzzard perched on a pinnacle of rock, staring down at me. It stretched its wings and settled in. I took its presence as a bad sign of what was around the corner, rather than an indication of what Mother Nature thought of my chances.

I wasn't accomplishing anything by standing still.

I ducked and went around the bend in a crouch. My Beretta preceded me into a widened section that functioned as the junction of two more arroyos.

The shushing sound grew louder, but I still couldn't identify it any more than I could divine its origin.

It grew louder still as I advanced, alternately scanning the area ahead of me and the canyon walls above for any sign of movement. Another fat black vulture alighted on a cholla skeleton thirty feet up to my right and tracked me with its beady eyes all the way to the fork. The branch to my left led toward the sunlight, where the rock walls petered to sandy hills bristling with cacti and yuccas. The branch to the right led into deeper shadows, at the far end of which I could see a bright sliver of sunlight where it opened onto the eastern slope. The sound was definitely coming from that direction.

I tried to picture Antone walking up here alone under the glow of the moon. A coyote howling in the distance. The faint *thupp-thupp-thupp* of helicopter blades to the north from the scene of a crime he had no idea had been committed. The scuffing sound of gravel underfoot. A notebook page of scribbled directions in his hand. Or maybe a GPS unit. This wasn't a blind walk for him. He had some idea where he was going; this was just the most direct route.

Sshhuusshhuusshhuusshhuusshhuuhhrr.

I pressed onward, wary of my surroundings. The light of the opening at the far end became larger with each step, limning the rugged rock walls a pale gray. Another buzzard watched me from its perch on a jagged ledge high above me, a black silhouette against the sky.

Sshhuusshhuusshhuusshhuusshhuuhrr.

I finally smelled what had drawn the vultures. Faint, but impossible to miss if you were familiar with the scent. Simultaneously biological and metallic. A sickly taste on the back of the tongue as much as a smell, one that told me something terrible had happened here.

It was blood.

Sshhuusshhuusshhuusshhuusshhuuhrr.

The world around me lightened by degree. The smell intensified. The air started to flow. Sweat rolled down my neck and back. I had to readjust my grip on my pistol.

The dirt beneath my feet softened several feet from the outlet. I risked a glance down and saw amoeboid splotches of mud that would have already been completely dry were it not for the shadows. To my right, an arterial spatter had ascended the canyon wall nearly to the top. Another led out into the sunlight where it dotted a palo verde like little red berries. It was almost a relief to step out into the open again. Ahead of me, the foothills led downward to the stretch of desert that passed through New Mexico on the way to Texas, beyond the horizon.

Sshhuusshhuusshhuusshhuusshhuuhrr.

Louder now.

This was where the Coyote had waited, just out of sight, for Antone to reach the end of the arroyo. I turned around and looked back in the direction from which I had come. He had stood to my right with his back against the escarpment, hidden from view by a thick saguaro. He had listened to Antone's heavy tread approaching until he was scant feet away and then made his move.

Antone had never stood a chance.

The attack had come directly at him. No time to retreat. No time to draw his sidearm. No time even to raise his arms in his defense. A slash across the throat from right to left, backhanded, by someone with considerable skill with a knife. And considerable strength.

Sshhuusshhuusshhuusshhuusshhuuhrr.

I looked up and to my left. The sound was coming from somewhere up there, above where the twenty-foot cliff terminated and the dirt and weeds and cacti resumed. A vulture perched on top of a rock formation shaped like a plow blade, beneath which I could see a dark orifice. Something small and metallic reflected the sun from the opening.

Sshhuusshhuusshhuusshhuusshhuuhrr.

It wasn't until I looked closer at the rock face to determine the best way to scale it that I saw what the Coyote had painted on it.

Comprehension struck me a physical blow, nearly driving me to my knees. I had been wrong about everything. This wasn't a stylized smiley face. It didn't incorporate any native symbology. This was something else entirely and I had absolutely no clue what it meant.

Sshhuusshhuusshhuusshhuusshhuuhrr.

As I stood there, dumbly staring at the design presumably painted in the blood of a man I both liked and respected, my mind rationalized the sound. It wasn't waves or the wind or a shushing sound. It was a voice. A man's voice repeating the same words over and over in a continuous loop.

'Bout time you got here.

'Bout time you got here.

'Bout time you got here.

'Bout time you got here.

THIRTY-ONE

I remember a time when I was maybe eight or nine. We were living in family housing on some base or other. Maybe Travis AFB in California. They all looked alike. Anyway, we had mice, and anything that entered our home uninvited was treated like an invading army. My father took it as a personal challenge to eradicate whatever pest dare violate the sanctity of his domain. My mother and I were happy enough to be party to the utter annihilation of spiders and earwigs and roaches and ants. My mother never really had a problem with his war on rats, either. I think it was because of their strangely fleshy tails, but it could just as easily have been their sordid history of spreading diseases like the black plague. But mice were a different story. Maybe it was their size or the fact that they had such cute, fuzzy little faces. I don't know. All I remember was walking into the kitchen one day in my pajamas and Spider-Man slippers to find her kneeling on the floor in front of the open cupboard beneath the sink where we kept the trash can.

She didn't hear me until I was right behind her. When she turned, she had tears in her eyes and I couldn't quite understand why, until she pulled me close and hugged me and I saw the little gray mouse snared in the trap. The wire rim had snapped down squarely on its face, all but separating the body from the whiskered snout and hooked yellow teeth that pointed in an entirely different direction than they were supposed to. The rear legs were stiff and held the hind quarters upright, as though it had tried to find the leverage to yank its head out. There was a puddle of urine underneath it, dotted with two small black pellets. A third poked halfway out of its rear end beneath its tail.

At the time, I didn't comprehend why it bothered her so much unless she was just grossed out by the fact the she was going to have to touch it. I mean, I had been watching my father set and bait the traps every night and this kind of felt like a respectable victory in an ongoing war. I remember asking her what was wrong, or maybe why she was crying.

"Because I'm sad."

"You wanted to keep the mouse?"

"No, honey, but I didn't want it to go out like that."

"You mean in the trash?"

She smiled despite the tears and ruffled my hair.

"Silly boy. In a trap like…that."

I remember looking at the mechanism, at the point where the metal had snapped nearly clean through its skull, at the gob of peanut butter that had flipped off of the pressure lever.

"It must have really wanted that peanut butter. It knew it was a trap and it still stuck its head right in. Why would it do that?"

I wish I could recall her answer, because right about now I felt a whole lot like that mouse must have as I stared down into the hole in the earth with the digital recording playing over and over in front of me.

'Bout time you got here.

'Bout time you got here.

'Bout time you got here.

It was the same model of recorder the Coyote had used before. There was blood smeared on the casing. The digital readout indicated there was only one recording and the two arrows forming a circle confirmed it had been looped.

Five words. Five ordinarily innocuous words delivered in a mocking tone by a man I hadn't even known existed three days ago, but one who had kindled the fires of hatred for me every day of his life. Why didn't he just come at me and be done with it? What could he possibly hope to gain? To prove he's better than me? To show me up in the media on a national stage? Those are some stupid reasons for so much death. There had to be more to it than that, something that was staring me right in the face.

And that damn painting on the wall below me…what the hell was that supposed to be anyway?

I grabbed the recorder and hurled it out across the desert. Probably not the smartest move from an investigative standpoint, but it did make me feel a little better hearing his voice plummeting into the valley below.

The opening itself was natural and had obviously been here since these mountains first reared up from the sea. There were scuff marks where a large rock had been repeatedly dragged in front of and away from the orifice. I assumed it was somewhere down the mountainside now that it was no longer needed. I clicked on the Maglite and directed the beam into the darkness. A series of irregular ledges led down to a point where the light diffused into the shadows.

I thought of the mouse again, with its skull snapped in half and its jaw askew, as I ducked my head and crawled inside.

Don't let anyone tell you I'm not paying attention to life's little lessons.

The first thing that hit me was the smell. Or the lack of the nauseating stench of death, to be precise. Not that it smelled wonderful, mind you. It smelled pretty much like any other cave: dank, earthy, and maybe a little like body odor, but, believe you me, I wasn't complaining. It allowed me to focus my senses on the main goal of keeping myself alive. I couldn't afford to work under the assumption that there was no one inside, despite what all of my instincts told me. That didn't preclude the possibility of springing some kind of trap, though. For all I knew, the entire cave could be slithering with diamondbacks without rattles or worse, although I had a hard time imagining anything worse than that. Not to jinx myself, anyway.

Maneuvering myself into a position where I could lower myself from one ledge to the next while still keeping the flashlight trained below me took some doing. The temperature dropped rapidly as I descended. I could feel the sweat cooling on my skin, raising goose bumps. It was both an uncomfortable and divine sensation.

When I finally reached the bottom, I was relieved to find nothing nasty already coiled and waiting to strike me. I stood in place for several minutes without moving, turning my beam and gun in unison from one side of the cave to the other. It reminded me a lot of Carlsbad Caverns just across the state line from here in New Mexico, only on a much smaller scale. The ground and the walls were smooth, seemingly polished by the great ocean as it receded millennia ago. Stalactites pointed down from the low ceiling like fangs, while stalagmites with the texture of melted wax rose against them. Petroglyphs had been carved into just about every available surface so long ago that minerals had accreted over them, preserving them behind a layer of semi-opaque limestone. I could hear condensation dripping from somewhere ahead of me beyond the light's reach.

I advanced slowly, placing each footfall carefully and silently, listening for even the slightest sound that might betray whatever trap awaited me. My pulse thundered in my ears and I had to consciously regulate my breathing. The conical features cast long shadows that moved in the opposite direction, as though trying to sneak around behind me, toying with my peripheral vision. The cave terminated ahead of me and I was forced to pause to evaluate my situation. I turned in a complete circle. Nothing. The only sounds were my breathing and the occasional plinking sound of leached minerals dripping from the ceiling. I smelled damp earth and an almost electrical scent I associated with the aftermath of a rainstorm, but that was—

Wait.

I inhaled slowly through my nose. It was faint, sure, but once I latched onto it, there was no mistaking it.

Kerosene.

I switched off my flashlight and the darkness swarmed around me. It was so dense it was almost suffocating, all except for a wan glow coming from a circular hole in the wall to my right, near the ground. I approached cautiously and lowered myself to all fours in order to see through the opening. It was a chute, maybe a dozen feet long. At the far end I could see the hint of the floor and the far wall flickering in the lantern light.

I was getting accustomed to squeezing through tight places like this. I couldn't help but make a Freudian connection to childbirth, which definitely seemed to fit with the whole scenario based on the way Roman reacted every time I asked about Ban's mother. There was something of importance there that I would eventually have to figure out, if only for myself and after the fact. I was closing in on him now and we both knew it. This was the start of whatever endgame the Coyote had in store for me.

It was a game I would not lose.

I squirmed through the smooth chute and into the smaller adjoining cave. While the framework had been nature's doing, the renovations had mankind written all over them. The stalactites and stalagmites had been shattered to jagged nubs by what I assumed to be a sledgehammer and swept somewhere outside of this chamber. A fine coating of the grainy residue glittered on the floor and prodded my hands and knees when I pushed myself up to my feet. I clicked on my flashlight to augment the kerosene lantern sitting on the ground to my right and used it to survey my surroundings.

I cleared the room down the barrel of my Beretta as fast as I possibly could.

There was a sleeping bag against the rounded wall to my left on top of what looked like a makeshift mattress made of a bed sheet stuffed with straw. Both were filthy. There was a small electric stove that had obviously seen better days beside a compact portable generator reminiscent of a lawn mower engine. Lights in little silver domes dangled from the ceiling by eye-hooks, their cords run around the stalactite nubs to an extension cord that trailed down the wall to the generator. There was an old HP inkjet printer behind it. I assumed that must have also been where he plugged in his laptop and police-band scanner and whatever else he used to monitor his tripwire beacons and the comings and goings of law enforcement agents and whatever various details I hadn't even uncovered yet.

He actually lived somewhere else, though. Or at least he must have until recently. There was no way he could have maintained the charade of his daily life from here. There were no clothes. No shower or bath. He was maintaining a residence somewhere else and I simply hadn't found it yet. This was just his den. His lair. I could only speculate as to why he had chosen to reveal it to me.

Until I turned around.

My mouth went dry and I had to remind myself to breathe.

Sociopaths tended to keep trophies or talismans they could return to again and again to remind them of the feeling they experienced in that penultimate moment of ecstasy, when they satiated the bloodthirsty demon inside of them. The kind of thing they could hold in their hands, stroke with their fingertips, caress with their lips. Something they could cling to when the demon started to rise from the depths, to drive it back down temporarily, until they were again in a position to give it what it craved.

This was where he kept his talismans, and judging by the looks of it, he'd been coming here for a long, long time. His was a demon as twisted as any I had encountered, but everything around me suggested that it had been tamed. The man was in control of the demon. There were no signs of dissociation, nothing to imply even a momentary loss of control. This was the lair of a man who had embraced his demon. No…

This was the lair of a man who had become his demon.

And it scared the living hell out of me.

I speak of endgames, but there's nothing even remotely amusing about this to him. This wasn't a game.

This was his life's work.

THIRTY-TWO

There were pictures. Hundreds of them. Pinned to a patchwork wall of plywood sheets. Lined up in floor-to-ceiling rows that had to be a good six feet wide. The ones on the left were faded and yellowed Polaroid instant pictures, which metamorphosed into crisper shots with finer detail to digital photographs printed on photo paper and laminated to preserve them. I couldn't see the subjects of the photographs. Not immediately, anyway. Not until I brushed aside the tufts of hair connected to the desiccated clumps of scalp that had been pinned to them. The majority of the strands were thick and black. Some still bore the luster of life, while others had dried to the brittle consistency of straw. Some were short, others several feet long. A couple dozen were blonde, mostly bottled, others brown or ginger. Others still were completely bald. The skin had shriveled, tightening the follicles and forcing some of the hairs to stand erect.

I really loathed the prospect of brushing the hair of the deceased away from the pictures in order to see them, but I didn't have much of a choice. Hair itself is composed of dead skin cells and keratin. Even the most beautiful locks are essentially little different than the skin shed from an old man's feet. They're just ropes of dead cells clinging to our heads. Evolutionarily speaking, their function is to keep us warm. In the more practical sense, they're styled to make us look good and attract the opposite sex. You don't run your fingers through a woman's hair and marvel at just how silky she managed to make her ropes of dead cells; you marvel at how it bounces with life when she moves, or how stunning she looks when it falls across her eye or sticks to the lipstick at the corner of her mouth. It is a part of her beauty. Her life. And yet these hairs somehow felt dead, as though whatever magic animated them had been rubbed off between the fingers of a killer who took them down from his trophy wall from time to time to stare into the faces of his victims while he caressed their hair and remembered how he felt while he was robbing the world of the promise of lives unfulfilled.

Faces. That was all the pictures showed. Faces, and maybe a little of the shoulders. Mostly taken at night, which caused the flash to wash out the skin tone. Close-ups of men and women alike, lying on their backs on dirt and rocks, their faces speckled and spattered and smeared with blood. Expressions of surprise and terror and pain were forever memorialized on their faces. Most were young, yet some were old enough to be gray. Some mouths were open. Others closed. Some were handsome or beautiful, others plain or downright homely. Some were fat, others gaunt. There was no one physical trait common to all of them, no pattern other than the fact that every one of these people had walked out into the open desert in search of the American Dream and found only a demon waiting for them. And now they would be forever linked together, thanks to this wall where they all now shared a single common trait. Mexicans and Guatemalans and El Salvadorans and Hondurans and Dominicans and Lord only knew how many others.

They were all dead.

I couldn't bear to look at the wall anymore. I felt tainted by its mere proximity. It was the kind of thing that made you wonder if we as a species wouldn't be better off if a good pandemic swept through and purged our inherent darkness from the face of the planet.

I had to move the flashlight away. It momentarily illuminated one picture that had been offset from the others. It was larger; a full sheet of photo paper. Printed so recently that the insane amounts of ink required still made the page curl.

Even though I could think of nothing I wanted to do less, I again raised the flashlight—

I squeezed my eyes shut as tightly as I could, but the damage was already done. I bit my lip to hold back the explosion of anguish that threatened to wrench loose from my chest. My grip tightened to the point I nearly fired an errant shot into the wall. I was certain I could feel my blood boiling in my veins. It took time to compose myself enough to open my eyes again and view the image with the kind of clinical dispassion I needed to properly do my job.

I recognized the face immediately. Despite the rivulets of blood that had dribbled down the picture from the oblong clump of scalp pinned to it. Despite the fact that the pin had been pressed straight through his face with such force that it had torn the paper. Despite the fresh sheen of crimson glistening on his cheek. Despite it all, I recognized Antone and felt a profound sense of sorrow that in no time at all blossomed into anger. The Coyote was going to pay for what he'd done. I was going to avenge Antone, avenge all of them. This was the kind of evil that could not under any circumstances be allowed to walk the earth for a single second longer.

I turned to my right and saw another display, which, in retrospect, I really should have expected, but wasn't even remotely prepared to encounter.

If I'd thought the collection of pictures my paternal grandmother had collected and displayed in her bedroom was a shrine, this was the freaking Louvre. There had to be more than fifty pictures and images and newspaper clippings pinned to another sheet of plywood, cobbled together from a dozen scraps. Some were so old they had the texture of parchment. Others were much newer. They'd been fitted together like pieces of a puzzle so that there was no space between them, nor any logical order that I could see, not even chronological.

My heart was beating so hard and fast that the edges of my vision pulsated.

There were photographs of me, color copies of old class and yearbook photos, enlarged and highlighted, going all the way back to my early teens, not long after I first came to live with my grandparents, when I first put down roots. Me with braces. Me in my various hockey jerseys. Me at homecoming, the prom. Me at graduations and parties and on vacations and doing the normal things that people do every day, entirely oblivious to the world around me, to the fact that I was being hunted. They had been drawn on with marker and scraped with pins to create horns growing from my forehead in some, threads sewn through my lips in others. Forked tongues. Black teeth. Various bleeding wounds. But there was one trait that each and every one of them had in common.

My eyes had been scratched out.

Every bit as disturbing were the newspaper articles chronicling my career. My involvement with the task forces that had tracked down the Boxcar Killer, the Delivery Man, and the Drifter. Pictures with me in the background in the field and on the front steps of courthouses. Articles with brief quotes and topical mentions. Printed stills captured from news feeds. All of them plucked out of the ether via the internet by a stalker who never even left the reservation.

I needed to get out of there. It felt like the cave was closing in and the weight of the mountain was about to collapse on me. There wasn't enough oxygen. The stale air was filled with carbon dioxide; the final breaths of the dead. The ground started to tilt from side to side as I staggered back to the hole in the wall and somehow managed to shimmy through into the main cave. The thudding of my pulse in my temples sounded like laughter in my ears. I wanted to vomit, if only to purge myself of the sensation that true evil was seeping through my pores. Ghostly faces flashed across my vision as I stumbled through the cave and hauled myself up the ledges. Faces I never knew, would never know. The faces of the dead. Faces that may have fit over the bleached skulls sinking into the desert sands or heaped in a hole under a trailer home or in some other pitiful resting place we had yet to find, and, in reality, might never find.

I crawled out into the blinding light, grateful for the sun and the heat, which cleansed me of the dankness and the darkness of that horrible cave. I rolled over onto my rear end, dangled my legs over the edge of the escarpment, and stared off across the seamless Sonoran.

I don't know how long I sat there with sweat covering every inch of my body. The shadow of the mountain behind me eventually started to creep down through the foothills below me. Finally, I stood and picked my way down the cliff and turned to stand before it. The design in Antone's blood looked like a K without the upper of the two diagonal lines, but that wasn't what it was, was it? I turned my head one way, then the other. I felt inadequate, enraged, but mostly I simply felt exhausted. Deflated.

Defeated.

There was something I was missing. Something I was too blind to see. Something staring me right in the face.

The eyes.

There was something oddly familiar about him, but I couldn't quite place it.

He had scratched out my eyes.

You have your father's eyes.

Scratched out my eyes in every single one of the pictures.

It's the eyes. You guys have the exact same eyes.

Just my eyes, not those of his victims.

I couldn't help but see the physical similarities between us, the parallels between our lives.

It wasn't just the eyes. It was *my* eyes.

His eyes.

I started to run.

THIRTY-THREE

It was full-on dark by the time I slewed from the gravel road and rocketed down Roman's driveway. His house grew larger and larger in my headlights until I stomped the brakes, skidded sideways to a halt, and leapt from the car. I beat the cloud of dust to the porch, lowered my shoulder just as the front door opened a crack, and barreled right through. Roman hit the floor with a loud thump. The door ricocheted from his feet. I swatted it aside and grabbed him by the shirt before his mind caught up with the situation. I hauled him to his feet, whirled, and slammed him against the wall. Framed pictures fell from the walls down the hallway to my right, shattering on the floor with the impact. I didn't give a damn. This entire godforsaken house could burn to the ground for all I cared.

I stared directly into Roman's eyes when he opened them. I stared long and hard. I scrutinized everything from the color of the irises to the shape formed by the lids and the pattern of vessels and the color of the sclera. I watched comprehension dawn on his face, followed quickly by panic, then, finally, resignation. I read all of this while staring directly into eyes that may have been similar to mine, but when it came right down to it, were clearly different than my fathers, than mine. Than Ban's.

I released Roman's shirt. He slid down the wall and crumpled to the floor. He looked old in a way he hadn't before, as though it had been the perpetuation of one lie that had formed the foundation for so many others. And now the whole house of cards was falling down on top of him.

The dust snuck through the front door like an unwelcome guest and settled onto the furniture and the floor. I felt the same heaviness and had to collapse onto the arm of the La-Z-Boy. I shook my head and rubbed my eyes. I was exhausted, physically and emotionally drained.

"What was her name?" I asked in little more than a whisper.

"Carmen," he said. "Carmen Chona."

When he looked up at me there were tears in his eyes. The expression on his face spoke of sadness and love, and something I couldn't quite interpret. Something like failure. Or maybe regret.

"Did you tell him?"

"Who? Ban?" He shook his head and looked past me. The dust that had settled on his hair made him look older still. "Pass me that beer, would you?"

I grabbed the bottle of Coors Light from the table behind me and handed it to him. He nodded his thanks, tipped it back, and drank everything but the foam, which he swirled around at the bottom.

I waited him out.

"He's a smart kid. He figured it out. But that didn't change the fact that he was *my* son." I nodded. There was a fire in his eyes that gave truth to his words. This was a man who loved his son unconditionally, regardless of the nature of their biological bond. "I think he was maybe fourteen when he figured it out. It was a few more years before he said anything to me, but by then I'm pretty sure he already had all the answers he needed." He sighed and finished off the foam. "Whatever you may think of me...I've always tried to do right by him. I don't expect you to understand. He's my son and there's nothing on this earth that I wouldn't do for him."

"Even cover up the murders of so many innocent people?"

Roman turned away. He whispered something that sounded like "None of them was innocent."

"What happened to his mother?"

"She died when he was three. Hit by a car while walking on the side of the road. Driver was doing fifty. The skid marks didn't even start until after the point of impact. Bumper, windshield, trunk, road. She was pretty much unidentifiable when I was asked to ID her."

I gleaned the truth from his face.

"She stepped out in front of the car."

A wistful smile, but there was no happiness in it. Only pain.

"The driver said he never even had a chance to brake. She just walked right out in front of him. Just driving along and then all of a sudden she was right there. Facing him. Eyes closed. A faint smile on her lips. Then shattered glass and blood. So much blood. Police said the evidence supported his story."

"And what do you think?"

He stared down into his bottle for a long time before he finally spoke.

"He just left her, you know? Just left her like that. Left me..."

"What are you talking about?"

"Rafael. Your father. He just left us both. Up and joined the Air Force and none of us ever heard from him again. Stole off in the middle of the night. Like a coward."

"My father was no coward." I could feel the heat rising under my collar, but at the same time, I had seen Ban's eyes and knew there was truth to the story, if not Roman's interpretation of it. "He took his responsibilities seriously. He never—*never*—would have left had he known—"

"That she was pregnant?" Roman stood and walked to the kitchen. I heard the refrigerator door open and close as I stared blankly at the wall in front of me, now cracked in the shape of the man I had slammed up against it. He handed me a beer before he again sat down on the floor and tipped his back. The bottle was cold in my hand. I just sat there holding it, uncertain exactly what to do with it. I eventually settled on resting it against my aching knuckles. "Of course he didn't know she was pregnant. And Carmen didn't tell him. She didn't want him to abandon his dream and return to her out of some misguided sense of duty. She wanted him to come back because of her."

"Why didn't she go with him? You said they were going to get married."

He stared at me with a genuine expression of confusion.

"You still don't get it, do you? This isn't just some housing development out here, some suburb misplaced in the desert. This is our home. Our parents lived here, and theirs before them, going back countless generations. There are traditions to uphold, beliefs that need to be passed on so they aren't forgotten. The world out there?" He made a wide sweeping gesture with his arm. "It has no i:bdag. No heart. It is a world devoted to greed and ambition and the usurpation of the individual. It is a giant bee hive where the drones don't even seem to recognize the fact that they're building a giant hive for a ruling class that doesn't give a rat's ass about them, all while destroying the traditions of the land—the very land itself—in the process. Of course she didn't leave. Regardless of whatever plans she and Raffi might have made, when it came time to actually do it, there was no way she could. Not for her child. Not for her heart. And in the end, not even for her life."

"But you were here for her."

He chuckled, but there was no humor in it.

"Yeah...I was here." He drew a long swill that emptied half the bottle. "I think she loved me, too. In her own way. I wasn't Raffi. But I was here. And I loved her. With all of my heart. I loved her. Maybe a part of it was because I initially felt obligated to do what my brother didn't. To right his wrong. Maybe at first, anyway. But it wasn't long before there were genuine feelings. I loved her and I loved her child. My child. Ban. My little coyote."

"Coyote?"

"Ban's O'odham for coyote. Carmen chose that name because the night Raffi left, she sat alone in the desert crying while coyotes bayed at the moon all around her. She thought it was an omen. More of a self-fulfilling prophecy, I guess."

"Why'd she do it?"

"Kill herself? Haven't you figured it out yet? Aren't you supposed to be the big shot investigator? She killed herself because of you."

I sat stunned for a long moment.

"Everything changed between us when Carmen heard Raffi had another child. Another life with another woman. I never tried to be Raffi. I couldn't replace him. I didn't want to replace him. I wanted my own family...and for a while...I had it." He released a long sigh. "Carmen was beautiful—the most beautiful woman in the world—but there was always a sadness to her. Something deep down. A hole she couldn't quite seem to fill. I think she must have filled it with Raffi. Or at least thought she had. I guess I couldn't fill it. Not for lack of trying. Hell, not even her own child could fill it. She was just one of those people always meant to burn really hot, but really fast."

"Ban blames me for her death. You both blame me."

"Can you fault him for that? Here he was, orphaned by his mother, raised by a father who wasn't his father by nature, and forced to watch all of those pictures of your successes accumulate on his grandmother's wall while he would never enjoy any of the same opportunities. He did the very best with what he was given. He breezed through school, earned his degree, and joined with Homeland Security to protect and patrol his ancestral land. It was noble and it was good, but many of our people viewed it as selling his soul to the enemy. He was shunned everywhere he went. And on top of it all, you had to go and one-up him every step of the way. He earned his associate's; you got your bachelor's. Mechanical engineering, if you can believe that. He had a mind for that kind of thing. But then nine-eleven happened and Gatekeeper closed down the established migrant routes and they started flooding across our land. All of them potential terrorists, you know? So he signed on with the Border Patrol. And you had to show him up again by joining the FBI. And to top it all off, the very same week he made one of the largest drug busts in history and was starting to catch the eye of the DEA, you go and get your face in every newspaper across the country by helping to take down the Delivery Man. I think that was what did it for him. In his mind, you guys were in a competition that not only could he never win, but one in which you would never even acknowledge the fact that he was competing against you."

He looked down at his now-empty bottle for nearly a full minute before he continued. "So he just quit. His job. His life. Everything. One day, it was all over. I could see the change in him, but it was a long time before I started to understand what had happened, why he had changed so suddenly. He had always been like his mother. He had that hole inside of him, too. I think he thought he could fill it with all of his accomplishments, with the way he thought people in the community would look at him. I guess he ended up filling it with anger. Hatred. And you personified everything that was wrong with his life and his world. His biological father was dead by then. We all knew that. He couldn't even track him down and try to get the answers he needed. And that left only you. Despite everything I had done for him. Despite the fact that I had assumed the role of father when no one else wanted to job. I *chose* him. But it wasn't enough. *I* wasn't enough. Not for his mother. And not for him."

His cheeks glistened with tears when he looked up at me. The expression on his face was one of unadulterated anger, though. I was in no mood to allow him his indulgences. I wasn't about to let him brush the responsibility off on me. I refused. He was Ban's father. By birth or by choice. It made no difference. He needed to accept that whether intentionally or not, he had helped create a monster.

"At what point did you learn he was killing people?"

"All you had to do was look us up. Come down here and show him that he wasn't alone, that you didn't think you were better than him, that you were—"

"Don't try to pin this on me."

"—brothers."

"You knew he was killing people and did nothing to stop it. That makes you every bit as guilty in my eyes."

"Your eyes…"

"This has to end, Roman. You have to—"

"I know," he whispered.

"Tell me where he is."

"I don't know where he is." He blinked away whatever thoughts had been distracting him, then looked up me with an expression that I easily interpreted as sincerity. "I don't know where he is."

"But you know where he'd go if he was out of options, don't you? Not that old abandoned trailer. Someplace where nobody would think to look for him. Someplace no one else knows about."

He nodded, closed his eyes, then hurled his bottle against the wall. Shards of brown glass shot in every direction. A gob of foam rolled down the wall.

"Where can I find him, Roman."

"There's another trailer." His voice became progressively softer as he spoke. "At the back of the property. By the wash. Used to belong to my mother's brother before he passed. Long time ago now. Long time ago…"

"The trailer, Roman. Where exactly…?"

But he was already gone, vanished inside of himself, or perhaps into another place and time altogether as I had seen him do before. A part of me wanted to hurt him even more, to vent my frustrations on him, but I realized that there was nothing I could do to hurt him more than I was already going to.

I was going to kill his son.

There was no other way I could see this playing out.
I was going to kill the Coyote.
I was going to kill my brother.

THIRTY-FOUR

My patience was spent. I was pissed off and frustrated and tired of being manipulated. I didn't care about the desert and I most certainly didn't care about the pool car as I drove away from the house across the open gravel and sand. If there was a road, I didn't see it. Then again, I didn't look too hard either. All of the deaths wore heavily on me. They always did. I think that was what allowed me to do what I did. Without that personal impetus, I can't imagine what wells of motivation an investigator draws from in order to follow the trails of blood and suffering so many sociopaths leave in their wake. This one drove me harder than I'd ever been driven before, though. Antone's death was weighing on my conscience. I don't believe it was merely the fact that I had known and liked him that caused his death to trouble me so much. Maybe it was because after enduring so much loss and heartache, he'd been trying to combat the bad guys within the constraints of the system, by the rules, only to find himself in the wrong place at the wrong time. A freak stroke of bad luck. My old nemesis coincidence. Whatever the case, something was nagging at me like the sound of footsteps behind me, but every time I turned around, there was no one there.

I found the trailer pretty much right where Roman said it would be. It made the previous one look positively futuristic by comparison. Like he said, this one had been set up right beside the wash. So close, in fact, that the bank had eroded out from beneath it. Either that or someone had dug such a large hole beneath it they had nearly toppled the trailer, which was a line of thought I had no intention of pursuing at the moment. Even from a distance, I could tell the trailer was leaning away from me.

I parked in front of it and climbed out of the car. I left the headlights on and directed at the dilapidated single-wide. I added my Maglite to the cause and drew my Beretta.

A coyote yipped and howled in the distance. Maybe just over the rise on the other side of the mesquite-lined gully. The wind rose with a scream, pelting the back side of the trailer with grains of sand that sounded like buckshot. I figured that was probably the reason for the lack of paint on the mobile home. It was just plain gray wood and cracked windows patched with duct tape and sealed behind a layer of dust and grime.

Red flagstones had been stacked in front of the door to form uneven stairs. Tumbleweeds clogged the skirt, a crosshatched pattern of thin wooden slats that had proved no match for whatever animals had tunneled under it and, in spots, straight through it. The way the trailer canted toward the dry streambed made it impossible for the front door to close in its frame. Which also meant there was no way to lock it. I'd caught so few breaks up to this point that I was almost surprised at my good fortune. Of course, all it saved me was a little wear and tear on my leg from kicking in a door a good solid knock would probably topple. It was held closed by a bungee cord stretched between the door knob and what looked like the handle from a kitchen cabinet that had been screwed onto the exterior.

I undid the cord and drew the door open. The smell that greeted me was one of tobacco smoke, sour sweat, dust, and rotting wood. The shadows fled from the flashlight as I ascended the uneven rocks and entered. Even my softest tread made it sound like I was stomping on the hollow floor. The carpet was so old that there was nothing left of the actual knap, only the crunchy matrix through which it had been sewn. It had pulled away from the far wall, due in large measure to the transverse ridge that bisected the main room where the settling of the trailer caused it to break its own back. The lone item of furniture was a threadbare couch that looked like it had spent more time outside than in. It had slid down the slope to rest against the far wall.

The wind roared and again assailed the wall opposite me with sand. The entire trailer shuddered with the gust. Dust shivered loose from the ill-fitting, yellowed acoustic ceiling tiles and sparkled in my light, lending an element of unreality to my already surreal surroundings. It was almost as though I had stepped across some magical threshold from the rational world I knew and loved into another reality entirely. There was something about this place that made me uncomfortable on a primal level.

The windows had been boarded over from the inside and painted bone-white to match the walls. Nothing hung from them. There were no pictures or speakers or bookshelves or plants or knickknacks. Only the flat white walls that served as a canvas for a tableau of an entirely different sort than the one in the cave, but somehow nearly as unsettling. There were stylized smiley faces painted on the walls. Every square inch, covered with variations of smiley faces. Some were red. Others were black or gold or brown. All of them had similar slanted eyes and that broad arched grin. Some had eyebrows, others nearly full circles for the heads. Some had what I took to be upward-curving mustaches, others various markings that seemed at odds with the overall motif. There were literally thousands of them, painted on every available surface, one on top of the other. All of them nearly the full height of the walls. There were some sections where it looked like he had simply practiced painting circles, over and over and over again until they were just right.

My first impression was that he'd made himself a modern cave similar to the ones through which I had been crawling; an enclosed space with walls covered with primitive artwork. And maybe that had been his intention, but it had the overwhelming sense of incompleteness, of a work abandoned before it was finished. It was the same sense I got from the smiley faces themselves, or perhaps because of them. There was just something inherently inconsistent about the nature of the designs. I found it hard to believe that anyone with enough talent to paint nearly perfect circles would content himself with such childish and meaningless expressions of his creativity.

I advanced deeper into the house. There were gaps where appliances had once been and the kitchen cupboards hung slightly open with the will of gravity. The counters were covered with dust. There was a black trash bag on the floor that smelled of the Dumpster behind a Taco Bell, crawling with black flies so fat I doubted they were capable of flight anymore.

Another gust of wind shook the entire structure. The sand and gravel sounded like hailstones.

The bathroom to my right smelled like an outhouse. The buzzing racket of flies sounded hollow, as though they were swarming somewhere beneath the sink, or possibly under the lid of the toilet. All of the walls in the hallway were painted in the same fashion as the living room, variations on the theme anyway. Even the master bedroom was white and covered with smiley faces, although it was obvious these hadn't been painted with a brush like the others had. I recognized the distinct paw pad marks. It was in this room that he taught himself to paint with the severed limb of a coyote. I shuddered at the thought of him unwrapping the stiff leg from a bundle of cellophane, turning it over and over in his hands, and then dipping it into the red paint for the first time, the charge causing the goose bumps to rise all over his body.

There was a military surplus cot with a large footlocker overflowing with clothes in the middle of the room. This was where he'd been living, all right. But there was nothing here that offered any sort of clue as to where he was now. At least not that I had found.

Yet.

I turned around and headed back into the living room. That was where all of this had started, where one day he had boarded over the windows, painted the walls, and begun creating his modern-day cave. Another Hohokam allusion? It certainly fit the established pattern, but why go to such lengths to actualize a small portion of a myth? It was only a story, after all, a story that eventually led to a mischievous creator god.

Don't be too quick to lay this at the feet of I'itoi. There are many gods of mischief out here in the desert.

A creaking sound behind me.

I spun around, my light tracing the wall as I aligned it with my pistol and sighted down the open front door—

The wind wailed and sand clattered.

An animal stood before me, its front haunches inside the trailer, its back legs on the makeshift stairs. Its eyes reflected my light like twin moons. One ear stood straight up while the other sagged against its cheek. Its gray fur was mangy and matted and the crescents of its ribs showed. It just stood there, looking right at me, its tongue lolling from its mouth.

Another gust rattled the trailer and it disappeared back into the night again.

I stared after it for a long moment before I finally turned around once more. As before, my beam swept across the smiley faces, seemingly animating them like a zoetrope. I was already attempting to mentally catalogue the differences from one face to the next when my brain caught up with my eyes.

I turned again, this time swinging my light across the opposite wall. I did it again. Faster. Watching one face metamorphose into another and another. I did it again. And again and again and again.

"Son of a bitch," I whispered.

It had been right in front of me the entire time.

I sprinted out the front door, cleared the stairs, and raced to my car. The moment I was in the driver's seat I grabbed my laptop, launched my digital photo manipulation program, and imported the pictures from the various crime scenes. My feet tapped restlessly on the floorboards while I worked. I needed to know for sure. I couldn't afford to go running off on another tangent. I found the clearest example of each smiley face, the winking face, and the armless K. I scaled and resized them and converted them into semi-transparent masks that allowed me to separate the designs themselves from the rocks upon which they'd been painted in the blood of the Coyote's victims. I arranged them in chronological order.

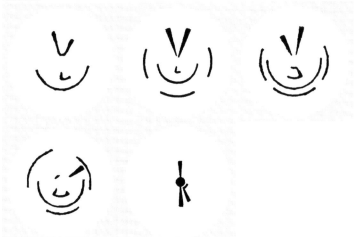

Then I took all five and placed them one on top of the other.

It was a mess, but I was getting closer.

I highlighted each mask in turn and started to rotate them in various directions.

Almost. I could positively feel the tumblers falling into place. I had it now.

I had *him*.

More rotation.

Closer still.

And then I saw it take form in front of me. I could see the moves I needed to make like a chess master surveying his board and recognizing there was no way his strategy could fail.

I made the final moves and held the screen up before me.

I knew where he was.
Ban.
The Coyote.
My Elder Brother.
I'itoi, that mischievous trickster god.
The Man in the Maze.

DAY 4

tash gi'ik

wia

Sir Francis Galton, first cousin of Charles Darwin, was the first to study the heritance of behavioral traits and is credited with launching the behavioral genetics movement, from which came the first twin studies and the resultant nature vs. nurture debates that will undoubtedly be waged until the end of time. It is an extension of this science that led to the development of Project Genome, which is dedicated to the understanding and advancement of humanity as a species. Conversely, from this science was derived the concept of eugenics and, by extension, Adolf Hitler's Final Solution. If that in itself isn't an argument for Team Nurture, then I don't know what is.

THIRTY-FIVE

Bobquivari District
Tohono O'odham Nation
Arizona

September 12th

I tried to recall Antone's words as I sped across the desert, my signal jammer making me invisible to the Oscars.

That mountain over there. Kind of looks a little like a top hat? That's Baboquivari. Waw Kiwulik *in our native tongue. It is the most sacred of all places to our people.*

There's a cave below the peak. That's where I'itoi lives. He's our mischievous creator god. When the world was first born, he led the Hohokam, from whom we descended, up from the underworld and to the surface. His home is within that cave, deep in the heart of a maze. Visitors to the cave must bring him an offering to guarantee their safe return.

I watched the eastern horizon as the Baboquivari Mountains grew taller and taller. It wasn't long before I identified the top hat of Mt. Baboquivari. I could see headlights far in the distance to both the north and the south, Border Patrol agents performing their nightly routines. Although judging by the fact that I could actually see them, there had to still be more of them out here than usual because of the death of Agent Matthews. Considering I didn't want to draw any unwanted attention, I killed my lights and navigated the arrow-straight roads by starlight until the rising winds eventually filled the air with sand and I had no other choice but to turn them back on. At least I was comfortable in the knowledge that if I couldn't see them, they couldn't see me. And keeping the Blackhawks in the air during such a ferocious sandstorm was an unnecessary risk. The only problem was that I could no longer see the peak. Dead reckoning was going to have to suffice.

The radio chatter was filled with complaints about the storm and jokes about the poor mechanics who would get to service all of the vehicles in the morning. It sounded like storms like this one cropped up out of the blue from time to time, but rarely tended to last for more than a few hours. Most of the agents were content to hunker down and ride it out, confident that whatever illegals were out there would no doubt be doing the exact same thing. Dispatch continued to coordinate the agents to the west along the I-85 corridor where the sandstorm had yet to hit in earnest. I would have preferred a few hours of sleep in my back seat and a hot cup of coffee upon waking, but I had a job to do. A job that only I could do.

I'itoi. My own Elder Brother. Christ. Only now was I beginning to internalize that fact. Ban—the Coyote—was the genetic expression of half of my father. Half of me. My own mirror image, to some degree. Me. Not me. Bizarro me. Similar life paths, but different choices at some of the crucial forks along the way.

I was at a disadvantage. He knew me far better than I knew him. I thought about his overt hostility the night we first met. The expression on his face had been more than anger and distrust for a federal agent on his native land; it had been directed at me specifically. And he had mocked me without me even recognizing it.

Without a body, you can't fix time of death. So there's no way you can pinpoint a date, let alone a time for which an alibi would be necessary.

What do you know about the body? I had asked.

Only that there wasn't one.

And what do you think might have happened to it?

A lot of things can happen out here in the desert. Could have been a coyote dragged it off...

I hadn't even been able to recognize his cleverness, which must have made him absolutely furious. Like Roman said, maybe all of this could have been averted had I tracked Ban down and acknowledged him earlier in his life and become something resembling a brother rather than a rival for the affection of a long-deceased father and the cause of the death of a woman I never even knew existed. Maybe. I wasn't willing to carry that cross, though. We all have to live with the choices we make. I couldn't change mine, so there was no point in dwelling on them now. I still had one last chance to acknowledge Ban, if that was really what he wanted, and I had every intention of doing just that.

And then I would have the opportunity to mourn him, although I doubted he'd take much solace in that fact. Fortunately, I simply didn't care. Not about him, anyway. Someone still had to speak for his victims since he'd robbed them of their voices.

I listened to agents running down UDAs in their cars and on foot and wondered if those immigrants understood just how lucky they were to still be alive out here in the desert with the heat and the Coyote. And I thought about the Tohono O'odham, living in the middle of a war zone where the battles were waged twenty-four hours a day and few people outside of their immediate vicinity were even aware of their struggles. Even I had scoffed at Agent Randall when he pointed it out. I remembered what Antone said in his quote from the newspaper on the wall in his bedroom. The entire country needed to be made aware of the plight of the people on this reservation. The public needed to know about all of the migrants dying out here under the blazing sun while simply searching for the dream we all took for granted. This corridor of death needed to be closed down before things got even more out of hand. Before more drugs could be funneled through here and into the hands of our children. Let the big corporations with their bottomless reserves and slick lobbyists find another way to supplement their largely illegal and woefully underpaid work forces. There were too many problems to make them go away by merely sweeping them under the rug that was my ancestral reservation.

The mountains offered some protection from the wind as I neared, but only a little. At least now I could occasionally see their silhouettes through the sand, which had to have been so high up into the atmosphere as to be visible from space. I tried not to dwell on the fact that asphyxiation was the primary cause of death during a sandstorm, as I'm sure I've pointed out, but it bears repeating now that I was preparing to climb out of my car to brave one. I had to focus on the positives. Of all the ways to die, I'd heard that drowning was probably one of the most peaceful, although I did question the validity of whatever survey gathered those results. Most people I knew who nearly drowned tended not to have too many good things to say about the experience.

I had to cut straight through the open desert to get from the drag I had thought would lead me there to an actual road that wended up through the foothills toward the peak. I crossed over a dry creek lined with what looked like massive ghostly cottonwoods through the dust and then through fields packed with so many palo verdes I couldn't even see a lone patch of bare ground. When I eventually emerged into a stretch of spotted shrubs and cacti again, I found myself nearing the end of the road. It widened into a parking lot of sorts. I assumed the sign nailed to the split-rail fence marked a trailhead, but it had been peppered by so much buckshot that it was impossible to tell for sure.

I rolled to a stop and parked. The windshield wipers flapped back and forth, drawing dirty arcs through the dust. I released a long sigh as I stared uphill beyond the range of my headlights. Saguaros and ocotillos materialized from the blowing sand only to vanish again. Just when I thought I had a handle on the topography and the route I was going to take, the wind shifted and completely altered my perception of the terrain. I was just going to have to trust my instincts.

I grabbed my laptop, looked at the Man in the Maze pattern one last time, then opened the Landsat files I had downloaded from the campus library. With the way the wind and the sand obscured my view, the three-dimensional elevation map wasn't going to do me a whole lot of good. Instead, I concentrated on the sonographic and magnetometric readouts. As with the majority of the mountains in the range, this one had several distinct subterranean features. One was larger than the others, but it was lower down and, if I was correct, the opening would be clearly visible from this lot under better conditions. If I were to interpret the myth literally, I was looking for something as close to within the peak itself as I could find. In my mind, that meant I needed to look higher. Unfortunately, that also meant greater exposure to someone coming and going and a higher probability of accidental discovery. I took that into consideration as I pondered the remaining two locations. Both were on the eastern slope, which meant that unless I wanted to backtrack to the highway and waste hours driving in from the other side, I had a decent hike ahead of me. One cave was significantly larger than the other, but that didn't exclude the possibility that the smaller one could be modified like the ones at the crime scenes had been.

Modified.

That was the key.

I examined the magnetometer readings, but both caves were enclosed within substrates of nearly identical density and mineral composition. One would be no easier to modify than the other. I overlaid the sonographic images and studied their shapes, which were little more than vague outlines. The only real difference was that one appeared to be more circular than the other. I zoomed in on the center. The resolution was grainy and pixelated and yet it still almost…almost looked like there were other densities in there. Nothing as solid as rock, but something nonetheless. Maybe I was just seeing what I wanted to see, or maybe, just maybe, I had found exactly what I was looking for.

There was only one way to find out for sure.

I donned my ball cap and windbreaker, killed off the bottle of water in the console cup holder and pocketed two more, and drew my Beretta and Maglite. I used the charger cord from my phone to tie the light to the side of the barrel in order to keep one hand free and the sightline unobstructed at the same time. I jacked the slide to make sure it still slid freely, grabbed two spare clips from the glove compartment, and tucked my cell phone into my pocket. I shut off the engine and sat there a moment longer, running through a mental checklist to make sure I hadn't forgotten anything that might help save my skin. I focused on slowing my heartbeat, on breathing slowly in and out.

A gust of wind struck the car with enough force to rock it on its suspension. It sounded like the sand pitted the glass.

I pulled the handle and the wind ripped the door from my grasp and hammered it against its hinge. I had to throw my full weight into it to force it closed. Sand and debris blew sideways through the headlights, limiting their range and effectiveness, but I was still grateful for even that little illumination. The sand pelting my jacket sounded like rain on an umbrella, only I can't recall rain ever smacking the side of my face and ear so hard I could feel it peeling off the top layer of skin.

I lowered my head in an effort to use the brim of the cap to shield my eyes and struck off away from the car. I found the trail without much effort and figured I'd try to follow it as long as possible. Eventually I was going to have to cross the dark ridge high above me. I assumed this path led either to a good vantage point from which to take pictures of the famous peak or to the peak itself. Whatever the case, I was counting on it to get me high enough that I could pick my way eastward between peaks.

I had to remind myself that my brother—that the Coyote—had been one step ahead of me the entire time. It was safest to assume that he had anticipated my choice of routes. Hell, for all I knew he could be watching me through the storm or otherwise monitoring my progress by other electronic means. Regardless, I was confident he knew I was coming and would be ready and waiting for me.

Coyote is the master of deception.

I needed to remember that more than anything else. After all, the Coyote fancied himself a mischievous creator god.

Good thing bringing down men who thought themselves gods was my specialty.

THIRTY-SIX

Ever been struck by a chunk of cactus hurled by a sixty mile-an-hour wind? It feels pretty much like you'd imagine. Worse still is the pain of prying it back out. Those needles may look straight to the naked eye, but I'm convinced they're covered with little barbed hooks that latch into your flesh and make them next to impossible to excise. It could have been worse though. The wind could have whipped up a rattler and slung it at me instead.

Don't let anyone tell you I don't know how to keep things in perspective.

Navigating the path was harder than I thought it would be. The wind did its best to shove me into the bushes and cacti and down hills slick with talus and over the edge of various precipices. Not to mention the fact that the sand it kept perpetually airborne made it nearly impossible to see. It also helped mask whatever subtle sounds lurked beneath it, and those were definitely the ones that were in my best interests to hear. It screamed through the valleys with an almost human voice, and, from time to time, made a high-pitched sound that reminded me of a horse whinnying. I slid the sleeve of my jacket over my entire hand and the majority of the pistol to keep any grit from getting inside and screwing with the firing mechanism. And I couldn't have that. I had a pretty good hunch I was going to need to use it.

I watched the ground for sign, knowing full well the wind would have already erased it, but I couldn't afford to take anything for granted. A footprint could potentially remain intact in the lee of a bush or a large rock. A bullet dropped while hastily attempting to load a gun would pretty much stay right where it landed. And heaven forbid I step down into a snake hole. There was no way I could scrutinize everything around me with one measly little light, especially since I was forced to watch my own tail at the same time.

The ground grew steeper and more treacherous. I didn't know how far I had come or how high I had ascended. My headlights had faded into the storm behind me long ago, and only occasionally was I able to glimpse Baboquivari Peak. I had to be nearing the top. At least I thought so anyway. Soon enough I was going to have to decide whether I was going to follow the trail, which was slowly starting to steer me to the right, or strike off away from it and utilize one of the valleys to cross over and onto the eastern slope. I had pretty much decided I was going to continue on the path for a little while longer when I glanced up and to my left.

My instincts kicked in and I hit the ground on my belly. I rolled to my left behind I boulder and leaned cautiously around the side to direct the beam at what I had seen from the corner of my eye.

It took me a few seconds to find it again. Up the hill along what almost looked like a narrow, cactus-lined animal trail I might otherwise have walked right past under the storm, maybe even under normal conditions. I had at first thought someone had been standing there, but as my brain sorted through the mental snapshot, I realized it couldn't have been. Not unless he was inhumanly thin and lacking things like organs and skin. My beam illuminated a thin post about four feet tall, on the top of which a canine skull had been fitted through the foramen magnum, the hole at the base of the occipital bone where the spinal cord connects to the brain. The skull drifted in and out of the blowing sand as I watched. It turned one way and then the other on the wind as though shaking its head at me.

I waited for several more minutes before I risked rising to a crouch and darting uphill behind another boulder that offered a better view. The pike had been staked into the crevice between two rocks, which held it tightly enough to defy the wind. A counterclockwise spiral design had been painted onto the dead animal's forehead. The majority of the teeth were intact, but it was apparent, even from a distance, that this skull had been sitting out under the sun for a long time.

I suppose I should have expected something like this. Maybe not the red-carpet treatment, but considering the Coyote's flair for the dramatic and questionable sense of humor, I really should have been prepared for some sort of macabre trail marker. We both knew how and where this had to end. No sense postponing the inevitable.

While the display had been left here to help me identify the proper route, it also served to let me know that had Ban wanted to kill me right here and now, he probably could have. Instead, he wanted to take this thing all the way to the end. I'm sure he'd fantasized about this scenario so many times that it had become almost an actualization of all of his hopes and dreams, of his very life, which meant that he had a very specific denouement in mind, one he'd gone to great lengths to plan. I tried to put myself in his shoes, to enter the mind of a sociopath whose brain undoubtedly worked in a similar fashion to my own. It wasn't as hard as I wish it had been.

It wasn't just me he hated. He hated himself. For allowing himself to be bested in life, for losing a competition against an opponent who had no idea he was competing; for his perceived sense of self-worth, which he derived from the abandonment first by one parent, and then the other. In his mind, neither of them had cared about him. His biological father had found himself a better wife and had fathered himself a better son. His mother decided she'd rather step out in front of a car than live another day with him. They had seen it in him, this inevitable failure, this culmination of all of his shortcomings. They had recognized that he would never be good enough, that no matter how hard he tried he would never be worth anything. But he had tried all the same. He had pushed himself as hard as he could to prove them wrong, if only in his own eyes.

And there I was, seemingly one-upping every little thing he did. I was the reason he would never be able to be proud of his own accomplishments. I was the son his father had wanted. I was the reason his mother was dead. I was the source of all of his problems. We shared the same genetic material, but I had utilized mine to greater advantage. I was just like him, only better. The version of himself he wished he could be. The version of himself that had been given every opportunity he had been denied. And there was only one way to prove he was better than me. He needed to beat me, head-to-head, in a competition of which we were both aware. And he needed to do so in convincing fashion on a stage for the whole world to see.

I found another coyote skull staked to a pike about a quarter of a mile up the slope and slightly to the north, in the mouth of an arroyo, which at least spared me from the brunt of the wind for a while. The walls weren't especially high, nor was the passage particularly steep. It gave me the opportunity to rub the grit from my eyes and lubricate them with tears, if only a little. I didn't realize how uncomfortable even the unconscious act of blinking had become.

There was a lone saguaro ahead of me, a perfect pitchfork framed against the distant outlet of the wash. A hunched shape rested on the ground in front of it. I could only see its outline, but I could definitely see the long hairs whipping away from it on the breeze. My first thought was that Ban was trying to trick me by playing dead, or perhaps he had even done the deed himself, but I quickly dismissed it. The shape was too large to belong to a woman either, to a human being for that matter. It wasn't until I was nearly on top of it that I recognized what it was.

A horse.

A slender mare the color of the desert sand, an almost rusty-brown. The wind tousled its mane and tail. I remembered hearing what sounded like a whinnying horse, but at the time had blamed it on the wind. It had been alive then, before its throat had been slit from one side to the other in a ragged, serrated seam, right to left, splashing buckets of blood onto the ground, more even than the greedy desert could absorb. My feet squished in the mud as I crept closer, sweeping my light from one side of the arroyo to the other before zeroing in on the carcass. Remnants of fresh vegetables were scattered around its head and spattered with crimson. The thought of Ban offering the horse the treats and then nearly decapitating it caused me to shiver involuntarily. There was something almost inhuman about the act. I was happy enough to leave that line of thought behind when my flashlight reflected from metal on the far side of the body, partially concealed behind the enormous cactus.

I'll cop to my prejudice. When Roman said Ban had earned a two-year degree in mechanical engineering, I kind of dismissed it as a fancy way of saying he had learned to be a grease monkey. Kind of like a custodial or a domestic engineer, you know? The contraption upon which I now stared might have been ugly and unwieldy, but the genius of its design was unmistakable. I had never seen anything quite like it. Thanks to growing up an Air

Force brat, I had a rudimentary understanding of how engines worked. There was a certain irony in retrofitting twin engines to a horse's saddle that would have been comical under other circumstances. Each unit reminded me of a garbage disposal with four intake valves in a ring formation on the forward end and a drive shaft on the back. Both were fueled by portable propane tanks small enough to be holstered on the saddle, their pressure control knobs within easy reach of the rider.

If I understood the design correctly, the propane served to create both heat and pressure on the power pistons in the piston shafts. The force of the air driven into the intake valves by the horse's momentum would drive the displacer pistons. The cooler air would then meet with the heated air, creating a miniature pressure front. Working in tandem, the two pistons would compress the pressurized air and displaced it laterally to turn the drive shafts on either side of the horse's flanks. The shafts themselves had been fitted with a series of chrome exhaust pipes that looked like they could have been ripped right off of a muscle car. Each pipe had been retrofitted with an array of miniature fans, which, when turned by the drive shaft, amplified the force with which the pressurized air was expelled from the pipes and channeled it across the ground behind the horse. It was essentially what I had theorized. A leaf blower. Only one that ran without electricity or the stink of petrol fumes and didn't emit a black cloud of exhaust. And it operated so quietly that I was almost shocked to see that the engines were still running. Without the force of the motion-induced airflow, it was only operating at a fraction of its potential, but that was more than enough to blow the sand a good ten feet across the wash.

I assumed the straps tethered to the back of the saddle were to tie down cargo, or, more specifically, the bodies of his victims.

The fact that he had dispatched the horse and left his means of covering his tracks behind was a giant neon sign that told me he had no intention of trying to escape. Either he killed me and waited for the police or the FBI or the Border Patrol to find my abandoned Crown Vic and ultimately arrest him and create a media circus, or I killed him.

I didn't like having my options dictated to me, but I couldn't waste any energy thinking about that now. I needed to remain focused on my surroundings if I was going to get out of this alive. And, believe me, I had every intention of doing just that.

I left the horse behind and continued eastward until I found another marker situated in the egress of the arroyo, where it began its steep journey down the red rock steppes toward the desert once more. I bumped the skull with my shoulder as I passed, causing it to swing in a circle.

The wind swatted me from the side the second I cleared cover, nearly knocking me from my feet. I turned into it and shielded my eyes with my free hand. Either I'd already forgotten how bad the storm was or it had gotten worse. I tried to get a clear view of the slope to my right, but the sand blasted me in the face. If I remembered correctly, and if I was where I thought I was, one of the caves should be roughly on my level and about half a mile straight ahead; the other would be close to the same distance diagonally up the mountain toward where the top hat rock occasionally materialized from the storm.

I had to use my free hand to maintain my balance on the slick boulders and scree to keep from toppling into the cacti lining what appeared to be an old animal trail. I looked for tracks, but had there been any, the wind would have obliterated them a long time ago. At least my instincts were telling me I was heading in the right direction. My heart beat faster with each step and it was getting harder to keep up with my body's oxygen demands with the increasing altitude and the wind blowing directly into my face. The adrenaline was starting to fire from my fuel injector, as well. My mouth was dry. I took a drink of water and used the momentary respite to calm my nerves. One way or another, this would all be over soon.

I peered uphill during a rare pause between gusts and saw what I had hoped to see.

There was another marker up there, at the top of an escarpment and nearly concealed by an enormous nopales. The pike and the skull leaned forward, away from the wind and toward me. When another gust rose, the skull lifted its chin and started to nod. I could barely see the upper crescent of what looked like a dark orifice behind it.

I turned my back to the wind and racked the slide of my pistol to make sure no sand had gummed up the mechanism. I couldn't afford for it to jam at a crucial moment.

I pressed onward, never once taking my eyes off of the shadows behind the cactus. Somewhere back there was the man I had come to find. The Coyote. My brother Ban. He was waiting for me somewhere down there in the darkness. I was walking right into a trap and I knew it.

I hauled myself up onto a ledge maybe four feet deep. The mountain grew even steeper from there as it headed up toward the peak. The cactus battled against the yellow grasses for a small patch of soil, into which a hole had been dug. The lid of the hatch that had formerly sealed it rested against the cactus. One side was bare wood; the other molded to imitate the contour of the slope and covered with sand and rocks that had been affixed to it with clear epoxy. This had once been a coyote den, no doubt. I had seen enough of them by now to know. It seemed almost poetic from a certain point of view.

The wind screamed past me. It made a hollow whistling sound from the mouth of the tunnel.

I shined my light down into a darkness so deep it swallowed the beam.

The coyote skull squeaked and nodded on the pike, almost as though it was laughing at me from beyond the grave.

Coyote is the master of deception.

I drew a deep breath, blew it out slowly, and crawled into the hole.

THIRTY-SEVEN

The smell hit me the moment I was out of the wind. It was a hundred, no…a thousand times worse than anything I had ever smelled in my entire life. This one would haunt me for the rest of my life. I retched several times before finally seizing control of my stomach. I had found where he had taken the bodies of his victims. No doubt about that. The stench of decomposition was so thick I felt like I was swimming through it as I wriggled deeper into the mountain. I couldn't afford to let it distract me. Nor could I spare a thought to figure out how to cover my mouth and nose. Anything that divided my attention was liable to get me killed.

I had squirmed maybe ten feet when the light from the outside world faded behind me. I stopped where I was and waited until my eyes adapted as well as they were going to. The bluish glow of my light reached out ahead of me to the point where the tunnel opened into a larger space. I gripped my pistol with both hands to steady my aim and used just my knees and feet to scoot forward on my belly. Progress was slow and laborious, but it allowed me to keep my finger tight on the trigger and my eye even with the sightline. I cleared the earthen tunnel and recognized immediately what the Coyote had done. Walls had been erected to either side of me from the dirt floor clear up to the rocky roof, maybe six feet tall. It wasn't quite high enough for me to stand fully erect, but I'd had enough of crawling to last me a lifetime. I rose to a shooter's stance and entered Elder Brother's maze.

The passage was perhaps five feet wide, not quite wide enough to allow me to raise my arms to either side. The circle of my flashlight grew smaller and smaller against the wall ahead of me. The only opening was to my right. I leaned against the adjacent wall, glanced around the corner, and ducked back.

Nothing there.

I went around the corner in a crouch, just in case, and walked straight toward another wall. This time, my only option was to turn left. I flattened to the wall, slid down lower, and peeked quickly around the corner. My beam flashed across an arm and a leg and threw a man's shadow across the ground. I squeezed the trigger three times in rapid succession. The report was deafening. It echoed back at me in the confines like pencils slammed straight through my eardrums.

The figure bucked and jerked and flopped backward to the ground with a clattering sound. I barely heard the faint tinkle of my spent brass over the ringing in my ears.

I fully rounded the corner and approached the body, which lay perfectly still on its back. The feet were bare and marbled purple and black. The jeans were crusted and bloodstained to match the checked western button-down shirt, the bottom of which had risen just enough to reveal the ragged wound on his abdomen. The ends of a long wooden dowel poked out of his sleeves. The entry wounds were plain as day: two roughly circular holes at center mass and a third in the upper chest. No blood flooded to the surface. No puddle expanded beneath the body. I raised my beam to the face and took an involuntary step backward.

The man's head had been replaced by a coyote's.

No. A coyote's head had been skinned to create a mask for the man underneath it. Such care had been taken that it was nearly impossible to tell. The snout and the teeth had been left intact, presumably on the original bony framework. The man's milky eyes stared up at me through the black-rimmed holes where the coyote's had once been.

I guess I now had a pretty good idea what he'd done with the heads he'd taken from the dead animals I found in the den yesterday.

I nudged the snout with my foot to lift it from the man's face. The wound on his neck looked like a great black bedsore through which I could see slimy liquefied flesh. I hadn't seen his face before and doubt I would have been able to recognize it even if I had. His cheeks were in such an advanced state of decomposition that I could see his bones and teeth through the rotten holes. His skin sagged from his facial architecture and drooped from the left side as though he were having a posthumous stroke. The moment I saw something start to crawl out through the shriveled ring of his severed trachea, I jerked my foot aside and let the mask fall back down.

I could only imagine Ban sitting somewhere nearby, trying to stifle his laughter. Or maybe just running his fingertips along the edge of a sharp blade and summoning his own blood in some sort of painful release.

The shots had undoubtedly given away my location, so I needed to get a move on.

I stepped over the corpse and followed the passage. Slowly. Allowing my light to do the exploring for me. The corridor wound to the left. The walls were choppy, not smooth, as though pieced together from scraps. Dropcloths had been nailed over them to cover whatever holes or seams remained. I imagined my light probably showed through on the other side, but I wasn't about to give it up. Not until I absolutely had to. I kept walking, letting myself continue to be guided in a wide arch until my light focused on another wall in my way. I felt like I was roughly parallel to the point where I had initially turned left and found the first body. This branch opened to the left, as well.

I tried to envision the maze in my head. I imagined it had likely been built as a replica of the one I had reconstructed from the crime scenes, but I hadn't paid close enough attention to it to be able to recreate it in my mind. I cursed my lack of foresight.

I slid along the wall to my left and stopped at the turn.

I had an idea.

I fished my cell phone out of my pocket and opened the mirror app. If I held it out and away from my body at the right angle, I could use the forward-facing camera to look around the corner without having to stick my neck out. It obviously wasn't a perfect solution. The phone would make an easy target for anyone with a weapon, but I'd rather lose my hand than my head. The digital "reflection" was a split-second slow, the tilting movements slightly blurred the image, and it was so dark I could see little more than grainy shades of black and gray. Considering the alternative, though, I figured one remaining hand would be sufficient to pat myself on the back for my ingenuity.

I used my phone to clear the corridor, then ducked around the corner to the left. Slid sideways along the wall with my light sweeping ahead of me. From here, I could only turn right. I held the phone out in my left hand this time and watched the dim, jerky reflection. The passage bent sharply back upon itself. I could see where it terminated roughly ten feet away. Nothing in between. I rounded the bend, flattened myself against the wall to my right, and scooted all the way along it until I reached the end, where my only option was to turn right again. I held out my cell phone—

Someone was standing right there.

I pulled my arm back as fast as I could. My heart was beating so hard and fast it pounded through the high-pitched ringing, which was slowly beginning to diminish. I tried to listen for the sound of breathing from around the corner, but it was a futile proposition. I shined my light at the ground. There were footprints in the dirt. Sporadic partials at best, but I was getting better at picking them out. Large. A man's footprints. Utilitarian tread. All of them headed deeper into the maze; none coming back. Of course, that didn't help me in my current situation, either.

If I assumed that each of the five victims was somewhere in here, as both logic and the nauseating smell suggested, then I still had four more to encounter, presumably on my journey to the center of the maze where I'itoi himself waited. Based on the level of decomposition, I was confident that the corpse I had shot was the first. If I was right, then the body around the corner belonged to the second victim, the woman whose murder had initially brought me here. What had Randall said? Knockoff Keds? Small feet.

I stuck out my phone again and tilted it downward. The bare feet were dainty and dangled several inches above the floor. The toenails glimmered subtly with chipped polish.

I retracted my arm and slowed my breathing. I went around the corner low and fast, swinging my light from right to left. No movement. No one else there.

I shined my light on the poor girl's body. Her sweatpants were torn and stained. Her shirt was crisp with a bib of blood. I could tell by her shape that she was still young, perhaps late teens or early-twenties. Her arms were stretched out to either side. A long wooden dowel had been run in one sleeve, across her back, and out the other. The dowel was fitted to brackets on either wall. The way she'd been hung almost made her look like a scarecrow. The snout of her coyote mask rested against her chest. The ears pointed forward. Her dark eyes looked down at the ground, unblinking.

I had to avert my gaze.

Anger flared inside me and I had to resist the urge to sprint headlong into the darkness to force the confrontation. He wanted me to see these people like this, to know that he had been the one who did it and I hadn't been able to stop him. He wanted me to see the next three lives that had been snuffed out on my watch. He wanted me to face my failures and realize that I'd been beaten. Over and over and over.

I picked up my pace as I walked, my gun held out in front of me. The passage guided me around to the right until I felt almost like I'd come in a complete circle around the damn cave before I finally encountered the end. I used the mirror function on my phone to clear the area around the bend and then went maybe another dozen feet before the maze doubled back on itself to the left.

Phone. Reflection?

Empty corridor.

Clear.

I went around the corner fast and quickly saw the next turn coming to my left again. Fifteen feet. Flatten my back against the wall. Lead with my light; follow my sight.

Phone. Reflection?

A human silhouette.

Pull back my arm. Blood thundering in my ears.

Wait.

Listen.

No sound. No breathing other than my own.

Footprints? Still only one set. Leading deeper into the warren.

Phone again.

No sign of movement. First impression? Male. Short. Five-foot-eight. Feet touching the floor, but just barely. Up on his toes. Suspended by his arms? Check.

Move.

I tried to vary my maneuvers to eliminate the element of predictability. Tuck and roll. Rise to one knee. Light, left to right. Exhale, slowly. Stand and ease forward. Based solely on the style of the pants and the curve of the hips, I assumed it was another woman. Not a man as I'd initially thought. The feet could have gone either way and the lightweight hoodie was black and crusted with dried blood. As with the last, a dowel had been run through the back of her sweatshirt to suspend her like a scarecrow. I could barely see the gash above her waistband. Her coyote face hung forward to hide the deep laceration across her throat. The dead animal's tongue was still clenched between its bared teeth. One of its ears was split and withered and resembled an artichoke leaf. I raised the light to her dark eyes. Soft and brown. Barely visible beneath the half-closed lids. Definitely female.

I had to keep moving. Soon enough these victims would come down and I'd make sure they were identified and given a proper burial if I had to do it myself. And even then, they deserved so much more.

A mental picture of the maze was starting to come together in my mind. I was now in the outermost ring. I could feel a slight difference in temperature from the outside heat radiating through the rock wall to my right. I figured this passage ought to take me nearly all the way around the cave and to the opposite side of the wall to the left of the entrance. I'd pretty much navigated the rest of the periphery; a left from there ought to lead me into the heart of the maze, where the passages would become much shorter and narrower.

I walked as fast as my shooter's stance would allow, following the leftward curve all the way around as I had expected. The wall of the cave remained to my right, although any number of side passages could have been hidden by the drop cloths and patchwork construction. The turn at the end was to the left. Again, as I had expected.

Back against the wall.

Phone out. Tilt. Reflection?

Nothing.

Come around high, leading with my light and pistol.

Clear.

It was a straight shot ahead to another left turn. Fifteen feet. Follow my sweeping light. Another left.

Phone. Reflection?

Maybe five feet to another left turn. Nothing in between. I covered the distance in two long strides. Flattened to the wall.

Phone. Angle. Reflection?

Clear.

Move through fast.

Next left.

Phone. Reflection?

Empty.

Round the corner in a crouch. Rise to shooter's stance again.

The corridors were getting shorter and shorter. This one was maybe eight feet long and ended in an abrupt right turn. I was nearing the center. I could feel it.

There were still two bodies left to find. It reeked so badly I couldn't have trusted my nose to guide me to either.

Still only one set of tracks, leading inward. None leading out.

Back against the right wall.

Phone. Tilt. Reflection?

No one there.

The bend was sharper and wound back to the right, out of sight. I swung around and followed it to a point on pretty much the opposite side of the cave. My heart was racing. I had to readjust my grip on my pistol. The light had begun to dim. I couldn't help but think about how long my escape route would be from here.

Coyote is the master of deception.

As I neared the end I identified a turn to the right. I approached cautiously. I was running out of turns almost as fast as I was running out of space. He was so close I could almost feel his presence.

The Coyote.

I'itoi.

My Elder Brother.

Right-hand turn.

Phone. Reflection?

Damn it!

I yanked my arm back.

Another body.

Should be Agent Matthews.

I knelt and held my arm out again.

The bare feet were a livid purple and rested flat on the floor, causing the knees to bend. Green pants, black splotches. Green jacket. Nameplate on the breast, insignia on the shoulder. Definitively CBP. Arms out to either side, although they were too long. The dowel had been forced through the jacket over his elbows, leaving his forearms and hands to dangle like his coyote head. The lips of the mask had been peeled back and glued in place to expose the savage teeth.

I ducked back. Deep breath. In through my nose, out through my mouth. Choke back the stomach acids. I rolled around the corner and cleared the passage with my Beretta. Maybe eight feet long. Nearing the end.

I shined my beam into the coyote's eyes. Blue irises, sclera shot through with blood. Vacant stare.

I ducked under his right arm.

Back against the wall, slide sideways.

Phone. Steeper angle. Reflection?

Another passage. Four feet long. Another right turn. Nothing in between.

I came around high and fast. Darted to the next turn.

Phone. Reflection?

Again, nothing. Another four-foot stretch. Left-hand turn.

Pulse thumping in my ears, shaking my vision.

Breathe. For God's sake, breathe.

Coyote is the master of deception.

Crouch. Hustle. Back. Wall.

Phone. Reflection?

Six feet. Arched passage. Left turn at the end.

Go, go, go.

Phone. Reflection?

Three feet. Right turn.

The quarters were getting tight. No room to move. To make a mistake.

Duck left. Already there.

The right turn bent back in the opposite direction, one-hundred-eighty degrees.

Phone. Reflection?

Nothing.

Three feet. Right turn.

Phone. Tilt. Reflection?

Ten feet, arched passage.

Clear.

Come around low and slow.

Right turn at the end. Back against the uneven, rounded wall.

Phone. Reflection?

Three feet. Nothing. No one.

Roll and rise. Two strides. The left turn merely rounded the wall to my left.

Phone. Reflection?

Clear.

Coyote is the master of deception.

Swing around. Five feet. Left turn. Back against the wall.

Phone. Reflection?

The curved corridor bent beyond my range of sight.

It was the final long stretch and I knew it.

Round the turn, hard and fast, sweeping the light, finger tight on the trigger, pressing it into the sweet spot.

Footprints?

Still one set, continuing inward. None coming out.

My heart, jackhammering.

Respirations, shallow, jerky.

Mouth dry.

All over soon.

Swallow hard.

Reach the end. Left turn.

Coyote is the master of deception.

Back against the wall, slide down low.

Phone. Tilt upward. Try to keep from shaking. Reflection?

Body. Large.

Arm back.

Steady breathing.

In. Out. In. Out.

Roll around.

Pistol up. Light up.

Black shoes, tan slacks. Universal cop special. Bloodstains. Belly holding shirt open, missing buttons, bloodstained undershirt. Glimmer from a badge on the chest, in the middle of a crimson Rorschach. Arms out. Just tall enough to remain standing roughly flat on the floor, not suspended or leaning. Doubtful dowel would have held otherwise. Antone. Without a doubt. Raise the light to the coyote mask. Jaw molded wide open, as though preparing to snap. Wrinkled skin on snout. Look up higher for the eye—

"Took you long enough to get here."

The words came from around the corner to my left.

I froze. The voice was hollow, haunting.

It reminded me of my father's.

"I can't tell you how long I've been waiting for this...*brother*."

THIRTY-EIGHT

I swung my light toward the source of the sound and held perfectly still, keeping Antone's body between me and the bend just past him. A faint red glow, hardly discernible, from around the corner. I waited in vain for Ban to step out of hiding and into range. No sign of movement. I crept to the opposite side of Antone's body, under his left arm, and peered around his back toward the lone remaining turn.

Only darkness and shadows.

I eased all the way around the chief and approached the bend slowly, silently, placing each foot softly and carefully so as not to make a sound. I opened my mouth to further quiet my breathing, although I was pretty certain I'd ceased breathing altogether. I didn't so much as blink as I stared straight down my sightline and through the heart of the flashlight beam.

Another step.

Another.

The corridor was only three feet long and terminated in a left-hand turn.

The final turn.

Another step.

"Are you ashamed of your native blood? Is that why you never even bothered to look for your roots? Or were you ashamed of your people, living on this patch of uninhabitable desert and subsisting on the scraps your government cast aside after stealing everything else from us?"

Another step.

I entered the short passage and watched the circle of my beam shrink on the wall as I closed the distance. The light betrayed my location. I paused long enough to untie the charger cord with my left hand and let it fall to the ground. I held the light in my left hand, away from my body, directed as far as I could angle it around the corner. If he had a firearm, he would get my hand, but the shot would pass well in front of my chest.

Coyote is the master of deception.

"It only seems fitting that our fates should be joined here, in this most sacred of places, where our people were first led from the darkness and into the light, where our blood bubbled up from the heart of the land. Here, in the home of our creator. Where your blood can return to that very same heart."

Another step.

My pulse was a non-stop thunderclap in my ears. I had to concentrate to keep my hands from shaking. Considering the way the light jiggled against the wall, I wasn't doing an especially impressive job.

"It's said that the maze is a metaphor for one's life journey. That we are birthed into hardship and only by navigating the various perils will we reach our ultimate destination. Here, at the center of the maze, where the sun god blesses us and ushers us into the afterlife. This is how things were always supposed to be. We were always meant to take this journey together...brother."

I held my light sideways and directed to my left, then threw it forward. It landed on the dirt in front of me and shined back into the center of the maze. No shots rang out. I listened for movement, but heard none. I was hoping he would immediately extinguish my light in an effort to seize the advantage, and, by doing so, reveal his exact location. Keeping the light was fine by me, too. I took a double-handed grip on my pistol and inched closer. I figured speed and the element of surprise would afford me one shot, and I needed to make it count. I knew he was back there. He wasn't making any kind of effort to hide that fact. In his mind, this was our shared destiny.

"There is one incontrovertible truth about journeys. They all must come to an end. Metaphorically and literally. No life journey would be complete otherwise. And you know what that end is, don't you...*brother?*"

Coyote is the master of deception.

The muscles in my legs tensed with potential as I lowered myself closer to the ground, into something resembling a compact sprinter's stance. Hopefully, he hadn't seen through my ruse and he'd be spotlighted in my beam when I dove around the corner and started firing.

"The legend says there's only one way to ensure your safe return from the maze. Do you know what that is?"

Coyote is the master of deception.

I glanced down at my flashlight, at the stretch of ground illuminated by the golden beam, at the very edge where the red glow turned it a subtle shade of orange. At the footprints heading inward.

And at the other set that crossed right over the top of them in the opposite direction, back toward me. Behind me.

"You need to bring a gift for I'itoi."

Coyote is the master of deception.

The red light.

The shoes.

Jesus.

I dove forward, flipped over in midair, and aimed my pistol between my feet, back toward the direction from which I'd come. I was firing before I hit the ground on my back and still firing as I slid up against the makeshift wall. The strobe of the discharge silhouetted the large form sneaking up on me from behind. I watched it buck in reverse, watched its coyote head snap backward, watched a mist of blood freeze in time behind it, watched the reflection of the knife as it fell from its hand. The report was painful and lanced right through my eardrums.

I grabbed the flashlight from the ground beside me and scurried to my feet. I shined it down at the body sprawled before me. Bloody cotton stuffing bloomed from above the collar of Antone's uniform shirt and the entrance wounds on his gut. A black puddle expanded beneath his head. The coyote mask had flopped back from his face.

"Did you bring a gift for Elder Brother to ensure your safe return?"

"Yeah." I turned away from the dead man's face and the entry wound between a pair of eyes that were nearly identical to mine. "I brought him exactly what he deserved."

I walked around the corner and stomped on the digital recorder before I was forced to endure another word uttered in the voice of my dead elder brother.

DAYS 5 - 9

tash hetasp - humukt

mahch

Albert Camus said that man is the only creature who refuses to be what he is.

I only wish that were true.

Man is a creature that embraces its animal roots and never misses an opportunity to demonstrate evolution's predilection for violence and depravity.

THIRTY-NINE

Sells District
Tohono O'odham Nation
Arizona

September 13th-17th

Everything kind of passed in a blur from there. I remember finding the remote trigger Ban had used to activate the voice recording on the ground beneath where he had been suspended by his arms. Or at least where he had been pretending to be suspended. The dowel had really only been two pieces, each of which had barely been two feet long. I remember seeing the knife, the way my flashlight glinted from the serrated edge, and having to look away before I envisioned what he had intended to do to me with it. I remember stumbling blindly through the maze, well after my light finally gave up the ghost, until I emerged from the tunnel and drew a deep breath of fresh air for what felt like the first time in my life. There were already flashing lights streaking over the eastern horizon when I sat down on the ledge in the lee of the cactus and drank my final bottle of water to the accompaniment of the coyote skull squeaking on the pike as it nodded its approval. I don't think I've ever tasted anything as wonderful as that water tasted at that moment.

By the time the first Border Patrol agents arrived, the windstorm had waned to sporadic gusts that pretty well left the sand on the ground where it was supposed to be. I hoped it stayed that way because the only thought that stood out from the chaos of unanswered questions in my mind was an almost physiological need to watch the sun rise from the flat desert ahead of me and abolish the darkness. It wasn't even a pink stain in the sky when

agents from the Phoenix Bureau arrived with a Crime Scene
Response Team, which promptly set up portable generators and
light arrays that evaporated the shadows as though they had never
been. I barely caught a glimpse of the fiery red orb over the
shoulder of one of my fellow agents, who was doing his best to put
me through the wringer. He could scarcely contain the stench of
ambition seeping from his pores, at least until he realized I wasn't
about to say a word to him. As far as I was concerned, my
involvement there had come to an end.

My SAC, of course, had other plans for me. I was still the ace
up his sleeve that promised promotion, but the personal nature of
my entanglement in the case made it difficult to thrust me too far
into the limelight, at least not until I'd been formally cleared of any
potential collusion with my brother and wrongdoing in his death.
The whole situation couldn't have played out any better for
Nielsen, who still got to trot his prize pony out in front of the
cameras, while ultimately being the one who held the reins.

By then, I couldn't have cared less. Getting my picture on TV
or in the papers was just about the last thing I wanted to do. Trust
me, that revelation surprised me, too. I think I just needed to put
this whole business behind me. The sooner I was able to scrub the
reek of death out of my skin the better. But there was also the
matter of the spin the powers that be were putting on the situation
that positively made me sick to my stomach. While there was truth
to the story the reporters were fed—and utilized to their advantage
with about a million breaking news segments—it was anything but
the whole truth. And I figured there would be no misinterpreting
the expression on my face had I been forced to regurgitate it in
front the press.

Don't let anyone tell you Lukas Walker is any man's puppet.

A Native American male—*coincidentally* of blood relation to
one of the lead investigators on the case—snapped and murdered
five innocent people, including a decorated Border Patrol agent
and the chief of the tribal police force, before being tracked down
by one of the Bureau's finest field agents with the help of
Behavioral's top profilers. Ban Rafael Walker was shot and killed
during his attempted apprehension. The maze he constructed was
used to illustrate his progressive sociopathic dissociation in
response to his inability to find work, his animosity toward the

federal government in general, and the Department of Homeland Security, his former employer, specifically.

By the time all was said and done, there probably wouldn't be a soul alive who couldn't recite the myth of I'itoi, the Man in the Maze, almost verbatim. That was the part of the story that made it sexy and surely sent screenwriters everywhere scrambling. The bodies unearthed from beneath his trailer warranted a passing mention, with particular emphasis on the number exhumed. Considering the paperwork involved with feeding them into the bureaucratic machine and how long it would take to identify them, if at all, the general consensus was that the victims would eventually make fine stories somewhere down the line to keep the Monster in the Maze, as the Coyote had been dubbed, in the headlines.

Despite the sketchy nature of the "truth" as it was told, some good did arise from the fallout. The plight of the Tohono O'odham people was placed front and center for the whole world to see. The everyday tales of survival in the middle of a war zone brought both humanitarian and federal aid in the form of money, food, jobs, and a whole slew of other promises I really hoped the government would keep this time. O'odham culture also reached the masses, albeit initially in a negative light, but that quickly faded as the general public developed an appetite for Hohokam lore and a people who were largely unknown, even though they'd technically been American citizens far longer than most other bloodlines. Of course, the political machine couldn't give without exacting its due.

A hundredfold.

The suffering of the O'odham was used to railroad Congress into appropriating increased funding for the Department of Customs and Border Protection to the tune of roughly two billion dollars annually, none of which would actually be used to fortify the Arizona-Mexico border that cut right through the middle of the reservation, I'm sure. At least the Tohono O'odham Nation would be receiving an annual stipend in the low millions, which would undoubtedly get a few politicians reelected, but would also allow the tribe to build and staff an eight-bed hospital and outpatient clinic, a new casino in Sun City, closer to Scottsdale money, and rebuild its police force into something more reminiscent of an actual force. There would probably even be enough left over to buy the staff honest-to-God ceramic mugs with their names printed on them in some medium other than Sharpie.

Antone would have been proud. It may have cost him his life, but his plea had eventually reached the rest of the country. No longer was the misery of his people a political mess to be swept under the rug. The entire world was now aware of the sheer volume of drugs being funneled through his reservation and the Department of Justice, the only actual loser in the situation, had been forced to make shutting down its designated High-Intensity Drug Trafficking Area its foremost goal. In doing so, it had to sacrifice even more of its power to the Department of Homeland Security. The liberal media had also latched onto the human interest angle by exposing just how many migrants died out in the Sonoran every year, a statistic that brought to light the nature of the coyote human smuggling network and its ties to the Mexican drug cartels.

I thought about Antone's quote from the newspaper article on his bedroom wall, about how he would put an end to this situation, even if he had to do so himself. And maybe he hadn't ended it, but his sacrifice certainly signaled the beginning of that end. I only wished I could have learned what it was about his facial expressions that had so totally mystified me before his passing.

My Uncle Roman quickly negotiated the sale of the rights to his story for a sum large enough to allow him to disappear. He was the reservation's pariah, the man who had created the Monster, and there would never be anything he could do to change that. He was the one who would forever bear the brunt of its wrath. I felt badly for him. His initial mistake had been in loving a child who wasn't biologically his and the boy's mother, who had never stopped loving someone else. He had made mistakes along the way, but his only real crime—and it wasn't an insignificant one—had been in looking the other way and allowing the murders to continue. If I were to be totally honest with myself, I don't know if I would have done anything differently with my own son. I hoped to track him down one day and tell him I was sorry for the lot life had given him, if he would even listen to the nephew who had robbed him on his only child; the son of the man whose shoes had proved too big to fill.

Me? I had a straight shot into the hallowed halls of Behavioral and could have cut just about any deal I wanted, financial or political, if I decided to play the game. Instead, I used the capital I had earned to negotiate a year off, with pay. I had made a promise I intended to keep. Someone needed to speak for the dead, and that someone was going to be me. I had already made arrangements with both the Pima County Medical Examiner's Office and the various Mexican and Central American consulates to serve as a liaison of sorts in the effort to coordinate the identification of the victims and the notification of their families. It had all the makings of a sad and depressing year, but don't let anyone ever tell you I'm not a man of my word. It also afforded me the opportunity to learn a little about my heritage, which delighted a certain librarian, who was more than happy to share her seemingly unlimited knowledge with me, even if I, like my father before me, had more than my share of coyotes nipping at my heels.

And I figured I owed it to the man whose death had brought about all of these changes to make sure his twelve year-old granddaughter, who fancied herself twenty-two, knew that her grandfather had loved her very much. And that he died a hero. Besides, I was starting to think I might not mind spending a little time with her mother, when things eventually settled down. Whoever would have thought I would potentially find what I was missing right where my father had left it for me.

There was just one little problem.

I couldn't let the case go. There were too many inconsistencies, too many questions and too few answers. Too many coincidences. As far as the Bureau was concerned, this one had been tied up with a big bow, but there was still one glaring hole right at the heart of it.

The mixed metaphor.

Ban had thought of himself as the Coyote.

Coyote is the master of deception.

But it had been the legend of I'itoi that had been the theme of the endgame, which had captured the attention of the entire world.

Don't be too quick to lay this at the feet of I'itoi. There are many gods of mischief out here in the desert.

Which was exactly what I feared.

And with each day that passed without the recovery of Antone's body, I feared it even more.

FORTY

By the fourth day following the breaking of the story, I'd had enough of cameras to last me several lifetimes. I'm pretty sure the feeling was mutual. I was too close to the story and it was in everybody's best interests to let me fade into the background, lest they inadvertently humanize the Monster. The bogeyman was no longer frightening when you turned on the light to find that he looked just like anyone else. Everyone else. The world needed him to remain a monster for fear we might look at him and see a reflection of ourselves.

The victims, however, needed to be humanized. They needed to be seen as somebody's children. As husbands and fathers or wives and mothers. The whole of mankind needed to be made aware that the world was poorer for their absence from it. At least, the ones we were able to identify.

The first victim, whose skin had nearly drained from his bones, was identified by a rather conspicuous tattoo of La Santa Muerte, the patron saint of sinners, which covered the entirety of his chest. His name was Juan Valarosa, and was a known member of the Mexican gang *Mara Salvatrucha*, or MS, 13. He was currently wanted in Arizona for the trafficking of both controlled substances and human beings. His profile read like the resume of a coyote. The DEA was hopeful it would be able to use the news of his death to draw out known associates who could be coerced into leading it higher up the chain.

The young woman was portrayed as a good little Catholic girl searching for a fresh start in life. That the bruising on her shoulders suggested she'd been carrying an extraordinarily heavy load and her remains tested positive for tetrahydrocannabinol, THC, and methamphetamines had been withheld from the press. Even I would never have known about it had I not been working with the ME on the process of identification. Nor would I have otherwise been there when the fingerprints of the third victim matched prints found at the scene of an arms deal gone bad in Houston that had cost an undercover DEA agent his life. These facts would never see the light of day, though. John Q. Public couldn't afford to think, even for a second, that the Monster might actually have been doing something that could be perceived as beneficial to society.

Despite his repeated attempts on my life, I was starting to have my own doubts.

Agent Brian Matthews broke the pattern. At least superficially. There would undoubtedly be books written about the heroism of the lone agent who struck off into the night to face the Monster. And while there was an element of truth to the story, a tiny element anyway, the papers weren't privy to his personnel file, which I'm sure was now confetti at the bottom of a shredder in some back room. Agent Matthews did have an exemplary record, with one minor blemish. A blemish that, were I not an investigative agent, I would never have bothered to uncover. For, while the DHS had taken full responsibility for the incident and compensated the reservation with the new Tribal Council Building, the identity of the agent involved had been withheld, for obvious reasons. Withheld from the media, not from the other law enforcement agencies involved. Namely, the tribal police. It was, however, a blemish that had led to an extended leave of absence and the derailment of a career that appeared to be on track for bigger and better things. A blemish caused by an overzealous agent playing cowboy out in the desert while chasing down a bad guy like it was the Wild West all over again. He had run down a modern day Jesse James in the Jesus Malverde mold, in fact, and made a bust that had led to the confiscation of more than three-quarters of a million dollars in marijuana. Unfortunately, it had also led to the death of a school teacher whose vehicle just happened to be in the way when they launched across I-86. The teacher's name?

Eloise Maria Antone.

Which brought me again to Chief Raymond Javier Antone, and the reason I was currently standing inside his house. The CSRT, under the oversight of Interim-Chief Louis Abispo, had performed a fairly cursory examination of the house. They'd confiscated Antone's maps, opening whole new worlds of underground fun for the forensics agents to explore, once they recovered from the shock of Ban's talisman cave, anyway. I'd been more than happy to absolve myself of every bit of knowledge I had about the underground warrens. After all, best they hear that I was down there from me. Besides, between all of the crime scenes and caves and the corpse pit under the trailer, they were going to have their hands full for the foreseeable future without having to run down all of my prints and tracks.

They'd left the tables in the middle of the room covered with fingerprint powder, but the place otherwise looked just as it had the last time I was here, which was one of the few facts I had kept to myself. The CSRT had undoubtedly found exactly what it was looking for in here, while I had broken in once more in hopes of finding something no one had thought to look for. And even then, I wasn't quite certain what that could possibly be. All I knew was that something was really starting to eat at me and I was beginning to think that regardless of how long or how hard anyone searched, Antone's remains would never be found.

I needed to know why I felt that way. My instincts had served me well so far; I'd be a fool to ignore them now.

It's about time. We've been expecting you.

I remember thinking at the time that he hadn't been referring to me as a federal agent, but to *me* specifically.

I wandered through his house. Leisurely. As though I were an out-of-town guest merely killing time while I waited for him to come home. Looking for signs of his life, for what he had been doing during the previous years. This wasn't a home; it was a way station. This was where he satiated his biological functions and plotted his subterranean investigations. Little more.

And you're here because of the report I faxed to the Phoenix office last month...

The same formal request for assistance that ended up lost in the shuffle.

If it had ever been sent at all.

I stared at the timeline of the pictures, at the conspicuous gap I could only attribute to the death of a wife and mother and the wedge it had somehow driven between a father and daughter. I couldn't presume to know how either Antone or his daughter had chosen to grieve, but it was obvious they hadn't done so together and little effort had been invested into reparations. I understood that. He had become a man on a mission, one that led him to look for hidden stockpiles of drugs in order to strike back at the cartels that had stolen his wife from him. Was it so farfetched to think he had also plotted revenge against the Border Patrol agent who had been in pursuit of the drug runner?

The Oscars function just like any other remote transmitter. They generate an RF signal that's amplified by the cell towers and relayed to a receiving station. And I just jammed the signal with the push of a button.

He had given me the ability to move invisibly across the reservation. The jammer had granted me investigative freedom, but it had also effectively isolated me from all of the other agencies and cut me off from my backup.

That mountain over there. Kind of looks a little like a top hat? That's Baboquivari. Waw Kiwulik *in our native tongue. It is the most sacred of all places to our people.*

He had pointed it out to me, hadn't he? We'd been on our way to Fresnal Canyon. I hadn't asked, nor had I cared. It was information volunteered out of the blue to serve a purpose I hadn't recognized at the time.

And if he was spending his nights spelunking, what did he do with whatever he found? He hadn't turned it in to the DEA or any other federal entity, nor had he delivered it to his own station. So where were the drugs?

There's a cave below the peak. That's where I'itoi lives. He's our mischievous creator god. When the world was first born, he led the Hohokam, from whom we descended, up from the underworld and to the surface. His home is within that cave, deep in the heart of a maze. Visitors to the cave must bring him an offering to guarantee their safe return.

I never would have known about the legend had Antone not planted it in the back of my mind. I wouldn't have learned of the significance of Elder Brother or been familiar enough with the concept of the Man in the Maze to piece together the smiley faces. Without that knowledge, I wouldn't have been able to bring about the endgame.

Don't be too quick to lay this at the feet of I'itoi. There are many gods of mischief out here in the desert.

And there was the root of the problem.

The mixed metaphor.

The coyote. I'itoi.

Two distinct mischievous entities. Two distinct MOs.

One was a killer who engaged me directly, who used coyote urine to obfuscate his trail, and who removed the bodies of his victims so he could replace their faces with those stolen from a family of coyotes. The other fancied himself a god. He used the most famous legend surrounding the most recognizable symbol on the entire reservation to bring the trials of the Tohono O'odham into the collective consciousness of a nation and orchestrated this entire affair from start to finish, but he never had complete control over his own puppet or his dark nature. He was a god who could have easily and willingly allowed a section of his head to be scalped and pretended to be dead for the picture that would serve as proof of his demise, who could have used the copiously bleeding wound to cover the inside of the cruiser he had driven across the reservation himself and abandoned a mere half-day's walk from his house.

The cartels must be stopped and held accountable for their crimes, whatever the cost. Even if I have to do so by myself.

They might have been the words that propelled him into the chief's office, but they were also a declaration of war.

I was searching for something easily overlooked, seemingly innocuous. I perused his bedroom, the shrine to his wife. The woman who revealed her upper gums when she smiled, who had taught her students about the history of the Hohokam and the O'odham. The woman who never aged past her early fifties, whose face revealed only the lines of laughter and smiles around her eyes and mouth.

The lines around her eyes and mouth.

I stood perfectly still and repeated the words in my head.

The lines around her eyes and mouth...

What was it about them? I looked at her picture again, at the wrinkles around—

I ran to the bathroom and threw open the medicine cabinet with enough force to crack the mirror. Damn it. I should have recognized it earlier. I was stupid and arrogant and allowed myself to be manipulated. I knocked the entire row of prescription bottles from the shelf and had to crawl around on the floor until I found the one I was looking for. I grabbed the box of

OnabotulinumtoxinA and held it up before me. One hundred units of purified neurotoxin complex. OnabotulinumtoxinA was the generic name for Botox, a purified form of the neurotoxin responsible for botulism. It was used to treat chronic migraines and neck pain, not to mention cosmetic applications like reducing wrinkles and erasing the signs of aging. It worked by blocking the nerve impulses between the brain and the muscles at the site of the injection, essentially paralyzing the muscles.

Paralyzing the muscles.

I remembered the nicks and cuts on Antone's face that I had mistaken for sloppy shaving or a butcher job from a dull razor. He had hidden the sites where he had injected the Botox perfectly among the real cuts he must have deliberately inflicted upon himself. That was why I had never been able to read him. He'd paralyzed certain groups of facial muscles to mask his expressions.

He'd known the Bureau would send me in from the start and he'd known about my skills. He'd been manipulating me since I first set foot on the reservation. He'd been in league with my brother, who he must have discovered was out there killing people in the desert, and had decided to put Ban's skills to use for his own ends. That's why Antone hadn't appeared threatened by him when we found Ban waiting with Roman near the first crime scene, the one they had discovered.

Master and puppet.

I'itoi and Coyote.

I bellowed in frustration and spiked the bottle against the wall. The plastic cracked and the top snapped off and I felt fluid spatter my cheek, but I was already in motion.

Out of the bathroom and down the hall. Through the main room and the kitchen. Out the back door and onto the porch. Past the lone chair in which I assumed Antone sat to watch the setting sun, where I had sat only days before and noticed the nearly invisible tracks in the sand leading toward the distant ridge, beyond which I had seen the roofline of an aluminum outbuilding. The seat where Antone had sat not to keep an eye on the majestic desert sunset, but rather the outbuilding itself, so as not to make the tracks any more visible than absolutely necessary, because he really only needed to drive back there when he had a full trunk. A full trunk brimming with packages he didn't want anyone to see him unloading.

It took me twenty minutes to walk there. The building reminded me of a small airplane hangar with a low, flat roof. The kind of thing someone could find on an abandoned Air Force bombing range, disassemble under the cover of darkness, and reassemble on his own land where no one else knew of its existence. It was situated in a narrow stone cul-de-sac formed by the convergence of the hills on the opposite side of the ridge from his house. It had been painted a reddish-brown to match the surrounding sand, but the wind had scoured it back to the bare metal in spots. There was a garage door on the face of the building. I gave the handle a solid tug. It didn't budge in the slightest. Locked from the inside. Or maybe rusted shut. I walked around the side. There were no windows. I found the main entrance on the rear of the building, abutting an escarpment that kept the front door in perpetual shadow. I used the same lock rake that granted me entrance to Antone's house to make short work of the main knob. The series of deadbolts running nearly all the way up the height of the door above it took a bit more finagling.

When I finally drew the door open, the smell swatted me in the face. Not the stench of rotting flesh or anything even remotely resembling death. Still, it was a smell I recognized immediately.

Marijuana.

I pulled out my flashlight and shined it around the interior of the building. There were large wire cages to either side of a central aisle. It reminded me of evidence lockup. Each of the cages was packed with bricks and bags and crates of drugs, all of them carefully catalogued and documented with their weights on the clipboards hanging from the locked doors. I was no expert, but the street value of this one building was probably enough to buy a small country. Or maybe even a large one. Antone had gathered it all here to be found and seized by the proper authorities. And my gut told me that everything he had accumulated was still here, right down to the last gram.

I strolled down the aisle, glancing from one side to the other. Marijuana, cocaine, methamphetamines, Mexican tar, crates of semiautomatic pistols and assault rifles. Everything that could possibly be smuggled across the reservation shy of a cage full of undocumenteds and an insulated case of plutonium. Or maybe I just hadn't come across them yet.

It was an impressive collection by anyone's standards. I couldn't imagine how much time and effort Antone had invested into confiscating this amount of contraband. It was a wonder he hadn't already been hunted down and killed by the cartels. I shuddered to think that this volume of drugs could be considered too small to actually be missed.

I found it hard not to respect Antone for making it his mission to help rid his reservation of at least a portion of the drugs being funneled across his land and into the public school system, but that didn't change the fact that he had crossed the line. No matter what crimes these criminals had committed, they didn't deserve to be hunted down in the desert by someone like my brother.

Or maybe they did. Was not the definition of morality a code of conduct that served the greater good of society?

The cages ended with about fifteen feet remaining before the garage door. I smelled the faintest hint of gasoline. There were oil stains all over the floor. The concrete was lined with tire tracks. Rubber imprints. Three close together. Parallel. Like a tricycle would make. Or perhaps, more accurately, like an ultralight "trike" one-man aircraft would make. The kind that looked like a hang glider attached to a go-kart with an engine-driven propeller mounted to the back. The kind that could fly at more than thirty miles-an-hour and stay under the radar where the Border Patrol couldn't see it. The kind that the cartels used to make nighttime drops in remote locations where collection teams were ready and waiting. The kind that could easily get a man across the border and into the kind of town where he could disappear in less time than it took for all of the inept law enforcement officers swarming the desert to find his abandoned police cruiser.

I unlocked the garage door, rolled it upward, and stepped out into the night. The tire tracks led about four hundred feet away from me to a point where they vanished altogether.

Who in his right mind would leave the 'States and risk his life crossing the desert to get into *Mexico, you know?*

Somewhere in the distance, a coyote howled at the moon.

Coyote is the master of deception.

Coyote.

I'itoi.

This infernal desert was positively crawling with gods of mischief.

EPILOGUE

Sonoyta, Sonora, Mexico

It took me nearly a full week, but I finally tracked down Antone's Scout XC Navajo ultralight trike at an airfield on the outskirts of Sonoyta, in the Mexican state of Sonora, maybe ten miles south of the line from Lukeville. It had been abandoned. No one had seen the pilot. I wondered why a forty thousand dollar piece of equipment was still sitting out there, untouched. The man who took me out to see it explained that if it belonged to a drug runner for one of the cartels, stealing it would be a death sentence for whoever did so, and anyone who shared even a single drop of their blood. I imagined that was a reasonable enough deterrent. I thanked the man and left him to a life I wanted no part of.

If I knew anything at all about Antone, it was that he wasn't about to leave his reservation. It was his heart and his home. And just because he'd left the country didn't necessarily mean he'd left his reservation. The two weren't mutually exclusive. The boundaries of the southern portion weren't as clearly defined, but the O'odham Reservation occupied nearly as much land in the Sonoran Desert this side of the border as it did to the north. My instincts told me he was somewhere out there in the vast expanse of sand and cacti to the east of Sonoyta.

I spent the majority of the afternoon cruising roads that were little more than footpaths. I passed small homes more chicken wire than adobe, trailers that appeared to be a stiff wind away from collapsing in upon themselves, and ramshackle houses cobbled together with scrap wood and tarps. The impoverished reservation to the north was positively rich by comparison. Eyes tracked my vehicle wherever I went. Children were ushered behind nervous mothers and fathers who studied me with open hostility. Whatever their families on the other side of the border might have thought about the constant presence of the Border Patrol Explorers, their Mexican relatives obviously suffered for their absence. I chose not to contemplate the daily terror they must have endured, having no one to stand between them and the merciless cartels.

By the time the sun prepared to set behind the mountains in my rearview mirror, I had seen enough to know desperation and depression. It was a singularly draining experience. I was physically and emotionally exhausted and wanted nothing more than to cross back over the border again.

A dirty white Econoline van bounced straight through the desert where no road existed. The people inside were packed so tightly I could scarcely distinguish them through the windows. There were even people sitting on the fender, their legs hanging out between the open rear doors. A spray-painted sign affixed to the side read simply "Los Angeles," but I was confident the passengers would be let out well shy of their destination.

The setting sun reflected from its flank as it streaked past, painting the dirty van blood-red. I read that as a portent. It swerved around a saguaro fringed with ocotillos and vanished into a field of palo verdes. I watched their rooster tail of dust settle over the trees and the crest of an adobe roof, which I could barely see through the branches. And might never have, had the man working bareback on the roof not stood to wave the dust out of his face. The large man raised his hand to shield his eyes against the sun and followed the van until it was out of sight.

I rolled behind some shrubs and waited, listening to the air conditioning blow and the engine tick.

The man turned in a full circle, surveying the entire area, before again ducking down out of sight.

I reversed the car and backed slowly away so as not to raise the dust. The gravel crunched under my tires. I eventually passed a rocky knoll crowned with nopales and backed off the road behind it.

I thought about Antone as I waited for the sun to set, pondered exactly what I was going to do. I didn't think he'd be inclined to come with me voluntarily, nor did I feel as though I was ready to take this thing all the way. I didn't know what I was going to do, so I did nothing. Just sat there in my car, watching the sun slip behind the horizon until I found myself alone in the darkness. Or at least what felt like alone. Lord only knew what all was skulking around out there. And what might be hunting it.

Antone emerged from hiding after about an hour. Maybe longer. I was still pondering my play when he drove past me in an old Ford pickup that was more rust than metal. I thought it was Antone anyway. I wasn't close enough to be able to tell for sure. I followed the truck regardless. All the way to Obregón, east of Sonoyta. Considering how little traffic there was, I couldn't be too obvious about it. I ended up losing him, but I eventually tracked his car down in front of an old whitewashed building that looked like the kind of place where you could count on being tattooed, pierced, or stabbed. Maybe all three.

I guessed that wasn't where he had gone; merely where he'd parked. Ever vigilant. I was proved right when I found the bar on the other side of the block, in the transition zone between the vile and the victims, where there was no problem that couldn't be fixed with cheap liquor and even cheaper women, as long as you had the cash. I still wasn't certain what I was going to do, so I stood on the opposite side of the street and watched Antone's back through the window.

For the chief, there was undoubtedly no greater punishment than a life in exile, but who was he to believe he could choose his own penance. People had died. A lot of people. Maybe not innocent people, per se, and not by his hand—directly, anyway— but he'd been the sheriff and had been derelict in his duty to protect them at best, and an active accessory at worst. And while perhaps in some circles the end could be used to justify the means, I refused to live in a world where black and white were swirled into a vague grayish smear where the dregs of society turned my ancestral home into a Serengeti for predators.

The mere fact that I'd worn my pistol to our reunion probably spoke volumes about how I expected things to play out. Then again, I wore it most places.

Don't let anyone tell you I don't know how to accessorize.

In the end, I decided there was no way of knowing for sure what I was going to do until I was already doing it, and walked across the street. The hinges squealed when I opened the door.

"'Bout time you got here," Antone said without turning around.

He was sitting alone at the bar with a mug of cerveza. I caught the reflection of his eyes from the cracked mirror behind the racks of hard alcohol.

I pulled up a stool beside him, spun around to face the window, and braced my elbows on the bar.

"Looking good, Chief. Death appears to agree with you."

I glanced over and saw the smile on his face. A genuine smile, unhindered by the toxins he had used to partially paralyze his facial muscles. I still found it impossible not to like him.

"What was my mistake?"

"The mixed metaphor."

He nodded to himself.

"Unavoidable." He looked up at the television bolted to the wall above a bartender who could have scared a hell's angel straight. I recognized the footage on the screen. I'd seen it all before, many times over. I didn't have to understand the Spanish reporter. I had lived it. "Things are going to change."

"They're already starting to."

The smile on his face was now wistful. I could see the longing in his eyes. He might have effected that change, but he would never be a part of it.

"You come alone?"

"Just happened to be in the neighborhood."

"No one comes to Obregón on purpose."

"Must have taken the wrong turn at Albuquerque."

"You plan on taking me in?"

"Your daughter and granddaughter think you're a hero."

"I appreciate that."

"They also think you're dead."

"I was dead to them a long time ago."

"You could have found a way to fix things within the boundaries of the system."

"We both know that's not true. Illegals mean big profits for American corporations and drugs—more specifically, the war *against* drugs—is a trillion dollar business. Despite the rhetoric, it's the government that would have been the big loser in that scenario."

"The government's like the house; it never loses. It just changes the game."

"Ain't that the truth."

We sat, unspeaking, for several minutes. I heard the clanking of bottles from the back, the din of a dozen different conversations from booths shrouded by shadows. I watched the people walking by on the sidewalk in front of the rundown bar and wondered how many of them were preparing to risk their lives crossing the war zone.

"So why did you come?"

"Honestly? I'm not entirely sure I know."

"Can't let it go, can you? It's in your blood, you know. I figured you'd show up eventually. In fact, it's almost a relief that you're finally here."

"I don't suppose that means you're going to turn yourself over to a federal officer, does it?"

"It would have all been for nothing if I did. You know that."

He drank from his beer as the report on the tube switched from the improving conditions on the reservation to the newest batch of butchered remains dumped in the middle of the street, not incredibly far from where we were now. The Beltrán Leyva or Los Zetas, most likely. They had a thing for taking the heads and the hands. They'd probably wash up on some stretch of tourist beach in a month or two. Not the direction the hippies thought the whole flower-power movement would take, I'm guessing.

When the newscaster finally cut away from the more-than-graphic images of the carnage, Antone pounded the last of his beer and spoke into the bottom of his glass.

"I don't suppose you're going to pay my tab either."

"The thought never even crossed my mind."

"Then let me make this easy for you. I'm going to walk out the front door and down the street to my car. I won't turn around. You won't have to look me in the eyes. I guarantee you that no one will hear or see a thing. Not in this neighborhood."

"That's not how I work."

"Then maybe you need to change with the times, Special Agent Walker. This isn't the same world it once was. There's no more honor, least of all among thieves. The best any of us can hope for is to remind the others of their humanity from time to time so maybe they don't forget about it entirely. So none of us forgets that we were once a proud people."

"The O'odham?"

"Mankind in general."

He eased his girth from the stool and walked out the door onto the street.

I followed him outside and watched him walk away, right down the middle of the gravel road. He knew full well that I wouldn't shoot him in the back. That I couldn't kill him in cold blood. That I was nothing like my brother.

"Antone!" I shouted.

I waited until he turned around, drew my pistol, and sighted down his chest.

I hadn't followed I'itoi all the way down into the black depths only to risk not finding my way back. If he demanded a gift, then I'd give him his choice of what that gift should be.

I closed my eyes.

Counted to five in my head.

Pulled the trigger.

One way or the other, when I opened my eyes, he would be gone.

MICHAEL McBRIDE

is the bestselling author of *Ancient Enemy*, *Bloodletting*, *Burial Ground*, *Fearful Symmetry*, *Innocents Lost*, *Sunblind*, and *Vector Borne*. His novella *Snowblind* won the 2012 DarkFuse Readers Choice Award and received honorable mention in *The Best Horror of the Year*. He lives in Avalanche Territory with his wife and kids.

To explore the author's other works, please visit
www.michaelmcbride.net.

Printed in Great Britain
by Amazon